Joseph L. Coleman

Dime's Worth
of
Dog's Meat

Dime's Worth of Dog's Meat

Joseph L. Coleman

ISBN (Print Edition): 978-1-54393-506-6

ISBN (eBook Edition): 978-1-54393-507-3

TABLE OF CONTENTS

PART 1

CHAPTER 1

Some thirty-five years ago, Maggie Mayo lay on the floor of a ramshackle four-room country shack in Gallia County, Ohio. An old sheet lay under her, her legs spread far apart, her knees propped high on the staves of a wooden barrel. The pain of childbirth was intense, yet she made no sound as an old country midwife probed the woman's vagina, searching for the child's head. Finally, she extracted the child and cut the umbilical cord. Holding the baby high, clasping it by its heels high, she slapped it smartly on its bottom. After a gurgling cough the baby cried out lustily. It was maybe five pounds...scrawny, but alive.

"Well, she's alive," the midwife proclaimed.

After giving the baby a quick sponge bath she approached the makeshift bed.

"Do you want to hold her?"

"No"

"Maggie, she's your child."

"I hate her."

"Maggie, don't say such things. God will punish you."

"I hate God. Where was he when Ira was dying? No just God would have taken Ira from me."

The midwife stood holding the rejected child. Then, without another word, she turned toward the fireplace. Wrapping the child securely in a blanket, she placed it near the warm glow of the fire then, picking up her shawl, she stepped toward the door.

"Maggie, I'll be back tomorrow. You and the baby sleep now."

Without another word, she stepped through the doorway, closing the door securely behind her. She did not walk away at once. Instead, she remained very quiet, listening for a moment longer, the silence broken by the wailing sound of a low moan and Maggie's voice crying, "Ira, Ira, why did you leave me?"

Pulling her shawl close around her to ward off the evening's chill, she moved away, knowing she should have consoled the grieving woman. Only God himself could answer Maggie's question. Only God himself knew why a young man in the prime of life should have that life washed away, floating down the Ohio River. She knew the story well, as did all the neighbors, for it had swept through the neighborhood community of Riverboat like a tidal wave. For Ira Mayo, though young, had been one of them.

Ira Mayo, twenty-three, a riverboat man for five years, husband to Maggie for almost two years, and father of a daughter he would never see, he had been a crewman aboard the steamboat *Simon Blank* that day, on a routine run upriver. From out of a low-hanging, nearly black sky, a thunderstorm had swept sheets of rain across the boat. The captain, anxious to deliver a cargo of baled cotton to a textile mill, steamed on through the storm but suddenly saw that a tarpaulin covering the cargo had broken free; the cotton would become worthless if soaked. The captain ordered the men to go into the sheets of driving rain to secure the cargo. The crew refused. All, that is, but Ira.

"Captain, I got a baby coming and I need money. I'll tie down the cotton, but I need extra pay before I do it."

"I'll pay any man fifty dollars if he ties down the canvas and saves the cargo."

Ira turned to the other crewmen.

"You all heard him. I get fifty dollars to tie down the canvas."

"Ira, don't do it," a friend said.

"It's too dangerous, you got a pregnant wife."

"That's why I'm doing it."

Without another word, he donned a slicker, crawled up onto the deck, and made his way onto the cargo. He inched toward the flapping canvas. Half kneeling, he reached for the broken rope. At that moment, a gust of wind keeled the boat sharply...and he was gone.

When Maggie heard the news, she became hysterical. Three strong men were required to hold her and forcibly lay her on the bed as she sobbed and waved her arms frantically. For several days, neighbors remained with her, watching, forcing some water into her body to maintain her sanity, even life.

Then, quite suddenly, Maggie went into labor, two months early.

The midwife returned each day and ministered to the child as best she could, until finally it became obvious that without nourishment, the child would die. Being the midwife for the entire community, she knew of many nursing mothers. And so, this frail little woman with piercing eyes and trained hands took command of the baby's survival. Skillfully, sometimes by doling out praise, sometimes resorting to manipulation, she maneuvered the community's young nursing mothers into eagerly participating in bringing Maggie Mayo's child back to health.

The midwife used her daily ministrations to Maggie as an opportunity to bring mother and daughter close. Not that Maggie acknowledged the presence of the child; she could ignore the child's wails and its gurgles of well-being. But occasionally, as time passed, Maggie sneaked glimpses of the baby. Apparently oblivious, the midwife continued her routine, almost without alteration; but with increasing frequency, she found reasons to absent herself from Maggie and the child.

Sometime, after some three and a half months, the midwife finally made the announcement.

"Today is the last day I will be here for some time. A lady several miles from here is giving birth and needs my help. The wet nurse will continue to come for several days, but after that you must feed and care for the child, or she will die. I'm sorry, but that is all we can do."

The next morning the child cried and cried and cried until, exhausted, she went to sleep. When she awoke, she cried again; but still Maggie would not touch her, and she fell back asleep.

Maggie retreated to her pallet and slept as well.

Then, while she was still half asleep, her breasts aching with breast milk, whether in semiconsciousness or dream, Ira suddenly appeared to her. Without accusation or remonstration, he reminded her he loved her, and he loved their child, and he knew she loved and cared for the child as well.

Now, fully awake, Maggie rose and approached the baby. As before, her breasts ached, and pieces of a rag she had stuffed into her dress were wet from dribbled breast milk. Other days, she had clumsily squeezed, pressed, and manipulated the milk out, until the pressure was relieved. Now, stooping, she lifted the child, who was wet from her excretions. The stinking child, weakened from lack of nourishment, rested limply in her arms. Slowly, she inserted a nipple into the child's mouth. The child sucked eagerly, famished from three days' lack of nourishment. Looking on as the child fed itself, Maggie felt the surge of love and affection that would last forever.

CHAPTER 2

With a final glance at her sleeping daughter, Lilly Ann turned and climbed up the not-so-short flight of stairs from the basement to the kindling. As she stepped through the doorway, the ninety-five-degree swelter of the mid-July day engulfed her.

Perspiring freely, she opened her mouth to call her son, and then snapped it shut, fearing the sound of her voice would awaken her daughter. Shading her eyes, she surveyed the yard, down the hill toward the garage, then to the small garden, where her eyes searched the rows filled with red ripe tomato plants and rows of green beans. Then she shifted her gaze and ran her eyes along the rows of tasseled sweet corn.

Nothing.

Her eyes still searching, she walked down the yard to the street bordering the garage. In a modulated voice she called, "Junior! Junior!"

Almost immediately a young boy appeared from around the garage.

"Yes, Mother."

Seeing him, Lilly Ann smiled.

"Son, I need you to go to the grocery store for me."

"Yes, Mother."

"All right, go in and wash up. I laid out a clean shirt. Put it on and come back to me."

Without a word, the boy scampered off.

Still standing at the street Lilly Ann called again:

"Everett! Everett!"

Again, from around the garage, a little young boy appeared. This one was smaller and younger, perhaps eight years old, to Junior's ten.

"Everett Elwood, what were you doing?"

"Playing catch with Timmy and Ron. May I go back?"

"Son, I'm sending your brother to the store."

"May I go with him?"

"No, son. I need Junior to hurry. Yes, you may go back to play, but I want you to stay right in the field. Your father will be home soon and we'll be having dinner."

With that the little boy turned and trotted back around the garage, calling to his friends: "Mother says I can play some more!"

Satisfied, Lilly Ann turned and walked toward the house. As she approached the back door, her son appeared. His hair was combed, and he was wearing a clean shirt. Seeing his mother, he asked, "Mother, should I take Rover with me?"

"No, son. In fact, please go and fasten him up so he will not follow you."

The boy trotted away and was back almost immediately.

"Mother, may I take my wagon?"

"Yes, but only because your package may be too heavy to carry a long way. And be careful that no blood ruins your clothes."

"You want me to get dog meat?"

"Yes, son, here's a dime. Tell Mr. Krugman you want a dime's worth of dog's meat—and be careful not to lose your money."

Together, they walked around to the front of the house, where the boy had left his red wagon. Without hesitating, he placed one knee in the bed of the wagon, pulled the tongue and the handle back over the bed to steer, and pedaled himself by setting his other foot on the ground and pushing off.

When he reached the curb down to the street at the bottom of the sidewalk, the boy gingerly let the wagon thump over it then pedaled strongly, continuing down the street. As he pumped onward he could hear his mother's voice calling to him to be careful.

Still standing at the curb, Lilly Ann thought she heard her child acknowledging her calls. She turned toward the house, and for the first time in a very long time she said it. *Her house. The house that Roy had built for her.* Even now it seemed strange. *Her House.*

Lilly Ann watched with pride as her son pedaled up the street. Her firstborn, her son Junior. It was strange, her having a son.

Even more strange: she, Lilly Ann, had a husband.

The reverie into which Lilly Ann had slipped was broken by the sharp clatter of a horse's hooves. The Moores and Ross milkman approached the house. Across the street Mr. Reid's pony neighed. The pony was in his small barn, kept there to be taken out by Reid as he plied his trade as a child photographer. Closer, on the flagstone street, the blaring sun had melted the tar beneath the stones; it clung loosely to the wheels of the wagon.

The wagon stopped in front of the house. The white-suited milkman stepped down with three-quart containers of milk.

"Shall I leave it on the porch, Mrs. Coleburn?" he inquired.

"Set one by the door and the other two by the steps and I will carry them in."

As Lilly Ann watched the milkman set the milk containers on the porch, a huge Mack truck, its chain-driven rear wheels churning through the alley behind, stopped at each house to empty the garbage cans. Once the milk wagon and the Mack truck had moved on, Lilly walked to the curb to watch Junior as he pedaled his wagon out of sight. Then she looked back to the house.

It was a new house, five years old, built by the Dorgan Construction Company. Five years earlier Lilly Ann had been living with her parents: Maggie, her mother, and Jimmy, her stepfather, brother to Ira. Maggie had married Jimmy after Ira's death. Having acquired a position with the U.S. Postal Service, Jimmy had moved the family from Gallia County to Columbus, where Maggie carefully nurtured her child to young adulthood.

One Sunday morning while attending church, Jimmy, dressed in a fine dark suit with a vest, met Roy Coleburn. A gold chain lay draped across the front of Jimmy's vest. A fob was attached to the chain, and Jimmy had slipped the Omega gold pocket watch that was attached to the fob into the left-hand pocket of the vest. Introduced by a neighbor, he shook the hand Roy extended to him.

"Pleasure to meet you, Sir."

Jimmy nodded as he looked the young man over. About six inches above five feet, he was strongly built, with wide shoulders, a heavy chest, and muscular arms.

The neighbor spoke:

"We are having a small gathering at my house—and, Jimmy; we want you, Maggie, and Lilly Ann to come, about five-thirty."

"It would be a pleasure," Jimmy said.

"Come here to the Shiloh Baptist Church," the neighbor said, giving Jimmy directions. "Turn right. Then four blocks to Sixteenth. You can't miss it."

That evening, when Jimmy and his family had arrived, a new Hupmobile sat parked in front of the house. The neighbor came to meet them as they stepped out of their car.

"That's Roy's car," he said, seeing Jimmy and his family standing in the driveway and eyeing the car. "He drove it down from Toledo, where he works at the plant. Nice, isn't it?"

Jimmy nodded.

In the house, they greeted Roy, who was impressively dressed in a suit, a high white collar, and gold-rimmed glasses.

After a pleasant afternoon, Roy indicated he had to leave to be at work tomorrow.

He approached Jimmy. "Sir, with your permission, I would like to call on your daughter."

Slowly, Jimmy looked him over, and then said, "You may."

A year later, Roy Coleburn and Lilly Ann Mayo were married.

CHAPTER 3

Two years passed. During that time, Roy made arrangements to leave his Toledo job, loaded his belongings in his automobile, and moved to Columbus. Once there he found employment at the Buckeye Steel Casting Company, and for two years he lived in a room in his father-in-law's house and saved his money religiously.

One Sunday after church, he said to Lilly Ann, "Please ride with me; I want to show you something."

After a ride of about half an hour they arrived at a vacant, corner lot.

Pointing, he said, "This is ours. We will build a house here."

"A two-car garage—there." He pointed slightly downhill.

"We'll have a garden—there." Again, he pointed.

Overwhelmed, Lilly Ann was speechless.

Then, she said, "Roy, I love you."

Touching her, he said, "Did I mention we'll have a full basement underneath, with a furnace and room for a washing machine?"

Now, standing on the curb looking back at the house, she was reminded of that day and the promise of the house. As Roy had promised, the home had risen from the full basement. Above the basement, there was a living room, a kitchen and dining room, a bathroom, and three bedrooms. Slightly downhill from the house, a garden provided a safe playground for the children.

Hearing a sound inside, she moved quickly to gather up the milk and go back inside.

Meanwhile, Junior pumped his wagon toward the grocery store. He stopped under the mulberry tree to eat a few of the berries, being careful not to stain his shoes or clothing as his mother had warned.

Shortly after, he parked his wagon close to the grocer's and entered the store.

"Mr. Schmidt," he greeted the grocer.

"Junior, glad I am to see you. Where's Rover?"

"At home, my mother wanted me to hurry."

"Fine, I have a package already for you. It's a little heavy. I put five pork chops inside. When they have been on the counter too long and changed color, customers won't buy them. With the other pieces, Rover will have a feast."

Taking the package, Junior thanked Mr. Schmidt. He left the store, put the package in the wagon, and made his way home. On the way, he felt inside his pocket and remembered he had not given Mr. Schmidt the dime. He would give it to him next time.

At home, he discovered his father had returned from work and was in the bathroom washing up.

"Did you get meat?" his mother asked.

"Pork chops," he replied.

"Give them to me so I can cook them, then go get Everett—and you two wash up. Dinner will be ready shortly."

An hour later, dinner was over, dishes were washed, Lilly Ann and Roy were sitting close on the ground, she, holding the small child, the other children playing about them.... She, detailing the day's activities; he, indicating he had had another day's work. When twilight fell they knew it was time to turn in. Gathering the children, they moved into the garage. Here, the heat was overwhelming. Then as they moved to place the children on pallets on the floor, with all settled, they themselves crept to their pallets and, despite the oppressive heat, slept.

CHAPTER 4

Travelers approaching Columbus from any direction could not miss it: the structure soared five-hundred-and-fifty feet in the air. The American Insurance Union Building. The company held one hundred million policies by the end of World War One. Only *magnificent* could describe the fifth tallest building in the world—the creation of the architects and workers employed by John J. Lentz, Founder and Chief Executive of the American Insurance Union.

Approaching the building, Lilly Ann could only marvel, and now, suddenly, she was entering. Holding onto Roy, she asked, "Do you know where we are going?"

He nodded. "Sixteenth floor."

At the Otis elevators, a sharply dressed starter inquired, "May I help you?"

Roy handed him the card he had received in the mail.

Yes, you will find Mr. Rhodes on the sixteenth floor. Turn left as you exit."

He ushered them into the elevator, pushed the button for the sixteenth floor, and stepped out. Almost silently the Otis car sped to the sixteenth floor; the doors opened. The receptionist in the office across from the elevators asked, "May I tell Mr. Rhodes you are here? "She left the office then quickly reappeared.

"Mr. Rhodes will see you now."

Inside, the office was lined with mahogany and walnut wainscoting. The chairs—and even a couch—were leather. Mr. Rhodes sat behind a huge ornate desk. Looking at the gold watch he drew from a vest pocket he said, "You're on time. I detest lateness."

Lilly looked closely at him. He was short, of a medium build, and steely eyed.

He opened a file the receptionist had handed him.

"Ah. Your balloon note is due. You have six months to pay the balance or evacuate. Is that clear?"

"But, Mr. Rhodes I don't understand," Lilly Ann said. "We have scrimped, almost gone without food—but the mortgage has been paid."

Settling back in his chair, a half smile on his face, Mr. Rhodes reiterated what he had just said: "I repeat myself. Your balloon payment final payment is due. Now! Either you pay the balance or get out. Do I make myself clear?"

Once outside, Lilly Ann said to Roy, "Does this mean what I think it means?

"If you think it means we must move, you're right."

Lilly Ann said nothing else.

That night, toward evening, but not quite dark, she sat outside on the steps of the house, her youngest child in her arms. A Model T Ford approached from down the street and stopped in front of the house. Thinking the driver might have been lost and needed directions, Lilly Ann stood and approached the car.

The driver rolled down the window. "Mrs. Coleburn? I am Nettie Barnes, Mr. Rhodes' receptionist. I met you earlier today."

Lilly Ann rocked her child in her arms as she stood by the driver's window. "Yes, I remember."

"I know what went on in the office. I have three children, too, and I know what it would mean to be homeless. So, if I may, I came to help you, here." She raised her hand and extended a plain sheet of paper to Lilly Ann. "I've written the name and location of a person who might help you. You and your husband need to contact this man right away. I told him you might."

Lilly Ann took the paper and looked at it briefly. Then, she thanked the receptionist. The receptionist smiled, and with that, she was gone.

The next day, when Roy returned from work, Lilly Ann gave him the message. Roy read it and agreed to investigate. The family was desperate; he would try anything. Over the last several years he had ridden the coal cars of the Pennsylvania Railroad, throwing off coal and gathering it up in burlap sacks to keep the house warm. Once he had lined the basement walls with oilcloth, brought in card tables with chairs, and installed a bootleg still. With the white lightening he distilled for a number of months he paid the mortgage and kept the family with food.

Then a drinker rolled a cigarette and struck a match on his trouser leg. The flaming portion of the match broke off and flipped across the room, lighting the oil cloth, which immediately set the entire room on fire. Seeing the smoke, a neighbor called the fire department. Once they arrived, the firemen broke the basement windows and pumped in water, extinguishing the flames. Standing outside with her children, Lilly Ann watched, horrified at the thought that the still would be discovered, and Roy would be arrested and sent to prison for bootlegging.

Instead, the head fireman said to her, "Lady, the fire is out. All of the oilcloth was burned, but no part of the house burned. The water made a mess but the rest was saved." He wiped his brow, charred from the smoke, and nodded quietly to Lilly Ann. "We're going now."

And they indeed were gone. When Roy and his friends arrived, Lilly Ann confronted Roy angrily: "You and your friends nearly burned down our house, and if they discovered you were bootlegging they would have thrown you in federal prison. I want that thing out of my house. Now!"

"But Lil...."

"Don't 'but Lil' me. Our children would be without a father. We would be on the street.... *Now!*" she repeated bluntly.

With the help of his friends, Roy removed the still and cleared the fire and water filth. He knew she was right, but he was distraught.

The next day Lilly left Roy in the house alone. She pushed the baby buggy with the two youngest down to Jimmy and Maggie's house. The third child walked beside them. After visiting her parents for several hours, she returned home, pushing the buggy as before. After settling the children, she entered the closed door of the bedroom. Roy was sitting on the bed, manipulating the twelve-gauge Winchester pump shotgun she had given him for Christmas, the barrel under his chin, his bare foot reaching for the trigger.

Rather than panic Lilly Ann reacted calmly. "Roy," she said. "Roy."

He raised his chin off the barrel.

"Roy, this is no solution to anything. We need you."

Moving slowly, she came to the bed and grasped the gun.

"We need you," she said again.

With the gun now firmly in her grasp she placed it on the floor. Then, grasping Roy, she broke down, sobbing loudly. Then, without another word, shotgun in hand again, she left the room.

The incident was never mentioned again.

The next day, when all were seated for supper, a knock came at the front door. Roy answered it.

A stranger stood on the porch. He held his hat in his hand. "Roy Coleburn, I am Bernie James," the stranger said. "I'm sorry to interrupt your dinner, and I apologize. But this is very important. I am a bandleader. We are playing an engagement at the Beacon Club and we promised six pieces...but we are one short. Our guitar player is sick. I understand you play. We desperately need a player. We need you if you are willing. We start at eight tonight."

By this time the man had stepped inside, where Lilly Ann could both see and hear him. Roy turned toward her.

"Lilly, this is Mr. James, you heard of him."

"Mr. James," she said, "two questions. How late must he be there and what does it pay?"

"We play eight to twelve and we pay four dollars a night."

Knowing their desperate need for money since the Buckeye plant had laid him off along with many other employees as the depression had deepened, Lilly Anne said:

"If you can do it, do it."

The position lasted for three months, and the mortgage was paid.

For a moment, all seemed well. Some month and a half had passed. Roy was still doing double duty. He, with others, was erecting a brick wall for a wealthy neighbor; plus, he was playing at night. Finally, Lilly Anne's curiosity got the best of her. Having persuaded a friend to stay with the children for a few hours, she prevailed upon Roy's friend Lemanual to drive her to the Blue Moon Night Club, where Roy was playing.

Once there, Lemanual turned to face her.

"Lilly Ann, I'll wait in the car. Maybe they'll let you go in. I know they won't me."

At the door, the doorman halted her.

"I'm sorry ma'am, nonmembers are not admitted."

Unabashed she said, "I did not come here for pleasure, my husband is playing in the orchestra and we have five children that I'm concerned about and I must talk to my husband before I do anything. It will only take two minutes."

"Ma'am, I could lose my job."

"And I could lose a child."

Unprepared for such a response, the doorman relented.

"Ma'am, the set will be over in a few minutes. As soon as the music stops I'll tell Roy you're here. For now, please go inside; you'll find a chair I use to rest. Sit down and make yourself comfortable." He paused and looked gently at Lilly Ann. "I do hope all of your children are okay."

As directed, Lilly Ann stepped inside. The interior glowed lavishly around her. The sound of the orchestra guided her eyes to the bandstand.

Still standing, she saw Roy strumming his guitar. Soloing, the trumpet player stood in the spotlight. As a unit the orchestra laid a smooth melody, while on the polished floor couples glided effortlessly. The dancers were flanked on three sides by tables of well-dressed patrons who sipped their drinks between half-heard remarks. All around the club were the accoutrements that spoke of money and influence.

As the orchestra ended its number the leader stepped to the microphone. "We will now take a fifteen-minute intermission. In the meantime, ladies and gentlemen, if any of you have a favorite tune you'd like to hear, we will try to satisfy your request when we return."

Immediately, the doorman led Lilly Ann outside. As Lilly Ann walked over to Lemanual's car, the doorman scurried back to the orchestra, where he whispered to the leader. The next moment, the leader rushed to Roy and whispered the doorman's message into his ear. As if electrified, Roy, almost running, made his way out of the club. Seeing Lilly Ann in Lemanual's car, he hurried over.

"Lilly Ann," he half shouted. "The children?"

"All fine."

"But?" he said, looking at Lemanual.

"She persuaded me," Lemanual said.

"I wanted to see the Blue Moon and you playing, so I exaggerated a little."

Relaxing a little, Roy said, "And…?"

"It's gorgeous, and imagine: my husband is playing here!"

Roy briefly laid his hand on hers then said, "I must get back. It's time for the next set."

And he was gone.

CHAPTER 5

The tent appeared as a complete surprise. Once it was erected, Roy said to Junior, "I can't give you a playhouse but I can give the tent that was given to me to you."

"You mean it's mine?"

"You do want it?"

"Oh yes," Junior said then hugged his father.

He slept in it on hot nights, with some old quilts spread across the tent floor. Once, he slept there with two of his friends. A time or two, he played hopscotch with Mary Jane, who lived next door. She had long brown hair; everybody thought she was pretty.

One day he was out in the tent by himself. While Everett played down the hill with his friends, Mary Jane came down the rise of her house and waved for him to come to her.

"I want to show you something," she said. "You must be very quiet."

She led him behind her house. Because of the heat, every window was open. Gesturing for him to be very quiet, she led him to one of the bedrooms' windows in the back. Stooping, then peering in, Junior saw them. The assistant butcher was on top of Mary Jane's mother, his bare behind pumping up and down. Mary Jane's mother moaned, her legs up in the air. The movement suddenly became frantic, the groans and grunts frantic, as well. Then it all stopped. The assistant butcher rose, his limp penis dangling in front of him. Mary Jane's mother lay there, covered in sweat.

"I've got to go. I can't be late." The assistant butcher slipped into his pants and then started buttoning up his shirt. "I'll be back in a couple of days. I'll try to bring steak next time but I must be careful. The boss sees me and I'm fired."

Dressed, he rushed out to his automobile and was gone.

Putting her fingertips to her lips to indicate silence, Mary Jane crept away. Junior followed.

When they reached his tent, Junior asked, "What were they doing?"

"Funking."

"Funking?"

"Funking. I've seen them do it many times. Want to try?"

"Sure," he said, trying to sound confident.

"Can you go and get a penny?"

"Sure."

And he did.

"Give it to him—" she pointed to her younger brother "—let him use your wagon." She turned to her brother. "Tommy," she said, "use Junior's wagon and go get candy."

Penny in his pocket, Tommy pumped the wagon—and was gone.

Inside the tent, Mary Jane laid down, pulled her dress up, and pointed between her wide, spread legs.

"Put your peter in here." She pointed between her legs.

He knelt between her legs, his hard peter in his hand. He put it between her legs as she guided it. At first it would not enter.

"Press harder," she said.

He did. She made a low hurtful sound, and he felt something give way, and his peter entered.

"Now, funk me like I see them do. You press down and I'll press up."

He did not know why, but it felt wonderful.

After that first time, as often as he could, he took pennies from the dish Lilly Ann kept on the kitchen window sill and gave them to Tommy, and he and Mary funked. After several days of funking, Junior sat on the top step of his parents' porch...and when Thelma Rice from down the street came up to greet him she sat down beside him. Being a couple years older made her feel superior. But today, she sat down and talked in a friendly fashion. After a while he suddenly blurted out what was on his mind so often these days.

"Have you ever funked?"

She heard it. Momentarily shocked, she feigned ignorance.

"Funked? What's that?" You know, put your peter in a girl and wiggle."

Still amused, she said, without answering his question:

"Have you funked?"

"Lot of times" he bragged.

"With who?"

"Mary Jane."

"Where?"

"In the tent."

She decided to play him, having "funked" a boy named Leon from a few streets away several times.

"Would you show me how to funk?"

"Sure."

"Not in the tent."

"Well, I know a good place. Come on." He went to the side of the steps. "We used to play here."

Rounding the porch steps, he raised the trellis on the side and motioned her to stoop under. She did, he followed. She started to speak; he touched his lips to indicate silence.

"I can't get this dress dirty," she whispered.

He sat down and motioned for her to sit on his legs, facing him. She raised her dress to squat on his protruding peter.

"Where's the hole?" he whispered, pointing to the hairy thing that spread darkly where Mary Jane's hole had been.

Suddenly determined, Thelma said, "I'll show you."

And holding his peter she eased it into herself, moving it in and out as she did. The sensation was such that he hardly heard the call:

"Junior!"

Thelma pulled her dress down while Junior, his peter dangling, buttoned his fly.

"Yes, Mother," he answered.

"Where are you?"

"Under here."

"Who's with you?"

"Thelma."

"What are you two doing?"

For once, for the first time, he lied. "Nothing," he said.

"Come out here!"

Junior pushed the panel out, permitting Thelma to exit. Sill holding the panel, he followed.

Lilly Ann stood with her hands on her hips. "What were you two doing?" she demanded.

Before Thelma could speak, Junior blurted, "I was showing her our secret hiding place."

"You certain?"

"Yes."

"Thelma, you go home. Junior, you go around back with the others."

Both youngsters scrambled to carry out their orders...

In bed that night, Roy asked, "Do you think they told the truth?"

Lilly Ann sighed despondently. "We'll never know, we'll never know."

For some time, Junior had heard talk about moving, but he didn't know where or when. Meanwhile he faithfully took his wagon to the butcher to retrieve meat, often excellent meat, always good. Sometimes he brought Rover with him, sometimes he left the dog at home.

An illness in the family suddenly altered Lilly Ann's packing plans for the move. Harold, who had been born prematurely, had come down with some upchucking, diarrhea, and fever. Still needing the food from the butcher to feed the family, Lilly Ann chose an option she had deliberately avoided to that point, that of having an older child seeing to the well-being of another.

Summoning Junior, she said, "Your brother is very sick, and I know we can trust you. Here is a dime for the butcher...only this time, I want you to take your sister in the wagon."

"Shall I take Rover?"

"No, that would be too much for you to manage."

While she chattered further instructions and pointed to make sure Junior did not stray from his appointed path, he pulled his little sister into the wagon. At the butcher's, he held her hand and went inside. The butcher greeted him kindly, handing him the package.

"And whose little girl are you?"

Softly, Junior's sister murmured, "Mommy's...Do you know Rover?"

"Yes, this is Rover's meat. Do you feed him?"

She stared at the butcher and shook her head. "We eat the meat and give the dog the bone."

Without a word the butcher snapped erect and walked off.

Over the course of the few remaining days that Lilly Ann and her family had at the house, Roy and his friend Abe carefully removed the furnishings from out of the garage and loaded them into Abe's large flatbed truck. Harold healed; the dimes bought fatback and bones.

Finally, Roy said, "Keep only the necessities you'll need for two days. We're moving."

Then, the Hupmobile, filled with all the members of the Coleburn family, followed the truck with its final load. They headed to Sunbury.

Lilly Ann sat in front, turned sideways in her seat to watch her children on the backseat, the youngest on her lap. They were followed by the real estate agent, who had insisted on accompanying them to show the wife the property, some twenty miles up the 3C Highway. The highway's route began north, on Lake Erie in Cleveland, then passed through Columbus's center and ended at the Ohio River in Cincinnati Some twenty-five miles out, the convoy turned onto a graveled country road and continued for four more miles before they came to a house set back from the road and stopped. Looking about, Lilly Ann saw several buildings.

"We're here," Roy said.

Before Lilly Ann could react, the real estate agent approached them.

"Mrs. Coleburn." He smiled pertly to the new homeowner. "If you'll accompany me I'll show you your new home. I'm sure your husband will stay with the children."

Lilly Ann looked back toward Roy, who nodded his assent.

"Since we're down here by the barn, I'll show you this part of the property first and we'll work our way up to the house."

He led Lilly Ann toward a large building.

"This, of course, is the barn. It has stalls for six cows or horses, further on are open spaces for the animals to rove around. On further, you'll find space for farm implements and tools. Above, a good size hayloft has the track and equipment to lift the hay off the wagon and slide it back in the loft." He paused. "I'm sorry; I didn't mean to bore you."

"Mr. Donald, "Lilly Ann said, "You do not bore me. A whole family on a farm needs to know these things. What with my husband working in town, the more I know, the better off we'll be."

Shocked, he stared at her. Suddenly respectful, he said, "Yes, ma'am, shall we continue?"

Patiently leading the way, he showed her the corncrib and other buildings on the fifty-two acres as they walked about the property.

"And here," he said, pointing, "is the new outhouse, over a freshly dug cesspit."

Understanding his meaning, she asked, "And what happens in the winter?"

He smiled modestly and said, "Oh, of course you have a cesspit in the house and carry the contents out here to empty."

Moving on he led her to a small rise behind the hill the house stood on. A smattering of short, gnarled trees spread out over the grassy landscape.

"Here, you'll notice a small orchard— and in season, there are cherries, peaches, apples and pears. Before she left, the former owner and her family and friends picked fruit as it ripened. But you can see the Grimes Golden apples are still starting to ripen."

He led the way around the house and stopped at a water pump.

"This pump works all winter, never freezes."

The pump stood about thirty-five feet from the front door of the main house. Looking up, she could see the house stood two stories tall, with a faded, red tin roof. Later, she learned it had six rooms—three up, three down. Inside, the agent pointed out the four-burner, cast iron heating rack over the oven, all clad in white enamel. The other two stoves on the first floor were ornamental, heavy cast iron and black, with pipes protruding through the ceiling and from there (the real estate agent told her) on up through the roof. Between the bedrooms, on a metal platform housed in a thin enclosure, was a stove designed for quick heating.

"You'll notice," the agent said, "the walls are lathed and plastered. The floors are split pine, the doors are solid pine and—I didn't show you—there is a root cellar that holds at fifty-five degrees the year-round." He handed Lilly Ann the keys to the house and smiled modestly again. "Mrs. Coleburn, I think you will find this wonderfully satisfying. I welcome you."

After Lilly Ann thanked him, the real estate agent said, "Now, I'll be gone. If I can be of any more service, please contact me."

And he was gone.

Leaving Junior to care for the children, Lilly Ann moved about as she and Roy unloaded the truck. Then she had Everett help make up the beds and shelve dishes neatly into the kitchen cabinets.

After all their belongings had been unloaded, Roy guided her outside and into the root cellar. They descended the creaking wooden steps; the temperature suddenly became fifty-five degrees, almost forty degrees cooler than the exterior air above.

Roy pointed to bags of potatoes, stalks of fresh vegetables, containers of grain and sugar. Lilly Ann guessed he and Abe had moved all of that here in recent days. "We've stored several days of food for you and the children, plus there's milk, flour, lard, beans, and side meat. There's enough for Abe and me to be here to help you get settled. I'll start a fire in the stove, and while you cook, Abe and I will wash up."

Dinner quietly took shape despite her unfamiliarity with the wood-burning stove. Biscuits baked quickly, the yellow sweet corn boiled in minutes. She sliced red tomatoes with leaf lettuce soaked in vinegar, let green beans boil in a pot until tender. The water from the well came up fresh and cool.   Later, after dinner, with the children all settled, Lilly Ann listened intently as the two men sat talking in the kitchen.

"The president said on the speech he gave over the radio, 'You have nothing to fear except fear itself.'"

Roy nodded. "I like that. We weren't afraid when I was a boy on the farm—and now I'm back on the farm." He paused thoughtfully. "No," he said, "I have no fear."

Lily Ann, hearing the conversation and knowing what she knew, felt grateful. But as she served the men a simple slice of apple pie, she found she wasn't certain.

For three days the men continued to implement plans they had discussed several days earlier. Weeds that had grown too high had been cut. Clotheslines were stretched between trees. Repairs were made to the cellar door. Roy slept in the house, and Abe slept in the flatbed truck.

"We'll have to leave today," Roy explained on the fourth morning. Lilly Ann was sitting with Roy at the kitchen table, enjoying the quiet of the house while the children were still preparing to come down. "Abe has to get back home, and I promised Jimmy and Maggie before I left I'd be back to start work on the janitorial force starting Monday." Seeing Lilly Ann's startled look, he apologized. "Honey, I promised Maggie I would tell you...." He continued, explaining that Jimmy had secured him a job at the American Insurance Union Building. "I'll room at Jimmy and Maggie's until I can do better. You know I love you and the kids, and I'd stay with you here if I could. But now...we're lucky to have a little money coming in. It will pay the mortgage and buy school clothes, and maybe a few other things." He stared at her affectionately. "Everything will be fine. You'll see. I'll come home once a week."

Lilly Ann sat perfectly still and silent. Then, without a word she rose and started to cook.

After dinner, with hugs and kisses, the men were gone.

Later, after the other children were in bed, she sat with Junior on the front steps. They talked by the light of the lantern.

"Mother.... Daddy's gone?"

Lilly Anne nodded. "He is staying with your grandparents."

"When will he come home?"

"Nobody knows, son; nobody knows."

For several weeks, always on Saturdays, Roy returned home, bringing whatever goods he deemed desirable, including clothes that he could afford. The weekly homecoming brought eager kisses from Lilly Ann and affectionate embraces from the children.

The Saturday morning ritual continued, until the weekend a Model A Ford drove up to the house. The family observed quietly from just outside the front door of the house, wondering who the stranger was. Then, Roy stepped out of the car.

Lilly Ann balked. "A new car?"

"No, it's three years old."

"How did you get it?"

"I was able to trade the Hupmobile to a man who wanted it—and I received cash for it, too." Lilly Ann's reticence receded. "We can finish buying school clothes. It starts soon, you know."

Lilly Ann did know. Two days earlier a school bus, long, yellow, emitting blue smoke out the back, stopped in the road in front of the house. The bus driver got out and approached the house. He took off his driver's cap and nodded to Lilly Ann. "I just wanted to let you know. Your children will be picked up at seven-twelve, *sharp*. They'll be returned at three forty-three, *sharp*. The school they'll be attending is Sunbury Consolidated School— they take children grades one to twelve." He nodded again. "I'm Allen Barnes, the driver. Is there any other information you need?"

Lilly Ann said, "I think not. Thank you."

The driver and his bus disappeared and Lilly Ann conveyed the schedule to Roy. For a long moment he hesitated.

"Lil, I know it will be hard for you, getting up so early, feeding breakfast, seeing all their clothes are right; but your effort will be rewarded by our children being educated. I know I don't need to tell you, that's critical."

*   *   *

Jesus loves me, the voices sang out. *This I know, for the Bible tells me so....*

Junior stood beside his desk, careful not to touch the steel-nibbed pen lying in the groove just above the inkwell near the corner. He watched Miss Rosen as her feet and legs pumped vigorously on the pedals that provided air to the organ she keyed as she sang the words to the hymn. Not really knowing the words, Junior tried to join in. For nearly a month now he had sat in her class and followed her instructions in Geography, Reading, Writing, History, Arithmetic, and Science. All interesting classes, he found, especially Current Events. He had heard the word "Depression" so often he knew the time it referred to had started in nineteen twenty-nine. He knew that Herbert Hoover had been the country's secretary of commerce and had then become president of the United States. That the stock market crash had led to millions of jobless, homeless, half-starved people. He had heard it said that the president insisted private charities were sufficient to assist the needy.

When Junior mentioned to his father what he had learned about President Hoover's solution, his father said, "Son, he is president. But I would have him sleep outside, on the ground, in freezing weather. And I would have him eat out of garbage when he is starving. Or I'd have his family die from malnutrition and illness without a doctor's treatment. Say that to your teacher and see what she says."

Junior knew his father was right, but he did not dare repeat his words to his teacher.

After several weeks of school, he still did not know any of his classmates well. Oh, he had said "hello" to several of them, but had not developed any true friendships. But one day, with his biscuit lunch in hand, he strolled outside. Clouds hung overhead. The wind was brisk. The first hints of fall lay about in the piles of red, yellow, and tan leaves that the janitor was raking up in the school yard.

As Junior approached the janitor, he raised his hand in greeting.

The janitor nodded. "Hello, young man."

Junior responded with a few words and then asked the question that was bothering him.

"Sir, they call this Sunbury Consolidated School. Why?"

The janitor stopped raking and leaned on his rake.

"Because all grades—one through twelve—are here. Before this school, children went to one-room schools scattered about the county. Now the school buses gather them from about and bring them here. What grade are you in?"

"Seventh."

"Oh yes, the junior high school building." He pointed. "Over there are grades one through six." He then pointed in the opposite direction. "And over there is the high school. Down there is the football field with the quarter-mile track around it." He turned back to Junior and smiled. "Anything else you wanna know?"

Junior shook his head "no" and thanked the man, who quietly resumed raking. Eating his lunch—a biscuit and sidemeat—Junior a short distance around the school. But a gust of wind suddenly chilled him, and he scurried back into his building.

When he returned home that afternoon, his mother met him at the door. She was wearing her heavy coat. Her hair was tucked up into a wool cap.

"Son, I want you to take a walk with me. Your brother will stay with the little ones." She turned briefly back to the house. "Everett," she instructed, "you and the children stay right where you are until I come back."

She led Junior across the road and under two strands of barbed wire, through the wheat-stubbled field, to the trees beyond. As she suspected, numerous dried limbs lay scattered about; but she did not stop there. Walking on some little distance they came upon a meandering creek. At its bank they stood watching as the water frothed and rippled between the six- or seven-foot banks. In the crystal-clear water, fish lazily undulated their tails against the current, holding their positions on the creek bottom. Hidden away in cattails, several startled frogs leapt into the stream. Junior exclaimed, "Look, Mother, fish!"

"Yes, son." She allowed Junior to savor his new-found diversion for a few minutes. Then she indicated it was time to return to the house. "Let's head back now, son."

Dragging long branches tucked under each arm, they stumbled and tramped back under the barbed fence and into their backyard.

"Leave them here," she said, "We'll try to cut them up later."

After supper and homework, just as they were about to go to bed, Junior asked Lilly Ann, "Mother, why are we out here?"

Touching her son on the arm, Lilly Ann said, "We were about to be set out into the street, homeless, Junior. God Almighty saved us with a safe place to stay and keep warm. When you're older you'll understand. Now, go on to bed and get some sleep."

She kissed him on the cheek then walked away.

* * *

October blew in frosty, but in each classroom the radiators emitted a pleasant warmth. At the front of the classroom, a sheet on which the alphabet was printed hung above the chalkboard, capital letters above, lowercase letters below. At each desk a student dipped the nib of a quill pen into the inkwell and copied the letters onto a clean sheet of paper, while Miss Rosen strolled about the classroom, making corrections. Quietly but firmly, the classroom door opened. Miss Dennis, the school's current music teacher, entered. She approached Miss Rosen, and the two began talking in close whispers. After a moment, Miss Dennis drew away; Miss Rosen in turn walked to the front of the classroom and spoke.

"Students, if you will…please put down your pens. Miss Dennis has something to share with you."

Miss Rosen turned to Miss Dennis. Miss Dennis moved beside her.

"Some of you may already know what I'm about to say, but for those who don't…. Each year, the eighth-grade class presents a musical before we are excused for Christmas. I'm here to determine if any of you seventh graders would like to sing one of the minor songs or be a part of the chorus."

The classroom was silent. Some students shifted uncomfortably, not wanting to be singled out. Junior stood up abruptly, surprising himself.

Miss Dennis smiled to him. "Junior, would you like to participate in the performance?"

"Yes, ma'am."

"And what would you like to sing for me?"

"If it's all right, I would like to sing a song from church."

"Oh, of course."

Junior nodded to convey his confidence. From the first note, his voice came out surprisingly lyrical. He projected his first tenor-soprano voice boldly through the classroom:

Jesus loves me…that I know…for the Bible tells me so….

The classroom again grew silent after Junior had finished.

"Junior," Miss Dennis finally said, "please bring a permission note from your parents to school tomorrow. What you sang for us just now was wonderful; I would like you to be in the show." She smiled warmly to her student. "You must arrange to attend practice after school and find a way to get home."

On the school bus home, Junior sat beside a fellow classmate named Neil. Junior mentioned the play and the fact he had no way to get home. Neil said, "I'm going to be in the chorus. My parents are picking me up after practice. We can take you to the corner and you can walk the rest of the way home."

When Junior excitedly told Lilly Ann, she smiled, saying, "You'll have to discuss the matter with your father when he arrives. Now, come help me bring in some firewood before the dark sets in."

Grimly, she trudged with him. That day, as with all other days, there were chores to be finished before breakfast. The children had to be cared for, the older ones washing, dressing, and eating in time to catch the school bus. The smaller ones were washed, fed, and dressed. Once she had taken care of each child's needs, Lilly Ann straightened and cleaned the house. Soiled clothes were scrubbed on the washboard then rinsed and wrung out by hand. The slop jars were carried to the outhouse and dumped. As on any other day, Lilly Ann and the children trudged across the stubbled field to drag home limbs to be cut up for cooking and heating.

That Saturday, Roy arrived while they were gathering wood. When told of the school program, he asked Lilly Ann's opinion. Despite herself, Lilly Ann said, "It's an opportunity for the community to get to know him—and us," she added as an afterthought.

Roy nodded. He granted Junior permission to stay after school for practice.

As the school musical progressed, Junior stayed longer each day, proving less helpful at home. Soon, the days became shorter, the evenings darker. Wood from across the way took longer for Lilly Ann and the other children to find and drag home.

Black walnuts appeared on the ground, succumbing to the frosts. Lilly Ann dared, now, to take Everett along with her, carrying gunnysacks in the wagon to gather the nuts and haul them back. Then, shelled husked, dried, and broken apart, she wanted to use them in fudge, provided she could obtain enough sugar before Christmas. For one short moment she felt a touch of happiness in the simple grimness of staying alive. Once Everett and the wagon of walnuts were safely back home, Lilly Ann and Junior scurried back to secure the wood so desperately needed for heat and cooking.

As the days grew darker and colder, Lilly Ann saw to the family's survival. Once a week she saw to bathing. Water was heated on the stove then poured into the same big tub used for washing clothes, with the bigger children washing one at a time, the smaller ones bathing together. On Saturday nights, Lilly Ann took the first bath while the children were upstairs. Out and dry, her long hair rolled up in a long, white cloth, she called for Junior to come have his turn. Like clockwork, Junior complained of having to stand naked in front of his mother. Lilly Ann chuckled at her son's shyness, saying that he looked the same as the day he was born.

One by one, she put the others through the same routine.

During the week she baked biscuits, fired salt pork to eat for lunches, saw to it that homework was prepared each day. With persistence, the family not only survived, it persisted.

Then, without warning, a morning sickness began to occur. Mild, but unmistakable. Despite her every effort, she was pregnant.

When Roy heard the news, he held her, saying, "Our celebration for not losing everything was a little exuberant."

She responded by saying she was not sure exactly how far along she was, but that it was at least three or four months, for certain.

The next Saturday, Roy summoned Junior. Together they crossed the road not once but a dozen times, dragging out as many fallen trees as possible, the larger the better. With a small crosscut saw, they cut and stacked wood for the stoves. On the weekends that followed he arrived with gunnysacks of coal. Along with his sons, he ground corn in the small grinder he had attached to the corner of a shelf in the corn shed.

On Thanksgiving he brought a small turkey, cranberries, and fruit he had somehow acquired. The holiday resulted in the family gladly gathering together, warm, and well fed. The Christmas season approached without fanfare. With school out for the holiday, Lilly Ann managed the required household functions but made certain to involve each younger member of the family in an activity that advanced their learning of the three Rs.

Later, the entire family filed into the school auditorium to see the eighth-grade play for which Junior had been practicing. Once the audience was seated and quiet, the curtain rose and the play went on. Then, Junior's voice rose sweetly and clearly.

Now every honeybee a warning take from me....

A tragedy most awful I will now relate of a curious bumblebee who flew out one day with a zoom, zoom, zoom....

Pie spied an open window near and flew into a room a maid was sweeping vigorously with a broom, broom, broom.

Spying the bumblebee she wacked him once, she whacked him twice, and there he met his doom....

And there he met his doom....

All the while that Junior sang, the eighth graders carried on the action accompanying Junior's song. Junior stood confidently onstage, fluttering his costume wings and singing sweetly, his voice entrancing the audience.

The curtain fell, the audience erupted in sustained applause, and the young actors bowed to the audience—not once, but twice.

On the drive home, Lilly Ann turned to Junior, who was seated in the back.

"Son, your father and I are proud of you. You performed well. You sang beautifully."

Junior smiled and nodded.

Christmas Eve came, and when the children were asleep Lilly Ann and Roy brought out the presents they had hidden when Roy had brought them home. For the boys, popguns perhaps eighteen inches long that broke open and *popped!* when the trigger was pulled. The girls were to receive an off-red baby carriage.

"I had to buy coal, four gunnysacks' worth. Those I piled on the porch."

There was little debate over what they needed most. Coal was coal.

*　*　*

Christmas day broke grey and gloomy. A light snow misted over the frozen ground. Inside, the children woke to warmth and the comfort of family. Dinner included a roast chicken that Lilly Ann had stuffed with a cornbread dressing; the corn had been ground by the boys. Sweet potatoes, apple and blackberry cobbler, biscuits and gravy…the family ate and spoke quietly to each other. When dinner was over, the children played while Roy and Lilly Ann sat quietly by the corner where the drophead Singer sewing machine sat.

At one point, noticing her husband gazing at the Singer, Lilly Ann said, "If you can, I need muslin cloth. The children are growing and I need to make some new clothes."

"All right…maybe I can buy a sack less of coal and buy the material."

Lilly Ann smiled. Thinking of his job at the American Insurance Union, Roy rose and gestured to the windows.

"I think I should go. Holiday or not, the work at A.I.U. goes on. I should leave now, before I get snowed in."

Nodding, Lilly Ann said, "And I want you to be safe."

Hugging his children and kissing his wife, Roy drew on his high-collar, sheepskin coat and his cap…and then he was out the door. Through the window she watched as the Ford moved down the driveway and disappeared down the road.

Morning brought no real surprise. The sculptured flakes had fallen throughout the night, bringing snowdrifts that covered the path the children used to reach the school bus. While the children got ready for school, Lilly put on her winter coat and snow boots and shoveled the path to the road. The school bus, its tires wrapped in chains, approached.

With the older children safely on their way, the younger children slept on. Lilly Ann warmed herself by the stove then sat at the Singer,

peddling stitches in the muslin garments she was preparing for her growing children. She paused and let her mind drift in reverie to the past.

CHAPTER 6

Finally driven to nurture, protect, and raise Lilly Ann, Maggie knew she couldn't do it alone. As neighbors and family drifted away, Jimmy, Ira's older brother, persisted. Bringing batten, clapboards, and nails he sealed the house against the approaching winter. Each time he returned from working the riverboat he brought goods, cloth, thread, needles, even baby shoes. Maggie grew quite fond of Jimmy. Her instinctual womanhood told her she needed a husband and father for Lilly Ann. Three years had passed; and while various neighbors had intimated at that a more-than-casual relationship was developing between them, Maggie kept Jimmy at a friendly distance. Then, after returning from a riverboat trip, Jimmy rushed to Maggie's home, looking forward to the supper Maggie had prepared. After supper, he rose, thanked her, and said he had to hurry home because of the cold and darkness.

Standing near him, she replied, "You're right. It is late and dark. Why don't you stay the night? You can go home in the morning."

Shocked, he stood speechless. What he had thought about often was now being offered. He moved closer to put his arms about her, saying, "I will."

Maggie went to Lilly Ann and, after preparing her for the night, placed her in the little crib she had been given.

"The slop jar is in the corner, if you need it."

Maggie moved quickly to the backroom and put on her nightgown. Without Jimmy seeing, she inserted a bacon-greased oil rag that she had prepared into her vagina. She then brought out the featherbed, lay herself down upon it, and waited. Jimmy came in, wearing only his long johns. Under the covers, they held each other for a long while. Then, he entered her. She responded, feeling him inside her. She moved with him, the pleasure started. In a building frenzy she increased her effort as encouragement until, suddenly, he collapsed.

Holding him close, she said, "Oh Jimmy, keep Lilly and me."

In his exhaustion he muttered, "Maggie, I will."

Three months later they were married, and she knew that she and Lilly Ann were safe.

Months later they came to her with the news that her father, John Pete Watkins, had been arrested and placed in the Ohio State Penitentiary. She had seen the prison, a vast city block enclosed by twelve-foot high, native-stone walls. Inside, sectioned off from the two cells from which a Civil War general and his men had escaped, stood a vast wood-working foundry. The forge produced school desks, chairs, tables, and wood-handled products such as axe and pitchfork handles. John Pete and a group waited on the assembly floor, where the steel parts were attached to the wooden handles. Assembled pitchforks and the like were tossed down the stairs at anyone who attempted to climb up to the forge.

Word had leaked out to reporters at the *Columbus Dispatch*, the city's newspaper, about the strike that had broken out among the prisoners due to rotten food, often dished out in inferior amounts, being served to the prisoners. The warden and many staff members were fired.

John Pete received an additional year of incarceration from his role in the strike.

Maggie's father was a full-blooded Cherokee Indian whose family had drifted up from North Carolina, across the Ohio River, into southern Gallia County, Ohio. Since his youth he had made a living hunting, fishing, trapping, and, occasionally, stealing. Fathering his daughter from birth after her mother had died, he had seen to her growth and development. He himself had been educated in a one-room schoolhouse on the reservation. He was taught by white Christian women who felt it their Christian duty to educate the poor, lost souls.

John Pete continued trading beaver, mink, fish, raccoon, and whatever else landed in his traps. His family survived on staples such as flour and sidemeat. From various ladies he knew he obtained dresses, shoes, and socks for his daughter. Summer brought potatoes, carrots, onions, kale, and other vegetables that he cooked for himself and his family. Cold weather brought ferret hunting and catching rabbits by covering their holes with a gunnysack. As Maggie grew she came to know her father for all that he was, and for his straight black hair, high cheekbones, and warm temperament—and for all that he wasn't. Their love and affection for each other would last forever.

CHAPTER 7

Permanent winter set in with quiet fury. The snow drifted deep in places, whipped around buildings, obscured vision at times, or lay in white silence. Lilly Ann managed fires, food, school, and family life.

But one essential for the family's well-being was missing—milk. Knowing the farm next to hers had cows, she instructed Junior to mind the children then set out for the farm. Pulling Junior's wagon loaded with the biggest jug she possessed, she set out. Even dressed in her warmest clothes she felt the chill as she walked. The wagon bumped over the uneven and snowy surfaces of the road even as she was buffeted by the winds. Arriving at the neighbor's house, she knocked at the door. Almost immediately a woman answered. Seeing Lilly Ann, she pulled her inside then closed the door, saying, "Please…come in."

Somewhat startled, Lilli Ann blurted her name and told the woman she was from next door.

"Gorsuch," the woman volunteered. "Eliza Gorsuch is my name. My husband is Jacob. We have lived here thirty-seven years. Our children have grown. They have places and children of their own." She paused, staring at Lilly Ann carefully, "Now, you look distressed. How can I help you?"

"Milk. I need milk for my children."

At that, Eliza smiled.

"Milk? We have too much milk. We milk six cows and feed two year-ling calves. We sold two calves to Natole in town, as well. Maybe you have noticed their plant? The railroad tracks cross the road to it, where the bed goes under the road just as you come into town. Once we made reasonable income, now they don't pay the cost of hay and grain. Milk?" she repeated. "Oh yes, I will be glad to give you some. Now and every day. But, please: take off your coat and come in by the stove to warm yourself. I will get you something warm to drink."

She left but returned shortly with a clay cup of cider, into which she inserted a hot poker from the stove. Coat off, now, sitting and drinking warm cider in the kitchen, Lilly Ann spent long minutes in comfort, then remembered her family and their needs. She rose. Eliza halted her.

"Lilly Ann, remember, I'm your friend. I've needed a neighbor-friend for a long time. If you allow me, I'll be yours and you can be mine."

Lilly Ann reached out her hand, and Eliza grasped it. For a long moment they clasped hands, then Eliza said, "You must hurry; the children must be fed. If you send Junior, I'll send milk back with him."

Lilly Ann nodded. "And we have food enough, stored or canned, we can share with you."

"I am grateful," Lilly Ann said as she left for home.

For the remainder of winter, every several days, Junior called on Miss Eliza and returned home with the milk.

As the days passed menacingly dark grey, Lilly Ann knew that snow, ice, and distance were keeping Roy away. Through frost and snow, Lilly Ann was nearly constantly hungry with the growing weight of her pregnancy. Her Singer whirred on as she maintained the family. And the winter's intensity continued on.

CHAPTER 8

Onward, Christian soldier, marching as to war—
with the cross of Jesus—marching as before....

The choir of Shiloh Baptist Church rang out. Alongside the reverend deacon, Jimmy Mayo sat in the pulpit. Jimmy wore his three-piece suit with the vest, his gold watch on its fob, the gold chain extending from pocket to pocket across his chest. Sitting with ten-year-old Lilly Ann in a pew nearby, Maggie, in a long gingham dress, sang along with the congregation.

Jimmy could not be certain of just how or when his transformation occurred. Before each trip upriver and after coming back, he spent his time at home with his wife and the child of whom he was so proud. While spending time with Lilly Ann, it became clear that he himself needed to increase his education if he was to teach the child. Increasingly, as time permitted, he read the Bible, books, and papers. At home, he spent time in the classes his reverend taught, duly passing his learnings onto his wife and child. Almost accidently, in one of Jimmy's church classes, he met a member of the state legislature, and they became fast friends. Jimmy took his wife and child to the member's home. He became familiar with his friend's political status. Over time, the two exchanged information about the family, the neighborhood, and local politics. As a result, Jimmy made the politician aware of his desire to come off the river; to accord himself a stable situation encompassing home, school, employment, church, and friends.

Several weeks later the politician approached Jimmy. "My friend, if you are willing to move to Columbus, I may be able to help you. How does a place in the post office sound to you?"

Impressed, Maggie nevertheless voiced her concerns. Jimmy smiled to her; her concerns were issues he could assuage with appropriate answers. In the end, they agreed her concerns had been met.

Sixteen Thirty-three Wheatland Avenue. One story, five rooms: living room, dining room, kitchen, and two bedrooms, in what she thought was a cute pattern that Maggie admired, the move from Gallia County had been accomplished effortlessly—an exchange of two rooms for five, with electricity, kitchen, closets…and Lilly Ann with a bedroom of her own.

Maggie knew her having accepted Jimmy had accomplished her purpose—a stable home for his brother Ira's child.

Shortly after their arrival, the postmaster of the local post office, Jimmy's boss, had invited the family to inspect Jimmy's workstation. First, they were shown the flow of the mail from pickup to sorting stations to carrier. Here, the postmaster said, was where Jimmy would work. He pointed to the strong, wood device, some five feet tall, with four sides, each side having a series of enclosures of various sizes into which the mail would be sorted.

"Jimmy will sort the mail in the cubicles to the carrier."

Jimmy's boss accepted smiles of gratitude from Jimmy, Maggie, and Lilly Ann. He shook their hands fondly then dismissed himself.

"That job's for life?" Maggie asked.

"For life," Jimmy said. "With pay each two weeks."

Silently, as the streetcar back to their new house rolled on, Maggie clutched Lilly Ann to her body, feeling, at last, that Ira's Lilly Ann was safe.

CHAPTER 9

Dark clouds clung to the earth. Winds howled during moments of ferocity while snows seemed to choose their moments to slowly drift down then swirl. Lilly Ann cooked the food she had on hand, which was gradually diminishing.

Apples, in good supply yet, were fried, cooked into sauce, provided in lunch pails. Flour into biscuits…little pork, the salt boiled off, fried… cooked beans. All slowly vanished. Hearing a strange sound Lilly Ann approached the window to see Rover half carrying, half dragging a large hog's head. Going to the porch she called Rover; the poor animal dragged the head to the porch. Lilly Ann lifted the head, along with the attached shoulder piece, and carried it inside. In the tub she washed it while saying a small prayer of thanks. Over the next several days, from the root cellar where she kept it for preservation, she sliced neck and upper shoulder meat to flavor the beans and fry the potatoes, and to provide small pieces to accompany the biscuits in the children's school lunch. Despite the gloom of early darkness, deepening cold, and a general uneasiness brought on by her pregnancy, Lilly Ann provided her children both protection and safety.

A knock at the door distracted her from the Singer. Outside on the porch, standing with her children, the school bus driver removed his cap. "Mrs. Coleburn," he said, "I am bringing your children home. They have the measles and must be kept home for two weeks."

"Do they all have the measles?"

"For now, only the middle one, but they have all been exposed. I myself have had them— and if you had them, we can't get it again, but your small children may."

Thanking him, Lilly Ann gathered her children inside while inspecting Everett. The red, bumpy lesions were profuse on the boy. With all her children close, Lilly Ann comforted them as best she could while deliberately exposing each of them so that they were each infected but would be immune to a later outbreak. Having all five itching, scratching, and whimpering during the two weeks of quarantine nearly overwhelmed her, but she persisted, knowing this one period would render them immune forever.

When two weeks had passed the school bus driver again stopped at the house. At his knock, Lilly Ann opened the door.

"Ma'am, tomorrow I will stop for the children."

She thanked him. When the next day brought the school bus, the children were ready.

Life resumed, resembling as closely as possible the life Lilly Ann wanted for her family. When chicken pox came, she again made certain all children were infected and cured while she prayed the mumps would never come.

Winter wore on in full fury. Snow, ice, wind, endless days in step with her pregnancy, which proclaimed itself with morning sickness, cumbersome movements and burdensome restlessness. The demands of each day were constant. Reading, writing, arithmetic at all grade levels occupied early evenings, while meals were prepared between washing, ironing, and sewing. Every day she doctored herself and her children with Vicks salve and Sloan's liniment, as deemed necessary, medicating each exposure as it occurred. She nursed herself, the children, and even Rover through the winter.

As usual Lilly Ann bumbled about in her pregnancy, going through the daily chores, cleaning, lamp filling, wood carrying, and then resting by the heat of one of the stoves before it was time to start again.

One day as she sat she watched through the windows as a long, black, four-door Packard droned into the driveway and rode across to the barn. She realized it was strange of her to somehow know the make of the car. Junior had taught her by saying, "Mother, you must know some cars.... I could teach you." She had smiled and hugged him. "My son," she had told him, "I will if you will teach me."

And, day after day, he did.

* * *

Now, that day, she knew that it was a very expensive automobile, indeed. Donning a derby, the driver wore a three-piece suit made of what appeared to be quite expensive material. A gold chain looped his Verve gold watch into his vest pocket. As he approached, he removed his hat and spoke:

"Mrs. Lilly Ann Coleburn. If you don't remember me, I am Mr. Rhodes. We met in my office in the A.I.U. Building in Columbus. Now of all things, I find you here."

She simply stared at him.

"Is your husband home?" Mr. Rhodes said.

She shook her head "no."

"Well, when he is, please convey my message to him. I intend to acquire as much farmland as possible. Germany and Italy are at war. They will need corn and meat and other farm products. I intend to be among those selling them. I intend to be very wealthy. Your land will help me do that—and I intend to have it. I've researched the county courthouse records to acquire it and I find you own it; maybe not for long. Tell your husband what you know of what I have told. I'll be back."

Turning, he donned his derby again and marched off unconcerned whether or not Lilly Ann had understood each and every word he had said. Lilly Ann quietly watched him leave; she found little comfort knowing that when they acquired the property they had acquired the warranty deed of ownership. Despite the hardship of acquiring money, they had managed to be current on their payments for the land. Although the property was theirs, she wondered what tactics she would be confronted with next.

* * *

Despite the cumbersome bulk of her pregnancy, Lilly Ann continued with the daily chores. Oblivious to outside sounds, she was unaware of a person in the room with her. Startled by the sound of creaking floorboards, she looked up to see Roy standing there.

Bursting into tears she shouted "Roy!" and, dropping everything, she stumbled into his arms.

Much later—after the children had arrived home from school, dinner had been put away, and time had been spent together as a family—did Lilly Ann have time alone with Roy. She listened with interest to multiple explanations of the circumstances that had kept him away.

After apprising Lilly Ann's condition and feeling assured of her well-being, Roy reached into his pocket and handed her a billfold. "Count it, some nine hundred dollars."

She looked at the billfold uncertainly. "How did you get it?" she asked.

"I was promoted to section foreman. I worked Saturdays and Sundays. I also worked in the restaurant, cleaning up. When some people needed a man to do odd jobs, I did them, and I saved, knowing we needed the money."

Praising him, Lilly Ann shared the joy of the evening with him. Only when they were at the breakfast table after the children had gone to school the next morning did she mention the visit from Mr. Rhodes.

"I'll look into it," Roy said after listening intently.

*　*　*

Back in the A.I.U. building he had a lunch break, during which he went to the post office, tucked away in an obscure space on the ground floor of the building. There he sought the postmaster, whom he knew from inspecting that space to make sure the janitors complied with the strict rules that particular area required.

After exchanging greetings, he asked how he could be assured a letter had been received.

"Return receipt required," the postmaster replied. "When you request it, the clerk will give you half the receipt, and when the letter is delivered the recipient will sign for it, and that signed half will be returned to you. You'll pay a little extra, but you'll know it was received."

With that knowledge Roy now mailed each payment for his land and paid for a return receipt.

Back at home, Roy and Lilly Ann discussed plans for the use of their land. Lilly Ann spoke of market day in town and her growing a garden large enough for produce to sell. Roy, for his part, revealed that while he was in town a man had approached him asking if he knew anyone who wanted to buy a Fordson tractor and all of the equipment needed to plow, plant, cultivate, and harvest corn and wheat. When questioned as to the price, the man indicated his age no longer allowed him to farm; he would sell for a few hundred dollars, a portion of which could even be paid after the crops were harvested and sold.

Seeing Roy's interest, the man then said, "My daughter will kill me, but if you're interested I'll even have it delivered to your place and spend a little time showing you how to use it, if you don't know how."

With a handshake Roy was an owner and farmer. Lilly Ann, when told, wanted to convey her joy. She even tried; but her problem was more intimate and urgent. She knew the symptoms well.

When Roy returned Friday evening, Lilly Ann told him the baby was coming.

"Can you hold on until tomorrow? The doctor's office is closed and I do not know where he lives."

The morning brought a grey, overcast sky and rain. Roy drove through intermittent rain, almost even through darkness, to secure the doctor who, fortunately, had no other patient.

Labor was short; the baby arrived.

The doctor took Roy aside.

"It is not news I would give anyone—yours is a blue baby. It will live for a few days, maybe a week. Please help your wife to understand: when the baby is gone notify the coroner who is also the undertaker. He will come and arrange burial. If I can be of more help, please don't hesitate to get me."

And he was gone.

When Roy approached Lilly Ann, she stopped him. "I heard," she said. "I know."

The doctor, before he had left, had helped Roy roll Lilly Ann onto her side, replacing the oilcloth that she had used many times before to prevent soiling the mattress.

Nine days later Roy brought the coroner–undertaker to remove the body and arrange a burial. Following the Model A hearse into town, Roy felt anxious. He had in no way prepared mentally or financially for a death. But once in town the doctor took charge.

"Sam," the doctor said to the undertaker, "I want a pine box, two feet long, one foot wide made for the burial. I will issue the death certificate; you will dig a proper hole in the cemetery."

"Roy," the doctor continued, "you will go with the body to the cemetery. You may say a few words, if you wish. You and Sam, with two ropes, will lower the box into the ground, pull the ropes out, and fill the hole. Do I make myself clear?"

Roy watched as the undertaker, a grimace on his face, said, "Ruben, you may be the doctor but you would deny a man a living."

"Yes, I know. You would have your brothers drive their cars and act as pallbearers and then charge whatever you think you could get. Oh, I forgot the cost of a fancy casket; these people have just moved here. They have little or no money. You will handle this matter as I have directed."

Two days later the doctor's instructions were carried out. Junior watched as the undertaker helped lower the box into the ground, filled the hole, and Roy paid him the fifteen dollars he asked for.

*   *   *

After Lilly Ann had given birth, Roy and the doctor carried her to the tub they had filled with warm, soapy water. While she bathed they stripped the bed, carrying the bloody sheets outside, where they washed them and hung them to dry.

Back in bed, Lilly Ann had persuaded Roy and the doctor to move the bed a little so she could see out the window. She had been instructed by the doctor to remain in bed for two weeks. And, because Roy had to return to work, he persuaded Mrs. Gorsuch to care for Lilly Ann during his absence. Mrs. Gorsuch, in keeping with the rural tradition of the time, felt it a privilege to help a neighbor, and she did.

Propped up by pillows in the bed, and with a comforter about her, Lilly Ann could see a great portion of their land. Having heard the men talk about land she, in her mind, envisioned a great swath of corn and wheat, and a pasture with cows, a pig pen with hogs, and a field of timothy and clover for hay.

Without knowing why, her mind shifted to the knowledge she had gained by reading *The Dispatch* and *The Citizen*. She knew when Herbert Hoover had become president. She had heard the president on the radio— his message, as best she could grasp it, that the Depression would soon be over. Timidity was his approach. Minor precautions were needed, but no unemployment relief from the federal government. He insisted private charities were sufficient to support the needy. The ultimate solution, he insisted, was a great poem, something to lift people out of their fear and selfishness, something a great poem could do more than any single piece of legislation. Finally, he did say the government should establish a Government Reconstruction Finance Corporation to provide loans to help finance properties, houses, and businesses.

Her mind still wandering, she thought of George Everett Coleburn's insistence that Roy vote Republican.

Roy respected his father. He did not want to engage in a political debate with him. He had listened as his father praised Abraham Lincoln for holding the country together and for allowing there to be a United States today.

When he had finished, Roy touched his father's shoulder.

"Dad, I'm certain you are right, but the nation is starving, and Hoover touts words with no actions. Something concrete must be done, and Roosevelt is trying to do it. Things are like the three Cs, choices, chances, and changes. People are accomplishing things while they are eating and sleeping and staying alive. Yet the Supreme Court continues to try and attempt to take down every one of his accomplishments. You are my father. I honor your judgment...and most of the time I agree with it. This time, I feel something must be done to save the nation. The New Deal Roosevelt speaks about on the radio is trying. I agree with him, and I vote democratic to support him. I'm sorry that we disagree, but Lilly Ann and the children must have a chance not only to live but to survive with hope for the future. If I offend you, I'm sorry. But that is how I see it and how I feel. I am a Democrat."

George Everett Coleburn and his son parted the conversation as political opponents, but loving, lifelong friends.

* * *

Still staring out the window Lilly Ann thought back on her life. While living with her parents she had received loving care. Maggie had coddled her; indeed, she could not do enough for her. Lilly Ann was fortunate to grow up in a stable family, and Maggie ensured that her daughter had the skills to provide Junior and the other children with everything they needed to succeed in school and in their community.

PART 2

CHAPTER 10

Time passed. Lilly Ann grew and learned with the stability Jimmy provided; and with Maggie's nurturing attentiveness, she received high marks in school. She participated in school plays and other school activities.

At twelve, with other female friends, she asked her parents' permission to volunteer as an aide at the tuberculosis hospital located on the southern edge of the city. The infirmary was a low, sprawling edifice with nearly all windows always left open, even in inclement weather, in the theory that fresh air, along with the hospital's other treatments, would assist healing. Driven there by Jimmy on weekends, Lilly Ann dressed in a long-skirted, close-fitting uniform, complete with face mask. She moved among the beds, administering the medicine supplied by the doctors, emptying bedpans for those patients who were bedridden, sponge-bathing some, carrying away soiled clothing, providing clean clothing, and being of general assistance to the staff.

One afternoon in school, when she was near the age of fifteen, Lilly Ann found her panties, skirt bottom, and chair soaked in blood. Embarrassed, she tried to shield herself as she approached the teacher, who helped her through the door and kindly sent her home. There, Maggie consoled her daughter, relieving her discomfort of her schoolroom shaming; then, with patience and understanding, she explained the menstruation process. While for a few days, some teasing and "bullying about" occurred; her friendships remained. Knowing the birth process, she now felt herself a woman.

Lilly Ann progressed contentedly toward high school graduation. Perhaps, given the nation's economic conditions, she would be an office employee? Perhaps, too, she might marry? But one day, returning from school, she found her mother crouched in a chair, clutching her side, softly groaning.

When Jimmy arrived home from work, he questioned Maggie.

"My side aches something fierce," Lilly Ann's mother said between moans. "I can hardly breathe from pain."

The doctor arrived somewhat later, after Jimmy's call. He examined Maggie.

"She must go to the hospital. It may be a kidney problem."

It was the campus hospital of the Ohio State University, a vast complex of science, medicine, and dentistry with the ability to accommodate patients overnight. Jimmy and Lilly Ann visited as often as permitted. After nearly a week, they were asked by the lead surgeon to meet with him. By then, he had studied the data collected from the medical examinations.

The surgeon said, "I asked to meet with you to seek your permission to operate. Without the operation, she will surely die. The kidney failure will progress until it proves fatal. With the operation, there is a good chance she will live. Note that I say 'good,' not 'sure.' All operations are dangerous, this one doubly so. But she has a good chance, as I say."

"You mean she could die?" Lilly Ann asked.

"Yes," informed the surgeon carefully. "But we must take that risk."

Jimmy looked at Lilly Ann reticently.

Lilly Ann blurted, "Pa, we must! It's our only chance. We must take it."

After a moment, Jimmy nodded. Lilly Ann had decided for both of them.

Convinced by hospital staff, friends, and neighbors, Jimmy carried on with his normal activities, despite the stress of the operation. Hospital visits were permitted after Maggie emerged from the emergency ward.

In her hospital room, she was in and out of consciousness. When awake, she smiled feebly before slipping back into semi-consciousness. After three weeks, she briefly sat up when greeting them, before slumping back down on the pillows of the hospital bed.

At home, Lilly Ann carried out the house chores—sweeping, mopping, and making the beds as best she could. What meals she knew how to prepare she did. In turn, Jimmy rushed straight home from work. When Lilly Ann asked him to set the table, he did, as well as clearing the table after dinner. As she washed dishes, he quietly sat smoking his pipe while scanning the newspaper. While completing her homework, Lilly Ann would hear her father snoring a bit too loudly in the living room. Despite their generation gap, they effortlessly grew closer as father and daughter.

CHAPTER 11

"Mother, please, persuade Daddy," pleaded Junior.

Lilly Ann touched her oldest son on his arm.

"My son, you're not too young to understand. We are still very poor. We barely have food to eat and clothes to wear…and you want a suit with long trousers? What a request."

"Mother, please!"

"Ask your father when he comes home. That's final. Glee club, long pants…what's next?"

"It's in Westerville," Junior explained when his father came home. "You'll have to drive me. Anyhow, it is not a glee club. It's the school choir, and I'm a soloist. Please, Dad, please."

Roy looked at Lilly Ann.

"Don't look at me," his wife said. "We need so many things. A suit is not one of them. I told him to ask you. So, don't ask me."

He could tell by her tone she was irritated.

"My son, where will this event be held?"

"At Otterbein University, in the auditorium."

Roy knew Otterbein University, a private Protestant institution, which was located in the historic uptown district, whose buildings dated back to the mid-1800s. It was near the county courthouse and other government buildings. He knew a little bit of its theology—asserting that human dignity required an unimpaired freedom of will.

He furthermore felt it was an honor for his son to be asked to perform. But Lilly Ann's feelings concerning money—and, for the entire Coleburn family, its scarcity—were justified. Yet he felt honor-bound to make it possible for his son to perform.

On performance day, Junior was dressed in a white shirt with a large collar that Lilly Ann had tucked so that a tie down the front looked proper. The sleeves were a bit short, as were the matching trousers, but it would pass as acceptable. Roy had searched through pawn shops and thrift stores to produce the suit.

As for himself, Roy had on his only suit. Lilly Ann had her best dress on. The other children had their best outfits on as well.

The Otterbein auditorium was an affair with what appeared to be two thousand seats slanting from the stage, up toward the rear. The family sat halfway up. After the professor made staff introductions and read several announcements, he led the audience through a rendition of the national anthem. Then, he ushered in the choir of which Junior was a part. The lights dimmed, and the performance started. The singers, covered in robes of the school colors and under the direction of the head of the Music Department, commenced. After a number of songs, about halfway through the program, a particularly pretty melody started. Junior stepped forward; and in a lilting, first-tenor voice, he sang his solo, with the choir beautifully backing him.

Amazed, Lilly Ann regretted that she had opposed his appearance. Now, she simply allowed herself to listen.

The concert over, Junior, sitting quietly, rode the entire time required for his father to drive home with eyes closed. No one uttered further praise. Instead, the parents mused over their previous fears, their apprehensions, fretting over their conduct and their uncertain dreams for Junior and the other children. The siblings sat quietly, too, and spoke only when spoken to by either parent.

Junior reminisced about his parents hugging him after the concert, saying loving, prideful words…and him saying to them, "You will be more proud to come see me play football next year."

Without notifying his parents, he had been playing during the intervals before classes began, at lunchtime, even during brief periods with fellow classmates while waiting for the school bus. During some of these sessions, Coach Lawrence Whipkey observed him before he finally decided to approach Junior. "You'd be welcome to try out for the team next fall," he said, and moved on.

Junior welcomed the invitation, but he had no knowledge of how his parents would feel about it. So, as he proceeded up to bed, once again he floated the notion of playing football to them, but he received no response.

* * *

As the early spring faded toward summer, the blue Fordson tractor, its plow, and the other farming equipment sat where they had first been delivered. Despite Roy's frustration, and his job at the A.I.U. Building, he remained tied to the farmhands' chores as well when he returned to the farm. One of his men had suffered an accident and was not able to work. Another remained confined in a tuberculosis clinic. Roy was forced to assume their tasks since management permitted no hiring. The brief periods he was home were spent with Lilly Ann and the children. For her part, and with the permission of her doctor, Lilly Ann attended the chorus outings and oversaw the half-acre garden, which she had paid fifty cents to a man with a team to plow and harrow. She even paid a small sum for seeds, plants, and cow manure. The plants, with sufficient rain, thrived in the rich loam. Having left Harold and DeVerne playing near the house with instructions not to leave the area, she hoed weeds in the garden.

Suddenly, Harold ran toward her, screaming, "Mother! Mother! DeVerne put the kitten in the cistern!"

Lilly Ann looked in the cistern to see the kitten frantically swimming, attempting not to drown. Only her canvas gloves saved the poor kitten as it clawed into them, fiercely holding on for dear life. Uncontrollably, Lilly Ann flung kitten, gloves, and all to the ground. Wide-eyed, she turned to DeVerne.

"I wanted to see if it would swim!"

Exasperated, she hugged him tightly, feeling blessed he had not climbed into the large cistern to see if he could swim. Once again working in the garden with her floppy hat to shade her face from the sun, the worn shoes Roy had bought her, and a long, loose dress to catch pockets of air to cool her, she continued to chop at the weeds. Until the man spoke, she was not aware of his presence.

"Good afternoon, Mrs. Coleburn."

Startled, she rose up, staring at him.

"I am Reverend Daniels of the local Baptist Church. Several people have informed me of you and your family moving into our community."

Lilly Ann acknowledged his presence with a half-smile and a mumbled greeting.

"I thought I would stop by to meet you and to invite you and your family to church," the reverend continued.

Recovering, Lilly Ann hesitantly accepted the reverend's invitation.

"Would this Sunday be too soon? If not, I will inform the parishioners."

"I'm not fully certain," Lilly Ann replied. "My husband works in Columbus, you know."

"Yes, I have heard. Please try."

When Lilly Ann told Roy that they had been welcomed to church, Roy said, "A good idea. Good for the children."

"They want you to play guitar and the children to sing. They heard about Junior's performance at the university.

Roy nodded. "I'll make certain I'm off and here this Sunday."

The small, white church with a cross copula on top had a capacity of perhaps one hundred and fifty or so. Standing in the pulpit, the reverend greeted the entire Coleburn family and announced them to the congregation. Lilly Ann had no knowledge what regular attendance at the church might be like and wondered how many were there out of curiosity.

"My friends," the reverend began, "as you may know, I have invited the Coleburn family to attend our church on a regular basis. But now, I have invited them to perform—as their son did at the university. Mr. and Mrs. Coleburn, if you please…."

Quietly, they assembled.

Roy played a few chords on the guitar, then, with Junior's tenor soaring and all family members joining in, they sang.

I shall not, I shall not be moved.

I shall not, I shall not be moved.

I shall not; I shall not be moved just like a tree standing by the water....

Other verses followed; and, when they had finished, there was stunned silence at the gravity of the performance. Then, thunderous applause.

After church services were over, the reverend and the congregation greeted and congratulated them at the door.

At home, Lilly Ann and Roy praised the children. Then Roy said, almost as an afterthought, "I wonder if that message will be conveyed to Mr. Rhodes."

Lilly Ann stared at him but said nothing.

* * *

As summer moved on, they came—Grandpa George Everett and Jenny, his new wife since Grandma's untimely death. Ed was a large, kind and jovial man. His wife, Virginia, was a kind and loving woman. Brenda, their daughter, eleven and a half years of age, was a sweet girl who was kind to her parents. Aunt Lil, Myron Lil, and Yvonne, as well as other invited—and uninvited—friends. Out of love and curiosity they came to see what fifty-two acres plus a creek had wrought. Often young chickens and blue-gills caught by the dozen were fried. Any available green vegetables, white and yellow ears of corn, ripe red tomatoes, and red cherries; almost anything edible was served. Laughter, gaiety, affection, and occasional hugs ruled the day.

Roy gave them a tour of the farm, and the equipment, Blue Fordson and all, and explained how the corn and wheat shared acres of land. They were shocked that, with his farm living and with so many children, he was able to make a good living and have retail income, while those living in the city were struggling still more. Loved ones went home surprised and happy that such fortitude existed among one of their own.

* * *

Confusion reigned. Parked directly across the street was a small army of chain-driven Mack trucks, drilling rigs, and trailers loaded with poles. After checking to see if the noise had awakened the small children, she opened the front door.

Men swarmed about. They set down survey equipment. They unloaded the poles from the truck. They laughed and swore generously.

Seeing her on her porch, one of the men crossed the road, came up the hill, and approached the house. "Progress, Lady. About time, progress."

Lilly Ann drew back carefully. "I don't know what you mean."

"Them poles will go in the ground. On top will be crosspieces, on them will be electric wires. You will have electricity. Roosevelt, you know, and his congress, passed something called the Rural Electrification Act—or something close to that. You will have electricity. No more kerosene lamps." He nodded kindly, "Well, I've got to get back to work." And he walked back down the hill and then was gone.

Lilly Ann mused. No kerosene, no danger of knocking a kerosene lamp over and setting the house on fire.

Although the government brought the wiring across the street to the house, the wiring in the house was up to the homeowner. Enterprising electricians, who had been unemployed for years, approached with offers. Roy, having discussed the matter with knowledgeable men in Columbus, selected one he trusted and could afford, and the house was soon wired.

To Lilly Ann, it meant a great deal, in spite of having to purchase on credit. The children could see better to do their homework and she would no longer have to wash by hand on a board. No more heating the iron on the stove. *Better, oh my, yes.* She didn't think, she knew.

* * *

A pick-up truck stopped near the barn while she nursed Harold's hacks, which had been brought on by a bout of the croup. "Please don't be frightened," the driver said as he approached. "I just want to talk with you. I'm Jackson Murphey."

He sat down on the step below her. She could see he was dressed in coveralls and scuffed, high-topped shoes. A farm cap sat lazily on his head. "Maybe you heard of me?"

Lilly Ann shook her head.

"I have a few acres near here," Jackson Murphey explained.

Again, she shook her head. Later, it became apparent to Lilly Ann that his few acres, if you call one hundred and eight acres a few, were what he referred to.

"Perhaps you know of Nestlé?"

Again, she shook her head.

Dismayed, he said, "Nestlé owns the plant on the other side of that dip in the highway as you drive into town. It's a Swiss company that chose our community to build a plant in which milk is powdered. You know, dried then sold in packages in grocery stores to provide cream for coffee in powdered form. Grocers can keep it on shelves while milk can be kept maybe a week at best."

She listened but said nothing.

"I have noticed that your husband bought the Fordson and equipment but hasn't used them."

"He works in Columbus," Lilly Ann replied.

"Will you give him a message for me?"

She nodded.

"You have maybe fifty acres of fine loam. I would like to plant corn, wheat, and hay seeds. I can furnish both the labor and seeds in exchange for use of your land. At harvest time, my men can harvest it and share one-third of it with you and your family. Do you know when to expect him?"

"He has had to stay in the city because some of his men are ill."

"I'm sorry, but please convey my message to him. I will be back in three days to receive his answer."

She nodded.

"Thank you for talking with me."

He tipped his cap and walked away.

When Lilly Ann relayed his message to Roy, she saw his head drop.

"Fine farmer I am."

Touching him, she said, "Someone once said 'half a loaf is better than none.'"

Roy nodded.

She didn't relate how she and Junior still dragged bundles of tree branches whenever they could to use for cooking, even though he had coal trucked in for heating.

When it started up, Murphey's operation was watched by Lilly Ann and the children in awe. Four teams of horses, harnessed to large pieces of farm equipment, made short order of the plowing and planting. Tending and harvesting were accomplished with equal efficiency. Corn was shucked, a steam rig trenched the wheat; hay was cut, allowed to dry, and stored in the loft.

One day, Murphey approached Lilly Ann with a request. "I have a cow that is less productive that I must replace. I wonder if you would accept her."

Bossie, as Lilly Ann and the children called her, arrived: a fawn and white Guernsey that Lilly Ann learned gave milk not as rich as a Jersey but richer than a Holstein. Junior learned to milk plenty for the whole family. Shortly thereafter, Murphey came by, guiding a club-footed horse. "I wonder if you could accept him. He has been this way since the day he was born. The children might enjoy riding him."

Lilly Ann knew the entire community felt sorry for her. Somewhat embarrassed, she nevertheless knew that she and the children needed the help. Her appreciation knew no bounds.

"But, Mommy, what kind of horse is he?" the children would ask.

"I'm told he is a gelded Percheron."

"But what happened to his foot?"

"They told me he was born that way. That his hoof was turned out instead of flat."

They looked at him. He was big, a plow horse, dappled brown. From the beginning, they called him Barney, and they soon discovered he would eat most anything they fed him. Climbing the fence that enclosed the hogs, they rode him, using only a halter to steer him. Concerned, Lilly Ann held him at first; but, in time (given the horse's crippled gait); the boys caught and rode him around the curve to the end of the upper section then down the straightaway to the barn without injury. A new way to have fun.

* * *

Jake, the youngsters called him. They didn't know where he came from. But, in the pigpen their father had repaired, they fed him. And when he flopped down, they scratched his belly. Roy had bought him for three dollars; he had a plan in mind. He believed that despite the depressed state of the nation, people had to eat…and pork was a favorite food. The hotel and the restaurant in town threw edible garbage away every day. Hauling it home and feeding it to Jake would be almost without cost; selling hogs would bring income. His plan included building a trailer to haul the hogs and sell them in Columbus. And, beyond doubt, they needed the money. His paycheck paid the mortgage, but beyond gasoline and other necessities, little else.

But a sow?

When he told Lilly Ann of his plan, she asked, "Are you sure?"

"People have to eat," he said.

Days later, as summer approached its end, the clouds hung low with the first autumn chill tinting the air. Lilly Ann queried, "The Fordson… what do you intend to do with it during the winter?"

She had asked Roy this same question several times before but had received little response. Now he said, "You're right."

"Don't you have to start it at least one more time?"

"Yes, and park it and take the water out of it."

"Junior is with the children. I want to ride and watch you start it and run it."

"You don't mean it? Women don't do that."

"I do."

At the Fordson he showed her the instruments that she had to set before cranking. Started, she stood on the small platforms behind the driver's seat, her arms tight about him. In the cornfield he set the plow, upped the throttle, and lumbered the vehicle across the field.

After he had completed a full round, she asked, "Can I drive?"

Again, he was shocked; but again, too, he nodded. Changing positions, he muttered instructions. She got the Fordson under way, keeping her eyes on the furrow he had just plowed. She made a second furrow near the first. After plowing several more furrows, she stopped near their start-ing point.

"Roy, thank you." She added: "I know women are not supposed to do things such as this. At least people say so, but they give no reason, except we are women. Does that make sense?"

Roy shrugged.

"Women are as capable as men," Lilly Ann continued. "Yes, we have babies and nurse them. We wash clothes and make them. We cook food and help grow it. We do so many other things, like hoeing, planting, and harvesting. If anything happens in a family to the man, women carry on. Expectations for women are high, credit for them is low."

She stopped, a little shocked by what she had said.

"We better get the Fordson up to the shed and drain the water so that it won't freeze over the winter."

With that they took the machine with its equipment to the shed. They parked it, drained it, and covered it with a sheet of canvas. Then they closed the door to the shed and went into the house for dinner.

* * *

Without realizing it she saw her son for the first time. He stood in the helm of the four-oared cardboard boat. An officer's cap on his head, he sang as the other actors crept across the stage.

> *Pull ashore, in fashion steady,*
> *Hymen will defray the fare,*
> *For a clergyman is ready*
> *To unite the happy pair!*

Thrusting his arm out from his body with palms extended, he continued.

> *Silent be,*
> *Again, the Cat!*
> *It was again the cat!*
> *They're right, it was a cat!*

DeVerne turned to Lilly Ann. "Mother, what is a cat doing on a boat?"

"Shush," Lilly Ann whispered. "*Cat* means a whip with nine leather straps that ship captains used to punish their men."

Roy looked at both of them, and they went still.

The family sat quietly in their seats in the school auditorium. They were watching the eighth-graders perform Gilbert and Sullivan's operetta, *H.M.S. Pinafore*. Junior had a leading part and now performed a solo in his lilting, first-tenor voice, filling the hall with a pleasing melody.

For Lilly Ann, it seemed as if she had never seen her son Junior before. Even on his knees, he seemed tall— not gigantic, but perhaps five-foot-eight or -nine. His body had filled out, muscular, now, from farm work. *Handsome,* she thought. Her son was handsome, even to her, as she watched him perform. And, although she hadn't thought about it, he would be in high school soon.

High school?

Yes, she thought. *He will be in high school.*

*   *   *

That year, winter slammed in on a fierce wind. Leaves, twigs, and refuse swirled about while wet snow came down hard, pelting faces. Roy, Lilly Ann, and Junior clutched their garments tightly as they hurriedly completed the feeding and milking.

After his chores, Junior came back to the house, to find his mother bent over and clutching herself.

"Mother," Junior asked, "are you sick?"

"I have what I think is a stomach flu."

"What can I do?" He embraced her and eased her into a chair.

She told him to get the castor oil and to place heated cloths over her mouth, then she watched as he followed her instructions.

"Shall I stay home from school?"

"My son, no. I never want to keep you out of school."

"But, Mother...."

"My son, no, never."

"Shall I rush?"

"No, go get the bread as usual."

She meant the sliced bread from town. She gave him fifty cents from the coffee tin and had him walk the short distance into town to the grocery store, instructing him to buy the bread. The grocer's bread was for their lunches, instead of biscuits. But it was *only* for lunches. He and Everett still spent endless hours in the corn shed grinding shelled corn in the crank grinder his father had installed for cornmeal to be baked into cornbread.

Bitter winter clung to the house. Yet Lilly Ann and Junior crossed the road through the shucked corn field, venturing into the woods, where they gathered smaller, fallen trees to drag home for the kitchen stove. The coal from the small pile was carefully hoarded for the main stove and the stove upstairs, both of which were kept burning during the day. Banked at night and re-flamed by day. While Lilly Ann continued to see to the needs of the family as best she could, she could not deny her slower step, her pauses, her hand sliding along the wall or the staircase banister to stabilize herself as she went about the house while leaving Junior to milk and slop the farm animals.

CHAPTER 12

"With your permission, I will carry the garbage you threw in those cans to the farm to make slop for the hog."

All of the waste from the tables was dumped into the garbage cans that were kept outside.

"Sure, Roy," the owner said, "help yourself. Just make sure our garbage cans and their lids don't go missing or get damaged."

Roy removed the back seat in the Ford to permit two ten-gallon cans to fit upright.

At the pigpen, Jake rushed the trough and gobbled noisily.

That evening, Roy talked with Lilly Ann and said they had to buy a sow so they could raise and sell pigs and hogs.

"Maintain a hog farm?" she questioned.

"Anything to produce income."

"But everybody who wants to raise hogs has them."

"Oh, we'll not sell them in Sunbury. We'll take them to Columbus. On the northwest, just outside the city, there is an auction yard."

"But don't they get plenty already...?"

Once he had all the answers she knew he had his mind made up. Anyway, her stomach flu, or whatever it was, forced her to grasp the rocker, sit gently, rock, and say nothing further.

* * *

Winter was in full swing, now. Grey skies clung low over the fields as the cold intensified. Junior traversed the distance between the house and barn, tending to his chores. To keep his family safe, Roy fixed a rope between the two buildings, to prevent anyone being blown off course, lost in the blinding snows, or frozen to death in the relentless cold. Mornings, Junior clung to the rope as he moved back and forth, milking, slopping, feeding hay, cleaning manure. All the while, Lilly Ann assured the other children made the school bus. Roy acquired wheels and axels—long two-by-sixes—to be hammered and sawed. He gradually formed the pieces of wood into a trailer in which to haul the hogs to the marketplace as often as possible—which was not often, as Roy remained keeping the A.I.U accessible.

* * *

Despite the howling wind, Lilly Ann heard the knock. Clutching her shawl, she opened the door to find Mr. Rhodes standing alone outside, his Packard half on the road, half on the snowcapped lawn.

"Please, Mr. Rhodes, come inside and out of the cold."

He did as Lilly Ann bade him, with hat in hand.

"Mrs. Coleburn," Mr. Rhodes said, "I was in the neighborhood and thought I would check on your welfare."

"We are as well as can be expected."

"Think how much easier it would be to be in the city."

Before responding, Lilly Ann paused, understanding Mr. Rhodes' implication.

"Mr. Rhodes," she said, "perhaps you're right, but we have established a life here. And, unless Roy says differently, I intend for us to stay here. But I appreciate your concern. Thank you."

Taken aback for a moment, Mr. Rhodes was speechless. Grasping his hat, he turned toward the door.

"Thank you for your graciousness."

With that he quickly stepped out of the house as she held the door open for him.

When Roy arrived home, Lilly Ann informed him of the incident.

"Damn him!" Roy exploded.

"Roy, the children…,"

"Honey, I know, but it makes me so mad."

Lilly Ann put her hand on his arm.

"You know he means it, Roy. You have made the payments fully and on time."

"Fully and on time."

"I was certain you had but he means business. I could tell by the tone of his voice."

Sensing her concern, he went to her, wrapped his arms around her, and muttered soothing words. Then, still reassuring her, he said, "Honey, I know you're right. When I come back, I'll bring the small strongbox I have in my office space here for your keeping. Be at ease. I have kept up all payments, including taxes, and made sure all the deeds and other papers are up to date."

*　*　*

Fortunately, while the weather remained cold, the snow ceased. Dutifully, he brought the strongbox with the critical papers to her. He hauled trailer parts along with garbage. Cold or no, the outside activities demanded Lilly Ann's and her sons' attention each day. Roy, for his part, made it home every Saturday, and carried on the duties of farming. Outside in the cold, Junior often worked hard, frequently seeking the warmth of the house at Roy's urging.

Often, in the cold, the hog slop carried steam. Jake gobbled down the slop with satisfied greed. Then one day, Jake found he had a companion: a sow, grunting, gobbling slop with satisfaction as she shared the trough and the pen with Jake.

When slop no longer captured Jake's attention, Junior stood watching as Jake circled the sow until she grunted and circled about the pen then stopped and raised her tail. Jake mounted her, and Junior watched as he thrust a corkscrew-shaped penis rapidly into her, dismounted then mounted again, repeating his actions. Then both Jake and the sow issued satisfied grunts and fed for a long time at the trough.

The next day, while they waited for the school bus, Junior related to a friend what he had seen. His friend scoffed, "That wasn't nothing!"

He told Junior that he did it to Sarah, who was seated on the bus. Junior, incredulous, said he didn't believe him. The friend, taking him by the arm, led him to the bus's window, where Sarah sat. Knocking on it, he signaled her to lower the window. She did.

"Don't I funk you?" he asked.

She smiled as she said, "Yes."

"Now do you believe me?" the friend asked Junior.

Junior could only nod "yes." The friend got on his bus and was gone. As he moved to his bus, Junior thought about funking. He hadn't done it for a long time. Really, he hadn't thought about it for a long time.

Now he did.

*　*　*

There were six of them, piglets the sow delivered as he watched. Junior saw them suckle her hungrily. Since their birth, Roy had brought more slop for the sow.

"Now we will have hogs to sell," Junior stated.

"Yes, we'll have three when they weigh about two hundred pounds, more or less. We'll keep the sows to reproduce."

Almost unnoticed, one young sow, maybe a hundred pounds or so, went into heat, and Jake did his duty. Roy, dismayed, told Junior he hadn't thought about it, but they needed the money. And on a Saturday, the trailer was hitched to the Model A with the sow and the pigs and one boar; all were taken to the stockyard auction house. Roy talked with the yardmaster then unloaded the hogs as the yardmaster had instructed and handed his son a biscuit and an apple.

"Son," he said, "I'll be here as soon after work as I can. Go up there in the stands, watch the auctions; and when our hogs sell, collect the money."

October chill hovered over the stands. Though dressed as warmly as possible, Junior huddled several flights up to watch as lot after lot of beef cattle was sold under the bang of the auctioneer's gavel. Toward the end of the day, the field man who brought the lots out to the yard herded the hogs in.

Behind him, Junior heard a snicker and a voice saying, "Do you believe it? Hogs! Everybody's got hogs."

The auctioneer commenced, but instead of the rattle of voices as before, there was silence. The auctioneer's voice shouted his chant: "Do I hear a dollar? Do I hear two?"

"I'll give you five dollars for the lot," came a voice from a man who was sitting near Junior.

The auctioneer announced the price, asked if anyone would raise it, and then hit the gavel.

Sold!

The man said to Junior, "Son, you must go into the office to collect."

Junior, shivering, snot running from his nose, tears in his eyes, allowed himself to be guided into the office. A stove glowed with heat. Junior huddled against it, tears flowing. A man came to him with a chair. He sat Junior down close to the heat then stooped and removed his shoes. Then he massaged his feet and covered him with a blanket kept for the occasional woman who needed it.

"Son, have you had any food?"

"I had a biscuit and an apple."

Going to his own lunch bucket, the man retrieved a bologna sandwich.

"Here, eat this," he said. "I'll set your shoes close to the stove; they'll warm your feet when you put them on. And, here, before I forget, is the five dollars for the sale of your hogs. Normally, we take a commission...but not this time. Now you warm yourself until your father comes. I'll be over here, working at the desk. Anything you need before I go?"

"I need the use of the bathroom."

"Yes, of course. Right back there."

After going to the bathroom Junior sat with his shoes back on, warm and comfortable, until his father came. With the trailer hitched, they rode home in silence. Once home, Junior gave his father the five dollars.

"Is that all?" Lilly Ann queried after she heard Junior tell her of the auction house and the auctions of horses, cattle, and sheep—and then of the five dollars.

"Well, son, we tried," Lilly Ann said. "I thank you."

She hugged him close and then said, "Let us eat dinner."

* * *

He had no idea when he first noticed it; but each time, now, as he milked Bossie, she had less milk. When he told his mother, she told him to tell his father.

When he went to his father, his father said, "I want you to take the cow to the Schwartz's place. I'll stop by and tell him you're coming. If the weather's bad, don't go. Wait until it's pleasant because you know she'll go slowly."

The weather cleared, with a low-hanging sun. Junior led Bossie with a line from her halter and walked nearly a mile to the Schwartz's place. Leo Schwartz met him near the barn.

"Bring her through this gate."

The bull watched her come through the gate. Then, without hesitation, he snorted and mounted her, semen streaming. With lunges, he penetrated her rear. Hunching and moaning, she stood with her legs slightly spread. When the bull dismounted, Leo grasped the rope and led her out of the pen.

"Tell your father she is well bred. The calf will suckle the milk. Wherever you got milk from before you will need to go back to. Be careful going back home."

Junior walked back with a rise in his pants from watching the bull and Bossie. He wondered when he would be able to funk again.

CHAPTER 13

"God damn!"

The expletive sounded long and loud. The entire operating room stood nearly paralyzed as the surgeon, scalpel suspended in midair, stood staring down at the body on the operating table. The body he had opened heaved uncontrollably, its chest jerking up and down. On the table, Junior's ether mask thrust up and down with each heave.

"God damn," the surgeon yelled again.

Moving quickly, the assistant surgeon, the nurses, and the anesthesiologist all grasped Junior's body, attempting to keep him from falling off the table.

"Please…he could die," a nurse said.

Slowly, Junior's body relaxed. The operating staff resumed the procedure. Later, when told of the incident, a nurse's aide would stare absently at the surgeon, then excuse herself and walk quietly to the bathroom, where she rinsed her face with cold water and then took a hard look at herself in the mirror. She had been given instructions to have the patient swallow a pill dry; but she had proven unable to turn down his request for a glass of water to help him swallow the pill.

During a physical exam required before joining the football team, Junior was discovered to have a rupture. Being told of the rupture, Roy had questioned the nature of it. The doctor described the ailment as being an opening in Junior's groin that permitted his intestine to protrude through the lining. Now, the operation Junior was undergoing was to sew the opening closed. Without the operation, the doctor had said, the intestine would eventually protrude farther, causing the intestine to twist until it cut off the blood supply, possibly leading to death. Later, Roy angrily questioned Lilly Ann regarding Junior's signing up to play football against his explicit instructions that Junior *not* play football. But, secretly, Roy knew that Lilly Ann had probably saved his son's life. Still, he churned inside over the fact that she had disobeyed him. His only words after the quarrel were "Don't do it again."

Now, Roy and Lilly Ann took the elevator, which moved quietly to the third floor of Meroy Hospital. Seeing his parents, Junior smiled. "I know you heard what went on here," he said. "I'm sorry."

"Son, you were blessed," Roy said as Lilly Ann moved to his bed and hugged him.

"Son, we know that you were blessed."

Junior nodded to Lilly Ann then turned deliberately to his father. "Now I can play football."

Lilly Ann turned toward Roy to gauge his reaction; Roy nodded in assent.

* * *

It was a little over three-foot long. The leather portion was maybe two-and-a-half feet long, and was attached to a stout, wooden handle. He carried it in one hand while he gestured with the other. Coach Whipkey surveyed his players, Junior among them, his rupture fully healed.

He had survived a season of freezing rain, snow, and sleet, all of which had melted and frozen again to form black ice. He had hauled milk from next door. He had worked the hayfield for a payment of fifty cents a go and then drunk maple syrup for desert at lunch. And all of it had been accomplished with one goal in mind: football.

Rivulets of sweat drenched his uniform as he went through the running and stretching drills in the August heat while being urged on by the leather whip, which was often wielded with both hands. Coach Whipkey stood behind him some forty yards away, a punter stood between two ends. The coach had previously determined—after evaluating several players for eye–hand coordination, running speed, and general football courage— that Junior was his best choice to return a punt. Now the kicker's punt flew high toward Junior who shifted his position to receive it. Returning the punt, the ends closed on him. As Junior ran past Coach Whipkey, the strap landed smartly on his rear, causing him to take a quick stride forward, avoiding the ends.

"Yes!" the coach shouted. "Yes!"

Junior had been the coach's pick to play left halfback, replacing a player who had graduated from high school the year before.

As practice ended, the coach put his hand on Junior's arm. "I've decided that you will be my left halfback. I hope you will live up to my expectations."

"I will, Sir." Junior nodded confidently to Coach Whipkey. "I will."

Several weeks later, the yellow school bus with "Sunbury Consolidated School" lettered on its sides rolled to a halt. Through its opened door, the football players, helmets in hand, ran out. They gathered about the coach on the driveway. Slightly downhill, with chalk stripes ten yards apart, lay the close-clipped, green, one hundred yards of the football field. Along each side's full length stretched the bleachers, rising some forty feet. A short fence enclosed it all, with the ticket gate at one end and a concession stand that served popcorn, drinks, and candy at the other end.

Almost as if a signal had sounded, the teams trotted onto the field. Sunbury sat on the team benches lining the left side of the field, and then Crow Town entered and sat on the benches on the right side of the field. Two officials who would mark the placement of the ball after the runners' progress had been halted moved to the center of the field, along with the lead official, who would signal penalties. The teams' captains joined them; the coin flip followed, which Crow Town won. They decided to receive the ball. Junior played left halfback, making tackles beside his teammates. Nevertheless, by employing clever running plays, and by using their quickness and strength to gain a further advantage, Crow Town moved the ball down the field. One play was particularly unusual: the fishhook. An eligible receiver would rush toward Junior, as though to block him, then turn toward the passer and receive the ball. Twice the play was executed, with Junior making the tackle and limiting the gain to only a few yards. The third time Crow Town tried the play, Junior rushed forward, caught the ball, and ran sixty-seven yards for a touchdown. Although he made tackle after tackle and rushed as well, his team lost. As he lined up to board the bus with his teammates, a man approached him. "That was quite a scoring run," the young man said. Junior whorled around to face him.

The man stuck out his hand. "I'm Rodger Blunt, a reporter for the *Columbus Dispatch* newspaper."

Junior shook the reporter's hand while also instinctively saying, "Thank you."

"I'm sorry," the reporter said, "but I didn't catch your name."

"Junior Coleburn."

"Junior, you caught my attention. You played very well, but your team lost, so your name will not appear in the paper. But I'll be watching you. If you do that well each week…we'll see."

The team members behind Junior pressed him forward, and the reporter was gone. As the bus rolled out of the parking lot, Junior spontaneously started to sing.

An assistant coach rose. "I'll stop him," he told Coach Whipkey.

"No," the coach said. "It will lift the team's spirits. They may even join in."

They listened, but they did not join in.

*   *   *

"Go up under there and drag him out," Roy said to Harold and DeVerne.

"Daddy, do we have to?"

"Do what I said."

Roy watched as his small sons crawled on their hands and knees through the small opening created by forcing slats aside under the porch. Harold and DeVerne each grabbed a leg and dragged Rover to their father who shot him dead with a twelve-gauge shotgun.

Earlier, responding to the boys' question, Roy had explained why Rover had to be shot. Now he repeated his explanation.

"He went bad. He was destroying our livestock, costing us money; and he would not stop. Now drag him to the hole I dug so that we can bury him."

And they did while Roy shoveled.

"Daddy, will we have another dog?"

"We will see."

* * *

The football soared high into the late afternoon soon as Junior moved to catch it. He clutched the ball tightly, his arm pressed to his side, then quickly accelerated and raced up the field. Even at full speed he surveyed his opponents' positions. All about him blue jerseys closed in. He stepped right, then left, straight- arming his opponents, always moving forward. Then he had a clear path to the end zone. His teammates cheered, as did the young beauties with the long legs and short skirts who waved their pompoms ecstatically as the scoreboard ticked off the final seconds of the game. Sunbury had won.

She was there, his mother. She had arranged for the children to be cared for while she attended the game in order to watch Junior. Once the game was over, she hurried to reach the car where the driver who had brought her to the stadium was waiting. Suddenly, a man had a hand on her arm.

"Please let me speak with you for a minute or two. I'm a reporter for the *Columbus Dispatch*. I've seen Junior play now for a third time. He is quite good. I want to write an article about him. If he is as good at the next game, I would like to secure a few facts about him from you. Would you mind?"

They had reached the car where the driver was waiting to take her home.

"No," Lilly Ann said, "I don't mind. I'm quite proud of him, but I will not tolerate any derogatory remarks."

"I understand," Rodger Blunt said, "and I'm grateful for your cooperation. I will contact you after the next game."

On the way home, she wondered what she had committed herself to.

* * *

Sheets of rain fell on the team's bus as it arrived. Junior stepped off the bus, a plastic, hooded cloak covering him. The other players unloaded, walking over to the benches along their side of the field. The bleachers along the other sideline were already occupied by the members of the other team, prepared to brave the elements. The heavy wool Jerseys, canvass pants, and shoes quickly became soaked by the rain and mud; the players lumbered up and down the field, slowed by the awful conditions. Junior slogged along, running the ball and making tackles. But he felt as miserable as he ever had.

Finally, his team made one final score. Each player carried out his assignment. The line made a small opening. Junior stepped through with the ball, as the tacklers came toward him. Instinctively, as they moved left, he moved right. As they moved low for the tackle, he stepped over them and scored the only touchdown.

The sports column of the *Columbus Dispatch* posted the following article the next day.

> Franklin, Delaware, and surrounding counties have teams playing less than outstanding fall football. I've witnessed it as I attended the games; but, as the old man said, 'Even a blind hog finds an acorn sometimes,' and maybe I've found one. While we call him Junior, his name is Joseph Leroy 'Junior' Coleburn. I've traveled to game after game to see him play. I've watched him make touchdowns, intercept passes, and make tackles— in other words, play outstanding football. I've seen it, and I recommend that all you readers do the same. Only a freshman, perhaps five-foot-nine, but still growing…will we see him play at Ohio State? One never knows. To ensure your chance of catching one of the greats in action, go now.

Roy did not remember the first time he read about his own son, but friends and coworkers brought article after article to his attention, asking "Is this your son?" When an article finally made its way to Lilly Ann, she smiled but said nothing.

*   *   *

A doctor, summoned by the crowds, kneeled by a prostrate Junior. Treatment, administered slowly, helped him regain consciousness. Standing close by was the Coach, trainer, and his fellow teammates.

"What happened?" Junior asked.

"You got kicked in the head."

"How?"

"An equal part bad luck and timing."

"What?"

"When you went in for that tackle, the runner jumped and his foot caught you in the head and knocked you out cold."

"Did we win?"

"We're ahead, and it's almost over."

"Good," he said as he sunk back into half consciousness.

At home, his head ached terribly. His family, hearing the details of his accident, nursed him as best they could; but he insisted on attending school the next day. At school, friends sought him out to see how he was faring. Members of the coaching staff inquired into his well-being, and the coach asked, "Is he well enough to play this week?"

Crowds gawked as the Sunbury bus arrived at the football field on Friday night. Everyone had heard of the knockout. The onlookers settled into their seats as the teammates sat down on their benches. The excited chatter settled down only when the game began. Each team scored a touchdown. Then, in the last few minutes of the game, as the opponents were just about to score, they fumbled. But Sunbury had little success trying to move the ball quickly down the field for a touchdown. Finally, Junior, rushing forward with the ball, saw an opening. Moving with almost miraculous quickness, he darted left, then right, pumping his legs high and fast until only one opponent remained between him and the end zone. Junior raised a foot, as though to move to the left; the opponent reacted to the move. Then Junior moved right and ran past him, into the end zone.

Again, an article appeared in the sports column.

Yes, it happened almost as we told you in our previous column. His name is Junior. He plays

for Sunbury. Sunbury won as Junior finished the
game with a touchdown. Oh, did I fail to mention the final score—Sunbury 14, Quartertown
7—with Junior again being outstanding? Lest we
repeat…stardom beware.

They came in groups and singles, all bringing the most recent article
to Roy's small room in the A.I.U. building. Sunbury's victory had featured
Junior. Details described Junior's feats. Roy admitted Junior was his son,
thanked them for the copies of the article, and slowly swelled with pride.
Until then he had avoided going to the games to watch him play, making good on his word to not enable him. He would not be blamed for any
injury, no matter how serious or how small, as he had warned Lilly Ann.
Now Roy was watching Junior practice and driving him home.

One day Junior asked, "Do you mind if I drive?"

The question was totally unexpected.

"You want to drive?"

Roy eventually yielded to his son's persistence. "Go around and get
behind the wheel," he said.

"Now this is the clutch," Roy explained. "This is the gear shift. Moving
this in and pulling this from here to here changes the gears and makes it go.
Oh, yes, you must push the accelerator to give it gas or it will stall and stop."

Junior eagerly tried to do as his father had instructed. He promptly
stalled, killing the engine. Embarrassed, he looked to his father.

"Try again." He spoke the words slowly, solemnly.

Junior tried to follow instructions. The Ford jumped forward but did
not stall. Finally, as Junior coordinated the movements of the gas pedal, the
clutch, and the gear shift, they made it home.

To Roy's questions concerning Junior's driving, Lilly Ann simply
said, "You teach well."

Riding to Johnstowne the next week, Junior sat in the front seat, just
to the right of the bus driver, to watch his every move, hoping to improve
his skills. Johnstowne had grown large enough to have two high schools,
one on the east side of town, the other on the west side. Sunbury played

each school in alternating years. This year they played West, which was reported to have the better team.

Later in the season, the team arrived at Benton to find a crowded stadium overflowing with gawkers. They all cooed when they saw the star the newspapers called "not Junior." They gawked and yelled and pointed.

Sunbury led by a touchdown as the game was nearing its end. Suddenly, Junior threw himself forward and collapsed to the ground. An attendant quickly noticed his swelling left ankle. Removing Junior's shoe, he saw the left foot had swollen into an angry mass. Almost immediately, a doctor rushed down from the stands. He asked the Sunbury staff to carry Junior from the field and haul him to the small hospital nearby. X-rays were taken, revealing no broken bones; but further examination revealed several strains to Junior's Achilles tendon. A shot was injected and adhesive tape was applied, leaving the heel suspended, so that only the toes could touch the ground.

At home Junior limped about the house, holding onto crutches, tables, and walls. Often, Everett steadied him, walking him over to the dinner table. At school, teammates and friends assisted him as he walked between classes.

He looked up, surprised, when the coach approached him.

"Junior, how do you feel?"

"I'm doing well, Coach."

"I want you dressed with the team for this last game."

"Coach?"

"Dress and travel with the team."

"Travel, Coach? It's a home game."

"I mean dress, huddle, and travel to the field."

"Yes, sir."

It was homecoming. The homecoming queen arrived in a convertible Model A with the top down. Met by her beau and her court, she was paraded to the section reserved for them. The overflowing crowd applauded. The opposing team from Crestwood was a glorious spectacle in their dark and light purple uniforms. They filed out of their bus and marched onto the field, welcomed by raucous applause from their fans.

Lilly Ann was determined to see her son, even if he wouldn't play. Neighbors had agreed to meet the school bus and tend the children.

"There he is. That's my son," she said as Junior hobbled onto the field with his teammates.

"What's that on his foot?" someone asked.

"Looks like a tennis shoe," another answered.

Lilly Ann could only stare.

Near the game's end, the score was tied: seven–seven. A gasp went up as, to everyone's astonishment, Junior hip-flopped into the game. On the first play, Junior made two yards, with no opponent touching him but simply shrouding him.

A player on the opposing team warned, "Only a fool would be out here. This time I won't hurt you, but next time your leg will be in a permanent sling. Get to the bench. I've read about you, STAR. Do it again, and I will 'star' you!"

To everyone's surprise, the coach called a time out. Once the team was assembled, he addressed the players.

"Boys, this is your last play of the year. Make it a memorable one. Now, do this...." He detailed the play.

"Now, fellows, boys, team, go do it!"

The team returned to play. Signals were called, positions taken. Then, to a rising chorus from the stadium, Junior hobbled at surprising speed toward the end zone. Above, the ball sailed, just as the coach had directed the quarterback: "Do not throw it too far or too short, Junior can only catch it if you throw it to him perfectly."

Junior and the ball arrived together, when Junior was seven steps from the end zone. As he crossed the line with the ball in his arms, he collapsed. The crowd, as one, gasped in horror. Assistants reached him and helped him to his feet.

Unnoticed by everyone, the *Columbus Dispatch*'s Rodger Blunt sprinted to Junior. He had his camera and a Graflex Flash in his hands. Seeing Junior, he called out. Still clutching the ball, Junior looked up. The Graflex flashed, the shutter snapped...and the picture was taken.

In honor of Junior's ingenuity and resourcefulness, the *Dispatch* ran Rodger's photo and article. Two days later Rodger appeared at Lilly Ann's home. Reintroducing himself, he presented her with a framed photograph—the same photograph that had appeared in the article.

"Please," he said. "Accept this small token of the newspaper's gratitude. Also accept a copy of my article. It says, along with details and turns I added with reporter's license, that you have a remarkable son. As if I'm telling you anything." He smiled.

Pleased, Lilly Ann smiled. Then she thanked him and invited him to join her for a cup of tea. He accepted. While awaiting the drink, he looked around, noticing the simple, clean and comfortable surroundings. Lilly Ann returned with hot tea.

"Please, make yourself comfortable."

"Your house, your home is…so pleasant and comfortable."

"I thank you."

"Please, I am not here as a reporter but I have some observations I would like to share.…"

"I trust your judgment."

She had trapped him. *Judgment. Trust.* Had he had a reason to, he now could write more than just facts or pleasantries he cared to add. He smiled. *Touché.*

When the visit was over he left having no impression of Lilly Ann Coleburn other than pure kindness. At the newspaper's headquarters, he suggested a follow-up squib to the editor.

"My son," the editor said, "the season is over. You were given unusual latitude—and you made the most of it. I praise you. Now move on."

*   *   *

The sound rent the air, an earth-shattering explosion, followed by a fast, soaking rain. The school busses were lined up, waiting; the children were nearly invisible in the sheets of rain. Students rushed toward the busses; when Phyllis Coleburn finally boarded her bus, she was soaked. Shivering, she drew her coat tightly about her. When she was home, Lilly Ann helped Phyllis—and all of her other children—out of their wet clothes and into dry ones as they shivered and stood close to the stove. Only later did she discover it: Phyllis had the croup. She had experienced it before so Lilly Ann was not overly worried. Three days later the symptoms seemed worse. By the week's end Phyllis's symptoms were serious: she had coughing, chills, and a fever. Once Roy arrived, he saw her situation, loaded her into the Ford, and rushed her to the doctor.

"She has pneumonia." The doctor set his arm on Roy's shoulder. "You brought her in time, hopefully."

"Hopefully?"

"I don't mean to alarm you, but this condition is very serious. You need to leave her here. We have two rooms for emergencies like this. This way, I or my nurse can constantly watch her…."

"Do we have any idea how long she'll need to stay here?"

"Between forty-eight and seventy-two hours."

"You know, I must leave for my job in Columbus!"

"Don't worry. If she becomes well enough, we'll take her back home."

When Roy returned home he comforted Lilly Ann. "She's in the best hands. All we can do is wait and put our trust in them."

Lilly Ann, for her part, maintained faith that her daughter would survive. She loved all her children…but she held a special fondness for her daughter. Now that daughter's life was at stake. Still, she had no doubt regarding the outcome.

Two weeks later an automobile drove up to the house; the driver parked in the driveway, beside the barn. The doctor and his nurse stepped out, followed by Phyllis. Lilly Ann, busy kneading biscuits, heard them knock on the door. Hands brushed off, she answered. Seeing the group, she held the handle of the door tightly to prevent herself from collapsing.

"Mrs. Coleburn." The nurse smiled. "We thought that since you have no means of coming to town, we would bring Phyllis to you.

Lilly Ann hugged her daughter tightly. "I can't thank you enough!"

"You are welcome." The doctor nodded graciously. "We can't stay, as we have to get back to the hospital. Enjoy your daughter."

* * *

They arrived. As a part of the Rural Free Delivery service the Roosevelt Administration had put into effect, the box labeled Sears, Roebuck and Company sat conspicuously near the mailbox Roy had installed. Junior found a knife, removed his coat, and cut open the box as soon as he came home from school. Inside the box were ice skates—. black with silver runners, mounted on shoes he knew would fit. He couldn't wait to try the skates on the frozen creek across the road. He found Lilly Ann, who was busy loading laundry into the washing machine. With the countryside now electrified, Roy had paid traveling electricians to install outlets throughout the house.

Using the washer required considerable effort. Water had to be carried into the house from the pump, then heated and poured into the washer time and time again, until the volume of water was sufficient to wash clothes. *Troublesome,* Lilly Ann thought, *but superior to a washboard and tub.*

Junior and Everett often carried the water for both the wash and the rinse in and out of the house. During warm months, after the clothes were wound through the hand-turned ringer, they were hung on a line outside. Now, they were draped over various furnishings.

Lilly Ann looked up at the sound of Junior's voice.

"Mother," Junior said, "I want to go across to the creek and skate. I'll pull the wagon. Everett wants to go with me."

"All right, but be careful."

Dressed for the weather in their high-top boots, wool coats, and gloves, with wool caps pulled over their ears, they trampled, pulling the wagon with the skates. They made their way through the stubbled cornfield and ventured out to the creek. Testing the ice with a sturdy limb, Junior found the pond to be frozen solidly enough to skate. He took note of the areas where the rapids flowed and where the ice was thin.

"I'm going to skate," he told Everett. "Play, but don't go near the thin ice."

Sitting on a big rock, Junior removed his shoes and put on the skates. Once he was out on the ice, he tried to skate, his ankles wobbling, turning every direction. He was just figuring out how to maintain his footing when he heard Everett shouting.

"Help me! Help me!"

Turning in the direction of Everett's voice, he saw his brother in the water. Almost without thought, he hobbled to the ice edge, grabbed the limb he had used earlier, and thrust it to Everett.

"Grab it! Grab it!"

Everett grabbed the limb. Still unsteady on his skates, Junior pulled on the limb and, in turn, pulled Everett out of the icy river. Skates off, shoes on, he got Everett quickly into the wagon. Then, stumbling, lunging, running, he somehow managed to get home. Opening the door, he pushed Everett through.

"My God," Lilly shouted, seeing her son half frozen. "What happened?"

"He got over the edge and fell in."

They undressed him, wrapped him in a quilt, and placed him near the stove. Then they rubbed his hands and feet with the towels she had been drying.

"Mother! Mother!" he cried.

But he was safe.

*   *   *

Lilly Ann, with her children gathered about her, sat intently listening to the radio. Stations WLW in Cincinnati and WJR in Detroit came through loud and clear all of the time. Other stations came through only sporadically. Now, the family was listening to WLLN. As she later recalled, Franklin Delano Roosevelt had come on to give one of his fireside chats. "My friends—and you are my friends…" he had begun. At least, she had thought she heard the president call her family his friend—but she was unsure since he, a Democrat, had defeated Herbert Hoover, who, as the sitting president, had proclaimed that what was happening to the country was short-lived, to be replaced by a "chicken in every pot and a car in every garage." Despite his optimism, the 1929 stock market crash had progressively worsened, giving rise to the Great Depression, with over twenty-five percent of American workers unemployed. Thousands of people were homeless, hungry, and destitute. Once elected, Roosevelt, with his cabinet, introduced a law every day—at least, it seemed that way to Lilly Ann. Banks closed. The Works Progress Administration was founded and Social Security established. But as though it existed solely to defeat Roosevelt, the Supreme Court ruled each attempt to create solutions to the nation's existing problems unconstitutional. Frustrated, the president attempted to add additional members to the court. That met with defeat as well.

His Social Security plan however, was not defeated.

CHAPTER 14

Social Security, as Lilly Ann understood it, would eliminate the most hateful establishments that existed in the country: poorhouses. It would provide income to old people, people sixty-five and older. A portion of every worker's paycheck would be deducted from their wages and matched by their employer. At sixty-five, people would be provided income—income to help them live…income that, Lilly Ann believed, would forever close poorhouses. She now knew what Maggie meant when she repeatedly said, "Honey, if you love me, see to it that I am never committed to a poorhouse."

It was as if Roosevelt not only heard her but assured her that there would no longer be poorhouses.

With the radio shut off, the older children asked questions about what they had heard; for this was the first time they had heard about social security. While this was also the first time Lilly Ann had heard the term "social security" herself, she knew its meaning well. Conditions had worsened as the Depression deepened; people became homeless as their properties were foreclosed. Families were evicted; their homes seized by the banks, they were committed to poorhouses, where impoverishment was widely spread. While operated by either the local, county, or state government, the pay they offered their inhabitants was poor. People were desperate for jobs, whether qualified or not; many found work as a result of the relationships they had with certain people connected to their employer, not because their skills matched the qualifications of the position being advertised. Conditions throughout the country were harsh and horrific. People starved to death, people wasted away, emaciated to a near-death thinness, people froze to death, hunkered down under bridges. To be poor meant walking in lockstep with death. As Lilly Ann thought of these matters, she huddled her children closer, to fully absorb the heat of the stove. She thought again about social security, wondering if it would bring an end to debtor's prisons, or the poorhouse. God forbid if it didn't.

Lilly Ann broached the subject almost as soon as Roy arrived that weekend. After hearing her description of social security, Roy acknowledged that he had heard the president's fireside chat, listening to it alongside a group of workers.

"It's something of a miracle, Roy. I remember Maggie saying to never let anyone send her to the poorhouse. Now no one will ever be committed to a place like that again. "Even the price of milk had gone up so high by then; if our family hadn't had enough money back then, she might have ended up at the poorhouse herself!"

Later that night, lying awake beside Roy in their bed, Lilly Ann couldn't sleep. *Do you realize where you are?* she thought. *What you are confronted by? What circumstances? Do you know what is required to run a country? No,* she told herself quickly, *don't answer. There are problems that you will face. What do you do right now about anything anymore? It's a tough life for a woman, especially one with several children....*

These questions, along with scores of others, filled Lilly Ann's mind over the next several days.

She was not certain when the first answer came. The kitchen fire blazed under her largest pots, which were filled with boiling water. She cautiously removed the mason jars and set them beside the many others, to be filled with blackberry jam. The steam's heat made her perspire while she filled jars and jars of preserves and then set them aside to cool. Above the sound of jars rattling in the boiling water, a knock on the door caused her to lurch forward.

Opening the door, she saw a large man in a uniform. The man was flanked by two of her neighbors.

"Mrs. Coleburn, I am Deputy Sheriff Frank Robins." The deputy sheriff held his hand quietly in his hands and had an apologetic look on his face. "I'm sorry to bring you such news, but your husband died in an automobile accident."

The words hung suspended, penetrating Lilly Ann's consciousness but their meaning remained unclear. It was all too devastating and overwhelming. Slowly, she started crumpling to the floor. The deputy reflexively extended his arms, halting her midway. Almost simultaneously the two neighbors moved to the stove, finishing the cooking and canning Lilly Ann had commenced. The deputy guided her to a chair. While she slumped back in the chair, she thought of Roy, without even meaning to. *Dead. Dead. Dead.* The reality of the situation escaped her while the words continued to echo in her subconscious.

Dead.

CHAPTER 15

Somehow, she found herself on the twenty-fourth floor of the American Insurance Union building. The friend who brought her remained in the lounge in the building's lobby. She entered the offices of the Metropolitan Life Insurance Company to meet with agent Robert Johns and found herself escorted to a luxurious lounge...and then into Mr. Johns' office. Mr. Johns had excused himself for a moment. Lilly Ann looked around. Mahogany furnishings were spread all about the office. Lamps glowed softly. Soft music played from hidden speakers. As entrancing as it all seemed, her thoughts were only of Roy.

For days, knowing her children basked in the overwhelming comfort and care of friends and neighbors, Lilly Ann had stayed with her mother, Maggie. Visits had been made to the undertaker, the reverend, and the church that had handled the funeral arrangements. At the front of the Shiloh Baptist Church, the casket rested on a wheeled, shrouded platform. In the raised pulpit, the reverend stood with his head bowed softly, praying as the choir sang "Nearer My God to Thee."

Dressed in black, Lilly Ann and her children sat in the first row of seats. After the service, which had included testimonials by friends, fellow workers, and other audience members, the group moved to their automobiles and made their way to the Greenlawn Cemetery. There, six pallbearers carried the casket to the open grave, where, using canvas strips that stretched underneath the casket, they lowered Roy Coleburn's body into the ground while the Reverend recited "Ashes to ashes...dust to dust."

With that, the ceremony ended.

Back home, Lilly Ann sat silent and still while friends and family moved about. Food prepared by neighbors sat on tables that had been pulled together. For several days, this scene repeated itself. Then, normalcy prevailed while Lilly Ann's mind was still filled with half-formed thoughts. Some family matters she would handle right and some she would not, but to do nothing was not an option. Her children needed, as she did, to move forward, as if Roy remained, still guiding his family.

One afternoon, while she was deep in serious thought, Lilly Ann heard a knock on her front door. Getting up from her chair, she realized that the caller had been knocking for a while, but she was only just now becoming aware of it. Opening the door, she encountered Mr. Rhodes, wearing a calf-length overcoat and holding his derby in his leather gloves.

"Mrs. Coleburn," Mr. Rhodes said, "may I speak with you?"

She stared at Mr. Rhodes briefly, then said, "Please excuse me for a moment" and closed the door.

Inside, she donned her long overcoat, a wool stocking cap, and wool gloves then stepped out onto the front porch to confront him.

Reflexively, she thrust her hand toward him, saying, "Mr. Rhodes."

Surprised, he extended a limp and unenthusiastic hand toward her, his expression registering disgust. But, the next moment, recovering, he said smoothly, "Mrs. Coleburn, I came to express my condolences over your loss and to offer my services, which would be considerable, in helping you to relocate."

Lilly Ann said nothing.

Undoubtedly, he knew of her meeting with Mr. Johns, which had resulted in the insurance agent saying, "As a representative of Metropolitan Life, I am authorized to present you with a check for two thousand dollars, which the double indemnity clause of your policy authorizes. Your Sunbury National Bank will cash it for you, if you so desire. As a representative of the company, I am happy to say Metropolitan thanks you."

She had deposited the check in the bank. For the moment, she continued her silence.

"You will be moving. How soon? I am aware that you are the recipient of insurance resources, but as both you and I know, when they are exhausted, you and your children will have nothing. As you can see, moving is your only option. It's the only one."

"Mr. Rhodes, thank you for your concern." Then teasingly, she said, "One never knows what one will do, does one?"

Again, his face registered surprise and disgust. Donning his hat, he turned, saying, "We shall see."

The wheels of the Packard spun as Mr. Rhodes sped away.

As winter tightened its chilly grip the situation seemed grim despite Lilly Ann's courage. Five children to feed, clothe, and teach…. Yes, quite grim indeed! But various neighbors, knowing Lilly Ann would need assistance to get her family through the freezing winds and snows, provided help. Men chopped, dragged, and stacked wood while various women brought cooked meals, explaining they had mistakenly cooked too much. Lilly Ann expressed her gratitude, inwardly knowing this could not go on. Unexpectedly, a neighbor and his wife came, bringing food, neighborhood news—and a suggestion.

"Lilly Ann…" He paused, then said, "Please, may I call you Lilly Ann?"

She nodded "yes."

The man continued: "A group of us men are going to Nestlé's offices to discuss milk matters. Since you are a neighborhood member, we wonder if you would like to come along?"

Speechless, Lilly Ann nodded her willingness to go.

Sitting in the backseat of a Model A sedan, Lilly Ann felt the car go steeply downhill, under the railroad pass, then turn a short distance and climb up to the top of the hill, stopping at the front of the plant. She and her companions were greeted by a young man, who ushered them into the sprawling plant.

Inside, a well-dressed man introduced himself as Clyde Robertson. "I am authorized to both show you our plant and to explain its function," he said. Then he nodded politely at gazed quietly at the group. "Greetings. Now, please follow me."

He turned and motioned for the visitors to follow. During the tour, he explained the entire process by which Nestlé's milk was transformed into powder: how the milk was sterilized, the steps involved in removing the liquid and reducing it to canned powder, the methods by which the cans were shipped.

Lilly Ann listened closely to his explanation as she followed along with the tour. When it was over, Clyde Robertson asked if there were questions. Lilly Ann asked if the price of milk would remain so low. Robertson answered, "No, definitely not. "His company needed all the milk it could get, he explained. Demand for Nestlé's product had decreased at the height of the Great Depression; but, as conditions had improved, demand for powdered milk had increased, thus the demand and the pricing had continuously gone up.

"Then," Lilly Ann asked again, "if I can supply more milk, could I make enough to pay my mortgage, maintain my home? Can I—" she asked boldly "—make enough to live?"

The representative looked closely at Lilly Ann then smiled, and said, "By all means, Mrs..... I'm sorry; I don't know your name."

"Coleburn. Lilly Ann Coleburn."

"Yes, Mrs. Coleburn. If you produce enough milk, we will pay well for it."

At home, she did not change clothes. Rather, she instructed Everett to mind the other children while she asked Junior to drive her into town. There, Junior parked in front of the bank, as she requested. Inside, she was met by a clerk, who greeted her cordially.

"May I help you?"

"I would like to see the banker," she said.

"One moment, please."

The clerk disappeared into the inner office then reappeared with the banker, Mr. Fine.

"Mrs. Coleburn." The banker recognized Lilly Ann from several days before, when she had come in and deposited, what was for the Coleburn's a large check.

"I would like to speak with you," Lilly Ann said.

"Certainly, come in."

Mr. Fine opened the swing gate to the foyer and led Lilly Ann into his office.

Seated on a small couch beside Mr. Fine's desk, "Now," she said. "I want to borrow money."

"Oh, if you need a few dollars, I can lend you that from my pocket and you can repay me personally."

"No. I need a thousand or more."

With that, he grew quiet.

"May I ask why?"

"I am going to turn my farm into a dairy farm. I want to buy cows."

"And who will run this farm?"

Without hesitation, she said, "Me and my children."

"You are not serious?"

Instead of answering, Lilly Ann glared silently at Mr. Fine.

"But you have five children!" the banker exclaimed.

"My workforce. We will run and maintain that farm."

"I don't know…."

"Mr. Fine, I am borrowing against my savings. If I fail, you are covered. How can you lose?"

He had no further argument.

"Yes, I will do it," he said. Suddenly, he turned most grateful. "Thank you for giving us the opportunity."

Shortly thereafter, he had the loan forms prepared. He asked her to sign the papers, informed his staff, and bid her good-bye. Then he disappeared into his office.

On the way home, she remained silent, staring out the window, wondering, even praying that she had not made a foolish decision. At home, after supper, when the children had finished cleaning up and had done all their homework, she gathered them about her.

"Please listen and try to understand me. Starting soon, we will have cows, ten or more, to take care of, milk and feed; we will have to clean up the manure as well. We will sell the milk. The milk will pay us a living wage for most of our needs. So, sleep well knowing that Momma loves you." She kissed them all good night and said, again: "Sleep well."

＊　＊　＊

Days passed. Lilly Ann cared for her family. In the contemplative recesses of her mind she saw ways to execute her plan. With a few dollars, she could build the stalls in the barn to hold the cows. She could plant and harvest enough hay for winter. The manure could be spread to make the pastures richer. Twenty acres could be seeded for corn and wheat. The other forty-four could grow alfalfa, clover, rye, and other seeds for rich hay. As for cows, she knew she must find the most productive Holsteins, Guernseys, and, even, Jerseys.

At the Nestlé plant, the manager had told her the milk she sold them needed to be of sufficient volume as well as embody a certain richness. But the price must be right. And although she had some money, she knew she must spend it wisely.

Unexpectedly, a gift (of sorts) knocked at her door. A burly man stood beyond the threshold. "Mrs. Coleburn, I hear you're buying cows. I have four fine ones for sale. Cheap."

He said his name was Sam Claibourne and that he lived in the next town over.

Lilly Ann stared at him kindly. "Why for sale? Why cheap?"

"My wife died. I'm joining my son. Maybe to help him a little, maybe be helped...."

"What are the cows," Lilly Ann continued, "and where are they?"

"If you have time, I'll take you. It's only about three miles."

The trip proved short and quick.

"There they are." Sam Claibourne pointed.

Lilly Ann could see them: four young, reddish-brown, full-ud-dered cows.

"You buy them, and I'll throw in the milk cans that get picked up to deliver milk to Nestlé. And I'll deliver them to your place."

"I'll pay you when you deliver."

As promised, he delivered the cows as soon as he had them loaded onto borrowed trucks. Unloaded into Lilly Ann's barn, they mooed loudly and uneasily.

"Here are the cans. I notified Nestlé to pick up here tomorrow. You're in business."

Lilly Ann thanked him then paid him with the cash she had secured from the bank. One thousand dollars. Never before had she handled so much money. Shortly, though, the reality of the situation set in. The cows had to be milked this evening. Tomorrow morning, the cans had to be set out to be picked up!

*   *   *

"If I might, missus, I'd like to speak to you." Whoever he was, he stood there, hat in hand.

Lilly Ann looked up from her list for staples to buy from the store: flour, molasses, cornmeal, salt.

"Yes?"

"Ma'am, we know of your tragedy, and we are sorry...."

"Thank you."

"Ma'am, if you let us, we'll come to your place and butcher for a share of the meat. Ma'am, my family is near starvation. We have had no work for some time; and knowing of your situation...well, just like everybody for miles around does: we know you have hogs to butcher. If you let us for maybe a quarter of a hog, we, my brother and me, will do the work. Please, Ma'am."

Lilly Ann looked toward Junior. who nodded "yes." Then Lilly Ann turned back to the man.

"Yes," she nodded.

"Thank you, ma'am."

From that day forward, she could always hear the Flivver from some distance away before it arrived. Quickly and efficiently, the brothers set up Roy's and George Everett's equipment. Having spoken to Lilly Ann earlier, they knew which two hogs to slaughter. Lilly Ann chose not to watch as they proceeded with the gruesome business. Instead, she busied herself at the Singer, sewing clothes for the children who had outgrown things she had made a year or less ago.

For days, the brothers worked at rendering lard, smoking hams in a temporary smokehouse they had constructed, and storing the meat in the root cellar. After a month, the men helped Lilly Ann prepare for the winter's sharp winds. One blustery day, one of them approached the house and knocked. When Lilly Ann opened the door, the sharp wind rushed in. Lilly Ann gestured for him to enter.

"Ma'am, I'm Fred, the older brother. We have completed our service. Now I understand you are recently widowed, and I wondered if I could still be of some service to you? A woman with, I understand, five children has had regular service. I will provide it for you. Just say the word."

Lilly Ann felt the blood rise. Her face reddened, knowing full well what he was suggesting. Her first thought was to repel him in no uncertain terms. Then, and, later, when she looked back on it, she never knew where her sudden nerve came from; she decided, since she was safe in the house, to tease him a little.

"If you are thinking what I think you are thinking, what are you prepared to offer to a woman whose husband is dead?"

Encouraged, he rushed ahead: "Lilly Ann, I'll do anything, move in, do everything."

She smiled as she opened the door.

"I'll think on it."

As she closed the door behind the older brother she allowed herself to laugh inwardly. Maybe, even after five children, men still found her desirable…?

It came so suddenly, so sharply, the howl and shriek of the wind caused her to sit up with a snap. With her shawl about her, she moved to the window. Outside, blanked in white, all else invisible to the eye, the snow drove down in sheets. Her first thought was how to milk and tend to the cows, and get the milk to Nestlé? Suddenly chilled, she found the poker for the stove, stirred the coals, added more coals to the pile, settled in a rocking chair under a quilt, and promptly fell asleep.

Eventually, she was roused by Junior. "If you let me use the clothesline and all the rope," he said, "I can find my way to the barn. We can tend to the cows; when there's more daylight, we'll be able to warm the slop and feed the hogs, too."

"Son, can you do all that?"

"Mother, I have to try. If I don't, we can lose it all."

She looked at him, no longer seeing her son, but a man.

"Joseph Leroy, if you can get us to the barn, we'll all go do what needs to be done."

Dressed in a heavy coat, his warmest boots, and his glove and hat, Junior ventured outside. He clung desperately to the rope. Lilly Ann looked through the window, watching her son disappear into the haze of wind, fog, and snow. After a time, Junior returned: his hat, his coat, his gloves, his shoes—every bit of him—was covered in snow and ice.

Lilly Ann wanted to put her arms around him but simply said, "My son."

For four days, the winter elements reigned relentlessly. Every morning, Junior went out to tend to the cows. On the fifth morning, tire chains crunched in the snow and ice, and the Nestlé truck ground to a halt on Lilly Ann's driveway. The driver approached the house.

Lilly Ann opened the door.

"Ma'am, if I could speak to you a minute. My name," he said, "is Adolph Jiger. I am from Switzerland, but I have lived here for more than ten years. I am representative of Nestlé and am soliciting for milk. Without it, our plant will shut down. We are aware you have cows. If I may ask, what has happened to their milk during this time of the terrible storm?"

Lilly Ann smiled proudly. "Mr. Jiger, you have arrived just in time. We are running out of cans."

Mr. Jiger nodded. "We will pay a premium."

"My sons will help you load them."

Slowly and cumbersomely, one by one, the man and the boys loaded seven full cans into Mr. Jiger's truck.

Before leaving, Mr. Jiger came back to the door.

"Ma'am, I want to thank you. I don't know how much, but the company will reward you with a monthly bonus. Thank you again."

Then he was gone.

Lilly Ann put her arms around her sons as tears ran down her cheeks and she thanked them for their help. "Just think, with six or eight more cows, we can make enough to pay for our home. I love you."

The brutal winter reluctantly gave way to clearer days and warmer nights. Lilly Ann and Junior readied the tractor for its springtime tasks.

They topped off the water, oil, and gasoline then brushed off accumulated leaves and other debris.

"Mother, are you sure you know how to work it?"

"Your father and I plowed together. I know how."

The Fordson coughed at the first cranking.

"Be careful," she warned. "That crank could break your arm, backfiring…."

Sitting in the driver's seat, steering wheel in hand, she fearfully watched as Junior cranked. It sputtered, coughed again, and started slowly…just as Roy had taught her. She hitched up the plow and plowed as soon as she reached the ten acres of field Roy had designated for corn, then wheat: crops for both consumption and sale. The big job was tilling for alfalfa, rye, clover, and the other seeds. Slowly, she increased speed, feeling confident. Then suddenly, a female quail flew up from the weeds as the Fordson dug open the earth. Before Lilly Ann could react, the tractor passed over the nest of fledglings and eggs.

Lilly Ann stomped the brake and grabbed the gearshift, bringing the tractor to a halt. She slumped over the steering wheel, tears flowing. Never before had she brought death to an innocent creature. After she recovered, she started the machine forward, plowing with a controlled, fury laying fallow row after row, not stopping for lunch or water, almost without breathing. Finally, a sharp breeze signaled the approach of evening. She stopped, shut the Fordson down, looked about, climbed out of the tractor, and walked toward the house. Outside, Junior and Everett were going about the evening chores.

"Mother," Junior said, "you ran that tractor well…you plowed *acres!* The weather holding, and you working as you did, we'll get the crops in on time."

She heard him, recognized what he was saying, but remained nearly overwhelmed with remorse.

"Thank you, son."

She turned for the house. Supper had to be prepared, the children fed, homework reviewed, lunches prepared, and the clothes laid out.

Tomorrow, tomorrow, and tomorrow, she thought.

CHAPTER 16

Hearing his name being called as he neared home, Junior looked up. He had walked four miles from school, having stayed late to have the track coach teach him how to pole-vault. The coach needed a pole-vaulter, and had encouraged Junior, saying he had the shoulder muscle and the quickness that were necessary to succeed in the sport. Now, approaching his house, he saw Mrs. Gorsuch rushing toward him.

He stopped.

"Son, you cannot enter your house. It is quarantine; the doctor put the sign on it."

Junior looked curiously at Mrs. Gorsuch, who explained:

"Your brother DeVerne has the measles. He has a sore throat, fever, and aches. He also has severe pimples; they're breaking out all over. Your brother and sisters may have them as well. Please," she pleaded, "come to our house for supper. Then we'll milk, feed and clean your cows."

Knowing they had to do the milking along with the other chores, Mrs. Gorsuch and Junior approached the house each day but stayed the required distance from it. Music could always be heard through the windows, which had been opened a crack on the doctor's orders, to permit fresh air to enter the house and hasten DeVerne's recovery. Junior and Mrs. Gorsuch laid the hay down and spread the straw. While Mrs. Gorsuch needed Junior's help, she insisted that he not miss school.

The doctor soon discovered that some of the other Coleburn children had become infected, causing the quarantine to be extended. Junior attended school and participated in a few track and field practices, but not nearly enough to advance his skills. One afternoon, he walked to the grocers to buy bread, as he had promised Mrs. Gorsuch. While waiting in line at the store, he overheard two farmers talking, saying the time for plowing was coming to an end, the time to disc harrow and plant seeds had neared.

Hearing this, Junior realized the chores on his mother's farm were growing more and more behind every day....

At home, on Saturday, he ventured into the field where the equipment rested. Moving about he studied the Fordson. He had, in cranking it for his mother, watched closely as his mother had set the controls. Now, without hesitation, he set the controls himself, assuring himself the forward gear was disengaged. He cranked the gearshift as he had done before. It sputtered. He cranked again. It coughed, coughed again...and started.

Climbing aboard, he seated himself and grasped the steering wheel. He engaged the gear and slowly moved forward. He plowed row after row, until he saw Mrs. Gorsuch appear, waving at him. As he came around to her, he stopped.

"Son, it's time for milking and chores, then supper."

Together, they milked, fed, cleaned stalls, slopped hogs, and then went to her house, where she had bathing water and towels waiting. At supper, she related to her husband what she had seen Junior do. Nodding to Junior, the man congratulated him, and then excused himself while Junior helped Mrs. Gorsuch clean the kitchen despite her protests.

Excusing himself, he retired to his room, studied, then slept to the radio sounds of Wayne King and Guy Lombardo, with an occasional song by Louis Armstrong mixed in.

CHAPTER 17

Elegant, elegant, if he said so himself. Slowly, what he considered gracefully, he wore the Hickey Freeman custom-tailored, three-piece suit, fitted perfectly by some tailor located in some big city—a city, he knew, that must be important. Removing a Patek Philippe watch from his vest pocket, he opened the eighteen-caret gold case made in Geneva, engraved inside, as well. The watch face gleamed the time. He admired the timepiece as he strolled across the street to the Maramor Restaurant. Its elegance was renowned for miles around the city. With spats and a gold-headed walking stick, he strolled leisurely into the Maramor. Across from him, the tables were set for four, with sterling silver, bone china, and Irish crystal.

As Mr. Rhodes stood by the host's stand, the maître d' rushed to greet him.

"Welcome. Welcome, Mr. Rhodes."

Once he and his companions had been seated at their table, a waiter in a white half jacket and black, patent shoes rushed to the table; he was followed by a helper. In front of each diner he placed two martinis. There would be no interruptions.

"Gentlemen, greetings," said Mr. Rhodes. "Please enjoy a drink before we get down to business."

Slowly they drank their first drinks and exchanged niceties concerning family. Then Mr. Rhodes called the group to order.

"My friends, I'd like to call your attention to our small problem. For several years we have profited handsomely by foreclosing properties. Filling them with cows, we produce the milk the Nestlé Company needs and pays handsomely for. Our problem is that place Lilly Ann and her children occupy. Our plan is to own and convert that place to a hay farm. Planted, cultivated, and harvested properly, we will fill the lofts of barns all around the world. We will have plenty hay to last the winter. We will have a milk factory to supply Nestle. We will—" he boasted "—make a fortune."

"Now gentlemen, let's eat lunch and think about what I've said."

Swiftly and efficiently, the meal was served. Waiters moved about, serving bouillabaisse, oyster on the half shell with hot sauce, lobster, steak, mixed vegetables, baked apples with ice cream, and coffee.

"Now, gentlemen, over cigars, brandy, and—if you prefer—a final martini, let's pick up where we concluded.... Andrew, with your accounting skills, I want you to bring me any and all books and papers relating to her finances. Paul, your task is to search and review county and state records. Finally, Floyd, we need to keep watch on any of her activities that we might use to discredit her. Any questions? Anything you want to add? What did I leave out?"

The men sipped their after-dinner drinks, lounged (but listened) as they puffed Cuban cigars, each looking at the other but remaining silent.

"Very well. I am in no hurry; you shall have time to be thorough. I will inform you of the time and the place of our next meeting. Mind you, though, I expect each of you to be working. Now, I thank you for your time. Be safe as you go about. Take care of yourselves. Now, good-bye."

He half bowed to them all as he strolled out.

CHAPTER 18

The truck squeaked to a stop under a grey, heavily overcast sky. In the distance, thunder rumbled. The driver lowered his hat as Lilly Ann and Junior approached.

"I'm here to pick up your produce. My father isn't well. I have oranges and bananas. I hope you have tomatoes, green beans, perhaps sweet corn, any other vegetables. Please hurry. That storm will be a bad one."

Lilly Ann pulled the wagon they had loaded in anticipation of this visit, saying, "Junior, run to the henhouse, bring all the eggs laid since this morning."

"Hurry, hurry," the man said. "The storm. See? There's lightening."

Junior rushed and returned with a basket of eggs.

"I won't bother to count them. Just put them in the case. For them, here's another hand of bananas," he said, lowering them down from the truck bed. "Thank you. I'll tell my father. Good-bye."

The truck rattled away.

Just then the first drops of rain hit. "Junior, take Everett and drive the cows in. Harold, bring in some wood and coal. Take DeVerne with you. Phyllis, go to the meat cellar. Bring up meat, quarts of beans, and blackberries. Now go! The storm looks bad."

Hearing the urgency in their mother's voice, the children rushed to accomplish their tasks. Then, gathered in the house, they listened to the monstrous thunder. Vicious streaks of lightning flashed light throughout the house; rain swept in sheets. Lilly Ann moved the children away from the windows, fearing that the lightning, or the ever-accelerating winds, might blow out the glass.

For two days, the rain fell. Not as viciously as during the first terrible hours of the storm, but steady and soaking, nonetheless. Keeping the small children inside, Lilly Ann and the two older boys, wearing all the raingear they could find, splattered through the puddles. The animals—cows, hogs, chickens, barnyard cats—still had to be fed, milked, and slopped. Exhausted by the work, they nevertheless slumped through them, each tending to their own tasks, until everything was accomplished.

The storm over, Lilly Ann, in gumboots, walked solemnly through her fields. Often, she had heard the term "heartbroken"; if hers could be, it was. All about her the winds and rains had devastated the land. The corn, wheat, and hay fields were driven parallel to the ground.

She felt weak. Her life, the life of her children, lay blown over before her. She knew she needed help—but from whom? She remembered Fred. Recalling his words, she knew he would help. She would pay him—and his brother—of course.

In town, where Junior had driven her, she went to the general store to ask about the brothers. To her question, the clerk replied, "Oh, you mean Fred Ames and his brother. I can send for them. They would be grateful to work. They haven't had any. If you wait, I'll send for them."

Soon after, a boy appeared with Fred and his brother.

"Mrs. Coleburn, ma'am," Fred said, "you need workers, we'd be happy to work for you. We'll be there prompt and early in the morning."

Thanking him, Lilly Ann and Junior left the store.

The next day, the familiar roar and clatter of the Flivver announced the arrival of the Ames brothers. Fred tipped his hat in greeting Lilly Ann, and then moved on to inspect the damage from the rains. As far as the eye could see, the crops lay nearly parallel to the ground. Farther out, feet sank into the muddy, soggy earth.

Turning again, he said, "Please, we'll help you, but we need time. With the sun shining, the wind blowing, the drying will take place fast. That's what we need. Meantime, we'll dry out and start the Fordson, ready the tools to cut hay; if the Fordson's dry enough we'll rake the hay into rows to let it dry in preparation to lifting and storing it in the loft, if that meets your approval?"

Lilly Ann had been looking away, but his tone caught her attention. Looking again to him she caught his suggestive expression.

Deliberately expressionless, Lilly Ann said, "Come for as long as you're needed. Pay is one dollar. I will feed you dinner and, of course, you'll be gone before supper."

Dejected, Fred only nodded.

Each day during the ensuing weeks the men worked hard. The bright sun and strong wind dried the corn, the stalks rising up toward the sun. The wheat ripened, and the hay grew inches by the day. In turn, Lilly Ann prepared fresh, carved meat from the root cellar. The men ate heartily, praising Lilly Ann and her cooking. The Fordson roared as the men guided her across the fields, tilling, dragging, and hauling hay to the barn. One day, they hauled an old wagon over and filled it with hay that had dried nicely in the rows to which it had been raked. In the loft, Junior and Everett watched the fork being hoisted by rope to dump a load of hay to be pulled back in the barn. A worker dragged the hay from the entrance back into the barn. Sweating and grunting the workers pulled it back, stacked it nearly roof high, assuring a full loft and sufficient hay for the eight cows to survive the winter.

Inside, Lilly Ann had cleared away the dishes, swept and cleaned the house, when someone knocked on the door. She opened the door to find a young man, strikingly dressed in what she immediately knew were brand new country clothes, new overalls, a blue denim shirt, and high-top country shoes.

"Ma'am," he said, "I'm Jacob Mayhan. I noticed you have men working. I need a job. I will work for supper."

Wondering if she should hire another stranger but needing a man to do some woodwork around the property, she asked, "Do you know carpenter work?"

"Yes, ma'am."

"I need an extension for two cows built on the barn. I have lumber, hammer, and nails. Shouldn't take more than a couple of days. As soon as it is finished, the cows will be here."

"Do you mind if I look around?" he asked innocently.

"No," Lilly Ann replied. "Meantime, I'll make supper. If you come in with the boys and wash up, we'll eat then."

As he walked away, looking about him, she watched momentarily, and then moved into the house to prepare supper. When the boys came in, she made sure they washed up; then she left a clean washbowl, filled with water, and a clean towel, for Jacob.

Inside the house, Jacob looked about.

"Not a bad-looking house," he muttered to himself.

After he had washed up, he said, "There's a door there." His tone seemed purposefully innocent to Lilly Ann. "What's behind it?"

Lilly Ann looked toward the door.

"Oh, the master living room. We don't use it."

"May I see it?"

Without answering, she moved toward the door and opened it. The room might be considered large. In the middle of the far wall sat the stove. On the floor stretched a carpet from Columbus. Also from Columbus sat the upholstered furniture. Pictures from the previous house hung on the walls. The effect was attractive and created a comfortable ambience.

"Oh, how nice. Now…how about the bedrooms?"

Again wordless, she showed them to him.

"Again, nice. It's quite a nice house," he said again. "Well maintained. You're a fine housewife and mother." She thanked him, and started to go assist the children before bedtime.

"I shall head toward the loft," he said. "I thank you for your courtesy. Good night."

He disappeared toward the barn.

The next morning, she prepared to meet Jacob. Walking near the barn, she called out his name but received no answer. The barn held no indication he had been there this morning. Disturbed that he had not spent the night in the barn as he had said he would, she wondered whether he had perhaps gone for his automobile and would return later. Still fretting she returned to the house. Later, while the hired men worked, she prepared dinner.

It was then that a worker said, "Perhaps I was wrong, but I counted one cow missing."

Taking him seriously, Lilly Ann asked the boys to go count the cows as soon as they finished eating. They returned from the barn with the sad news that a cow had been found on its side, lying motionless.

"Dead?"

"No," they answered. "It was grunting."

"We must get the veterinarian."

Junior rushed into town in the Model A and returned with the vet. When they reached the cow, the vet told the boys to hand him his medical bag and to step back from the animal.

"What's wrong with her?" asked Everett.

The vet looked at him. "She's bloated," he explained. "See that little section of green, where it's low so that water can stand? Mosquitoes lay eggs. Cows seeking green grass and water ingest algae in the water, along with mosquito larvae. She is full of the gas that's generated. We must relieve her bloating."

With that he withdrew a slim, eighteen-inch knife. Then, feeling carefully with his finger, he found the area he wanted, plunged the knife into it, and stood back as a great explosion of gas erupted. The cow lifted her body then lowered it, shook her head…and relaxed peacefully. Using a paintbrush, the vet swabbed the wound with ointment then gathered his equipment and rose.

At the door to the house, he addressed Lilly Ann.

"Missus, if you can spare it, I need two dollars for gasoline. Your cow will be well in two days. A word to the wise: I would have that fence repaired to prevent other animals from ingesting that water."

Without a word Lilly Ann entered the house then returned and handed two dollars to the vet. "Is there anything I need to do today?"

"Her udder will fill. It needs to be emptied as soon as possible. Other than that, nothing. Thank you for the fee." He nodded to her quickly. "Good-bye."

He walked to the car and drove off.

*   *   *

Standing near a window in Rhodes' office in the A.I.U. building, Jacob looked down on the flow of automobiles far below. "I carried out your instructions exactly as you told me. I ingratiated myself into her confidence so that I could persuade her to take me into every room of the house."

"And?"

"It's a finely built house. They built it when two-by-four timbers actually measured two inches by four inches. They were joined together with spikes. The joining is flawless. The rooms are large. There is a large root cellar. The outbuildings, barn, chicken house, equipment building, and tractor shed were all built with the same care. In other words, they will sell or rent easily, in my opinion."

"Jacob, a good report. That you gave no indication of your purpose, that you were discreet, is to your credit. My assistant will write you a check."

"Please, sir, if I might, could I have cash? I have trouble cashing checks."

Rhodes hesitated…stared at him for a moment.

"Yes, I will see to it. Good day."

In the outer office, the telephone rang. The clerk answered, nodding several times, and then hung up the phone. He went to a safe behind him, took out a bundle of bills, counted out the instructed amount and then handed it to Jacob and bid him farewell.

* * *

On the farm, the hammering and sawing signaled the addition to the milk shed portion of the barn. At the end of the day, Fred spoke to Lilly Ann as she opened the door.

"We have completed the new addition. You have room for four more milk cows."

"Four?"

"We had the lumber, and the weather has held up. Now you have room for twelve milk cows…if you desire."

"I can't thank you enough," she said, handing him the pay for him and his brothers.

"It's a pleasure to be of service," Fred Ames said deliberately. "Any service…all services…."

Ignoring his innuendo, Lilly Ann nodded and closed the door. *Four more cows* she thought. Just to buy four more would be a strain. Even with the boys' help, it would mean being up practically at dawn. It would mean being home every day. The decision had to be a family one. After supper, she asked her children to gather about her, to shut off the radio first, and to listen to her, then talk.

"Some of you won't understand everything, but please try. This decision affects us all. My children, we have the opportunity to have four more cows. That means more milk. The manager at Nestlé assured me they will buy all the milk we can produce. With the new shed, we have room for twelve milkers. It means milking morning and evening. It means being up each day in time to milk, feed, and clean. It means being here evenings to do it all over again. Now that school is starting, there will be homework. Each of you must go to bed earlier and get up earlier. In other words, be part of a family farming unit."

"Mother," Harold asked, "will it mean more money?"

"Yes."

He nodded. "We can do it. We'll still be able to live here and have our friends; and nobody can take our home because we didn't pay our loan."

Shocked by her son's words, Lilly Ann said, "My son, where did you learn all that?"

"In something called 'civics' at school."

Lilly Ann then asked, "Does what Harold said make us all in agreement?"

In unison the group responded, "Yes."

Several weeks later, twelve milking cows stood in the barn. As Lilly Ann had predicted, the cows dictated the family routine. While the routine tended to be monotonous, the check it produced every month proved gratifying. For the first time, Lilly Ann brought home some store-bought clothes, to make her children more presentable at school.

And, for the first time since Roy's death, she opened the boxes containing Roy's effects, which a worker had gathered from his small office.

Receiving them, the tears still streaming down her cheeks, she had stored them away, unopened. Now, from the boxes, she extracted the records Roy had so meticulously kept in spiral-bound notebooks. Taking them into the living room, again tearfully, she closed the door.

Earlier on, she knew Roy had secured money orders from the post office in the A.I.U. building; now Lilly Ann saw that Roy had kept all of the receipts in his files. Whether he had paid in advance or on time, the transaction had been recorded and the receipt had been filed. At the end of each year, that particular notebook was closed. Year after year, the records were kept, maintained, stored.

As she read through the files, Roy loomed strongly before her. Her tears flowed again, as Roy was with her both in person and in spirit. As she delved further into the files, she relived many of the events that had led to everything she had spread about her. In that Lilly Ann had no previous experience with family business matter, surprisingly, her files revealed that, since his passing, she, too, had maintained records of receipts and expenses.

Slowly, she reinserted the files so that they were once again organized exactly as she had found them. Just as carefully, she reinserted her own files into the folders she had maintained. She felt a sense of pride, knowing she had—and would continue to—maintain the records that would clearly prove to anyone who asked that Roy and Lilly Ann Coleburn had maintained their mortgage payments. Carefully, she moved the files to corner behind the Singer.

It occurred several weeks later.

She came into the house from the barn only to find DeVerne sitting on the floor in the corner, many files spread open before him. Shocked, she scolded him sternly as she gathered the files back up. Several days later, having thought of the incident, knowing it might reoccur, she made a decision. Asking Junior to drive her, she took all the sensitive files to the Sunbury Bank and rented a safe deposit box in which she stored the files. Knowing the files were safe from the harm that curious children might cause, she stopped worrying.

CHAPTER 19

The school bus stopped and loaded Junior, Everett, and Phyllis. As usual, they sat at the far end of the bus, Junior on one side and Everett on the other. Phyllis sat a few rows ahead of her brothers. Since they were the first stop on the route, it permitted others to fill the seats more toward the front.

Two stops later, she got on.

Pretty...long blonde hair...perhaps five feet, four inches tall...full bodied (*and*, better, full breasted) ...her figure slender under the fitted coat she wore.

Smiling, she made her way to the back of the bus and sat in front of the brothers. Still smiling, she turned to Junior and said, "You're the football star, aren't you?"

Junior looked at her. "Yes," he said, noting how her smile made her look even prettier.

"I'm Becky Scott. My family and I just moved here. I know you from articles in the *Dispatch*. I admire you," Becky Scott said frankly, without embarrassment. "I understand there will be a school dance next Friday. You do dance, don't you?"

"No. I do not know how."

Becky smiled deliberately, now. "I'll teach you."

And she did, using short periods of time before school started, during lunchtime, and during the few minutes before they climbed into the school bus. By Friday, after receiving permission from his mother, he drove hurriedly back to school for the dance...and to Becky. With her guidance, they danced while his friends watched in stunned amazement and jealous envy.

Before the dance ended, the school principal approached Junior as Becky left to use the restroom.

"Junior, I know you know, or I think you know," the principal explained. "I own the farm next to yours. My daughter, who is ill, lives next door. If you're interested and can find the time, I would pay you to do some work for me. My hired hand who lives in the cabin behind the main house is gone because of an ailing mother. I'll meet you there, Saturday, and show you what I need. Interested?"

"Oh yes, sir."

The principal nodded. "Then enjoy the rest of the dance, and I'll see you Saturday after you've finished your chores."

He moved on, talking to the other mentors.

Becky returned, and they danced again.

Later, as he drove home, she leaned as close to him as the seat would permit. "I am *so* happy," she said, smiling up to him. Then, placing her hand on his crotch, she squeezed evermore tightly as she felt the rise strengthen in his pants. "Tuesday evening my parents are gone bowling until eleven o'clock," she said, softly stroking his erection. "Come to my house, and I'll show you some different dance moves...."

Startled, confused—and intrigued—he pulled the car up to her house. Smiling, she squeezed once more and got out.

"See you tomorrow. I mean Monday." Then she was gone.

Overwhelmed, he could not start the automobile. His penis throbbed; then his erection slowly receded.

At home, Lilly Ann greeted him.

"My son, did you enjoy the dance?"

"Yes."

"Did you dance?"

"Yes, they taught me."

"Did you make any new friends?"

"Several. I don't understand it. They think I'm a hero because of football."

"And girls?"

"I met several. In fact, a new one named Becky who lives not far away and who rides our school bus. She moved from Columbus. I've been asked to help her with schoolwork while she adjusts."

"Oh, I guess your all A's makes you eligible."

"Mother, is it all right?"

"You should be honored. We, as a family, certainly are." She smiled and then sighed tiredly. "We all need some sleep. Good night."

They rode the school bus each day. Becky spoke to him, she smiled to him, she greeted him and several others on the bus. At school, she underwent his tutoring, acted convivially, but gave no other sign of an intimate relationship. Finally, Tuesday arrived. The hours passed slowly until eight o'clock. They were alone at her house; her parents having left for town.

After a short while she excused herself from the room, returning in a full-length, satin robe, posing with the light of a table lamp behind her. She extended one leg toward him, with one knee thrust forward. Slowly, she allowed the robe to part, exposing her full breasts, with her nipples protruding, pink and fully erect. Her torso sloped to a slender waist that curved gracefully downward into hips that, in turn, rounded nimbly into thighs framing a packet of hair several shades darker than the warm, flaxen hair outlining her face. Observing this under her glowing and mischievous smile, Junior attempted to rise from his seat.

"No!" she said sharply. "Before we do anything, I want to tell you the rules. If you don't agree, we will do nothing. First, you will get prophylactics— 'rubbers,' to you—and you will wear one each time. We only do it on Tuesdays, when my parents are gone. You will tell nobody—no gloating, and no bragging. I will provide washbowl, soap, towels. You will go home clean. Finally, when we do it, you must do it more than once. My needs are considerable. Once is never enough. Do you agree?"

"Agreed," was all Junior could manage under his breath, his penis throbbing.

Closing her robe, Becky said, "I never give any the first time we are together this way. I will dress, and we will study."

She disappeared into her bedroom. Returning dressed, she calmly returned with her school books in hand.

"Let's study."

CHAPTER 20

"This is where you will be working. The team is in the barn. Have you ever hitched a team?"

"No."

"I'll show you."

Junior had gotten up early. Having finished his chores at home, he walked to Mr. Scott's farm, ready to work.

In the barn stood the Percherons.

"Here is where the harnesses are kept," Mr. Scott said, pointing to a rack filled with leather straps and brass fittings. Bridling one horse with deft movements, he fitted the collar, the body harness, and the thick leather that attached to the wagon.

"Now, you try it," he said, pointing to the other harness. With effort, Junior hefted the harness over the other draft horse and stooped to fasten the straps under the horse's belly. Then, Mr. Scott showed him how to hitch the horses together, to form a team, and then hitch them to the wagon. Aboard the team, Junior learned to say, "Gee," commanding the horses to go one direction, and "Haw," commanding the horses to go in the other direction; he learned how to command the horses to stop, and how to say "Giddy up! "in order to command the horses to go. Watching Mr. Scott, Junior learned to work the horses, and he learned how to control them. Day after day, he finished his chores at home first and then worked at Mr. Scott's farm next door.

One day, when the wagon was loaded with piles of briars, a large blacksnake crawled out onto the road and spooked the team. Their sudden lurch threw Junior off the seat and onto the pile of briars. The horses galloped, and the wagon reeled over furrows, rocks, and fallen branches. Junior, thorns piercing him with every bump, pulled on the reigns but was unable to regain control. Knowing he had to at least rise to his knees, he struggled against the pain and tightened the reins until he could feel the team's head movements. Then, shouting "Whoa!" at the top of his lungs, he sawed on the reins. The team slowed, and halted. Hurting with every movement, he pulled himself back onto the seat and guided the team to where he had been instructed to unload the pile.

At home, Lilly Ann, after being told of his pain, heated water in which he could soak.

Hurting all along his backside, Junior went to school the next day after completing his chores. Seeing him limping slightly, Becky asked what was wrong. When told of his accident, she empathized with him and asked, "Will you be healed by Tuesday?"

Assured he would be, she smiled, touched him soothingly, and moved on with the other girls.

On Saturday, at the Scott's farm, Junior harnessed the team, and went toward his worksite. Approaching it, he halted the team. Slightly down the grade, away from the Scott house, stood a small bunkhouse. Climbing down he entered it. Inside he found three bunk beds lined up at the far end. In the middle stood a flat-topped stove for both heating and cooking. Spread about were several chairs. Work clothing belonging to the hired hand hung on the wall: coveralls, warm jackets, a heavy topcoat. Heavy gumboots, ankle-high leather boots, and heavy work shoes were neatly aligned under the coats. A rack of wood was stacked behind the stove, and, in a bin, coal was piled high. Having seen all this, Junior retreated from the bunkhouse, knowing that lingering anything longer would invade the hand's privacy.

Back on the wagon, he went about his work. Later, he looked up to see Mr. Scott, heading his way.

"Young man, I'm proud of you. You have accomplished all I expected, and more. I want to pay you. Here is three dollars. Quit for the day. Next Saturday will be here before you know it. Care for the horses, hay, water… hang the harness…and anything else I may have forgotten. As you can see, it will be getting cold soon. I hope you are finished before then. Good-bye for now."

With that, Mr. Scott turned, made it to the house, and disappeared inside. Junior guided the team toward the barn, completed his final chores, and headed home for the final chores there.

*　*　*

Tuesday seemed to come swiftly. Work at home was finished, and he made it swiftly over to Becky's house. Once there, she greeted him as before, in her long robe.

"Come on. They're gone until about eleven o'clock." Holding his hand, she guided him into her bedroom. It was an average size, painted a light pink. The room was furnished with a bed and a chest of drawers. A small, bench-type chest sat under a mirror, which was accompanied by several pictures. An upholstered rocking chair in the far corner completed the look.

"You did bring the prophylactics…?" Becky asked.

Junior nodded and produced one from his pocket. He had remembered to search through his father's things in the parlor, where he found two boxes. Each box was filled with twenty-four rubbers, and he had put one in his pocket.

Taking it from his hand now, Becky said, "Undress. "Pointing to the upholstered rocking chair, she said, "Take off your clothes and pile them on that chair."

Moving to the chair, he sat, unlaced his shoes and slipped off his socks, then rose and stripped off his clothes. Turning, he found her naked, close beside him, holding the prophylactic.

"Let me put it on," she said. She grasped his penis in her hands. Placing the prophylactic onto its length, she remarked, "You have a long, full, nice one…just as I hoped you would."

Still holding his penis, she guided him to the bed on which she had placed a linoleum-like piece of cloth. Stooping, she set herself on the bed, her head resting on the pillow. Knees bent, feet flat, thighs open, her haired pussy exposed. She guided his penis skillfully into her moist opening. With equal skill, she thrust her lips up to take him fully inside. She lifted her hips to match his thrusting. Suddenly, with low, soft moans, she grasped his thighs, lifting him until only the head remained inside, preventing his ejaculation. Minutes later, she permitted re-entry. In response to the penetration, she could feel the throbbing. She grasped his behind, one cheek in each hand, pulling him tightly against her while she vigorously raised herself up and down.

Hearing his moan, she raised herself harder, faster until she felt his ejaculating penis soften. Then all movement subsided.

Three minutes later, she raised her head to find the clock, saying, "We must get up."

Reluctantly he rose, his limp penis dangling. She disappeared and returned with a pan of warm water, a washcloth, and a towel.

"Here," she said. "Wash yourself…wash and save the rubber for future use, as long as it's thoroughly cleaned, then dress and leave. They will be here in about half an hour. You must be gone before they arrive."

While he dressed, she washed, using the same soapy water, and then again donned her robe.

As he moved through the doorway, she held him a moment, kissed him, and said, "See you tomorrow."

At home, no one was up; he made it silently to bed.

*   *   *

At home several days passed uneventfully, until Everett said at dinner, "I need help." History was his problem. He needed a paper on the Depression for his midterm exam.

Lilly Ann said, "Son, your elder brother not only makes straight A's, it's his favorite subject. "Turning to Junior, she said, "I'm certain he will help you."

Junior nodded while saying, "I will, but we—you and I—must do the research to present proper facts. I will help, but you must work, too."

"I will," Everett said.

Days later Junior, with Everett by his side, brought the library books down to the kitchen table.

"Where do you intend to start your paper?"

"At school, we talk about the president. Maybe we should start there?"

Reaching into the stack of books, Junior chose one. "You might find what you want in here."

After a while, Everett said, "I think these facts are enough."

"All right, write them down."

Everett wrote:

Franklin Delano Roosevelt:

Born 1882 in Hyde Park, New York.

Graduated Harvard University, Columbia Law School, New York.

Senate 1910.

Appointed Secretary of the Navy by Woodrow Wilson.

Elected Governor of New York 1928.

Elected President of the United States 1932. This all after having contracted polio (1921). Spent years starting in 1924 in Warm Springs, Georgia, and after being elected in 1932, established what was called the Little White House there.

"Is that enough?"

Junior nodded affirmatively.

"Now, we must research what was called the Great Depression. The years were officially 1929 to 1932."

"Depression," Junior continued, "means *sunken,* and the U.S. economy became sunken. Fifteen million people were out of work, or thirty-two percent of the workforce, fifty-nine percent of pharmacists, sixty-five percent of engineers, three hundred thousand teachers, ninety percent of architects."

Each day on the radio Everett had heard of people jumping from tall buildings, putting guns to their heads, covering exhaust pipes to inhale exhaust fumes. Radios were filled with songs with lyrics like "Brother, can you spare a dime…."

Money provided under the Federal Home Loan Bank Act was to be loaned to people to save their homes…but instead it went to banks, savings and loans, and insurance companies; Hoover insisted it go to private charities, who would best care for the needy. In the Midwest, the KKK grew to nine million members, with the number of women members rising to a hundred and twenty-five thousand. Meanwhile, Roosevelt thought the business of government was to help people, so he appointed the first woman Secretary of Labor, Frances Perkins.

From 1923 to 1935, union membership rose by three to four million, while the Committee of Industrial Organizations split up, creating the American Federation of Labor, which unionized the growing body of automobile workers. Frances Perkins engineered a forty-hour work week while Josephine Roche became the second woman cabinet member when she became Secretary of the Treasury.

"Junior, I think that's all the notes I need," Everett said.

"I almost agree with you; but there is one more piece I think you need, that's mention of Roosevelt's wife, Eleanor. She's was—and still is—very important. She felt that, in response to extreme droughts on our farms, the economic pressure felt by farmers should be addressed. So, on April eleventh, ninety fifty-three, F.D.R. created an agency called the Subsistence Homestead Division. Harold Ickes and his Department of the Interior thought it was useless, but Eleanor, with F-D-R's assistance through her assistant, Louis Howe, thought highly of it. Twenty-five million dollars was budgeted, with the money to be distributed to twenty-five thousand farms at one thousand dollars apiece. I think it's critical that your paper shows the nature of their relationship."

Everett nodded and took notes vigorously. Finally, he said, "Thanks for your help."

"When it's written," Junior offered, "I'll review it."

"Again, thanks brother."

* * *

When Junior came home late one Tuesday evening, he found his mother waiting.

"Mom, you're up so late!"

"Son, I was waiting for you. Please sit down."

He sat nervously on the couch.

"Son, I don't want you out late like this again."

As he started to rise, her extended hand restrained him. He sat down again. "I want to talk to you."

"I don't have much to say."

"Then, I want to hear it all."

Lilly Ann sat close to him on the coach.

"I want to hear all about Becky, and I want to hear it *all,*" she repeated.

"Oh, you know. I help her with her homework."

"And Tuesdays until—'" she looked at the medium-sized floor clock "—almost eleven o'clock."

He started to speak. Her hand again restrained him.

"Don't."

He sank back onto the coach.

"My son, since your father is gone, I must see to the duties of both mother and father. So here I am."

She stared at him more closely to better gauge his reaction.

"You did wear one of those prophylactics I found missing from the carton Roy left for you?"

Color and heat rose in his face. His breath came out in gasps.

"Mother!"

"Son, I told you. I must be both father and mother. I must talk with you. Please listen. Today, starting the wash, I reached a pair of your shorts. The front of them was caked with the residue of sex, dried and caked. I knew you had sex. It could only have been you. I couldn't believe it. When I verified it with Becky's mother, she said this was one reason they moved here, to stop her from having sex."

"My son, an unused prophylactic or a ruptured one could result in a pregnancy. You, fathering a child, a forced marriage, a life of so much promise and ability, destroyed. My son, your life holds so much promise! Ohio State, a fine career, a family. Don't destroy it!"

For a moment, she held his hand in hers—and then, she was gone.

Junior remained slumped on the sofa. Trembling, his eyes tearing, his hands shaking. Slowly, he rose, made it to the bedroom, and fell into a fitful sleep.

*   *   *

Days passed uneventfully, almost without Junior's knowledge. "The Girl." She was now "The Girl" or "That Girl" among his friends. When "The Girl" passed, he was just another guy; they passed without speaking. Junior entered the library to return the books he had taken out for Everett, but before he did he fingered through them, jotting down previously unknown facts that Everett could use for another paper, should he need them.

In the notepad he wrote,

New Jersey had 60 million a day purchased.

The Federal Reserve made loans for as low as 3.5 percent.

1929 call rates rose as high as 20 percent.

Hoover's Secretary of Treasury, Andrew Mellon—hands-off economic policy.

Hoover's world is self-promotion. He is absolutely certain they are correct all the time, especially in the estimation of God.

W. E. B. Dubois founded the NAACP in 1909; the same year Hoover signed the Agricultural Marketing Act.

1930 Hoover's Smoot-Hawley Tariff Act provided tariffs as high as 50 percent on some 20,000 imported goods.

Roosevelt' social reform policy, the New Deal.

In 1933, banks in 33 states closed under Hoover.

Agricultural income down 60 percent.

Kerosene lamps were the only source of light.

Hitler Chancellor of Germany.

Feb. 1934, U.S. foreclosures 150,000; 1930, 200,000.

1932, farm income dropped 6 billion, to 2 billion.

United Mine Workers—John L. Lewis.

1933 Federal Emergency Relief Act

Frances Perkins, at a wage of eight to 12 dollars a week, was developing her duties as Secretary of Labor. She worked to develop plans for unemployment insurance, old age pensions, social security, so that they could be developed into law.

With that, Junior returned the books, thinking if Everett needed more information for his paper, he had it.

CHAPTER 21

"What have you been doing, all of you?"

Rhodes leaned forward over his desk and glared at the three men.

"I was certain you would have the information I ordered you to secure."

Nervously, the three men shifted in their chairs.

"You should know, sir," Andrew began, "we have carried out your orders. We researched the records on file related to the Sunbury property. She has legally conducted all business associated with the land, the crops, the animals. In fact, she has almost bent over backwards to see that the records are legal and on file."

Andrew stopped speaking, his hands raised and thrust forward in earnest.

Next, Paul reported on his activities: "As ordered, sir, I have researched the state, county, and city records. I found that, over the years, that property has been owned, bought, and sold legally, including the sale to Mrs. Coleburn. All required payments, taxes, and assessments have been paid and are on record. I know because I personally went to each establishment and secured permission to record the information we're interested in. Sir, I have brought copies for your inspection, if you wish."

"No, I have no doubt that you are speaking truthfully. We wouldn't dare lie...would we"

He turned to Floyd and leaned forward.

"And you?"

Floyd, responded, "Sir, as instructed, if she took two steps, I was one step behind. When she went to town for supplies or to the bank, her son Junior drove her. When she worked the fields or the garden, if she had visitors, I knew who they were and why they had been there. Despite it all, I could find nothing of the nature you sought."

"Damn it!" Rhodes said suddenly, standing and walking to the window. "I'm not buying it! There must be something!"

He stared out the window, his gaze falling on the automobiles running on the street below. Turning back to the men, he said, "Checks—"

Before he could finish, Floyd said, "Sir, if you want her out, a small fire would make her change her mind."

Rhodes' angry expression flared as he shot up from his chair. He started to speak, controlled himself, sat back down, and leaned forward again.

"Lest you don't understand, let me explain. I want to acquire that property as it is. Start a small fire? Right! And if the wind blows from the wrong direction it can't be controlled. It burns the house, barn...everything! Do I make myself clear? I want that property as is. Unless you don't understand, your jobs are to help me acquire that land as soon as possible. Now, as I was about to say, your checks are at the front desk. We will meet again in six weeks—or sooner, if you acquire information I need."

He rose.

"Good day."

CHAPTER 22

Dark clouds hung low over the countryside. Lilly Ann drew her shawl tightly around her. Everybody had left the house long ago, after their chores were completed. Now Lilly Ann sat in her rocker, thinking of her dead baby. In her mind's eye, she could clearly see Roy and the others bury her baby as she felt the biting wind meet them as they approached the cemetery. The undertaker and his assistant were carrying the tiny casket. The undertaker was assuring Roy that all legal requirements had been dealt with as he led them to the small opening in the ground. Wet snowflakes fell from the sky and whirled on the wind. Two men with a length of rope in their hands appeared. Without a word, the small casket was lowered into the ground. The undertaker intoned something about ashes to ashes, dust to dust. The flashback brought tears to her eyes as the memories of her dead baby overwhelmed her. For a moment longer, her mind lingered on the bitter past. Then, with a resigned sigh, she rose to gather the ingredients she needed to prepare supper.

*   *   *

Sitting on the edge of the porch, Lilly Ann both heard and saw the elegant automobile pull up. Later, she would learn it was a Cord, a brand she had neither seen nor heard of before. George Everett Mayo emerged from the vehicle, along with lady whom she later learned was to be her step grandmother. George Everett had sold the nearly forty acres of walnut, maple, and oak trees—in addition to some other varieties—to a lumber company in Gallipolis, making him quite wealthy since Matilda had passed. He moved from the country and acquired a duplex he rented out and a single-family home next door that was opulent — or nearly so. He lived in the single-family home with his wife, Jenny,who was from a well-placed family in Akron.

Lilly Ann rose to greet them. Jenny was elegantly attired, with a hat and white gloves. Once the introductions were over, Lilly Ann led them into the house. In her heart of hearts, she took pride in knowing that, earlier, after the children had gone, she had cleaned and made her home orderly.

"I did not recognize the auto when you drove up."

"Oh, yes. It's a Cord. Quite fashionable. Jenny helped me pick it out."

"Since you're here, I have green beans cooking. I will kill two chickens, and we'll have fried chicken."

Removing her hat and gloves, Jenny said, "May I help you?"

For a moment Lilly Ann did not know how to respond.

Then she said, "If you will. I'll bring in some tomatoes and leaf lettuce. If you'll braise the lettuce and slice the tomatoes, I'll fry the chicken and bring up a jar of peaches from the root cellar; we can have the peaches for desert.

"I will gladly help."

They enjoyed supper together as soon as the children arrived from school.

"Grandpa, Grandpa!" Everette exclaimed, come outside and see everything."

While washing the dishes, Jenny said, "I bring sad news. One of your aunts in Columbus has nearly lost her mind."

Lilly Ann listened silently. She had never met Aunt Gertrude, but she had been told about her. She knew she was a small but buxom woman, five-feet-one or -two. At a time when most women raised children and kept house, Aunt Gertrude had worked as a clerk for a finance company. She had invested her savings in stocks that she had been advised to buy, paying only ten cents on the dollar. With the earnings, she had bought and paid for a house with money provided by her gentleman caller: an attorney and head of the law firm Mellman, Water, and Kolterman. The firm dealt primarily in real estate but also serviced other legal matters. Their offices were on the twentieth floor of the A.I.U. building, whose proximity to the Deshler Hotel allowed Mr. Mellman easy access to the suite the firm leased to accommodate important out-of-town clients.

Then Black Friday occurred. Aunt Gertrude lost everything, except her house, which was paid for. Afterward, she was often seen sweeping the middle of the street with a broom, holding up traffic. Around this time, she had married a large man who worked for the city's street cleaning department. Her husband would guide her into the safety of the house after neighbors would call, informing him of her antics. Other times drivers would stop, knowing who she was, and gently lead her to the curb.

One Saturday after Jenny had told Lilly Ann about Aunt Gertrude, Junior drove her and the other children to Columbus to see her aunt. They all filed into Aunt Gertrude's home and greeted her and her husband, John. Knowing the children would be hungry, Lilly Ann had brought along a sack of crackers, cheese, bologna, and fruit. Shared by all, they sat talking when Uncle John rose, and retrieved a jump rope from a closet.

"I know they're restless in here. I'll take them outside to play."

After Uncle John had left with the children, Gertrude abruptly stood up, left, and returned with pencil and paper.

"I know you are alone with the children. With Roy gone, you have to see to all legal matters. If you need help, here's the name of a lawyer you can depend on. Here is his name—Aaron Mellman. His office is in the A.I.U. building. I've added a small note so that he will know who sent you. Please let this be our secret. Don't tell anyone."

Handing the note to Lilly Ann, she added, "You know, Lil, half the time I *am* crazy. Other times, like now, I'm not. But I'm so happy that you came and brought the children."

Later, at home, Lilly Ann thought about what had just occurred. She knew she must follow up. Seldom did she keep Junior out of school, but the next day she did. Parked in front of the A.I.U. building, she gave him a half-dollar.

"Buy something." Starting to enter the building, she turned back to Junior. "Please meet me in the lobby in about an hour."

She walked into the building, took the elevator to the twentieth floor, and entered the law office. Asking to see Mr. Mellman, she handed the receptionist the note from Aunt Gertrude. The receptionist stood from her desk and was gone a moment; then she returned and ushered Lilly Ann in.

Mr. Mellman's office was large and elaborate. The room was furnished with sofas and a small, round meeting table with chairs. A mahogany desk with a high-backed swiveled chair sat in front of draped windows.

As she entered the office, Lilly Ann was greeted by a nicely suited man with a large, warm smile.

"Lilly Ann—I hope I can call you that. I am Aaron Mellman. Please come in and have a seat beside me here on this couch. How can I help you?"

Lilly Ann hesitated.

"Please don't hesitate—I am here to help you."

"I can't pay you," Lilly Ann blurted.

Mr. Mellman smiled again. "I'm pretty certain you have never heard the term *pro bono*. It means "for free." Occasionally, attorneys work *pro bono*. Your legal work will be performed *pro bono*. Does that satisfy your concern?"

She nodded.

Hesitantly, she described Roy's death, her children, her land, and how she and her children worked to keep up the payments on the property.

"And do you have papers—all the papers related to the farm?"

"Yes. When Roy was alive, he kept them. Now I keep them in a safe deposit box in the bank."

"If you would, I want you to bring all of them to me. I will have my clerks copy them to establish a file on you. Then we will return them to you. Would you do that?"

Smiling, she said, "Gladly."

"We need to do this as soon as possible."

"I will go to the bank this afternoon and bring them tomorrow. Is that acceptable?"

Mr. Mellman nodded. "Splendid."

They rose together from the couch. Grasping and shaking her hand, Mr. Mellman said, "I will see you tomorrow."

As promised, Lilly Ann delivered the papers the next day. Mr. Mellman's receptionist made copies, and then Lilly Ann returned the originals to the safe deposit box at the bank.

* * *

The day glistened with a low-hanging sun. Lilly Ann sat alone on the Fordson. She was a novice at driving and operating the Fordson but Junior had cranked it before he left for school—before he steered together the last cuttings of hay for the year. She could not drive the thought from her mind—Roy on the bed, the shotgun under his chin, and her terrified yet calm instructions.

"My darling," she had told him later, "in every person there is some cowardice, in every person there is some bravery. This is a time when we must choose, and we, for the children, must be brave. Darling, they...*we*... need you. *I* need you."

And vividly remembering, too, slowly removing the shotgun from his hands and placing it on the floor.... She had saved him only to see him die, anyway. Quickly that thought faded into figuring out how to maneuver the Fordson. With some effort, she pulled it around the corner of the field and turned it back toward the house. As she neared the house, she saw a 1933 Hupmobile in the lane parked near her house. The convertible's top was down; spare tires were set in the front fenders. It had white walls on its red wheels, throwing the car's black fenders into sharp contrast with the shining, red body.

Reaching the end of the furrow in the field, she shut the Fordson's motor off. As she stepped down from the tractor, the driver of the Hupmobile approached her. "Please don't be frightened," the driver said. "In case you have forgotten, I am Aaron Mellman."

"Yes, of course, Mr. Mellman. I could not but admire your automobile."

"Yes, a Hupmobile. I bought it new; and on fine days like this, I drive it. Today, since I needed to air this one out, I thought I would stop by to see how my *pro bono* client was doing. Fine, it seems to me."

"Yes. I'm attempting to get the last hay in. The cows need a lot."

"Lilly Ann," Mr. Mellman said, "I have had members of my staff look into your situation. Perhaps you have heard over the radio of the drought in many of the Midwestern states, and I'm afraid some of the dry weather may start to occur here."

"Yes. I heard that on the radio, and the thought of it happening here makes me shudder."

"Then perhaps my *pro bono* client would accept a little help...? Starting next week, I will have workers come here to work on two projects. One, I have had experts look into your water situation. You have a well some forty or more feet dug into the ground and lined with stone; the well is fed by an underground spring. It will produce all the water you need for yourself and animals, forever. I propose, with your permission, running a galvanized pipe from your pump, underground, to the barn. Deep enough," Mr. Mellman added, "so it will not freeze."

"And, two," he continued: "We will dismantle a silo from an abandoned farm and attach it to your barn, then fill it with ensilage so that you can feed your cows all winter once it is mixed with hay. Oh, and one more thing. Lest you be accused of accepting charity, we will prepare papers committing you to paying for these services."

Seeing the dismay on Lilly Ann's face, he said: "Never fear, the sum will be small...but no one will be able to accuse you of accepting charity."

While Lilly Ann turned thoughtful, Mr. Mellman added, "You may not know, I own over two hundred acres just past Gahanna. I'm concerned about reports saying the drought we spoke about earlier might be coming our way. Your place will give me an opportunity to experiment with methods to save farms for many people, if they will follow our example."

Standing in the low, morning sun, he nodded kindly to Lilly Ann and said, "I must leave. Remember, the crew will start soon, so don't be startled when the workers appear to do their work."

Then he bid her good-bye and drove away.

*　*　*

They came. Crews to dig a trench deep enough for the pipes, galvanized two inches across, to lay in without freezing. Crews to erect the silo. Crews on Case tractors to mow and start harvesting the hay to fill the barn. Crews to grind some of the hay and corn from the cornfield, to fill the silo as it was being erected.

Lilly Ann could only watch in thoughtful amazement as they swarmed like ants to complete their tasks, including burying an eight-foot long trough, some four feet in the ground, leaving two feet above ground for the animals to drink.

Then: there it was, completed. "All done," as Phyllis would say.

Inside the barn, Lilly Ann watched as Junior and Everett carted the wheelbarrow filled with ensilage and hay to the newly built trough, which extended to each of the stalls that had likewise been newly erected.

When Lilly Ann had seen the work being done, she opened her mouth to protest to Mr. Mellman.

Before she could speak, Aaron raised his hand, "*Pro bono, pro bono!*"

Leaving Mr. Mellman to go to the house, Lilly Ann could only look skyward, thinking, "Thank you, thank you."

CHAPTER 23

It was the last game of an undefeated season. Each team had scored one touchdown in the last two minutes of the game. From the sidelines Coach Whipkey called time. Surrounded by his team, he looked at Junior and a fellow teammate and friend, Tom.

"Now," he said.

They knew what he meant. They should; they had been practicing the play all season, ever since Coach Whipkey had returned from Pittsburg, where coaches from all over the country gathered for a three-day annual meeting to greet each other, exchange ideas, and learn new strategies. Upon his return, Coach Whipkey detained Junior and Tom after football practice, so they could learn and practice the maneuver.

As the teams started to return to the playing field, the coach grasped Junior by his arm and repeated, "Now."

On the field, the teams lined up. The referee blew his whistle to indicate time had restarted. The center hiked the ball to the quarterback; the offensive line surged forward. Tom hesitated a count, then ran forward while the quarterback handed Junior the ball and Junior stepped backwards, raising the ball in his hand. Then he drew his arm back and flung the ball to Tom, who caught it and sped toward the end zone.

Touchdown!

The opposing team, once they realized what had happened, stood stunned. Then, protesting, they crowded the bench, where their coach also raised his voice in protest. Coach Whipkey was prepared with the rule book opened in his hand.

"Marv, here it is for you to see."

Marv read the relevant regulation and shook his head then said, "Okay."

To his players, Marv said, "What they did is legal. It's legal."

The game was over. Sunbury had ended the season undefeated.

* * *

It was dark brown leather, thick leather, maybe two-feet high by two-feet wide when fully loaded; maybe two-feet high, with a thick, leather shoulder strap.

Lilly Ann estimated the dimensions while Jimmy, with Maggie by his side, displayed it, smiling with pride. "I've been promoted," he said. "I'm a carrier, a mailman."

Later, Maggie told Lilly Ann, "He's so proud he has a route to carry. He'll have to pay for his uniforms, summer and winter. They'll take a small amount from each paycheck until it's paid for; but he'll start right away. The friend on the council got him the promotion, just as he got him the job in the first place."

Lilly Ann said, "I'm so happy for you."

"Yes, we have agreed that we will still live on his current pay and pay for the house, which will come to you if anything happens to us."

"Mother, don't talk that way."

"Honey, you never know. But enough of that talk. Let's eat. I know the children are hungry."

As with each time she and the children visited, the food was not often enough, but the farm work required the family's full effort to just keep up. So, Maggie cooked, and they ate.

Over dishes in the kitchen, Maggie said, "I'm a little afraid. Oh, yes. I'm happy, but I'm concerned with him being out in the weather—you know that slogan, 'neither rain nor snow nor dark of night.' I can't remember it all, but it means his being out there when I should have him safe inside. I've come to love him so."

She stopped, her voice choked up, tears easing down her cheeks.

Lilly Ann moved to her mother, put her arms around her, consoling her and murmuring, "It will be all right, it will be all right."

Later, at home, Lilly Ann thought about her mother and Jimmy, and of what he called *catarrh*, the inflammation he had in his nasal passages and throat. Silently, she said a small prayer, asking God to ensure Jimmy's well-being as he delivered the mail.

* * *

It came, as she had feared it would: relentless sunshine with low-hanging, dry clouds, day after day. Leaves dried on the trees and fell to the earth as an arid wind blew. The desiccated earth cracked open. Animals, wild and domestic, sought after water in every creek, stream, or pond. Water, they had plenty, Lilly Ann had been assured. And each time they pumped, the water came.

Soon, Junior pumped water for the neighbors. Now, chores done, arms tired from pumping to fill his neighbors' containers, he stopped to remind his mother that the celebration dance at school was that evening.

"Son, anything that hasn't yet been done the rest of the family can do. I'm sure. Get yourself ready and go."

After bathing he put on his only suit. He hadn't worn it since he last sang, and he found the jacket's sleeves a little too short, the fit of the jacket and trousers a little too tight. He buttoned up the shirt and knotted the tie. His father's hat fit after he stuffed a bit of paper under the lining.

"My, you look nice," Lilly Ann said.

"Thanks."

And he was gone.

* * *

Stepping inside the gym where the music was playing, he was met by Coach Whipkey and his wife, who chaperoned the affair.

"Junior, I'm happy you're here," Coach Whipkey said. "Meet my wife."

Junior stepped forward.

"Mrs. Whipkey, it's a pleasure to meet you."

She smiled. "Junior, I have watched you play. I'm happy to meet you, too. Now go have a good time."

As Junior approached his friends and classmates in the gym, a group of pretty young women approached, each saying, "I get the first dance."

For a moment Junior hesitated, then, gathering his courage, he said, "I don't know how to dance."

Almost as a group, each said, "We'll teach you."

And each, taking a turn, did.

Later, when he was relaxed and enjoying himself with some of his friends, a man he had never seen before approached him. He extended a hand to Junior. "Jim Worthington," the man said, introducing himself. "Assistant principal at a school up in Columbus. I have friends who live here, and I told them I would speak with you. Sorry to interrupt your conversation with your friends—" he nodded politely to the other boys around Junior "—but if you wouldn't mind lending me a moment of your time, perhaps you'll accompany me next door, where we can sit down?"

Junior looked around at his friends then looked back to the man. "But, sir...."

"I know your concern. They'll let us in."

At the Old English Bar and Restaurant next door to the school, they sat at a comfortable table. J.W. (as Mr. Worthington now told Junior he called himself) drank a gin and tonic and Junior sipped a water spritzer as they listened to a band—piano, bass drums, trumpet, tenor saxophone, guitar—play Irving Berlin's "Blue Skies." They listened to the music for a short while longer, enjoying themselves; then, the serious discussion began.

"I'd like to know you better, Junior," J.W. told Junior frankly. "I know a little about you from the articles in the *Dispatch*, but who are you really? What do you want to be?"

Junior hesitated, unsure of J.W.'s meaning. He averted his gaze and caught sight of several players from the team. He opened his mouth to call out to them, but he said nothing.

"Do you want to go to college?" J.W. asked.

Junior turned his attention back to the conversation. College? He had not entertained the thought. College required both good grades and money.

He thought he had neither.

Again, he said nothing.

"I've spoken with your coach. He monitors your grades, along with the grades of your teammates, to make certain they are eligible. I've checked yours. They're fine. In fact, they're outstanding. Since seventh grade, you've received one B—all the others are A's. As for costs, a scholarship would cover all tuition fees and books. And I'm told a team player would receive a campus room, and board."

For a long moment Junior was dumbfounded. Playing for Ohio State, or at least being on the squad...? Then reality set in. He thought of his family, his mother. Under no circumstances could he desert them. Reluctantly, he smiled. "Thanks, but no thanks."

J.W. smiled. "Son, I do not expect a decision now. What I have said to you is only for you to consider. And, I thank you for listening to me."

Finishing his drink, he rose, said "good night," and was gone.

Junior's soda had lost all its fizz. Letting it remain where it was, he rose and looked around. His friends were gone, or were involved with female companions. So, he walked out and made for home.

* * *

Lilly Ann sat in her rocker on the porch, watching friends and neighbors lug containers of water—big jugs, small bottles, containers of all sizes. Above her, the darkening sky hung tenaciously, preventing little more than hopes or prayers to comfort Lilly Ann. Rising, leaving the porch while acknowledging the greetings of the water seekers, she walked toward the barn then continued to the fields beyond it.

Perhaps it wasn't until now that she had felt loneliness. Before, when the children were smaller, their needs and activities demanded her attention every moment. Now, with all of her children in school, and the morning chores over, and the birds long gone in their migration, long, silent moments prevailed....*Roy...Roy....* Perhaps she hadn't permitted herself to miss him. Now that she did, tears flowed down her cheeks. About her the chill air, loaded with the coolness of the morning dew, caused her to gather her shawl close about her.

Back at the house, with damp feet and the bottom of her skirt muddied, her mind determined how she would revive herself. She would go to town on the school bus.

On the bus, the driver looked at her sharply but said nothing. At school, he reported her to the principal. Meanwhile, Lilly Ann simply walked away, toward town. But arriving at the quiet streets, she wasn't quite certain what to do. Instinctively, she sought the general store. There, she wandered through the aisles. She inspected, touched, and browsed the various goods, as the other shoppers did. She basked in the feeling of being herself—a feeling she had not experienced since she was married, and when Junior was born. Deep in her reverie she did not sense the man's presence until she heard his voice.

"No good deed goes unpunished. You can paint a pumpkin black, but that does not make it a bowling ball."

He said this with a straight face but grinned when she looked up at him.

"Aren't you that lady who lives on the cow farm at the end of the road?"

Lilly Ann stood straight. She tightened her shawl about her and studied the unshaven man dressed in coveralls, his body half-covered with a light jacket.

"I'm Ned Parker. I have a proposition for you...."

She stiffened, her face grim.

"I want to sell cows to you; and if you take them, I'll give you a bull. Please, I'm desperate. We're moving and need the money."

Lilly Ann relaxed a little. "What kind of cows, and how old? The bull, is he wild or dangerous?"

"They're Guernsey cows, two and three years old. Same goes for the bull. Not dangerous, has a ring in his nose. Twenty a piece for the cows, and I'll throw the bull in for free."

"These animals belong to you?"

"I had twenty acres. It's so dry we have no pasture or hay for the winter. We're moving to Columbus to live with relatives, and for me to try to find a job—anything to prevent us from starving."

Lilly Ann eyed the man a long moment then relaxed. "I'll buy your stock and pay you on delivery. When I leave here, I'll go to the bank."

"We'll bring the stock tomorrow."

"I'll be home."

Her pointless, aimless day had taken on a purpose. At the bank, she was greeted kindly. A teller at the counter carefully counted out fifty dollars and smiled warmly as he slid the small bills across to Lilly Ann. The ride home on the school bus was uneventful.

The next day, the stock arrived on an ancient, rusting Ford. After the animals were unloaded, Lilly Ann held out the fifty dollars.

"But you only owe me forty," the man said.

"I know, but I cannot take your stock for nothing."

Shaking his head, hat in hand, the man said, "God bless you.... God bless you!"

*   *   *

"I'm afraid I don't understand," the superintendent told Principal Scott.

"Sir, take my word for it. The mother rides the school bus to town."

"And why?"

"Sir, she lives on a farm close to mine. All of her children are in school. She is isolated there."

"And her husband?"

"Dead. Killed in an accident."

"How do they eat, and shop, and live?"

"The oldest son was taught to drive before he died, but he rides the school bus with the other children."

"Do you know this woman?"

"I do, a fine woman. Manages over fifty acres to raise her five children and keep them fed and in school."

"You would recommend this unique agreement of her riding the bus?"

"Yes, sir. In this case, indeed, I recommend it."

"Then I approve it."

"Sir, may you be blessed. I thank you."

"You're welcome...and remember, the condition with this privilege is her discretion."

"Thank you again, sir. I shall inform her."

Lilly Ann, when informed, felt a freedom, a lifting of her spirit; but she was not quite sure how to use her newfound privilege. Maybe once or twice a week? She would start out taking the bus that frequently and see if that was all that she required.

On her second trip to town, she went back to the general store to see what new goods were on display. Once there, she strolled through the aisles, moving about the counters, again picking up and examining the goods. She was amazed at how unaware she had been of the variety of colors merchandise was available in. Ladies moved about her, browsing and buying, the tinkling bell on the front door signaling the entry and departure of more customers. Timidly, Lilly Ann pulled a hat from a tall rack that stood in a corner and then looked at herself in a mirror. The hat was the latest fashion in ladies' headpieces…but suddenly she became self-conscious, admiring her appearance. She looked about to see if anyone was watching. No one was! After another moment, she set the hat back on its hook. Slowly, then, she moved about the store again, allowing herself to experience some of the vast array of goods available to those patrons who had both time and money. She had neither, just a newly awakened desire. The thought made her sad—and hungry.

"Is there a place where a person could get a bite for just a little money?" she asked a female clerk.

The clerk looked at her. She seemed to be assessing Lilly Ann: what food she meant by "a bite" and what her financial situation might be.

"Oh, yes. Mom Pickens Restaurant, three doors down."

Thanking her, Lilly Ann made for Pickens, a place she had passed numerous times but had never paid attention to. Inside, the pleasant odor of warmth and cooked food wafted over her. Hesitating, she was approached by a stout, gray-haired woman.

"Welcome." The waitress smiled to Lilly Ann. "Please seat yourself at any empty table."

Glancing around, Lilly Ann saw what appeared to be some eight or ten tables. Half were occupied with diners busily eating and talking. The place was pleasant, painted light blue and topped with a spectacular ceiling. Later, she learned the ceiling had been in place for many years; it had been imported from Germany and was made of tin that was cut into three-foot blocks of multicolored shapes. It simply *glowed*.

Lilly Ann sat down at an empty table and took in her surroundings.

The gray-haired waitress returned. "Please, enjoy the atmosphere," she encouraged. "But I know you must be hungry—would you like our special? Beef stew with vegetables; corn bread on the side. Twenty-five cents. May I serve you?"

"Please."

Several moments later, the waitress brought the stew. Hungrily, Lilly Ann started to eat her meal. After she had enjoyed several spoonfuls of the savory stew and a couple bites of the cornbread, the waitress returned and seated herself.

"Well?"

"Delicious."

The waitress smiled her approval then said: "Aren't you the woman from out on Cemter Road who runs the Fordson with all those attachments—who farms all those acres, milks all those cows, has all those children?" Breathless, she stopped.

Astonished, Lilly Ann nodded.

"Seems strange," the woman continued. "When Levi died, everyone just *knew* I would close the restaurant. When I didn't, everyone had an opinion as to my decision. Now it's the same about you. Many women admire you for continuing to care for your children, but many others feel you have no business running a tractor, or farming. They feel a woman's work is in the house. Having babies, cooking, sewing, and, oh yes, doctoring the measles, whooping cough, and all the colds while hoeing the garden so that the family can eat. A man works hard, farming or in town; but when his day is over, he comes home to eat and rest. After cooking, washing dishes and clothes, putting the children to sleep, the woman then must service her husband's needs, whatever they may be. Someone once said, 'a woman's work is never done.' That someone was right."

Then, rising from the table, the waitress said, "Honey, enjoy your meal," and returned to her duties in the restaurant.

For the next several days, as often as she could, Lilly Ann "discovered" Sunbury. At the library she learned the town was founded in 1816, mostly to keep life and death records for the farmers around town. The records building stood in the center of the town square. The building was a quarter-mile wide on each side; three floors were dedicated to warehousing the records of the town's residents. About it sat stone benches; the rest was grass and trees.

Roaming about the square, curious as to what was there in addition to the general store, Lilly Ann found the barber shop, a hardware store, and, curiously, a blacksmith shop, where farmers could go to shoe their horses—for farmers who still used shoes on their horses, that is.

On days when she roamed about the town, she returned to Mom Pickens for a bite to eat. Seated at her table, she again spent time enjoying the colorful beauty of the ceiling: the reds, yellows, blues, and greens. And, of course, the food. Each day the food was different. Today, the specialty was chicken and dumplings. But it didn't matter: chicken, beef stew, chicken and noodles…it always was delicious. While she enjoyed the food and the atmosphere, she also enjoyed meeting and socializing with other diners who frequented the restaurant.

A small radio on a shelf along the back wall carried news of the various happenings in the local areas and about the country—and, more and more frequently, news of Germany and the rest of Europe. How Germany had invaded Poland, Belgium, Holland, and France. Conversation about this drifted among the diners; the conversations were never in depth or carried on for very long, and were never discussed very seriously. But, fleetingly, Lilly Ann heard the conversations and was occasionally asked her opinion as to what was happening. Having studied World War I in her history class when she was in school, she understood the horrors of war. The hundreds of thousands of men killed, the devastation of populations, the murder of women and children. So, in response to the diners' questions about what was happening, she could only repeat what someone had said: "War is hell!"

The diners nodded in agreement. Then the subject changed to children, teething, rashes, and women's ailments. Lilly Ann listened and nodded, but she said very little.

* * *

Moving about quickly, Lilly Ann busied herself at home, reading, preparing lunches, and getting the children ready for school. Staying busy, she could not rid her mind of yesterday's parting conversation among the friends, the diners.

Someone had said, "That's Europe. They have always been at war. We're here across the ocean. Yeah, somebody else said we thought we were safe before. Never forget World War One…we thought we were safe then."

Suddenly, Junior had burst into the room.

"Mother, come quick. A cow is dead."

Dropping everything, she rushed into the barn alongside Junior to find a dead cow, with another on her side, heaving.

Quickly she said, "Son, take the Ford into town and bring the veterinarian. Please hurry!"

In town, Junior found the veterinarian in his office. Knowing how fortunate he was, he drove the Model A back to the farm as fast as he could, the veterinarian sitting anxiously in the passenger seat.

In the barn, the veterinarian quickly examined the nearly dead cow.

"She is dying of poison. What have you been feeding?"

"Hay and ensilage."

"Ensilage from your silo?"

"Yes."

Moving quickly to the silo, he opened the side door, thrust his head inside, sniffed quickly, and withdrew his face.

"This ensilage is rotten. It's killing your cows. You must throw it all out!"

Clutching a fence post, Lilly Ann felt herself go faint. *Dead cows.* How many others would die? Would she lose them all? Would she lose the farm? Losing everything would mean not being able to support her children—which would mean losing her children, and all of them going to orphanages. The thought devastated her. Only her grasp on the fence post kept her from collapsing. Sensing Lilly Ann's plight, the veterinarian grasped her arm.

"Are you all right?" he asked.

She could only stare at him as she slowly recovered.

"Will they all die?"

"I'm almost certain you have lost all that you're going to lose. We'll give each of your cows some medication and watch them. In two days, we shall know."

Carefully, he helped her to the house. As they entered through the front door, she suddenly asked, "The children? Where are the children?"

"Unless I'm mistaken, carrying out their chores."

"But their lunches!" Lilly Ann said. "I didn't finish packing their boxes."

Without saying a word, the vet brought Lilly Ann into the kitchen. After sitting her down at the table, he went over to the lunch boxes on the kitchen counter, put the correct items in each lunchbox, closed the boxes, and then returned to Lilly Ann. "I'll ride the school bus back to town. And I'll send men to remove the dead cows. Now, rest."

Only half aware of all that was happening, she watched the vet guide the children outside and board the school bus with them. Then, still half dazed, she sat in her rocker, rocked a little, and then slept.

CHAPTER 24

He had to do it. Junior approached the bull pen. Inside, the bull grazed on hay Junior had thrown in. Sensing Junior, the bull raised his head, staring at him. Satisfied, he returned to his grazing. Junior walked away from the bull pen, then returned, guiding the cow in heat. The veterinarian had pointed her out as he made his inspection after returning to the farm to administer shots. "You have a bull over there," the vet had told Junior. "Take that cow to him for insemination. Birth of a calf will restore her milking ability again."

Opening the gate to the bullpen, Junior led the cow in then let her go as he retreated and closed the gate. The bull snorted as he moved to the cow, penis erect, emitting semen. The cow moved a little then stopped, allowing the bull to mount. Snorting, penis inserted, he pumped away. Junior watched, feeling his own penis grow. The sensation made him wish, at least for the moment, that Becky were before him again, pink-nippled breasts, her hairy crotch inviting him in. Opening his pants, he let his throbbing erect, penis extend into his fist, eyes on the bull as he pumped into the cow. Junior jerked on the throbbing penis until suddenly semen spurted while he jerked faster. Then it was over.

The bull dismounted. Junior's penis went flaccid, his body relaxed. With a handful of grass, he wiped himself, pulled his soft penis back into his pants, buttoned them, opened the gate and gathered the cow, then went up the hill, to the house.

*   *   *

Oblivious to the days passing her by, Lilly Ann busied herself with her sons, using the Fordson to carry the spoiled silage to the fields and spreading it diligently. One day, a dump truck backed up, tilted its bed, and winched the farm's dead cows aboard. Though she didn't know how many days had passed, she should smell the stench of the dead cows. Almost obsessed, she and the boys made trip after trip into the woods across the way, hauling and dragging wood, piling it up to be broken up for heating and cooking. Milking time found them trying to get one last milking in, to have more to sell to Nestlé.

* * *

Over and over again, she combed and braided Phyllis's hair, no matter how much Phyllis squirmed and cried. Later, she oversaw study sessions each evening. Lilly Ann moved tirelessly between her children, advising, correcting; she even asked Junior if he needed help.

"Mother," Junior said, "you help us all. I talked with the veterinarian. He said the cows will be all right. *We* will be all right...."

He moved away from his books then stepped close to his mother, put his arms around her, and held her.

"Maybe we should go see Mom Mayo and see if she is all right?"

Lilly Ann nodded and gave Junior a tired smile.

When they arrived at Maggie's house, the children rushed to her and wrapped themselves around her. She held them but looked out at her daughter. As the grandchildren released her, she moved to her daughter and put an arm around her, too.

"It's so good to see you. How have you been?"

Tears flowed.

"Darling, what is it?"

She told the story of the lost cows and the spoiled ensilage and chattered on and on and on. It all flowed out in an anguished, choking voice.

Gently, Maggie led Lilly Ann to a couch. She helped her sit down while she sat beside her, silent, occasionally touching her daughter softly. As suddenly as it started, Lilly Ann's crying spell stopped.

"Where's Jimmy?" she said.

"Out delivering his route. Honey, earlier today I made a pineapple upside-down cake. There's way too much for Jimmy and me. Is it all right if I share some with the children?"

"Yes, if you'll allow me to cook and give them dinner and serve the cake for dessert."

"Oh, what a good idea. We'll cook together. Then we'll get Jimmy's supper ready."

While the older children played checkers, the young ones drew on pads their grandmother, Mom Mayo, had given them. Almost without a sound, the front door opened and Jimmy, keychain in hand, stepped in. Seeing him, the children rushed over to him, shouting, "Grandpa!"

Seeing his grandchildren, Jim smiled. He managed to remove his cap and the mailbag while the children surrounded him. Hearing the commotion, Lilly Ann entered the room, only to find the children huddled around Jimmy. Seeing Lilly Ann, Jimmy smiled and managed to free a hand to wave her way.

Maggie also entered. Seeing Jimmy almost suspended by the children, she went over to the group, saying, "Children, let him rest. He's had a long day," and then she led her husband to a lounge chair.

Understanding the situation, Lilly Ann said to her children, "Listen to grandma. After he's rested, he'll play with you."

They all rushed back to their previous activities.

At dinner, Jimmy, now in a subdued cotton shirt and corduroy trousers, said the blessing, thanking the Lord for his family, their health, and, of course, the bountiful meal. Having sliced the baked ham, he served it onto the children's plates, along with the succotash Lilly Ann had prepared earlier. This was accompanied by sliced tomatoes, boiled potatoes, and scalded leaf lettuce with vinegar dressing. As they ate, all was silent except Jimmy's continuous hacking. Turning his head, he hacked again and again. Finally, he excused himself and left the table.

When he returned, he said, "That darn catarrh."

Once dinner was finished, Lilly Ann helped her mother clear the table and clean the dishes while Jimmy and the children played. Then, recognizing the time and the chores to be done at home, Lilly Ann and the children bid the grandparents good-bye, and left.

Nearing home, Junior said, "Grandpa Jimmy's catarrh sounded worse."

Lilly Ann nodded, saying, "Yes."

CHAPTER 25

"Are you telling me cows are dying?" Bill Rhodes asked.

Once more Rhodes and his three agents were seated at his favorite table, which the maître d' at the Maramor had reserved especially for him. Sipping their glasses of chardonnay, the others anxiously awaited his reaction.

"Yes, sir," Floyd finally said, when Rhodes had not continued. "I saw the truck haul them away. They had a dump truck with some kind of drag line and hoist and dragged the two cows into the truck. That's all I could see without being detected."

"There could be more? The whole herd?"

"Oh yes, sir. They had the veterinarian out there more than once."

Rhodes took a full drink of the wine, set the glass down, and propped his elbow on the table. He rested his chin in his hand as he looked reflectively out into space.

Then, dictatorially, he said to one of the men, "I want you to find out specifically how many cows have died."

To another man he said, "Again, inspect the records. This time, sooner than later, she will have to go to that banker. He will have to foreclose on the house. You should be there, watching."

To the third man, Floyd, he said, "You did well, seeing the dead cows. Keep it up. Now, let's have some Cornish game hens." He nodded to the plates teeming with the juice of the small birds as the waiters just now set them down at each man's place setting. "Enjoy."

*   *   *

It's over, Lilly Ann reminded herself. The veterinarian had examined the cows, twice finding them well and healthy, but that did not replace her loss or her continued anguish. Not only had she lost the cows and the income from them, the silo that Mr. Mellman had so generously installed had proven defective, even fatal. Having looked at prices in town, she knew the price of necessities had crept up, while her income had gone down. That was not her imagination. It was real.

While she sat and worried, a navy-blue Auburn drew up, windows cracked, the radio playing Duke Ellington's song, "It Don't Mean a Thing." The driver stepped out of the car and spotted Lilly Ann.

"I hear you've had some difficulty," he said.

Recognizing his firm chin and resonating voice, she said, "Yes, Mr. Mellman." She invited him into the house and they sat down together.

"I'm told we reap good things by investing in others," Mr. Mellman said. Remember to think that before you thank me again. Also, remember I said my father was such a stern man that I grew up hoping, even praying to help somebody."

Slowly, she said, "You are a blessing to me."

He smiled. "Every blessing has its little burdens."

She smiled in return. "I know you don't want anything from me, but be careful. I'll give you beefsteak tomatoes. There's still a few left."

He smiled again. "That sounds like an aphorism. Whether one believes it or not, life often gets worse before it gets better."

She looked closely at him. "Do you believe that?

He smiled again, saying, "Life is not only full of sorrow, life is full of joy. Or, as it is said, nothing succeeds like success. Be careful, I'll tease you with more.... For example, there is one way to skin a cat—or maybe an onion? Or, maybe," he said, cleverly, "a lawyer. Then someone once said to me, 'I stand in blind awe for your gift of blind certainty.' Then, 'Be careful. It's a place you could catch death like a cold.' Someone else once said, 'Good men bend the law for just reasons, bad men bend the law for unjust reasons.' We lawyers like that one...if you're on the right side." He continued: "Napoleon said, 'History is a fable agreed upon.' To you, comparing your troubles is like comparing Noah's flood to a drizzle. Oh, I've heard thousands, I guess. But tell me what your husband was like. I mean both looks and actions. Does it bother you to discuss him?"

"No, it doesn't. He was short, barrel-chested, he had muscled arms, with the strength of a man brought up on hard work...He was handsome, with a shock of long, black hair. His word and a handshake were his bond. He was kind to me and his children, but strict."

"I understand Floyd visited you for facts about the silo."

"Yes, he appeared. May I be frank?"

He nodded.

"A frantic man who wouldn't listen, change his mind, or change the subject."

Mr. Mellman nodded. "I've warned him many times of a fact that even your fledglings know. Words can be like a treadmill that lets you walk for a long distance…yet you never get anywhere. Now, may I ask you another question or two?"

"You mean about the silo and the rotten ensilage?"

He nodded. "Shall I send Floyd and his men to clean it out? I don't want to interfere with you or your schedule."

"The boys and I used the Fordson to haul it out and spread for fertilizer.

"You mean…?"

"I mean the rotten smell; it smelled so bad we couldn't stand it, so we emptied it."

"You mean…?" He looked dumbfounded.

"Yes, I mean anything to get rid of—" she eyed him "—the stench."

He smiled, recovering his courtroom demeanor.

"Your family—but mostly you—amaze me. How can I help you now?"

"You mean it?"

He nodded. "Yes."

"With the money from Nestlé for all of the cows' milk, I—we—were just starting to get ahead."

"Please, permit me to loan you whatever you need."

"Money given…I know you call it a loan, but one that could never be repaid."

He shook his head. "Pride goes before a fall."

"No, not pride—and no, I'm not referring to you, but men have always compromised women one dollar at a time."

He looked hurt. "I thought you thought more of me than that."

Quickly, she said, "Oh, please, I did not mean to hurt you. I'm just a stupid woman."

He raised his hand. "I'm certain this foolishness has caused cows to be sold, farms abandoned, this drought…I mean, those left still have water and some money. But I will inquire."

She stopped him. "Rhodes."

Half-risen from his seat, Mellman looked at her eagerly. "What do you know of him?"

"It's a long story. I'll tell it to you sometime."

"Tell me now. I'll listen."

"No, the children will be here. Supper must be prepared, chores done."

Now standing fully, he looked curiously toward her, turned away, and then looked back. Then he said, "Very well," and was gone.

*　　*　　*

The next day there was a knock at the door. Lilly Ann answered.

Gaunt, with tobacco-stained teeth, some of which were missing: the strange man stood on the porch.

"I was told you had a silo spoilage trouble."

She nodded "yes."

"Mind if I take a look?"

She shook her head, "no."

He was gone fast—then back faster.

"It's empty."

She nodded.

"Understand you got cows."

She nodded.

He continued, "I got hay, no cows—either died or I sold them. I'll bring you plenty hay. Who's going to pay me…you?"

"Whoever hired you," Lilly Ann responded.

"Don't you get smart with me! I'll…."

She left him standing there, alone on her porch, then reappeared with Roy's Winchester.

"Or you'll what?"

Watching his eyes, she continued.

"If you try it, I'll pump two into you with a third in the chamber before you fall."

With quivering hands, he said, "Now, lady, you know I didn't mean nothing. I'll bring your hay."

He slowly backed up and was quickly gone.

The next day, a mistreated-sounding truck of some unknown make arrived with hay. She could see him up in the barn, forking hay.

Two similar trips provided hay for the winter.

Rain finally came in sheets from low-hanging, dark grey clouds. Violent lightning illuminated the countryside. From the barn, cows moved uneasily. Lilly Ann, sitting at the Singer, heard the steady drumming of rain on the tin roof. Despite it all, her fingers guided the cloth as the needle pierced and threaded the dress she was making for Phyllis. Slightly insecure but almost certain, the children boarding the school bus in crude but effective clothing were, and would be dry boarding and exiting the bus.

Her mind drifted back over the past few days. Suspecting that what was now here would, eventually, come, she and the big boys had crossed the road to the fallen limbs, dragging load after load to be cut and stacked. Though she believed he had tried, he had not replaced the last cows. More beans, less broccoli she thought she had heard. In any case, that prevailed. There would have to be fewer trips on the school bus, more baked bread and less city loaves. Using her ingenuity, she prepared meals from what they had and bought little or nothing from town. A violent streak of lightning followed by an equally violent clap of thunder shocked her back to the task at hand: the dress.

"I could quit school and get a job," Junior said later that night.

"For what?" She glared at him.

"Fifty cents a day and food. Carl Nester Craig, who prints the newspaper, said he would teach me to set type. He runs a printing business besides the newspaper."

Seeing his earnestness, her tone softened.

"Son, thank you; but the answer is 'no.' School is your future. You must not be denied. I've shared our groceries and hardships with you. I've had no one else to talk to. You and the children are my life. Your future is *your* life. School, learning, knowledge is your future. Please go as far in school as you can."

"Mother, if it means that much to you, I will. I will tell the printer 'no.'

She held out her arms. "You're still not too big to be hugged."

"Never," he said.

Rain drummed the tin roof, thunder roared, and mother held her son.

* * *

Four days' work at the Singer sufficed. Then cloth and thread were gone; and, despite her resolve, her mind grew restless. The next morning, she once again boarded the school bus. In town, she entered a building she had been told was the city hall. Inside, she entered a door labeled "Records."

Approaching the counter, she asked, "May I see records?"

The clerk eyed her as he said, "Of course, ma'am. What records do you wish to see?"

"Ones that will tell about where I live."

Still eyeing her he said, "You're the lady who bought the old McGuire place; the one who does a man's work?"

He walked back into the rows of shelves and returned with two large volumes. Then he came from behind the countertop, walked to a small table and placed the files on it.

"I think you'll find it all in there," he said. He walked away but returned with a stool high enough for her to sit on.

Lilly Ann, though somewhat clumsily, seated herself and opened a volume, waving the dust away with her hand. From behind his counter, the clerk called out, "If I can help you, please let me know."

Lilly Ann nodded while opening the volume. She didn't know when Sunbury or the county started to keep records. This one started in 1816.

As she turned pages, she, in her mind, envisioned the potato famine in Ireland, the flow, the almost endless rush of almost blank-eyed, staring Irish through Ellis Island. Mayos from Ireland furnished their share of immigrants to many counties, and Sunbury, along with the others, received them. The farm Lilly Ann now occupied was once large, extending on both sides of what was now the road. Some attorney general used what Lilly Ann now knew was the state's power of imminent domain to seize land for Sunbury Road. The McGuire land had been reduced to its present fifty-two acres. Turning the pages of the old volume made her think of the section in the Bible that reveals the *begats*—so-and-so *begat* so-and-so, who *begat* so-and-so, who *begat* so-and-so: it went on almost endlessly.

Finally, but only after going through the second volume, she came upon what she had hoped she would find. The McGuire family, like her own, had fled famine to come to the Ohio territory—to the very place her land was on; through nearly as many *begats*, families had passed through and lived on the land. Over time, she saw, various members of the family had acquired a better education and better jobs, and they had retained the land. Only when Lilly Ann and Roy's plight became known did the McGuire family agree to sell. After information regarding Rhodes' plan to buy up property was provided by an insider, Lilly Ann had had the visit from the real estate agent, which handled to the purchase of the farm. She sat back, sighing.

"Do you need assistance?"

Thinking she had been silent but suddenly realizing she hadn't, she looked at the clerk, shaking her head "no." He still smiled understandably. Extracting a pocket watch, he ascertained the time.

"I have an hour for lunch. If I can take you anywhere, I will."

"I've been reading that this area had a family of McGuires who helped develop it. Are any of them still here?"

"I don't know, but I do know that a half mile or so out of town there's an old man who lives alone named McGuire."

"Could we go see him?"

Rising from a faded, green, grass lawn, a two-story, red brick house revealed two windows on each side of a bright red door with a brass knocker. All about were dead perennials. The clerk rapped the door with the knocker. After a short pause, the door opened.

"Mr. McGuire, this lady would like to speak with you."

The man in the door was a big man, over six feet tall, broad of body, white haired, and smiling curiously.

"How can I help you, madam?"

Seeing his friendly demeanor, Lilly Ann felt encouraged.

"I did a little research," she explained, "and found that the land my husband and I acquired originally was part of the McGuire Farm. My curiosity has led me to you. Do you mind talking with me about it?"

"Not at all, on one condition—that you come in and have tea with me. You as well," he said, addressing the clerk.

Entering the house, Lilly Ann immediately saw the beauty of a mahogany banister...hardwood floors...oriental rugs...overstuffed divans and chairs artistically arranged about the large, bright rooms

McGuire motioned to seats in the living room then excused himself. He returned with a silver tray on which were set teapots, cups, saucers, sugar and cream, utensils, and a small platter of cookies. Setting the tray on a low, inlaid table he poured the tea, filling the cups, and indicated the cream, sugar, and cookies.

"Please, help yourself," he said.

When all were settled with their tea, he sat down across from Lilly Ann and the clerk.

"I don't know if I know what you want, but I will tell you what I know. I'm certain your general research has informed you of the history of Ohio—and even of Sunbury—but perhaps not much about the later years. The McGuire's, being Irish and Catholic, produced many children. So, many in my family who had a natural curiosity migrated to the big city, to Columbus. Various McGuire men worked on various construction projects, including that tower, the American Insurance Union building."

He paused, and the clerk removed his pocket watch to glance at the time. Interrupting, the clerk said, "Please, sir, I must be back at the top of the hour."

McGuire nodded, saying, "I'll skip some details. Our sister, Jenny, met and married a rather well-to-do lawyer, and they bought and moved into a fine house on the near eastside. After several years of trying to have a child, they adopted one, a boy. When they attempted to change his name, they were told that doing so might harm him. Later, perhaps, after he had grown accustomed to his surroundings, they could change it. But for now, he should remain Woodrow Floyd William Rhodes. Once in his new surroundings, even beyond some teenage scuffles, he remained a difficult student. Moved into a special class for both dull and extra-bright students, he attempted to prevail over his difficulties. Upon graduation, he enrolled at Ohio State University, majoring in accounting, and, on a whim, minored in real estate. Upon graduation, his father found him employment in the real estate office of a friend with offices in the A.I.U. building."

The clerk looked down to his watch.

"We have half an hour."

McGuire smiled and looked to Lilly Ann, who shifted in her chair.

"Am I boring you?"

"Oh no, I find it fascinating."

McGuire continued: "Rhodes was working as an accountant in the offices of Rostoive and Franklin, where the salesmen were continuously in and out. He heard them speak of commissions, large amounts compared to his salary. One day, after work, he took a notice to the home of a home seller, introduced himself as a representative of Rostoive and Franklin, saying he knew the property had been up for sale too long and that he would sell it in three days, with the owners' permission. The next day, he moved about the office, secretly securing potential buyers' names. Surreptitiously, he made calls and located the buyers. Still moving almost invisibly, he arranged for the interested parties to meet in the office and ask for him. While others looked on, the sale was completed. Informed of the occurrence, Mr. Rostoive, a man of some sixty or seventy years—grey-haired, stooped, wrinkled—approached Rhodes and offered him a part-time position in sales."

After a pause, McGuire again continued: " Whether through luck or his persistent drive, he sold properties while his accounting background permitted an accurate assessment of his growing wealth. When asked why he didn't marry, his standard answer was 'too busy.' His sexual needs were met with discreet visits to a brothel. Earning, saving, and investing, he acquired and sold properties, which made him very wealthy. Being recognized as Rostoive's heir made him powerful, but it wasn't enough. Overheard conversations, research conducted in his spare time, and ruthless fantasies allowed him to envision his becoming the exclusive representative to one of the largest corporations in the world. He could see himself meeting and negotiating with perhaps a vice president of a foreign power. Perhaps going to Europe, or to Switzerland. With that in mind, he set about acquiring farmlands, large and small, as much as possible, to gain recognition by Nestlé. Fascinated by the extent of his control as well as the recognition it wielded, he ruthlessly seized property, foreclosing with the sheriff's help, evicting without regard for families, mothers, children. Lounging at his desk, he listened as employee after employee entered, relating acquisitions, seizures, evacuations, until one clerk, trembling, related the continued inability to acquire Lilly Ann's property. Today, Rhodes remains frustrated by both his inability to acquire this one particular property and by not having the land for growing the sorely needed hay."

"Please, sir," the clerk said, looking at his watch one more time, "we must leave."

Rising, the white-haired old man said, "Yes, of course."

"Sir, you have provided so much information," the clerk said. "I thank you."

Back at the records department after speeding, the clerk found no one waiting to chastise him. From behind his desk, he told Lilly Ann, "I hope I have been helpful."

Smiling, Lilly Ann said, "Greatly.

The evening felt of the damp chill of heavy frost. Lilly Ann, having completed the nightly chores, sat cooking at the red glow of the stove. A blanket over her shoulders spilled into her lap. She was warm now, having dared to throw three more lumps of coal into the stove, but without knowing when she would be able to afford more. With a haste induced by the chill, she and the children had set the cans of milk outside for morning pickup.

Supper over, their homework accomplished, their mild playing finished, all the children were in bed, leaving Lilly Ann alone. It was at moments like this that she missed Roy the most. Their intimate times together, seeing him as she first saw him: high stiff collar, softly tinted tie, dark blue suit, glasses with plain glass lenses—unnecessary but needed to convey the near-formal look. He had begun courting her more frequently, then, her having prepared golden fried chicken, potato salad filled out with hard-boiled eggs, sweet pickles, red pimentos, the entire meal accompanied by lemonade. A white tablecloth with silver utensils for two…and following one of these suppers, a kneeling proposal of marriage, with Lilly Ann's trembling 'yes' in acceptance. A tear of remembrance slid down her cheek. With effort, she brought herself back to the present.

A sound at her door made her think the wind had strengthened. The sound came again, only louder this time. Lilly Ann wondered who could be at the door after nine o'clock.

"Who is it?" she called.

"Your next-door neighbor."

Lilly Ann opened the door. The woman, standing there, hooded against the cold wind, stepped inside. Once there, as she took the hood off, Lilly Ann recognized her.

"My, it's been so long, Mrs. Gorsuch."

"Do you have Paregoric?"

Lilly Ann did. It was medicine she had had for a long while to help her children as they cut teeth.

"Yes, I'm sure I do."

"May I borrow it? He has a rotten tooth. My husband, I mean," Mrs. Gorsuch said.

"I'll get it."

Lilly Ann moved to a small cabinet to retrieve it.

Standing close to the stove, hands thrust out to warm herself, her neighbor said, "Hear someone bought the place up the road, the place where you got your hay."

"Oh?"

"Yep. Drove up in a big car, got the bill of sale, paid cash."

"Oh."

"If he said his name, I didn't hear it. Just went on about his business."

Lilly Ann returned with the medicine, glad to help, but confused and concerned. Had the noose's knot just been tightened? Cows without hay would perish. With no cows, she would lose the farm. All would perish.

Seeing her concern, Mrs. Gorsuch said, "Is something wrong? Can I help?"

Lilly Ann managed a wry smile.

"You've helped enough with this information."

Mrs. Gorsuch pointed to the medicine.

"I cannot thank you enough."

"I hope this will help your husband," Lilly Ann said, opening the door. "Be careful out there."

*　*　*

Wind cut sharply across the open field, blowing Junior sideways as he stepped from the house to go to the barn. Reaching up, he caught hold of the line, held on, steadied himself while looking up at the lush, red–yellow leaves and clinging tenaciously against the sweeping force of the wind. Wind-driven as well, a flock of blackbirds swept by, banked sharply into the wind, clung for a moment, then sped past wind-blown, brown leaves fluttering in little whirlwinds on the ground. All about the farm, the atmosphere was grey, the grey that precedes the first while snowflakes of the season.

Feeling the wind's chill, Junior rushed to the shelter of the barn. Once there he seized the wheelbarrow, opened the gate to the bull's stall, shoved the wheelbarrow in, and closed himself in the stall. He started to load manure. Silently, with a rush, the bull butted him down, mulled him a little, then stood over him, watching, matching each move Junior made to get away with a move of his own. Seeing the pitchfork nearby, Junior attempted to slide his way over to it, using his arms and his buttocks and his feet. Almost reading his mind, the bull moved to the pitchfork, too, stood over it and snorted. Not knowing what to do next, Junior slumped back, exhausted. It was then he heard the sound of somebody moving about. Afraid to move with the bull lurking, he turned his head to see the newcomer's legs.

"Help me."

"Where are you?"

"Down here. Look down."

Everett looked down, saying, "What are you doing down there?"

"The bull, he's trying to gore me."

"What should I do?"

"Get a pitchfork, jab the bull until he moves. Be careful. Stay outside the fence."

Everett retrieved a pitchfork, jabbed at the bull, which looked toward him but did not move. Moving closer, Everett jabbed and jabbed until he pierced the bull's nose. The bull bellowed, jumped back, then turned and moved away.

With Everett standing guard, Junior crawled to the gate, opened it, and climbed out, saying to his brother, "Thank you. Thank you."

Raking, shoveling, hauling the wheelbarrow, load after load, the brothers worked together to clean the barn.

*　*　*

Working together despite the increasing cold they harvested the year's final crops. The family gathered, carried, wheeled the potatoes, both Irish and sweet…. beans, to be shelled and boiled…pork meat to be cured. Anything green that was left over was dried, to be ground up as spice.

Lilly Ann grew cold, and she knew the children were cold; but they labored on, to the finish. Finally, it came, glistening, silvery, fluttering, and riding the wind: snow. A little at first, then a deep blanket that covered the earth. Hustling, urging the children on, she moved quickly to complete the morning chores and get the milk out for pickup. She returned to the house to ready the younger children for school, while Junior and Everett filled their wheelbarrows with manure-loaded straw. All about the house a snow-blizzard wind whipped their clothing, forcing them to lower their heads, their eyes nearly closed against the sting of snow and wind.

Reaching his dumping spot, Junior emptied the wheelbarrow, allowing the wind to do the spreading. Turning against the darkened sky he could only just make out the barn. Struggling, he pushed the wheelbarrow to the barn, grasped the rope, and struggled back to the house. Once there, he spread his arms to absorb the heat and saw the concern on his mother's face.

"Where's your brother, Everett?"

"He was ahead of me. Isn't he here?"

"No," his mother said, approaching him. "He must still be out there. You must find him, hurry. The clouds have made it almost dark. Take a lantern."

Junior bundled up, took the lantern. Fearful the wind would blow it out, he grasped the line and made it to the barn. Calling his brother's name, he heard—and saw—nothing. He turned on the electrical light in the barn and set the lantern down. Whipped by the wind, he stumbled and moved on, calling out his brother's name. Continuing to move down the hill, he almost tripped over it—the wheelbarrow. And there, unconscious, was his brother. With almost superhuman strength, he pushed his brother right up to the wheelbarrow. Then, grasping the wheelbarrow's downed edge, he lifted the wheelbarrow upright, Everett's body sliding into the wheelbarrow with the rolling, upward motion. The lantern he had set in the snow, he now slid down one of his arms, lifted the handles of the wheelbarrow, and turned toward the faint light.

Against the wind, barely moving, he struggled toward the barn; reaching it, he followed the line to the house, calling out, "Somebody help! Help me!"

From the house, they swarmed out. Then, half carrying, half dragging, they got Everett into the house. All helped to remove his coat, his shoes, his socks. All rubbed his hands, his feet while keeping him covered as warmly as possible. As she helped minister to him, Lilly Ann knew that he was warm enough, now; still, they needed a doctor. While she was not certain the school bus would come, it finally did, chains grinding through the snow. With no one to car for Everett at home, the family boarded the bus with Everett in tow.

The four-door Model A sedan sat high and dry in the doctor's garage. And it was to the garage that the doctor took her after she had struggled to reach him, fighting her way through the blinding snowstorm, starting from where the school bus had dropped her off. Now they were on their way back home. Riding in the doctor's automobile, in which he now told her he had put alcohol to prevent freezing, she thought of the Ford and the Fordson parked in the shed, drained of water, and twenty-weight instead of forty-weight oil. They were protected, but she knew she had nothing, nothing to protect the engine of the Ford and Fordson from freezing. Looking at him, she said a small prayer for the doctor.

They arrived safely at her home and fought the storm to finally enter the house. The doctor immediately tended to Everett. "He is going to be all right," he said after long, anxious moments. "You did a fine job of saving his hands and feet. Feed him soup and then more solid food, when he will eat it. I'll be back when this blizzard is over. Take care of yourself. Good-bye."

She heard the Ford start. He was gone.

CHAPTER 26

"Entomophagous," she pronounced.

The English teacher, who sat in the chair, looked up at the two remaining students, who stood at her side. Previously, there had been twelve. Now there were just the two—Junior and Mary Sue Collins, both eleventh-grade students.

Gathered before them, on each side of Principal Scott, were the teachers of the various classes. They were sitting in the front row. Behind the teachers were the students, who were permitted to attend this once-a-winter activity designed to encourage learning and as a way to break the monotony of the fenced-in feeling of winter...

"Would you pronounce the word again?" Junior asked, half smiling and preening in his letterman's sweater.

The English teacher complied with his request. "Entomophagous, feeding on insects."

Junior swaggered a little.

"Entomophagous. E-N-T-O-M-O-F-A-G-O-U-S. Entomophagous."

"Junior," the teacher said, "that is incorrect. Now, Mary Sue, I will pronounce the word for you." And she did.

"Entomophagous." Mary Sue spelled, and then waited.

"Correct," the English teacher said. "You are the winner of this year's spelling bee."

Almost simultaneously, Principal Scott, bearing a small, gold-colored trophy, appeared onstage. "Mary Sue Collins," he said, "may I congratulate you. Students—our champion."

He proffered the trophy and raised her hand in his.

Mary Sue took the trophy and smiled. "Thank you."

For days Junior did not see her, but he saw them pointing and whispering ever since the contest had passed. Others had stopped saying "it could have happened to anyone. "Then, whether by purpose or by accident, he entered the library. There, among rows of other students seated at the tables, sitting quietly and studying, was Mary Sue.

Approaching her, Junior saw a copy of Herman Melville's *Moby Dick* open on the table. She, jotting notes and face turned downward toward the table, did not see him. From his vantage point, he had the opportunity to look—truly *look*—at her. He could see her shoulder-length hair, spilling over her shoulders, richly auburn. His downturned eyes glistened with intent. Looking farther down her body, he could see her breasts, which flowed outwardly, her wool sweater seeming to suspend them gently over the table. At about five-feet-six, her arms, though covered, conveyed the strength gained from helping on the farm. She was concentrating intently on her writing. When he moved, his rustling attracted her attention. She looked up into his intense, focused eyes.

Seeing her view him, he half smiled through his muttered, "Hello."

For a moment, she suspended her writing and, facing him, said, "Aren't you afraid?"

"Afraid? I don't understand?"

"In case you missed it, I am sitting alone."

He frowned and sat down in a chair across from her. "I'm afraid I still don't understand," he said.

"You, in your letterman's sweater—or without the sweater…they all recognize you. They point at you, they speak to you…. You get your name and your picture in the *Dispatch*. Me, I'm ignored, even resented. I defeated their hero, their big man."

He sat back as realization struck him. "Would you prefer I move?" he asked.

"Only if you want to."

"Want to what?"

"Want to leave."

Slowly it came through to him…. As someone had once said to him, women are for cooking, cleaning, washing, ironing, poking, and making babies. Women with brains, those who did well in men's work—obviously, farming included; but also, women who were doctors, lawyers, businessmen practicing in the big cities—were to be avoided like the plague. And she was watching, awaiting his answer.

Almost unconsciously, he reached across the table and grasped her hand.

"Of course not; if I wanted to leave, I would have left. I'm here because I want to be with you."

She pulled her fingers away.

"Thank you."

She returned to her *Moby Dick*.

"I'm writing a book report."

"On *Moby Dick*?"

"Yes."

"You do pick them, don't you?"

"I picked Herman Melville's *Moby Dick* because I'm interested in it; and if I submit a good paper, I'll get an 'A.' My father will be proud."

Glancing at the wall clock, he rose. "I have a class."

"You mean a big football hero still has class?"

Immediately seeing that her tasteless remark had wounded him, she said, "I'm sorry. That was tasteless."

He smiled. "Shall we walk to class together?"

They rose and walked together. As they walked, those seeing them together gave more than a curious glance. Later, Tom Hale, his blocking back, accosted him in the hall.

"Tell me you're not close with *that*, not after what she did to you?"

"What did she do to me?"

"Showed you up at the spelling bee."

"You mean she won the bee by spelling a word I missed."

"Exactly. Everybody's talking."

For a long moment Junior remained silent, remembering that Tom opened those holes for him to run through. He meant no harm…was only repeating the gossip that was going around. He said, "A good person did what we do when we play. Try hard to win. Sometimes you lose. Still going to open those holes for me next season?"

That broke whatever tension had arisen.

"Of course," he smiled.

Her school bus had just departed when the Ford truck pulled up. The driver waved for Junior to come on over. As he approached, the man called, "Hi, Junior. I'm J. T. Collins, Mary Sue's Father. Get in. I'll take you home."

Junior hesitated. While doing so, his school bus departed. He had no choice, now.

With both hands on the steering wheel, J. T. said, "I hope you don't mind if I buy you a pop before we leave. I want to talk to you a minute."

He drove straight to the restaurant. Parked. Inside, J. T. told Junior to order whatever he wanted. Junior ordered a root beer.

J. T. said, "That sounds good." He nodded to the waitress. "Bring me one, too."

Junior, trying to be polite, said, "I noticed the double-barrel hung overhead in your truck. Fine-looking gun."

"Remington, double twelve-gauge. I'm glad you noticed."

The waitress brought their drinks.

After they both had a few sips, J. T. said, "I know you don't know, but Mary Sue is my only child. Her mother died when Mary Sue was seven. She and I have been alone together ever since. I've been father, mother, and friend ever since, too. I've seen her through croup and measles—and all the rest. We've studied together, and we found help when I couldn't help her." He added, "I know you have chores to do. So do I."

They finished their drinks. Back at the truck, J. T. reached inside, removed the double-barrel, exhibited it to Junior, broke it open, and, from his pocket, removed two twelve-gauge shells then inserted them into the breech but did not close it.

"I know you're a country boy used to shooting rabbits, squirrels, maybe a groundhog or two. So, you know what a twelve-gauge can do to a man. That's what I would do to the man who got my Mary Sue pregnant before marriage. As you know, a pregnancy, a child, takes a woman in an entirely different direction—nursing, diapering, cleaning behinds. Mary Sue is very bright. You found that out. She has a chance to be a doctor, a lawyer, a congresswoman. Who knows, maybe even president. I don't have much, but what I have will go toward seeing she has every opportunity. I promised her mother."

He took the shells from the Remington, put them in his pocket, put the gun back in the rack, smiled and said, "Hey, get in. We both got chores to do."

At home, Lilly Ann greeted him when he arrived.

"Son, hurry with the chores. Supper will be ready soon. I heard you missed your bus. It was nice of J. T. to bring you home.

Junior nodded as he rushed off to change and do his chores. As he milked the cows he thought. So much had been pushed toward him. He hardly knew Mary Sue. As any young man would do, he had examined as best he could her sexuality, noting her full breasts, slim waist, protruding butt, good legs—much of what had been pointed out to him by his buddies, once they had accepted his interest in her. Who knew what fate held? Perhaps Mary Sue knew. Women had a knack for such things, but he certainly didn't.

A swift movement snapped him from his reverie. The cow he was milking attempted to kick the pail over. Half rising, half stumbling with the pail, he slapped the cow sharply on the rear.

Just as he arrived back inside the house, his mother began bringing food to the table.

As the meal progressed, he said to his mother, "In about two months there will be an alumni dance in the school gym. I have been almost ordered to attend by some of the former players. They want to meet the young man the *Dispatch* has proclaimed a hero. With your permission, I'd like to attend." He paused, watching his mother's reaction. "And I would like to take Mary Sue, if her father permits. I'm asking you first. Then, I'll ask him."

Lilly Ann smiled. "Son, of course. Go, but remember, I would like to meet her before the night of the dance."

The next school day Junior asked Mary Sue if she would go with him. Mary Sue smiled joyously, and then sobered. "You must ask my father and then introduce him to your mother."

Trembling inside, Junior rode the school bus with Mary Sue to her house, to again meet with J. T. He arrived just in time to catch him preparing to go outside to do the evening chores. Seeing Junior, J. T. paused, listened to him, and nodded.

"I would be pleased to see Mary Sue being accepted at school and mingling with her schoolmates. Now, if your mother will accept me in working clothes, I will drive you home, and Mary Sue and I will meet your mother."

Arriving home, Junior opened the front door, calling out, "Mother!"

In the kitchen, Lilly Ann, her hands white with the flour of the biscuit dough she was working, looked up to see Junior leading two strangers: a man with hat in hand and his pretty daughter, Mary Sue.

"Mother, this is J. T. Collins and his daughter, Mary Sue."

Lilly Ann nodded in acknowledgment.

J. T. started, "Oh, ma'am."

Lilly Ann interrupted.

"Please call me Lilly Ann. I have heard much about the both of you. Please, come in. I will be out of this dough in a minute. Please, sit down wherever you'd be most comfortable."

Junior led them into the middle room, where the stove radiated heat, warming them from the cold they had just left.

Shortly, Lilly Ann returned with her hands cleaned, her apron removed, and her hair pinned back in place. Proper introductions were made; small talk ensued. Finally, J. T. said, "We must be going soon, but Junior told us we must meet you and secure your permission for him to take Mary Sue to the school dance. Do we have your permission?"

Lilly Ann smiled. "Someone once told me a branch of our military service would meet a request with 'permission granted' or 'permission denied.' So, permission granted."

The two youths smiled warmly at each other.

"Now, honey, we must go," J. T. said to his daughter—and then they were gone.

As time passed, Junior and Mary Sue studied together in the library, lunched together, walked to class together. Until one day, J. T. took them home early then left them alone.

Knowing she had time, she advanced her curiosity, and her bravery. "Let me see your thing," she said without preliminaries.

"What thing?"

"You know, that thing between your legs. Your penis, your what-do-you-call-it?"

"Peter."

"Your Peter."

He hesitated.

"Please."

By now, he was aroused. He unbuttoned his pants and lowered his drawers until his Peter stood straight out.

"Can I touch it?"

He nodded. She touched it.

"Let me show you mine."

She pulled up her dress and lowered her panties, exhibiting the auburn-haired triangle. Then, lounging back on the couch, she lifted her waist and spread her legs.

"Put your Peter in here, between mine."

He moved to insert his erection, got the head in, but her hymen blocked further entry.

"Push," she said. "Push."

Her speaking reminded him of J.T.... the Remington... the admonition.

He withdrew.

"No," he explained. "Your father would kill me."

The thought made his Peter go soft. He stood up, replaced his clothes. Without a word, she did likewise.

When J. T. arrived, they were standing at opposite ends of the couch.

J. T. looked at Junior.

Mary Sue took a step forward. "He didn't do anything, Daddy."

J. T. glanced at his daughter, then turned to Junior again. He considered for a moment. "I know," he said, responding to Mary Sue but still staring at Junior. "A father can tell these things." Then, he nodded to Junior and said, "Thanks, young man, for making me not have to kill you."

CHAPTER 27

Trousers, spats, the full-length cashmere coat, the collar turned up, the fedora held tightly against the swirling wind: stoutly he approached the Maramor. Greeted warmly by the waitstaff, he was escorted to his table. He nodded gratefully to the maître d', settled in his chair, sipped the cocktail he was graciously served. Shortly, red-faced, blowing on their hands, his three agents presented themselves.

"Gentlemen," Rhodes said, "sit, have a drink, report."

As instructed, they did; but, as they reported their information, Rhodes raised his gold-crested walking stick, signaling the waitstaff once more. Two men, each dressed in a white uniform and a *toque blanche*, rolled a cart with a huge loin of beef to the table. Silently, they carved the beef, placed the slices on large plates, served the au jus, the roasted asparagus topped with cheese, and the Caesar salad they prepared on a small stand they rolled alongside the cart with the beef. Finally, they filled the diners' wine glasses with generous portions of the restaurant's finest cabernet sauvignon.

As the waitstaff retreated, the head chef appeared, dressed in his white uniform and his *toque blanche*, and pushing a cart on which rested a fragrant loaf of freshly baked, hard-crusted bread.

"May I serve you?" the chef requested.

Indicating "yes" and requesting the heel for himself, Rhodes settled in to eat.

Bread served, the chef now returned to his kitchen; the men settled in to eat. Again, Rhodes directed.

As the men ate, the murmurings of the other diners in the restaurant could be heard; otherwise, all was silent. Then, shattering the lull, a man burst in from the outside; he was immediately stopped by the maître d'. A whispered conversation ensued, then the strange man was directed to

Rhodes. There, a second whispered conversation, heard only by Rhodes and the intruder, elicited a muttered, "Damn."

Raising his walking stick as if to strike the man, Rhodes, half out of his chair, paused a moment, then settled back down and signaled the maître d'. While Rhodes' companions looked on in stunned amazement, the maître d' escorted the intruder away...

"Gentlemen," Rhodes said, addressing his agents, "a most intriguing event has occurred. When we have finished our meal, if you will, please join me for cigars. I will discuss it with you."

With a wry smile, he returned to his meal.

*   *   *

When Mary Sue's front door opened, Junior could only stare. Hourglass figure, full breasted, slim waist, full hips, raised heels, a touch of rouge, makeup around the eyes, a little face powder, and her hair pinned up...Mary Sue Collins was a sight to behold. J. T. had taken his daughter to the town's beauty shop, knowing that, in the right hands, a farm girl could be transformed into a thing of beauty.

Inside the gym, as Junior passed through the crowd with Mary Sue on his arm, one admirer questioned his friend: "Is that who I think it is?"

"Yes, it is," the friend replied.

At the front of the gym Principal Scott stood before the orchestra. He raised his hands, saying, "If I could have your attention, I'll say just a few words and make a few introductions. Then, we can all dance."

As he made the introductions, Junior danced with Mary Sue. He had practiced with his mother and his little sister enough that he didn't stumble over Mary Sue's feet.

"Hey," one of his teammates said, abruptly intruding, "can I cut in?"

After that, they came one after another, until Mary Sue finally said, "Keep me, Junior. I'm tired."

Moving her to a table with one of several punch bowls, they got two glasses of punch and sat down on chairs lining the gymnasium walls, Junior fending off two or three other classmates who tried to take Mary Sue away.

"Thank you," Mary Sue said.

"I thought you wanted to dance so you could be popular."

"I enjoy not being a toadstool, but there's a limit. Anyway, I came to be with you."

As she said this she leaned toward him, held his face, kissed him. Then, knowing the end of the dance was nearing, they danced again.

Riding home, Junior held her, his arm around her shoulders. Stopped at his house, he thanked J. T., squeezed Mary Sue's hand, and entered his house. To his surprise, he found Lilly Ann wrapped in a blanket, sitting in the rocking chair near the stove.

"Son," she said, "did you have a good time?"

He smiled. "Yes, and Mary Sue was the prettiest girl there. All the guys tried to dance with her. I had to claim her as my date."

"I'm proud of you. Her life was miserable before you. I've known about her before you started dating her. Now go to bed. Tomorrow will be another busy day."

The next morning, noise aroused Lilly Ann. She went to her window to see what it was.

Backed up to the hill of her yard stood a truck. The back lid of the truck was lowered, with J. T. leading a cow down from the truck. Standing in the bed of the truck, a second cow waited.

J. T. tied the first cow to the truck and went back up the ramp for the other. Then, both cows secured, he approached the house. At his knock, Lilly Ann opened the door.

"Ma'am," J. T. said, "I was told to deliver these cows to you. Where shall I put them?"

Seizing a shawl, Lilly Ann stepped outside and pointed to the barn. She walked over to it and opened the door, and J. T. quietly lead the cows in.

Inside, J. T. said, "Ma'am, a Mr. Mellman instructed me to deliver these cows to you. He paid me well, so, if you would, I would like to invite you and your son to have dinner with me and my daughter. We enjoyed being at the high school dance with him so much. If you would, I'll pick you and your son up in my truck. We'll be a little crowded, but we can make it."

Taken a little aback, Lilly Ann hesitated.

"Please, Mrs. Coleburn, my daughter wants it so much."

J. T., his truck shining, arrived a little before five. Lilly Ann sat in the middle; Junior, a heavy pad on his lap, sat outside, with Mary Sue on his lap.

At the restaurant, the owner recognized Lilly Ann but was busy at the cash register and sent a waitress to the table. Lilly Ann turned to J. T.

"Everything here is really good. I can vouch for that."

They ordered. And as they ate, J. T. said to Lilly Ann, "On next Saturday, there is a dance in the gym. If you would, I would like to take you."

Again shocked, Lilly Ann said, "I thank you for asking, but I'm afraid I couldn't."

"Please. I will arrange for Mary Sue and Junior to stay with the children. "Then smiling, he said, "I'll even wear a tie."

"I don't have anything to wear."

"It's not formal. What you have on is fine. Please."

Junior, hearing this conversation, said, "Please, Mother. Mary Sue and I will watch the children."

Lilly and smiled. "With so much persuasion, I guess I must."

And on Saturday, she and J. T. did. She hadn't danced in a long time; but, hearing the music, she—*they*—did.

Several times after that, they repeated the experience, and enjoyed it.

*   *   *

Lilly Ann, feeling almost youthful, almost happy, didn't know when or how it happened. She had heard it; it had been spoken like a ghost in the night. She knew what it meant—it was like what the jackass said, looking in the mirror: "I'm all ears. "Yes, from all around her, she heard they were in a recession without a depression. First Roosevelt's fireside chats had tried to lift the country's spirits—but her delivering more milk produced only smaller and smaller checks. And now, on the radio, she heard of farmers dumping milk, instead of selling it.

Yes, she heard of it! Whether it was the man who picked up her milk, saying "I'll pick it up, but Nestlé won't pay more "or more people being thrown out onto the streets, cold and starving: she heard it. As money lessened, she had the boys grind more corn for meal. For now, the root cellar provided food goods…but what would the new year bring? Junior had learned to half-sole shoes…but where would the leather come from? The smaller children were growing fast…. Where would the cloth come from to make new clothes?

* * *

The tree fell as the crosscut sawed through the final edge. At home, having been inched laboriously across the nearby frozen field, it yielded stove-sized pieces, which the boys carefully stacked. Only the truck backing into the drive to the barn stopped them.

Staring, they watched the ramp being lowered and two Guernsey cows being driven down it. Everett ran to tell his mother. Lilly Ann came out, saw what was happening, and approached the truck driver, who was in the bed of the truck.

"J. T.," she said, recognizing him. "What are you doing?"

"I was told to give these cows to you."

"I don't understand."

"We're leaving, my daughter and I, back to where we came from."

"But I can't use more cows."

He shrugged. "I'm only doing what I was told. When we leave here, we'll load up and be gone."

Saying nothing more, he drove the cows into the barn. Returning, he approached the truck again.

"Lilly Ann, it's been a pleasure to know you."

And he drove off.

Lilly Ann could only stand and stare, bewildered.

CHAPTER 28

Greeted by the Maramor's doorman, his near ankle-length cashmere overcoat and silk-lined Fedora were quickly removed and whisked away. Rhodes extended his leather gloves and gold-headed nightstick to a waiter, who bowed and backed away after securing them. Another waiter approached, bringing an olive-dunked martini in a stemmed glass on a silver tray.

Rhodes smiled. He took a swallow from the extended glass and asked, "Have my men arrived?"

"Not yet, sir. Perhaps delayed by traffic or weather."

"When they arrive, show them directly to me. Meanwhile, what has been prepared?"

"Lobster, clams, Lyonnaise potatoes, mixed vegetables, and, perhaps, a wine."

"I think I will stick with martinis. I'll have another."

"Very well, sir."

A short while later, the two expected men arrived.

"Sorry, sir. An accident delayed us."

"Very well."

"As you directed, we did the research. We discovered the man moved here from Oklahoma, where he shot a man over an incident with his wife. He claimed self-defense, because the man drew a knife when he approached with a double-barreled shotgun. The law being what it is down there, he got away with it. Took his daughter and moved here. Since no trial was held, nor court case opened, when threatened with a lawsuit, he fled. I don't know where to, Nevada or New Mexico."

"Yes, good work." Rhodes thought for a moment. "That Lilly Ann woman now finds herself with twelve cows not only to milk but to feed and clean the shit they leave behind. Gentlemen, it's only a matter of time. Now, shall we eat?"

At a signal from the maître d', a cart holding an oval tub, some three-feet high and perhaps four feet wide was rolled to the table. The tub was filled with lobster and clams. It was followed by a second cart, laden with utensils and tools for opening and cracking the shells. The second cart was followed by a third cart, filled with vegetables cooked to perfection. Moving swiftly, the three waiters tied lobster-printed bibs about each man's neck. Then, lobsters cracked, shells opened, vegetables and fresh bread served, the lunch was underway.

*   *   *

At his mahogany desk adorned with silver writing instruments and small photos, Aaron Mellman had been receiving reports from various young attorneys and legal aides on Lilly Ann since that day when he had learned that Rhodes was somehow involved in her property. At the home, inherited from his father, a sprawling three-story, ten-room affair with a barn behind it that had been converted to a four-automobile garage. He had discussed the matter with his wife. Learning of Lilly Ann's loss of her husband, her five children, her working as a man to pay for and maintain the small farm, his wife had said *pro bono* and every other way to save them. She, too, read and heard daily of the disasters that were overwhelming so many farmers.

As various staff members reported their findings, he learned about the cows—the cows that had succumbed to the spoiled ensilage, and the cows that J. T. had delivered. Staff reports triggered the delivery of hay, coal, and refuse from restaurants for the family to use as scraps for the hogs. Remembering a classmate from Yale, when he was as undergraduate or in law school, he couldn't remember which, he recalled the young man once said, 'No good deed goes unpunished.' He did not visit the Coleburn property often; but today his real purpose was to see how Lilly Ann and the children were faring. He also wanted to know if Rhodes had brought additional pressure to bear. Knocking, he was warmly received.

"Mr. Mellman, I'm pleased to see you." Lilly Ann gestured for him to enter. "Please, pardon my floury hands. I'm baking biscuits for dinner. Please come in. The children are not home from school."

He nodded. He knew. He had planned it this way.

Together, they sat on a couch.

"And how are things?"

"I have been well. The children are well, too. With a few odds and ends, we would be fine."

"Odds and ends?"

"Oh, you know, they're growing so fast. I have trouble keeping them in clothes. If I had material I could make clothes, and Junior could help sole shoes, if he had the leather."

It was the opening he had hoped for. Reaching into his pocket, he extracted a clip of bills.

"Oh," Lilly Ann protested, "I couldn't accept money from any man."

"I came prepared for that. It's not a gift but a loan. I will give you the bills. You will sign a note"—which he immediately produced. "You will repay a little at a time."

She looked at him skeptically. He took the bills from the clip and handed them to her, along with a pen.

"Just sign."

She complied, and he handed her the money.

"Now, about Rhodes…."

She nodded, wondering.

"Over a period of time, I have had staff members assemble information on him. "Reaching inside his coat, he withdrew several folded sheets of paper and unfolded them. "Please, may I share this information with you?"

She nodded.

"His name is Woodrow Floyd William Rhodes. He is forty-two. He has two grown children away at school. His wife, ever intimidated, maintains the household in a lovely Victorian among a neighborhood of classic old—but properly maintained—residences near Bexley. Ever since he was young, he was determined not to grow old and broken like his biological father working coal mines and steel mills that surrounded Pittsburg. A good student, he graduated high school, moved in with an uncle in Columbus; and, having a gift for salesmanship, he sold property for Rostoive and Franklin. Now in the vestiges of a midlife crisis, ever fearful of his own mortality because he has watched many others contemplate a plunge to their death rather than face the horrors of bankruptcy, he is currently living his life just as he wants, sitting in an ornate office, directing others to relentlessly seize property for the firm—and for himself."

Mr. Mellman continued: "Lately, seeing that he is now a stone's throw from the executive office of the Ohio branch of Nestlé, his interior avarice has become overwhelming. Knowing he holds vast—albeit seized—wealth, real estate, and impressive offices, he also now supposes himself to be within striking distance of a position according him international power; being appointed a board member of an international corporation would be proper and fitting, in his mind's eye—or at least in the minds of anyone who has read my staff's report." He paused briefly and looked at Lilly Ann deliberately. "This is a very dangerous and relentless man."

Lilly Ann was speechless but nodded. What Mr. Mellman had told her about Mr. Rhodes reinforced what the old Irishman, Mr. McGuire, had reported, too.

"What we have said to you is from actual words and inferences that various members of my staff have reported. Unfortunately, we do not know what his next step will be. Being aware of what he is up to will force us to pay strict attention—and, trust us, we will." He stood from the sofa. "Now I must go, but I will return."

"But how can I…?"

"Laissez faire."

"More Latin?"

"It's French, for 'free action.'

He smiled, retrieved his hat, and was gone.

*   *   *

On his way out of town, Mellman drove to the Nestlé factory. Inside, he asked for the manager. Informed the manager was not in, he spoke to the assistant. Handing him a check for one thousand dollars, Mellman instructed the assistant to provide a portion of it to Lilly Ann Coleburn, and not to tell her of it. Shocked, the assistant nodded; later, he complied. Lilly Ann, for her part, received increased payments from Nestle, knowing more milk earned more pay. No matter, she was grateful, as her food and clothing needs were now met and the mortgage payments were made on time.

CHAPTER 29

Along with other challenges, the family faced an early winter.

One morning, instead of slow, fluttering flakes, wind-blown snow piled high, making access to the barn and other outbuildings treacherous. To reach the barn, the family lined up, with Junior leading, Lilly Ann last, and the children in between. Inside it was cold, yet teats had to be pulled, bags emptied, milk gotten to the roadway, because all the while they knew the school bus, milk trucks, and any other vehicle with chains would make it through the snow. Inside, Lilly Ann moved efficiently, assuring milking and feeding were done properly, and that hay and straw were properly dealt with, too, then rushing everyone into the house to ensure they would be ready for school on time. Once the children were gone, Lilly Ann moved about, sweeping and dusting, and otherwise tidying the house and, of course, making it down to the root cellar to secure items with which to prepare supper.

The blizzard lasted three days. The wind-blown snow piled higher, to a height of maybe six feet or more. Lilly Ann wasn't certain. Nevertheless, early winter had turned into winter.

On the radio, Franklin D. was assuring the country that the nation was not in a depression, only a temporary recession, and that the price of milk—of everything, in fact—was temporary.

At one of the president's outdoor gatherings, someone had yelled, "Keep the faith."

He now repeated it: "Keep the faith."

The radio audience applauded. Lilly Ann could not understand why. Today, she had sewn the last of her last muslin; the children's soles, hers and Junior's, too, were not worn out but thin. Meanwhile, her rides into town provided her with occasional staples. They were surviving, but just barely.

Mail delivery was slow, foul weather making it slower yet; but, constantly Lilly Ann received letters from Maggie—three weeks late, but Lilly

Ann was always relieved when they finally arrived. The letters often said, in effect, "no news is good news." The news she received that day should have been no news. Jimmy had been—or was—in the hospital with pneumonia. She had to get there.

When she broached the subject with the children, Junior said, "It's your mother and father. You must go."

When she raised the subject of the farm and taking care of the animals, Junior said, "Mother, we'll manage. You taught us. Now, trust us."

She felt the pride rise up in her. He was right. She had taught them… now she must trust them.

A ride on the school bus took her to Sunbury…where a ride on the Greyhound took her to Columbus…where a ride on the streetcar took her to Maggie.

Maggie smiled, kissing her daughter briefly. "Honey, I'm so glad you're here. Your father is home, now, but he's still very sick. He was in University Hospital, near death. They saved him, but he is still not well."

Jimmy, sitting in a rocking chair, under blankets, smiled when he saw her. "I know your farm burdens, especially in this weather. But I have prayed to see you again."

"Oh, Pa, stop it."

Lilly Ann approached him, hugged him, and took a chair beside him. "I'm told you had pneumonia. Why? What happened?"

"Allowed myself to get soaked, delivering papers. I've been wet before, but with a result like this, maybe because I'm getting old. I don't feel old though."

"You know you're older," Maggie said. She turned to Lilly Ann. "Come on, help me to fix supper. He can tell you his tale as we eat."

Rising, she took her husband's face in her two hands, held it a minute, then made for the kitchen. Lilly Ann followed.

"I've started cooking applesauce, vegetable soup, biscuits…."

"Can he eat such?"

"As much as possible." She sighed loudly and nodded to Lilly Ann. "I'm so glad you're here. It's not been easy. I'll not bore you with it."

"Mother, you never bore me. Everything you do interests me. I'm listening."

"What you see here is only a small portion of what things are really like. I know you know this has several parts. The illness is one part; the living here is a part, the mail, of being improperly dressed, of getting soaked, of feeling pneumonia could not strike him. It did almost, like I told you; only the doctors at the hospital saved your father."

"Here I've been the man, the woman, cooking, cleaning, fetching on foot or streetcar all our necessities. Then serving as mailman."

"Mailman?"

"Oh, we did it together. When he went down, we walked, rode the streetcar, and put him in the hospital. They immediately put him in bed and started treatment. I heard someone say he's near pneumonia…and for three days, it was touch and go. Meanwhile the mail piled up in the pick-up box. An inspector contacted me, and when I told them of what had happened, they had the mail delivered. But after about a week, they contacted me again, saying, if Jimmy would not be able to deliver the mail himself, they would have to remove his route. Our source of income, his mail carrier job: if it was gone, we would lose the house, our belongings….

"I pleaded with them, I was almost on my knees, telling them of our circumstances, that Jimmy was better, that the mail would be delivered. They listened but were not persuaded; they granted us only one week. Jimmy, hearing it all, agreed to do it. I dressed up in long underwear, Jimmy's pants tightly belted to stay up, gumboots over heavy wool socks, his postal overcoat, sleeves rolled up. I braided my hair and folded it up under Jimmy's cap. Drop-off mailboxes were situated at corners for trucks to drop the mail for that section of town and for carriers to pick up mail for delivery. Jimmy, heavily dressed, drove to the boxes for me to pick up and deliver the mail: I walked up one side of the street and then back down the other side. Proceeding so, we delivered Jimmy's route. For five weeks we worked, keeping Jimmy's route until he fully recovered."

Lilly Ann listened intently and shook her head in wonder.

"How is he now?"

"Still weak but determined to work."

Feeling uneasy but knowing her mother needed consolation, as well as physical help, Lilly Ann stayed for three days.

When she returned home, she rushed to open the house door. Inside, the house smelled of fine, cooked food—but all that greeted her was silence. Assuming her children were doing chores, she carefully made her way to the barn. Silence greeted her there as well. More mystified than ever, she returned to the house.

Opening the door elicited a raucous loud "Ma!" and they swarmed around her. Behind her she again smelled the cooked food.

"Supper is ready."

Lilly Ann, having received a wash cloth from Phyllis and a towel from DeVerne, used them at the sink and then was seated at the table. At Junior's nod, Phyllis led the household in prayer.

Later, when all were eating, Junior said, "Ma, we're so glad to have you back. Tell us about Grandma and Grandpa."

"They are doing pretty well. Jimmy has been very sick. He's much better now. They have maintained his mail carrier job. In fact, they were determined to keep it. But how have things been here?"

The children looked at each other.

"Okay," one said.

Junior explained: "For a while now a man has snooped around. We don't know who he is, what he is doing, or why."

Lilly Ann stopped eating for a moment but then immediately resumed. "If anyone sees him again, tell me right away." She smiled confidently. "Now, tell me about school and other things."

Suddenly the atmosphere erupted, with everyone talking at once, through dishes, through homework, and then through bedtime.

CHAPTER 30

He arrived buried in a thick maroon wool headpiece, pulled down to meet the erect collar of a heavy cashmere coat; he wore thick overshoes as well. A servant quickly met him; helped remove the heavy garments then seated him in a round, leather chair located a proper distance from the glowing fire, and then served him hot chocolate laced with brandy.

"Anything else, sir?"

A head shake conveyed the answer. Shortly thereafter the servant reappeared. "Your guest has arrived, sir. Shall I show him in?"

"By all means."

As the man appeared, Rhodes rose, extended his hand, and said, "I'm having a hot chocolate." Then, a sly smile. "Laced with brandy. Would you like one?"

The nearly six-foot tall man, dressed in a pinstripe suit with a vest, smiled and extended his hand. John Guilligun. No, thank you. Diabetes won't permit...."

A servant brought a second leather chair and pushed it near where Rhodes was sitting.

"I hope, after our short meeting, you will join me for lunch."

"I would be delighted."

With that, Rhodes started right in. "First, I understand your firm is very expensive. I want you to know money is no object. Results are."

John nodded.

"Before we get to the crux of the matter, I would like to explain to you who I am and what this is all about. I hope you don't mind."

"No, of course not. The better informed I am the better I will know how to proceed."

What John Guilligun didn't say was that he had had staff members investigate the matter in some detail. He never took on a case without as much inside knowledge as possible. He had been told of Rhodes, an overly ambitious, middle-aged, white man. He had been told of his ruthlessness, of his ambition lacking all morality as he pursued wealth for his clients and himself. Still, Guilligun could not understand his being obsessed with one small plot of land, given that he had achieved all that the Depression had allowed him to achieve.

"I have at your disposal staff with various research and investigational skills, as requested."

On a silent signal recognizable only to Rhodes and his hired help, a servant approached, pushing a tray. "For an appetizer, beluga caviar and champagne. Please, enjoy."

After enjoying the appetizers, another silent signal produced a servant wheeling a roast of beef, followed by staff carrying silver trays of side dishes: salads, vegetables, bread fresh from the oven....

"Know I am engaging you. All that passes between us from now on will be confidential, between attorney and client. Now, shall we enjoy this repast?"

Jacob nodded, amused at the selection of words but sincere in his conveying of his services.

*　*　*

The radio conveyed the president's message: The Depression was over. Public service employment was being created, there were many jobs to be filled in many fields. Everyone in the country should feel that, like the song said, happy days are here again.

Perhaps they should feel that way...but that way was not the way for Lilly Ann. The family's needs were as great, the supplies were not. How could she know that the new economic downturn had caught Mellman's firm unprepared, that the seriousness of the matter had placed him in an equally serious condition at University Hospital?

Mellman's staff, while gravely concerned for him, worked nearly twenty-four hours a day to save the firm. Assistants who had been charged with working on Lilly Ann's case had no time for her, only for saving the firm. Some staff brought flowers and blankets and slept on the office floor to be available to execute any action whenever it was needed. Any questions that were raised concerning Mellman's condition were met with the same response—no comment. University officials answered inquiries from reporters and other members of the press with the same response. While Mellman's room at the hospital was not officially guarded, it was protected by a staff member, seated near the door. Slowly, meticulously, medical staff members nursed him back to health. First in the hospital and then at home, always with staff members reporting on the firm—its falling, and, with meticulous attention, its rising. Moving cautiously. with his staff hovering over him, he resumed his position in the office at the A.I.U. building. As reports were fed to him, he studied them then made notes relating to them, and placed them in the "out" box. Then, in a calm moment, he rearranged his desk, and in so doing, he found it—a slip on which he had jotted her name. *My God,* he thought, *what has happened to her?* Pressing a button on his desk, he summoned Anthony, his new driver.

"I want to go to our farm in Sunbury."

"Yes, sir."

Upon arrival, the driver inquired, "Shall I wait, sir?"

"It's much too cold," Mellman observed. "Besides, I may need the help coming or going."

The driver came around the car to his boss and helped him to the house.

At the knock, Lilly Ann opened the door. Half supported by his driver stood Mellman, gaunt, much thinner, hat in hand.

"Mr. Mellman, sir, please come in."

Moving slowly, allowing the driver to take his overcoat, Mellman made his way to the rocker near the stove. Seated, he raised his hands to absorb the heat while saying, "Lilly Ann, how are you?"

She gestured. "We are surviving, but it is tough."

He nodded.

"How are you, sir?"

"I have been in the hospital, but I won't bore you with details."

"Sir, it is the details I want to hear. Over the radio, I heard the president, who speaks encouragingly but *never* in detail."

"Then, perhaps you know the country is in another depression. While I have been hospitalized, my men have been developing strategies to resist the decline. Fortunately, I am blessed with brilliant associates who have skillfully managed the firm's assets, making proper moves as property is acquired or disposed of. No one expected to be mired in this type of action now. We were led to believe, as the song says, 'happy days are here again.' They seemed to be—the president had made all the right moves. Fireside chats were believed to be having the desired effect. For a long time, they did. Now, they don't. My own firm's experience can testify to that; and listening to WNBC or WLW, or reading the *Citizen* or the *Dispatch*, affirms it, as well."

"Sir," the driver said, "do not exhaust yourself."

Mellman stopped, put a hand to his mouth, and coughed.

Slumped back in his chair, he said, "I'm sorry. I didn't mean to run on."

"Oh no, sir. I understand, and you must save your firm."

He smiled. "Thank you. Now, food, clothing, wood, and coal…what do you need?"

"Sir, I can't…."

"*Pro bono,*" Mellman said.

"In that case, I need to get to the general store for food staples and to the bank to pay the loan and maybe some trifles for the children."

"And something for Momma!"

She smiled. "The work gloves have worn thin."

Mellman signaled for Lilly Ann to ready herself. The driver made the trip to town quickly and safely. Lilly Ann went to the bank first. "Milk money saved for the loan," she said, approaching the banker, her hand extending the payment.

The banker accepted the money with a friendly greeting: "Lilly Ann, it is so good to see you."

She had insisted on being called by her first name, "just like a man" …as a man had once said.,

"Thank you," Lilly Ann said to the banker. Looking about, she asked, "Where is Heidi?"

"I had to let her go. In these tough times, I couldn't keep her. It's a struggle to keep the bank. Too many people no longer bank, the little they make. But you seem to be making it okay."

"Yes, with the little milk money, I pay the loan; and we scrape by for the rest."

"Oh, yes, back during football season I read in the *Dispatch* of your boy. I kept the articles. If you have a minute, I'll show them to you."

He turned to find them, and she went out to the car.

"The banker wants to show me something," she informed Mellman. "Can you please wait?"

"Of course, we'll go to the restaurant and have a coffee. Will you please come there when you finish?"

"Yes, of course."

The driver and Mellman went off. Lilly Ann went back into the bank, where the banker met her again and guided her to his small office. Here, newspaper clippings were spread on a table. In striking football poses and postures was her son. Starting with his first season, Junior had excelled, one article describing outstanding examples of running and pass catching, another exhorting game-saving defensive moves.

"Ohio State is my school," the banker explained. "I graduated there in finance and banking. A brother and a sister graduated, too. In fact, the sister is a nurse at the hospital your doctor had Mellman in."

Again, she looked at the pictures, the articles of her son, the star. Slowly, she began to realize he was discussing Ohio State University, the university that required tuition, fees, and books, while she and her children barely had food and heat and clothing. She shook her head.

The banker read her thoughts.

"Room and board, clothing, meals, books, tuition, and a little expense money all come with a football scholarship. And he will grow an inch or two more, and build his muscles with training. With that, and his speed and quickness, he'll be perfect for the university. No—he'll be perfect for the Ohio State University!"

She sat down, overwhelmed. Her son...the Ohio State University...a lawyer, a doctor, risen to those heights on the virtues of football excellence.

She rose; so did he.

"Has anyone mentioned this to him?"

"I'm not certain. You're the only one I've discussed it with—but some reporter or a friend or a stranger, for that matter, has. I thank you," she said. "But I'm sure they are waiting. I must go."

The banker smiled again.

"Thank you for listening."

At the restaurant, she made a list of certain items, as fast as she could think of them. And after coffee and a small roll, the necessary items were gathered at the general store.

Then, Mr. Mellman had his driver return her to her home. .

* * *

"Depression," Phyllis recited. "A going down, a lowering compared to the surface around it. That's what the dictionary says; but in school, they call this—I mean what we're going through *today*— a depression. I don't understand it," she told her mother. "We're talking about it, but I don't understand."

Lilly Ann looked thoughtfully at her daughter.

"I'm not sure I understand it either, but it's on the radio every day; and if you listen carefully, stocks are...."

"Oh, I know. They're paper people buy, sell, or trade to get money. We discussed that in class, too."

Lilly Ann shrugged. "I guess that is all I know."

"Stocks are papers people receive for money," Phyllis explained, telling her mother what she had learned in school. "Money that people use to buy things to make their businesses better."

"But how can stocks be worthless?"

"I told you, stocks are only paper. More paper can be issued than the business is worth...or for many other reasons stocks may become worthless. Oh, and we discussed bankrupt businesses. A store sells dresses that suddenly no women will buy—customers, wholesalers...*no one*. And no matter how badly they feel about it, bankruptcy must be declared. Thursday, Black Thursday, bankers as a group tried to stop the crash; but in October, crash-selling occurred. The Hoover bubble, as he put it, was a temporary slowdown that would soon give way to twenty-five percent unemployment and breadlines, a collapsed stock market. Mother, did… *does*…the Depression hurt us?"

"Yes, but that is another story for another day. Today we must stick to what your teacher wants you to know and to discuss. The Depression forced the president to create organizations and take actions that were unheard of or never thought of before. Honey, I know this is your assignment, but you were not told to not seek help in finding out as much as you can about it. Your brother has been through this class and this same discussion; and I have asked him to help you. Please talk with him."

When Phyllis asked her brother, he smilingly said, "Of course I'll help you. I'll go to the library, research it, make a list of written facts for you from which you can discuss the Depression in class. Then you'll be able to write a paper. If your teacher requires it, I'll help you with that, too."

Phyllis smiled; and for two days in class she listened, then, having the facts on paper Junior had given her, she spoke up.

"I have some facts," she said, simply.

The teacher looked at her and smiled in approval. At eleven years old, Phyllis was a pretty girl, her hair in braided pigtails, her eyes bright and alert.

"Phyllis, I see you have some papers. Will you come up front and share them with the class?"

Almost timidly, Phyllis approached the front of the class.

"Stand anywhere near my desk," the teacher instructed kindly, "and rest your papers on it."

Phyllis did as she was told, then started:

"The economy was in freefall from nineteen twenty-nine to nineteen thirty-two. New capital was down ninety-five percent. Five thousand banks failed. U.S. Steel in nineteen twenty-nine had over two hundred and twenty thousand employees. Now, no full-time employees. Agricultural employees are down to half of what they were. Farm income was twelve billion dollars, now it's down to five. Many communities and states could not pay teachers. Forty-five percent of home mortgages were foreclosed.

Many banks limited withdrawals to five percent of deposits. April nineteen thirty-two ended Prohibition. In April nineteen thirty-three, Anheuser-Busch horse-drawn wagons appeared. The Agricultural Adjustment Act of 1933 limited acreage, restricted the number of hogs that could be raised, which resulted in offering other farm-raised products.

Phyllis continued: "Civilian Conservation Corps employed between two hundred and fifty thousand to three hundred thousand men and women in fifteen hundred camps. The National Industrial Recovery Act passed, the Tennessee Valley Authority was formed. Huey Long called socialism under AAA. One hundred and eight million acres produced corn, forty-four million acres produced wheat, thirty million acres produced hogs, eight million acres produced bales of cotton, the American Farmers Surplus Relief Corporation bought apples, butter, and wheat to raise prices. Franklin Delano Roosevelt said, 'Never let your right hand know what your left had is doing.' Roosevelt created the National Labor Relations Board, one hundred and ten thousand workers on strike. Men were killed. Five thousand national guardsmen with fixed bayonets were called to restore peace to the Teamsters' striking turmoil. The Grand Coulee Dam was constructed. The world's largest dam was constructed at Fort Peck, Montana. Flood Control and Reforestation, seventy-five thousand corpsmen were assigned to national parks."

Phyllis looked to the teacher.

"Shall I go on?"

The teacher replied, "Yes, but our time is limited, that will be all for now."

As she passed the teacher's desk, the teacher reached out, touched her, and said, "Fine job. Thank you," and smiled.

* * *

"Mrs. Coleburn, what a pleasure, and, I must say, what a surprise, to see you out in this…." the banker stopped midsentence, gesturing to the shimmering snowflakes as they joined those already on the ground.

Lilly Ann acknowledged the banker's greeting, shivering a little as the indoor heat struck her long, wool coat and wool-stocking cap.

"I needed a few things from the general store, so I rode the school bus with my children and stopped here to make my payment," she said. Then, she extracted an envelope from an inside pocket of her coat and thrust it toward the banker.

"Lilly Ann, please, come into my office. There is a matter I want to discuss with you."

With a concerned frown on her face, Lilly Ann followed the banker and took the seat he gestured toward. Then the banker moved to his desk and rummaged through a stack of papers. He selected one, seated himself, and laid it on his desk.

"Since you are one of my most faithful clients," the banker started, "I thought you might be interested. It's a law that was passed and finally implemented and disseminated to banks. It's called the Bankhead–Jones Farm Tenant Act. It allows banks to offer low interest loans to tenant farmers to permit them to buy their farms. I don't know, but you might be interested."

Lilly Ann relaxed as relief came over her.

"And your bank is prepared to offer such loans?"

"To carefully selected farm owners."

"I'm considered one of those?"

"Yes, that's why I'm bringing it to your attention."

Suddenly, Lilly Ann was nearly breathless; she could protect the children by owning their farm. She looked toward the banker, her mouth open, but no words coming out.

"Please, I did not mean to startle you. This is only for your consideration. If you were to decide in favor of pursuing this type of loan, members of my staff will prepare papers for your signature."

Soberly, Lilly Ann said, "And if I do it, I will own it? No loan where at the end of five years if I don't pay it in full my home will be repossessed?"

The banker smiled. "No bubble loan, or whatever you know it as. You will own your property free and simple, no caveats."

Later that night, at home, as was her custom more often, now, she discussed it with Junior, who inherited her excitement.

"You mean we would own it? No one could throw us off or buy us out? We could farm better when times get better.... The kids could finish school."

She nodded.

"Are you going to do it?"

"I'm leaning toward it."

"Lean all the way."

CHAPTER 31

The day lay bright around them, reflecting off the piled snow…lay bright, reflecting off highlights of buildings…lay bright on the wind that swirled about them. They were two little boys—Harold, the older by eighteen months, and DeVerne, seven years old. They lay on their backs, swinging their arms wildly, moving their legs from side to side, creating snow angels. Laughing, gurgling noisily. He appeared over them, looking down. When they looked up at him, he smiled, waved, and said, "Hi."

They stopped, sat up in the snow, and said a fearful, "Hi."

"Don't be afraid. I was just passing and saw you. Thought I would stop and say 'hi.' You live near here?"

They pointed toward their house.

"Live here long?"

"Always."

Then DeVerne blurted, "But we might live here forever. I heard my mother talking to my older brother. She said the banker told her how we could."

"Did she say you would?"

"She said we might."

The man smiled. "Thank you. I've got to move on"—and he was gone.

That same man, along with another man, appeared in the bank, where the banker, dressed in hat and coat, said to the cashier, "I will sign what you need on farms, you can fill them out afterward."

Then, seeing the men, he said, politely, "Gentlemen, welcome. I must rush to an important meeting. My clerk will serve you," and he moved toward the door.

The men, looming tall enough and wide enough in their black overcoats and hats, moved in front of him, saying, "Sir, this will only take a minute. Your office, please."

Once there, the man who had seen the two boys playing in the snow said, "Those children are sons of the lady we're interested in. We have learned you have discussed with her a way to own her own farm. We have also learned that you have two children. Any wrong decision would put them in danger…if you get my meaning."

Without another word, the men turned to leave, saying, "Enjoy your meeting."

* * *

Lilly Ann was at first baffled, then bewildered. No one at the bank would accept her payment. The banker himself hid out in the back and listened as a bank teller explained to Lilly Ann that instructions had been made to refuse her payment.

* * *

He sat in the Maramor knowing they had devised and schemed their way to success. Rhodes tasted the dry martini the waiter served him as he awaited his men. Upon their arrival, he signaled for the meal to be served.

"Well?" he questioned.

"Two down, only one to go," one of the arrivals said as he removed his hat and coat.

"Don't be flippant with me. I want details."

"Oh, sir, I'm sorry. I, *we*, in no way meant to be anything but respectful."

Then in detail he described their operation with the banker, how they had instilled such fear in him that he dared not disobey.

"Again, sir, if I may…two down, one to go."

For a long moment Rhodes only stared.

Then he said, "Very well. Let's eat."

* * *

About them the sky darkened; more storm clouds rolled in. Dry lightning pierced the sky, but Lilly Ann and another woman waited outside the phone booth, which finally emptied.

The man in front of her nodded. "Ma'am, if you are not too long, go ahead."

Lilly Ann, change in hand, entered the booth. She was cold, having walked from where the school bus had deposited her. Taking the paper from her pocket, she deposited a dime, rang the number, and waited. To the woman who answered, she asked to speak to Mr. Mellman, and gave her name when requested.

When Mr. Mellman came on the line, she said, "Thank God, it's you." And, half sobbing, she poured out her troubles. Then she said, "Remember, I must pay you later. I only have the mortgage payment."

"*Pro Bono*," Mr. Mellman, said, a smile in his voice. "*Pro bono*."

* * *

The Studebaker pulled into the lane and, a few moments later, a nattily dressed man came and knocked on the door. Lilly Ann opened it, finding a man with a firm chin, a wrinkled brow, and (as she learned the next moment) a firm voice. Introducing himself, he told her that Charles Davis, associate of Aaron Mellman, was there to help her. He must complete this matter today, he informed her, before the bank closed. He had papers for her to sign without her needing to read them. He produced the papers, a pen, and pointed to where she was to sign. Trusting the man without question, she signed. He thanked her, and was gone.

In Sunbury, Mr. Davis—or, rather, Charles—conspicuously drove around the town square three times, and then parked in the snow-shoveled space in front of the bank. Almost grandly he swept into the bank and introduced himself to the clerk, saying he was new in town and represented a named concern. The clerk was impressed, nearly bowing, and saying he was at his service. With a gesture that stopped just short of being overly grand, Mr. Davis swept open his overcoat, revealing a three-piece Hickey Freeman suit. From the vest pocket he extracted an 18-carat Patek Philippe hunting case watch attached to a gold chain threaded through the vest's buttonholes. Then he flipped the case open to check the time.

"Since time is limited, I have taken the liberty of obtaining five copies of the banker's signed forms, and filled them out. Before you, I will sign them, and, after you authorize them with your notary stamp, we will be finished. As you and I both know, time is of the essence."

From under his almost-closed eyes, he observed the clerk at this pivotal moment, when any hesitation would be fatal to his plans.

The clerk smiled, saying, as he rose and pivoted on his heels, "Let me get my equipment."

Charles, reaching the clerk's desk, produced the papers, then spread them out so that the clerk needed only to stamp and sign them. "I know you're a very busy man," Charles said, "thus, as I mentioned before, I have five copies, all that we need."

As the clerk proceeded, Charles used a favorite cliché, "You never miss your water 'til the well runs dry."

The clerk grinned broadly. "Ain't that so?"

As each copy of the document was presented, Charles signed, and the clerk notarized. The job was done as promised. Fees were paid, plus the promised bonus. Charles gathered the papers into his inside pocket, donned his hat and coat—and was gone, thinking, as he had discussed with Mellman, that what could not be accomplished through force could be accomplished through deception. And it had been. His final task was to ensure that each relevant agency or person, clerk of the court, the bank, the county sheriff's clerk, and Lilly Ann, had a copy. Finding the local boarding house, he had a meal, a night's sleep, then, the next morning, rose, bathed, had breakfast, then personally went to each relevant office, and each relevant party, to deliver the papers. His drive back to his office was a satisfactory one, if he did say so himself: a job well done.

* * *

"God damn, God damn, God damn."

The epithets streamed on endlessly, it seemed, until they finally stopped.

"How can it be?" Rhodes now screamed into the telephone.

"I don't know, sir. I only know that I went to the clerk's office and was shown a document that I was not permitted to copy. So, I can only paraphrase it to you. It said, 'I hereby authorize Charles Davis, acting in, for, and intentionally Lilly Ann Coleburn, shall pay and incur all mortgage payments, delinquent, current, and future, on the property she occupies henceforth and forever more.'

"Do you know who prepared this?"

"No, sir, I don't."

The line was disconnected, angrily, suddenly, and vindictively.

* * *

It was dark, or nearly so, on this mid-fall afternoon. The chores were done, supper eaten, dishes washed, and Lilly Ann sat in her rocker near the ornate cast iron stove. On the floor, lying on her stomach, her lower legs and feet raised, her head propped on her hands, which were raised to accept her small chin, Phyllis's eyes gazed at her mother. Both mother and daughter smelled of Ivory soap and cleanliness.

"The teacher asked the class about what we had heard on the radio. Recession. All of us, the whole country is in one—in a recession. What does that mean?"

Lilly Ann lay her hand on Phyllis's head.

"Honey, it's what's happening to us. Thankfully, we're still selling our milk, and with the money we pay our mortgage, buy the few essentials, like salt for both us and the cows. I bake cornbread from corn from our crib floor, which goes to biscuits you children take to school; your brother repairs your shoes when he gets the leather. In other words, we manage, just barely. We go to bed and close our eyes in our own house, just barely, honey. Thank God we, all of us, live—barely."

Phyllis rose, went to her mother, and flung herself into her mother's lap.

"Mother, we talk about so many things in history class that I don't understand. Why is Germany doing what it is doing in Europe now?"

Lilly Ann shifted her body to accommodate the load.

"Honey, you'll learn as you go forward in history, men have always fought each other. Someday you'll read the Bible, and you will find it to be so. What's going on now in what is now Germany, it was called the Austro-Hungarian Empire then. What Germany is doing now is an awful aftermath of World War One, when the rest of the organized world thought Germany should be punished for their actions. Hitler and the others didn't think so. The result is what is going on now in Poland."

She stopped, wondering if what little she shared was too much.

Almost miraculously, the child said, "Oh, thank you. Now, tomorrow I'll be able to talk in class. I won't feel so dumb."

Lilly Ann hugged her. She had so wanted a girl when she got only boys.

She hugged Phyllis again then slipped her off her lap, saying, "Now, to bed."

Normally, she herself would have been in bed. Now she sat in her rocker, covering herself with a multicolored quilt she had made, not rocking but merely tilting slightly back and forth, her mind unusually jumbled and cluttered. Yes, she had milk money to meet the mortgage and a few additional items...but so little else. The radio blared again and again. Recession, or call it whatever they may, she only knew she and the boys were once again crawling under the fence to drag as many tree limbs and trunks as possible to supplement what little wood and coal they had. Never had she been more grateful to Roy for erecting the hand-cranked grinder he had setup in the shop. With the cornbread and milk, they had some staples. She knew she had thought these thoughts before, but she could not remove them from her mind. Slowly, as her thoughts raced, her eyes grew heavy, slowly closing.

A rooster's crowing awakened her. Rising quickly, she groomed herself, packed lunches of biscuits, salt pork, and apples, made breakfast of rolled oats, milk, and cornbread.

Ready, Junior, when he saw her, questioned, "Mother, did you sleep?"

She nodded. He said no more.

Then, they were gone. She had hardly cleared the kitchen table when the knock came at the door. Opening it, Lilly Ann saw Melissa, a neighbor from two farms away.

Shivering, Melissa stepped in and moved toward the stove. There, she removed her ear covering, wool-stocking cap, and her long, heavy wool coat, revealing an ankle-length, long-sleeved wool dress.

Hands spread toward the heat, she said, "I saw your light on all night. I thought maybe someone was sick and maybe you needed some help."

"Oh, thank you. I'm fine. I admit I went to sleep in my chair and spent the night there. Would you like some coffee?"

"Yes, if you have some made."

"I don't, but it will take only a minute to make some."

She moved to the kitchen stove and returned shortly with a mug of coffee made sweet with a spoonful of sugar and colored by milk freshly milked.

"Please," she said, "sit in the rocker. I'll pull up a chair."

For a while they sat, Lilly Ann drinking the coffee she had prepared, exchanging tidbits of news. Then Melissa abruptly said, "Did you hear? Once again, we have strange men searching at the hall of records about the neighborhoods in town, asking questions."

Lilly Ann said, "No."

"They asked at the barber's shop. The barber told Luke and Luke told me."

"What were they asking about?"

"Seems they were asking about you or someone they described that looks like you."

"But why?"

"They didn't say. Oh, look. It's getting dark. I must go home to help Luke with the milking and the chores. Oh, yes, one other thing. We're milking, but for somebody else. They bought our cows, and Luke keeps the animals for them."

She rose, clad herself, and was gone.

Lilly Ann rearranged the furniture and started to prepare herself for evening chores while thinking about what had been said but not lingering on it.

CHAPTER 32

At intervals, the rain turned to snow. Constantly, the cold high wind blew, yet they were there. Their Ford van swayed in the gusts of wind. A crew of three were there, with the tape recorder that was being tested. Its inventor had said—and had hoped—that it would revolutionize the news business.

The inventor was a friend and former roommate of the son of the *Dispatch* editor; they had known each other at the Ivy League university they attended. Having persuaded him to accept and experiment with one of the recorders, hoping for a favorable report but willing to accept any feedback from a close friend. The friend, having assembled a crew of three —a cameraman, a spokesman, and a person to help drive them to their destination —instructed them to go to Sunbury to test the camera on the twenty-fifth anniversary of a small firm that printed and distributed sales books.

Having completed their assignment, while making their way back to the van, they saw the black smoke rising nearby. In the van, they drove toward it. Some four miles later, they saw it rising from behind a farm building.

Fearing another building might be on fire, they drove behind the first building and found a place to park. Removing their equipment, they approached the smoke. The high wind silenced any sounds they made. As they drew nearer they readied their equipment, plugging the microphone into the recorder in order to roll tape, and to listen, and to record.

Almost at the smoldering plumes of black smoke, the crew came upon a strange man cursing, pouring kerosene on straw, and trying to start a blaze. Glancing up, the man spotted them, hesitated, then decided to brave it out.

When asked what he was doing, he said, "Trying to burn this straw."

When asked why, the man said, "To clear the path to the barn."

All went well until he was asked, "Do you live here?"

With that, the man fled toward his automobile. Almost instinctively, the driver followed him, took note of the man's license number. Back at the equipment, he reported to the man, who was still talking into a microphone.

Back at the editorial room, he produced his recording. Tomorrow being Saturday—a slow day for news—they ran an article with a picture and the caption, "Know this man?" Calls came into the public relations phone, identifying the arsonist as Rollo Noonan, an associate of Bill Rhodes. Before leaving the firm, all three men had talked with Lilly Ann, informing her of what had happened and warning her to be on the alert for suspicious activities. She thanked them while privately wondering what was going on. Were these men, and the others her neighbors had made her aware of, attempting to harm her and the children? What could she—what *should* she—do?

*   *   *

"It was all I could do to keep him from being arrested," Rhodes said to the man facing him.

The man had walked in, tall and immaculately dressed in an ankle-length cashmere overcoat, a black Hickey Freeman suit with pin stripes, and a silk tie tastefully clipped to a gleaming white shirt. Opening his coat, he revealed a vest crisscrossed by a gold watch chain attached to a gold Rolex watch, which he consulted as he sat. Crossing one leg over the other, he revealed Cole Haan shoes under spats.

He had walked from his office on High Street to the A.I.U. building. Riding the elevator up to the thirteenth floor, he stepped off of the Otis car and was immediately escorted to Rhodes' office, at the window of which sat Rhodes behind an immaculate mahogany desk.

Seeing the man, Rhodes rose, extended his hand, and said, "You are timely."

"Always and precisely," the man said. "Before we start, *if* we start, let's lay down some ground rules. That way we'll both be happy. First, I am very expensive and immediately require a retainer of two thousand dollars, which, provided I take your case, I shall receive as I leave. Second, I require complete honesty. If you lie to me, you're finished. I'll drop you faster than a hot potato."

Then, from an inner coat pocket, the man withdrew a small notebook, saying, as he flipped it open, "I have had paralegals on my staff collecting information on you. What I am interested in is some of the tactics you have used to acquire your holdings, your positions."

Rhodes, who had sat relaxed in his desk chair, now leaned forward, over his desk, his arms out in front of him, his jaw muscles flexing but saying nothing.

"A matter I'm curious about. I'm told two strongmen approached the banker; and after they left, he refused to accept payments on her loan. Are you aware this occurred?"

Rhodes hesitated, and then the next question came.

"Just recently, a man using kerosene attempted to set a fire that, with the right wind—and I'm told the wind was blowing furiously—could have burned the whole place down. Were you aware of any of these things?"

With that, Lee Brazelton, sat back in his chair, awaiting an answer.

Rhodes hesitated and said, "Sometimes you make mistakes. I made a bad one. The man who carried out these things worked for me, but no longer. That is the reason I sought you. I want to legally acquire a property. I need your help."

Brazelton rose, gathered his coat and hat, and started toward the door. "I'll let you know."

He opened the door and was gone.

*　*　*

The sound—low, ominous, threatening—came with a sudden blast that sat her up with a start, eyes wide open, with only one thought in her mind: all of her important papers, all of them, were locked in her safety deposit box in the vault in the bank. Rising, she washed and dressed, pacing all the while that she was preparing. Attempting as best she could to not indicate her anxiety, she led the children through the morning chores, saw the milkman load the cans, and then, with the children, she boarded the school bus. In town, she sought the first public telephone, got Mellman on the phone, and, almost crying, frantically related her dilemma. Once again, he calmed her by promising to immediately assign someone to the problem and for her to return home. As if by a miracle, she saw a neighbor who had come to town for supplies and who indicated he would take her home as he went back.

She had been home perhaps an hour when the knock came. Opening the door revealed Charles Davis standing outside. Urgently, Mr. Davis indicated his mission. With the same urgency, Lilly Ann produced the key—and Mr. Davis was gone in the Studebaker, sliding out its wheels as he sped away.

In town, parking just out of sight of the bank, looking at his watch, he knew he was too early. Not by much…but too early. Entering the barbershop just up the street from the bank and hanging his overcoat on the rack, he rested his polished, brown briefcase and seated himself in the chair, saying, "Please, just a trim."

The barber smiled, one more fare on a slow winter day.

Going about it quickly, the barber continued when Charles asked, "The bank is still open?"

The barber, glancing at the clock he had set on the wall, responded, "Yes, sir. For twenty more minutes. Only the banker's second teller is there. The banker is gone, and his first teller left to take his daughter to practice for a school play."

Charles smiled. "Then we must hurry."

In the bank, Charles saw the clerk: gartered arms, green eyeshade, and money piled on the counter in front of him. He looked up, saying, "Sorry, sir. I should have locked the door. I'm alone since my partner had to leave early to take a child to practice for a school play. Thus, tomorrow the teller…."

"I won't be but a minute," Charles interrupted. "I won't be but a minute. It's a safety deposit box I need to extract some contents from. I have the key."

"Oh, all right. I'll open the gate. You can get what you need," the clerk said, moving quickly, watching the money on the counter. He pushed the gate open to let Charles enter, watching, holding close to everything, saying, "There, sir, but please hurry. If my boss were to see this, I'd be fired."

Charles entered, keyed the box open, and emptied the contents into his spacious, brown, leather briefcase and put blank papers in their place. He then closed the box, keyed it locked, tucked the briefcase under his arm, and said, "Thank you. I know you'll lock the gate."

Donned hat, coat, moved at normal pace, saying once more, "Thank you"—he was gone.

At Lilly Ann's house, he gave her the briefcase, saying, "Our mission was successful. Keep and protect the briefcase. It contains all of your documents, protect them."

He was gone.

Back at his A.I.U. headquarters, Charles reported to Mr. Mellman. "It worked as we had planned, but it isn't over."

Each day she checked her mailbox often, receiving nothing, other than the occasional piece of commercial mail, but today a letter came from Mother Maggie. Opening the letter back at the house, Lilly Ann glanced at the contents and then forced herself to quickly seek her rocker and read the contents more carefully. Beyond her expressions of love, Maggie came quickly to the point: "Your Father is suffering from a serious illness. He continues his mail carrying, but I have seen him spitting up blood. If you can, please come."

Lilly Ann went down the steps carefully until she reached the ground of the root cellar, where she commenced her inspection to determine if there was sufficient food for her to be gone for a significant period of time, the precise length of which she did not know. In front of her were rows of Mason jars filled with fruits and vegetables, canned and placed there in the fall. Rows of jars red with tomatoes, green with beans, yellow with corn, purple with blackberry jelly. Next to them, hanging, were two smoked hams. In fifty-gallon wood barrels filled with pork fat were layers of cooked sausage. Next was a barrel of flour half full. Satisfied, she climbed the stairs and closed the door, knowing that Junior could find food in her absence. The flour could make biscuits for school lunches, and corn could be ground in the grinder in the corn shed.

When the children were home from school, Lilly Ann gathered them together and told them the news.

"I must answer Mom Mayo's letter. I must go to Columbus. Grandpa is very sick. I know that or she wouldn't have asked."

Facing Junior, she said, "Son, I know you'll go on as if I'm here." Facing the other children, she said, "Help Junior in every way you can. Grandma, Momma Mayo, is counting on it. Now, let's hug and love each other."

The next morning, after having participated in the morning chores as usual, she boarded the school bus with her children. At school, she waved good-bye to them and then waited for the Greyhound bus to Columbus. There, she boarded the right streetcar, exited at the stop she knew, and walked to Maggie's house.

Knocking, she waited. The door opened, and Maggie appeared. In one movement, she flung her arms around Lilly Ann.

"You came."

Then, feeling the cold, Maggie backed in, holding her daughter's arm. "Come in, come in."

Once they were fully inside the house and the door was closed again, they exchanged the usual niceties before Maggie launched into it. "It's Jimmy," she said. "I caught him spitting up blood. He denies it, but it is so."

"Has he been to the doctor?"

"He says he doesn't need to go."

Lilly Ann hesitated, knowing her mother often exaggerated and frequently became emotional.

"What can we do? I don't want to lose him."

Lilly Ann knew doctors made house calls, but it cost money—money they didn't have. As she thought about it, a thought came to her; what if they brought the doctor to him? She didn't know what the Ohio State School of Medicine needed patients for. Student doctors needed patients to practice on. Would they come here? She could ask, but who?

"Would you let me try to bring a student doctor from Ohio State here?"

"Could you?"

"I don't know, but somebody once said, 'do things that are hard while things are easy.' So, we'll try. They can only say no."

When she arrived at the School of Medicine, Lilly Ann had to insist she be allowed to see the appropriate official. Once she was sitting in the executive's office, she tried to carefully explain her mission. The executive listened carefully to her and said, "And you have done all this to try to save him?"

"Jimmy is the only father I have ever known."

The executive reached for a button on his desk. When a voice answered, "Yes, sir," the executive said, "Please send in intern Ben Ewing."

When doctor Ewing appeared, he was introduced to Lilly Ann and her mission. "Of course," the executive said, "you must be subtle when explaining your visit; perhaps say your visit is simply a visit to the neighborhood to perform an examination on each person without charge, and is sponsored by the Ohio State School of Medicine. And, of course, you will drive Lilly Ann back to her mother's home in the university's Ford."

Lilly Ann couldn't thank the administrator enough.

He said, "We thank you, ma'am. We need more citizens to practice medicine on."

At Maggie's house, Lilly Ann led doctor Ewing into the room where Jimmy was sitting with Maggie. Lilly Ann introduced them to the doctor, and doctor Ewing explained that his internship required him to examine everyone in the neighborhood; he then asked permission to examine Lilly Ann, Maggie, and Jimmy. Placing his medicine bag on a table and slipping the stethoscope from around his neck, he removed a small book in which he could take notes and started with Lilly Ann.

To Jimmy he said, "Please understand that, as a doctor, I will be placing my hand in places on your daughter that are medically necessary to conduct an examination." He proceeded to do as he had said. Finally, he drew blood with his hypodermic needle then injected the blood into a small test tube. He capped the test tube, made certain the cap was secure, and shook the test tube. Satisfied, he placed it in a small rack and wrote Lilly Ann's name beside it. Then, securing new rubber gloves and new implements, he proceeded to examine Maggie, subjecting her to the same routine.

He then moved on to Jimmy. "Sir," he said, "I can't express my gratitude to you enough. Often, men prove reluctant to deal with a doctor. They think they're infallible while, in fact, they're flesh and blood, as are all humankind. Sir, do you have on long johns?"

Jimmy nodded "yes."

"Please, these ladies have seen such many times. Please strip down to them. My professor will grade me on how thorough a job I did."

Jimmy stood and removed his shoes and socks. Sitting on the divan, he removed his pants, and his shirt, grinning a little sheepishly as he stood again. The ladies, meanwhile, had walked into the kitchen, leaving Jimmy alone with the doctor, who kept up an endless chatter to keep Jimmy calm. He proceeded with the examination, including the drawing of blood. Finished, he removed his rubber gloves and grasped Jimmy's hand, saying, again, "Sir, I can't thank you enough. If only more citizens would get involved...."

Doctor Ewing gathered himself and his gear, nearly forgetting the stethoscope around his neck. When Lilly Ann, who had returned to the room, pointed it out, he said, "Thank you. I wear it so much I forget it. It is a part of me."

She led him to the porch, where he asked, "Jimmy is gone each day?"

"Yes. You know that thing about rain and sleet and the rest of it. He claims he keeps nine-to-five, department-store hours."

"It will take perhaps a week to have all the results, including my report. Will you be here that long?"

She hesitated, answering, "Yes, I must," even as she considered the chores and the children back home.

"When I have the results, I'll come here and talk them over with you. For now, as somebody once said, 'keep the faith.' He was gone.

Inside, Jimmy, now comfortably dressed, queried, "Well, what did he say?"

"He thanked us for lending ourselves to a poor intern."

"You know what I mean, the blood stuff."

"Oh, the blood must go to a laboratory."

"The results will tell us a lot about ourselves."

"And?"

She went to him, held his face in her hands.

"Know I love you. From a little girl I have loved you. Nothing has changed. Now I must help with supper," she said, pressing his face fondly once more. She went back to the kitchen.

Lilly Ann, though uneasy over conditions at home, spent time over the next few days with her mother. Time she had not had for quite a while... time spent talking...time spent touching and smelling and sharing every minute in ways she had not experienced for years. It was as though she were renewing the acquaintance of someone she had forgotten, or rediscovering something she had forgotten but was now quickly reminded of.

Her mother was always cold when she was in the house. The house had a furnace and registers. Maggie often talked with her while sitting wrapped in a blanket, her feet on the register while Lilly Ann, perspiring, edged as inconspicuously as she could toward a window that, although not open, allowed cool air to leak around the frame and through the single-pane glass. Despite their discomfort, mother and daughter enjoyed each other's company.

PART 3

CHAPTER 33

"I live the dream of the future rather than the failures of the past.' I read that in a paper we were given today at school. It was Thomas Jefferson."

Lilly Ann stared at her son as she said, "And you remembered it?"

"Yes."

"Why?"

"I hope we have a better future than this."

Everett said this to his mother as they dragged a tree limb across the field. Lilly Ann managed a smile as she tugged and pulled the wood toward home.

"Is it all right if I hope it with you?"

Everett smiled and nodded his "yes."

The heavy, overcast sky seemed all about them. Though the year was moving toward spring, winter still exerted its fury, bringing wind and clouds and, even now, snowflakes. For a day or two longer the thought of the family home on Cleveland Avenue and the gracious living they had enjoyed there. Now the harsh reality of Sunbury set in; the farm, the cows, the hay, the manure. The utter, bitter harshness of it all.

At home, the radio blared news of Adolph Hitler and *Mein Kampf*—the autobiography he had written while in prison. His elevation by the Nazis and the Gestapo to *der Führer*. Everyday carried news of the occupation of Poland, the rounding up of the Jews, their deportation to prison camps; brutalization was the common denominator underlying it all. *Der Fürher* had come to the conclusion that without resistance, Nazis, under his command, could take over the world.

Lilly Ann could barely muster enough willpower to hide such awful news from her family. In no way did she want her children to hear it, nor in any way be associated with the Gestapo or Nazism. She continued to take pride in her children. Each time parents were invited to her children's school, she rejoiced in the congratulations she received that her children were "straight A" students. She had watched Junior interrupt his own homework to help one of his younger siblings. And it was reflected not only in the children's grades but in the pride they displayed when they shared papers and projects with her. True, not only the weather but the recessionary times weighed heavily on them all. More often than not, when Charles Davis appeared, handing her an envelope containing the money from the cashed check from Nestle, her fear rose up inside her; for against her better judgment, she always worried that, when she opened the envelope, she would find less money in it than the time before.

So far, her feelings were groundless.

The letter was unexpected. So strange that it was real, Jimmy was gone. From her mother, once again requesting her presence. Again, discussion of the matter with her children produced a similar concerned response.

"Grandma needs you. You must go."

Going through the familiar routine, she left her home with reassurances from Mrs. Gorsuch that her children would be safe, but (her neighbor added) she had to be home for suppertime to feed her husband. That would only take two hours, and then she would return to Lilly Ann's children and stay the night.

*   *   *

The knock at the door was long and purposeful. Answering the door, Junior was confronted by a large man in an overcoat. Without introduction, the man thrust several folded documents at Junior.

"Kid, where's your parents?"

"Not here."

"Then where?"

"Dead and gone."

"What?"

"You heard me. One is gone and the other is dead."

"How old are you, kid?"

"A teenager."

"When will the one gone be coming back?"

"Nobody knows."

"Smart aleck, I'll...."

Junior reached behind the door for the Winchester twelve-gauge pump shotgun and leveled it at the man. "You'll do what?"

Falling back, the man said, "Hey, kid, don't shoot me, I'm gone."

And he was.

"Did he leave? Did he leave?" Everett wanted to know.

"Look!"

Everett looked out the window. The man was running to his automobile, and—climbing behind the wheel—quickly drove off.

* * *

It lay there, blue–black, meticulously shaped, with its grooved, walnut forearm—the walnut the same tone as the other wooden pieces composing it—the stock with its trigger pistol grip. Close by sat a box of twelve-gauge number 6 shot, which could be propelled out of the full-choke barrel with deadly ferocity. Near the table on which the shotgun rested, in a straight chair, sat Junior. He had spent the night sleeping, yet he had remained aware of all sounds. Now, the sound at the door alerted him. Hand on the shotgun he watched the door slowly open. The figure that pressed the light switch revealed itself to be his mother.

"My son," she said. "Why are you already up?"

"I'm protecting our home."

For a moment, her mind flashed back to the day she saw him coming across the field in front of the house carrying the shotgun and dragging a groundhog he had just killed.

She smiled. "I'm proud of you. Someone gave you a reason?"

Yawning between words after he had answered her, Lilly Ann related the event that had occurred, especially the part about the papers. Leaving the shotgun still loaded but making certain it was on safety she returned it to the other room.

"My son, get yourself ready and help the others. It's time for chores and then for school."

Quickly she changed, cooked breakfast, saw to the meal, assured chores were completed. When the school bus came she boarded it with the children. In Sunbury, she went immediately to the telephone booth to contact Mr. Mellman to tell him of what had occurred. She sought information as to what she should do. Told to remain at the restaurant, she hurried there, hoping to once again meet with the owner, but she was informed she had the day off. Over a cup of coffee, she waited as she had been instructed to do. Nearly an hour later, Charles Davis arrived. He escorted her to her home, drove away but returned with Mrs. Gorsuch, then waited for Lilly Ann to make arrangements for her absence for an extended period of time, during which she was to reside with Maggie. As she had been instructed, she gathered all of her records, papers, and invoices, and she set them in Roy's valise. Dressing appropriately, bidding farewell to her family, she departed.

Early the next day, she was delivered to the American Insurance Union Building and escorted to the offices of Mellman and Associates, and to Mr. Mellman himself, who greeted her, received the valise filled with the papers he had requested, handed them off to accounting, and moved to a plush chair near her.

"And how are you, my dear? Frightened? Don't be, you are among friends here."

"But they sent a man who frightened my children. I'm so proud of Junior, who drove him off with Roy's shotgun."

"I know. I'm sorry we didn't move sooner. The man was a process server. He, or possibly *they*, will serve you in Columbus as soon as they can."

"What does that mean?"

"You are being sued for something. We guess it to be the farm."

"But that's our home."

"We know, but Rhodes doesn't care. He wants that property and he's willing to do anything to get it."

Lilly Ann suddenly shuddered at the thought that she and her children were being confronted with the possibility of losing their home, their farm, their income. With those thoughts, bile arose in her throat. What schools would her children go to? What workplaces would she be qualified for?

"Please, if I may," Mr. Mellman said. "I want to discuss with you what will be done next. Never fear, process servers will always find and serve you. Please see to it that my office receives a copy of any forms they give you or ask you to sign. Then we will request that you permit us to properly prepare you for a court appearance. May I be more specific? Lee Brazelton, the attorney who will represent the party or parties bringing this action, will appear in the courtroom. He will, as the old people used to say, 'be well laid out': groomed to perfection, from head-to-toe uses this tactic to impress the judge and the clerk of the court, and to intimidate the opposing party. We must do likewise."

At that moment, a beautifully dressed woman appeared.

Mr. Mellman rose from his chair. "May I introduce Natalie Sharpton of my staff...."

Natalie came forward, young and gorgeous, addressing Lilly Ann with a smile:

"Pleased to meet you. I have been instructed to accompany you to the Lazarus Department Store downtown, to assist you in fulfilling Mr. Mellman's request."

Stunned, Lilly Ann assented. She gathered her coat and let Natalie escort her out of the office. An automobile deposited them in front of a huge, eight-story department store with large industrial glass windows displaying beautifully garbed models wearing the latest styles. Inside, an elevator delivered them to the third-floor women's department. Immediately, a professionally groomed clerk accompanied by an assistant approached.

"Ladies, how may I serve you?"

Natalie Sharpton answered, "Yes please, we would like to see outfits appropriate to wear for court."

"Indeed, we shall display ten outfits for you, including hats and gloves."

Almost on signal, dresses, undergarments, stockings, shoes, headpieces, and gloves were brought out by the staff. Prices were not mentioned; Mr. Mellman's staff had taken care of all the details. To Lilly Ann's protest, he had silenced them with a raised hand.

"*Pro bono. Pro bono.*"

Lilly Ann could only stare in wonder. Never, not even as a young girl at home, had she been able to shop at Lazarus. Several times before, with friends, she had walked through the store, admiring the beauty of it all, especially the automated displays in the windows during the holidays. But prices of even the least costly items were beyond her means.

After leaving the store, the driver delivered not only Lilly Ann but her purchases to Maggie's home. He carried garments on hangers, garment in boxes, garments in storage bags to the room made vacant by the loss of Jimmy.

For several days afterward, mother and daughter relaxed, enjoying each other's company. One morning, a telephone call instructed Lilly Ann to make herself available to be driven with Mellman to the recently constructed post office and federal courthouse in downtown Columbus. Met by the automobile, Lilly Ann, accompanied by Mellman, arrived at the building. Inside, they climbed the stairs to the second story, which housed the federal court. Standing before the ten-foot doors to the courtroom, Mellman said, "I acquired permission to familiarize you with the courtroom we will be in soon. I am informed you will be served with a summons. I want you to be comfortable once our action is underway."

With that he swung the ten-foot door open, and they stepped in.

Inside the courtroom, Lilly Ann was impressed by its grandeur. The president, in effort to restore employment to every field of labor—in this case, construction—was indirectly responsible for the fine woodwork decorating spaces such as the one Lilly Ann saw before her. Mahogany appeared throughout the courtroom.

The judge sat at a large desk, raised above the floor of the rest of the room, so that he could be seen by all. Directly behind the judge, the jury station, consisting of twelve chairs fronted with ornate, turned posts and topped by mahogany railings, had been arranged with an imposing austerity. The witness box, just below the level of the judge's desk, opened on the rear. Mahogany tables and chairs, indicating where the opposing attorneys were to sit, had been placed in front of the judge's desk...

In admiration, Lilly Ann said, "This is...."

"A courtroom," Mellman interrupted. "This is why I brought you here. So that you would grow accustomed to it all, in order to not be intimidated and distracted by your surroundings. Above all, you must be totally aware of what is going on, of what is being said by every person testifying—and even why they are saying it, if you can discern their reasoning. Remember—please remember! —that what is at stake here is your life, you children's life. If there is to be a future for you and yours, it will be decided by how we perform here."

Abashed, Lilly Ann remained silent. Touching her elbow, Mellman asked, "Shall we leave?"

At home, Maggie rushed her out the door. "Two men were here to see you! They said they will be back!"

Lilly Ann touched her mother gratefully. "It's all right. I know about them. They will only comeback. They only want to serve me papers."

Later, the semidarkness of early evening brought a heavy knock on Maggie's front door. Suspecting who it was, Lilly Ann, with Maggie at her side, greeted two burly men in overcoats.

Determining Lilly Ann was their target, one thrust several folders at her, declaring the simple words, "You have been served."

They then turned and left.

"What is it?" Maggie asked.

"These are the papers ordering me to appear in court."

"What do they want?"

"The farm."

"Will they get it?"

"We hope not."

"You mean they might?"

"Possibly."

"Oh, my darling." Maggie embraced her daughter tightly. They clung together.

*   *   *

Lilly Ann had ridden up to Maggie's in Columbus by mail truck. Once inside Maggie's home they embraced. Being certain that Lilly Ann would answer her summons, Maggie had prepared supper; and so, smiling lovingly, they shared the chicken and dumplings, the hot biscuits, the green beans that Maggie had canned, then, after the main meal, enjoyed Maggie's golden-crusted apple pie, which she served with tea. Without great haste the kitchen was cleaned. After they had settled in the warmth of the parlor, Maggie said, "He asked me."

For the first time in her life Lilly Ann decided not to be straightforward with her mother. Feigning ignorance, she inquired, "What man, Mother?"

"Why, Sandy Stevenson of course."

"What did he ask?"

"For me to marry him, of course."

"And what did you say?"

"That I would think about it and discuss it with you."

Instantly the burden her mother had set on her shoulders weighed heavily on Lilly Ann. "Why me?"

"You are all that I have. You, I trust."

Lilly Ann felt nearly overwhelmed. "But I've never met him. I know nothing about him. Especially for such an important decision."

"Then if I telephone him will you meet him, ask him questions? This is the most important decision I will make since I lost your father. Maybe for the rest of my life."

Lilly Ann felt bowed by the weight of the decision but she knew she must comply. "Yes," she said. "Telephone to see if he will meet with us."

Maggie's telephone call not only arranged a meeting but also secured the automobile to deliver them to Sandy Stevenson's door. At the residence, a maid opened the door. She offered her greetings then ushered them into a less grand sitting room. Almost immediately, Sandy appeared in a sport coat, odd, crisply creased trousers, blue shirt, and a proper tie.

Saying greetings and almost on the same breath offering refreshments. Maggie declined while Lilly Ann remembering the dryness of her mouth requested a glass of water. The maid disappeared only to return immediately with a sparkling glass.

"Ladies, Sandy said, "I am so pleased you came. Please make yourselves comfortable."

After a few additional pleasantries were exchanged, Lilly Ann said, "I understand you want to marry my mother."

"With her permission," Sandy acknowledged, "and yours."

"Please, why? She's only a widowed old lady."

"Would it be all right to say I love her? We, as two couples, were friends: my wife and I, and Maggie and her husband, Jimmy. My wife admired your mother's grit as she fought through their hardships, and, overtime, I came to share her feelings. I still do."

"Your wife?" Lilly Ann asked.

"She developed cancer that penetrated her lymph nodes. I was told by the doctors who treated her that it had spread throughout her body and swept her away. That's been over two years. Now that your mother has lost Jimmy, I have asked her to marry me."

Lilly Ann smiled. "I know it is not romantic...but I see all this," gesturing toward the house and the help.

"By dumb luck, or perhaps God's grace, I graduated from Ohio State's law school, then secured a position in a legal firm that dealt in, among other things, stocks. Overtime, my holdings became more than substantial."

At that point Maggie suddenly broke in: "He told me he is rich."

Sandy smiled as he raised both hands and both arms.

"Tell her," Maggie said.

He nodded toward her saying. "With permission.

"With my wife's illness in remission I cashed my holdings, knowing I wouldn't be in position to tend to them, and took her on a trip around the world. She enjoyed it. Little did I know that that would be our last trip, she saved me and all of our holdings."

Maggie began to speak but hesitated when she noticed Lilly Ann's scowl.

Smiling to Maggie, Sandy said, "Please rest assured I have resources sufficient to maintain this lovely lady in a style to which she could grow accustom. And, I can cook."

Laughter broke out, relieving the tension that remained.

"Now, ladies, as we have talked, I have asked supper to be prepared. "He rose. "If you will join me," he said, and moved toward the dining room.

*　*　*

One evening while having tea, Maggie voiced her concern to Sandy Stevenson regarding Lilly Ann being sued and her difficulty in getting court. Hearing Maggie's consternation, Sandy smiled then laid a hand on her arm in affection, calming her.

"Not to worry, I'll have an automobile here each morning to take you to the courthouse. When I'm able, I'll accompany you."

When Maggie told her daughter, Lilly Ann touched her hand and smiled.

*　*　*

"What the hell do you mean you couldn't find her...or seize the farm...or at least serve the papers?" Rhodes shouted. He had ordered the man to meet him at the Maramor for lunch.

"Sir, let me apologize. Let me try again. This time I'm sure I'll succeed."

This had occurred several weeks earlier. As punishment, the man was made to stand and watch as Rhodes had sipped his martini, quietly spooned up his chowder, and, finally, taken up his knife and fork to cut into his bacon-wrapped filet mignon.

Looking up, he snarled loudly, "Are you still here?"

Embarrassed, the man scurried from the dining room.

CHAPTER 34

As they mounted the witness stand one after another, they mouthed the statement, "I shall tell the truth, nothing but the truth, so help me God."

The courtroom filled with Lilly Ann' neighbors: the Shoensies, Schields, Hoffmans, Schielers, Schoenbrums, DeiterSchillers, Ernst Braun, and a host of others—friends, townsfolk, curiosity seekers, victims of the recession who, as the country neared a second depression, had nothing more to do. Before the court session began the conversation among the spectators centered on the upcoming trial.

"Do I understand this is for the farm?"

"Yes," somebody said.

"And what will be done to the family?"

"Evicted. I believe that's the right word."

"To where?"

"Obviously, that's of great concern to the family, but there are those who could care less. Possession of the farm is all they care about."

"But why?"

"It has been learned that a Mr. Rhodes owns or has leased all surrounding properties except the one occupied by Lilly Ann and her children. They have lived on, maintained, developed, and otherwise cared for it for a number of years. Now Rhodes and others hired by him are suing to repossess it. That is the basis of this lawsuit."

"Do they have proof of ownership?"

"They claim so, they claim so."

CHAPTER 35

"Please rise, the Honorable Silas Hertz presiding."

With those words, a white-haired man cloaked in full judicial robes entered the courtroom through a door behind the judge's desk. While everyone in the courtroom was standing, he began the recitation of the Pledge of Allegiance. When it was over he said:

"Please be seated."

As soon as the courtroom was quiet he continued.

To all in the courtroom, Judge Silas instructed, "Before we proceed there are a few rules I ask you all to observe. First and most important, I ask for complete silence at all times." To the jury, the Judge continued, "Please pay attention to each and every one appearing before you, the case, the testimony, the materials presented, the attitude of the presenter as they answer the questions. I have no axe to grind. Any question I ask is only to clarify a point so that can be fully understood. With that, lest you not know, seated at the table to the right of the aisle are the attorney Lee Brazelton and his client, Mr. William Rhodes. Across the aisle are the attorney Aaron Mellman and his client, Ms. Lilly Ann Coleburn."

The judge cleared his throat and then continued. "As most of you know, we are here to decide ownership of a piece of property claimed by both contestants. So, without any additional loss of time, let us begin."

With that, the clerk of court rose from his chair and said, Adam Micholson, please approach the witness chair."

"My name is Adam Micholson. My brother Tom and I are professional surveyors and were hired by Mr. Rhodes to survey Mrs. Coleburn's property. When we started, we were challenged by a young man as to our right to be on the property. Mentioning Mr. Rhodes permitted us to accomplish our task. Now, with your permission, sir—" nodding to Judge Hertz— "I will display the fruits of our labor." And with that he nodded at his brother, who promptly produced the surveying chart, which was mounted firmly on a stiff board.

"Here on the left runs the full road beside the property, right here along the border of the property next door." Then, with the assistance of his brother, Adam pointed out all the features of the entire property—the area around the house, the area around the barn, and various outbuildings. A small pointer indicated each area while Adam described it in detail, delving further when requested by the judge. Once the judge was assured no further clarification was needed, he dismissed the surveying team to allow for the testimony of new witnesses.

As the surveyors returned to their seats, Ora Fishburne blurted out, "I would have told them that without charging all that money." Upon hearing the outburst, Judge Hertz snapped his gavel. Ora simply lowered her voice, continuing to whisper to her neighbor while glaring back at the judge. Judge Hertz decided to ignore her and signaled for a disheveled and uneasy Fred Ames to take the stand as the next witness.

Lee Brazelton stood up and strolled to the witness stand. Looking out at the jury and then to Fred Ames, he began, "Good morning, sir. Please sit tight and be easy. This is not an inquiry; we just have a few questions. Would you please tell us what you do?"

"Handyman, sir," the witness replied with a tone of deference.

A spectator yelled out, "Why don't you kiss his feet? You're low enough!"

Judge Hertz glared about but could not identify the culprit.

Lee Brazelton continued: "And what kind of work had you been doing on the property?"

"Everything to help her, and I mean *everything*."

"You mean of the personal nature? Tending to a woman's natural desires?"

"*Everything*. I mean *everything*."

An outcry arose throughout the courtroom. Aaron Mellman rose to object.

"Your Honor, please prevent Mr. Ames from making statements suggesting that the defendant had anything other than a business relationship with the witness."

The sharp, quickly injected statement caught Judge Hertz somewhat off guard. Recovering quickly, he replied: "Mr. Mellman, you will abide by court rules. Rest assured you will be permitted to cross-examine the witness once Mr. Brazelton is done. Mr. Brazelton, please continue."

Still casual, Lee Brazelton continued as if he had not been interrupted.

"And Mr. Ames, suppose you were to marry Mrs. Lilly Ann Coleburn?"

Seeing a glimmer of hope, Fred Ames continued: "Why, yes, sir, marrying would bring both Lilly Ann and the land."

"And if you knew the land was owned and coveted by another?"

Crestfallen, Fred Ames stammered, "B-but with others, we built the barn, added to the silo, repaired the hog pens…we maintained the place."

"Interesting." Lee Brazelton slyly, and casually continued: "And Mrs. Coleburn and her children, they did nothing?"

Trapped, Fred Ames replied, "Sir, they helped some, but me and the other men did much, much more."

Nodding to Judge Hertz, Lee Brazelton dismissed the handyman. "That's all, sir."

Looking toward the defense, Judge Hertz beckoned Aaron Mellman forward to cross-examine Fred Ames. "Mr. Mellman, if you're of a mind to…."

Aaron Mellman stood up. "Sir, I'm not of a mind to."

A chuckle rolled over the gallery. Rather than permitting Judge Hertz to be mocked, Mellman said, "Sir, with your permission, I would like to thank Mr. Brazelton. He did a rather complete job." He nodded cynically to Lee Brazelton. "I thank you."

With a smirk, Lee Brazelton half saluted Aaron Mellman. "Back at ya' my friend."

Bringing the courtroom to order, Judge Hertz announced, "Because of the late hour, the court is adjourned until nine o'clock tomorrow morning."

Sitting in the backseat of his limousine with Maggie and Lilly Ann after leaving the courtroom, Aaron asked Lilly Ann, "Well, what did you think?"

"Confused. Why did it require all of that?"

"Make no mistake. Brazelton is clever. In proceeding the way he did, he has outlined the case without wasting precious time."

"Precious time," Maggie said. "Can he be convicted now? He looks guilty, sounds guilty, *is* guilty. Convict him now."

"You don't understand. This is not a criminal matter. We do not convict. We only hear testimony to rule who will win possession of the property."

"But...."

"Please accept that I know of what I speak; we must move on."

"But...."

As the vehicle neared Maggie's home, Aaron addressed both Lilly Ann and Maggie: "At this point, our next move is to start anticipating Brazelton's next move and thinking of possible statements, answers, approaches to this matter. You can rest assured that Rhodes would not have brought this action without being assured of a victory."

"What should we do?"

"At this moment, nothing. Just be prepared to speak. You must be adroit when the conversation changes directions and adapt to Brazelton's questioning as the situation requires."

Lilly Ann said no more. *Adroit.* She could guess the meaning but was not sure. Back at Maggie's house, Lilly Ann was handed a letter addressed to her. Upon opening and reading it, she was somewhat surprised by the quality of the writing, even in pencil, by her son. To Maggie, she said, "He wishes you to be well. He says they are well there, that Mrs. Gorsuch is taking good care of them. The cows are producing and the milk is being shipped, so the income is being maintained. He concludes with words of affection for us."

Lilly Ann put the letter down.

"He's growing up. He wants me to be comforted in knowing they are all well. Notice that he does not mention the possible loss of the farm."

Somberly, Maggie nodded, uncertain of the consequences of it all.

The following morning, back at the courtroom, Lilly Ann and Aaron were informed that the hearing had been postponed.

"I'm sorry," the clerk of the court explained. "Judge Hertz has been reported seriously ill."

Aaron turned to Lilly Ann.

"It looks like we'll be adjourned for several days—fortunately for me. A friend of mine has been selected to head the forensics department at the Federal Bureau of Investigation. I don't know what railroad to take—the Baltimore and Ohio, the New York Central, or the Pennsylvania, in order to reach Washington, D.C. I need to check into the Willard Hotel before I go to his swearing in. I'll take you home and send a car for you when court resumes."

On the ride back to Maggie's house, Lilly Ann was silent, longing to return to her home. Maggie, as if intuiting her daughter's mood, had supper ready, the table set with steaming collard greens, roast beef, candied sweet potatoes, and freshly baked bread.

"Please freshen up and come to supper. No matter what has happened, everything will be all right."

What Maggie didn't say, even though she found it hard to keep these matters from her daughter, was that Sandy Stevenson had visited with her on several occasions. On several of these visits, Sandy had remarked how Maggie's daughter, with her five children, needed a large, roomy house, and that since his children had moved on with their own lives, he no longer needed, nor wanted, ten rooms. Having discussed the situation with Maggie, he was glad to find Maggie agreed with his proposal. Now, though, Maggie's concern was for her daughter. Having asked around since her naïve assumption that all was well, she had now acquired a new set of assumptions as to what could happen—and all of these new assumptions seemed to have dire consequences. Now, though, she conveyed as much confidence as possible.

"After supper and dishes, I'll rub your feet," she said, remembering how, as a young woman, Lilly Ann had gained relief from troubling matters the moment Maggie began to rub her feet. Lilly Ann, laboring under the weight of losing all she had, followed her mother's instructions, removing her shoes and stockings. Slowly, as her mother rubbed her feet, she relaxed, perhaps even nodding off, she wasn't certain. But she rested.

CHAPTER 36

Days passed in the comfort of her mother's care. Just when she was beginning to feel like a young girl once more, a telephone call returned her to reality. It was a call from Aaron's secretary, informing Lilly Ann court would resume in two days. She was instructed to dress as was previously agreed; an automobile would pick her up and deliver her to the courthouse. If she desired, Maggie could accompany her.

On the second day, groomed to Maggie's satisfaction, Lilly Ann was ready when the automobile arrived. At the courthouse, Aaron greeted her warmly, nodding approval at her appearance.

"Please rise."

The voice boomed in the courtroom as the assembled throng rose. Judge Hertz strode in, strong, though looking gaunt from his illness. Still standing, he announced, "My fellowship, I apologize for the delay my illness has caused."

Once the Pledge of Allegiance was recited, the first witness of the day was called:

"Mr. Hermann Mitchell, please take the stand."

A corpulent man waddled to the stand. Sworn in, he was seated. Lee Brazelton stridently approached him. Lee was handsomely suited in a Hickey Freeman, complete with linked cuffs and spats.

"Please restate your name."

"Hermann Mitchell."

"Mr. Mitchell, what is your occupation?"

"Head recorder of court records."

"All records?"

"Yes."

"Records since when?"

"Records since the eighteen hundreds."

"Thus, if we were inquiring about say, the nineteen thirties, the records would be there, even the nineteen twenties?"

From the gallery came a loud whisper, "They want to place every property eligible for repossession!"

Another outburst added: "They want to steal your property!"

Ignoring the interruption, Lee continued.

"What do the records contain?"

"Property lines, records of ownership, ownership transfers," the recorder replied.

"Are the records accurate and up to date?"

"They are."

At that moment, the clerk arose and announced, "Ladies and gentlemen, the judge has ordered a twenty-minute recess, starting now."

All rose. The judge disappeared into his quarters.

Someone from the gallery commented, "The judge has to use the bathroom, no doubt."

Lilly Ann turned to her attorney.

"What is going on?"

Aaron smiled. "This recess is to our advantage. Why don't you go freshen up? When you come back, we'll review possible approaches Brazelton may take and prepare ourselves to counter any claims."

Upon her return, Aaron removed his glasses and cleaned them.

Smiling, he said, "When I was a little boy I shot marbles. Before we shot we declared 'fun' or 'keeps,' meaning if either of us got the other's marbles we would either give them back, *fun,* or keep them, *keeps.* If you consider this hearing a game, it is not. This is for keeps. The farm goes, or stays, with you. If during the trial I ask you a question that appears meaningless or that the answer is obvious, please remember. All questions have a purpose. Please answer them fully. Now. Any questions?"

"What am I to do if some matter being discussed is not brought out fully and I think I can add something?"

Aaron rose from his seated position and leaned toward her.

"Please, please do not do that. Many a case has been lost with just one inadvertent or superfluous comment the opposing side has been able to manipulate." He smiled. "Just trust me. No matter how strange it seems, have faith in me. Can you do that?"

Lilly Ann nodded and smiled faintly. While she said nothing, she knew from the beginning her fate rested with Aaron. For the moment, she said a silent prayer, thanking God for having Aaron to defend her.

Upon Judge Hertz's return, a new witness was called to the stand. Despite her effort, Lilly Ann could not understand Hans Rophyney, the head of Nestlé's manufacturing plant, which was seated at the top of the hill. In broken English, he attempted to describe the company's operations. Lilly Ann learned that the Swiss company was strategically located in the center of the country, from which it could access supplies from every direction and ship product for distribution throughout country—supplies that would permit the company to expand into other products such as butter and sour cream—and products that could go nationwide, producing both vast resources for the country and vast profits for the company.

Lilly Ann noted the deference with which Brazelton handled Mr. Rophyney. She wondered if Rhodes saw or could see himself aligned with this international corporation, perhaps being invited to Switzerland, where he would be handled with similar deference.

"And you say this plant produces dried, canned milk. Would you mind describing how?"

"After a fashion I would. It is a patented process, quite intricate. The product is a rich powder—richer than raw milk—that can be maintained months, while, as you know, raw milk will spoil after several days. In our current times, such waste cannot be tolerated."

Brazelton nodded in agreement.

"Would you agree with a hypothetical statement asserting that control of the milk supply lines could control volume, quality, price—provided that whoever controls the supply lines controls the entire supply? That, over time, whichever organization controls the supply lines could control the United States' milk supply, and the head of that organization could become elected to the International Board of Directors in Switzerland?"

This last item had been insisted upon by Rhodes. As soon as Brazelton said it, a frightening scowl tightened on the Swiss gentleman's face. Hans muttered to himself, "Board of directors!"

Standing, he grabbed his coat and hat and half-bowed to Judge Hertz.

"I thank Your Honor for having me, but I must go. My board duties require my immediate presence. Again, I thank you."

Judge Hertz dismissed Hans, "Thank you, you may be seated." Hans hastily departed the courtroom. As he left, the courtroom filled with murmurs. After a few raps of his gavel, Judge Hertz finally achieved order. He then dismissed the court with orders to reconvene at nine o'clock the following morning.

At Maggie's home, Lilly Ann found a short note from her mother. Maggie and Sandy had gone to the movies, and supper awaited her in the warm-up rack. For the first time since she could remember, she found herself alone. After having eaten and cleaned the kitchen, Lilly Ann enjoyed a leisurely bath. Sitting in her gown and robe in the rocking chair near the still-warm stove, she thought of Roy. In her reverie, and with her throw around her shoulders, she walked to the sofa. Passing a small mirror, she halted to gaze at herself. She still had the pronounced cheekbones and slim, aquiline nose, the pert mouth, and the almost black hair. In the courtroom, men had stared at her as though they found her to be a gorgeous woman, perfectly made up by the make-up experts sent in by Lazarus. Certainly, her children had induced a wrinkle here, a sag there, but men still stared. Resting on the couch, covered and warm, her mind returned to her plight. What would ten years, even five years bring? In the worst case, there would be no farm, no home. The Depression meant no jobs would be available to provide her family an income; the children could end up in a children's home, or adopted and split apart from each other. In the best case, all she could look forward to was the farm, daily chores, driving the Fordson from spring to fall, canning fruits and vegetables, the older children gone and married, grandchildren, and hard work slowly breaking her down....

Having dozed off, Lilly Ann awoke to the sound of the front door opening. Maggie stepped in, followed by Sandy.

"Did you have a good time?"

Maggi's broad smile faltered when she saw Lilly Ann's expression.

Sobbing, she cried out, "Mother, I'm lost. Always before I knew what I was doing. I had Roy, a father, a home for my family. Now I might end up with nothing. Nothing for my family, nothing for myself. What am I to do?"

"My daughter, I have never had great wisdom—mother-wit maybe, but no great schooling. Nevertheless, the fact is, things change based on people's opinions changing. Right now, all the opinions are based on a set of facts; but remember there are other facts yet to be presented. Have faith."

Maggie held Lilly Ann until her sobbing stopped.

"I'm sorry. Thank you for everything you are doing for me."

Bolstering her self-confidence, she stood taller.

"Now, we must prepare for court tomorrow."

*　*　*

"Uneventful" characterized the opening the next day. As he took his seat, Judge Hertz looked out into the gallery. With a gesture to the court clerk, he quickly brought the first matter of business before the court: the clerk read the rules on conduct in the courtroom. When the clerk had finished, Judge Hertz reminded the courtroom to please observe the rules that had just been read. The clerk then turned to a short, wiry man seated in the jury box and reminded him to remove his hat.

Lee moved smoothly around the courtroom. This morning, his Hickey Freeman three-piece suit was topped by a tastefully patterned navy and green necktie. Turning to Billy Wasick, the current witness, Lee said, "So, Mr. Wasick, sir, you have extensive knowledge regarding farm equipment?"

"I should, been some thirty years in them."

"Tractors, plows, planters and the like…."

"Got 'em all."

"And 'all' includes those items found on this contracted piece of land?"

"All you see was sold, given for less than a dollar, or little more. At a time when many where still following a team."

"What was that?" Lee asked. "I fail to understand."

"It's not complicated. Did you ever hear of, 'all total, every piece'?" Billy said with pomposity, tilting backward and raising his feet to the rail—from which a court officer rushed those same two pompous feet down.

Ignoring Billy's behavior, Lee asked a final question. "Now Mr. Wasick, would you advise a person to purchase this equipment?"

"Why, yes, of course. While most around here are still using horses, Mrs. Coleburn was farming with a Fordson tractor and regular equipment. Darn good job of it, too."

"Could you estimate its worth?"

"Not offhand, but it could figure the worth in a little time."

"Thank you, that won't be necessary. I thank you again."

Hearing the usual noise and clamor accompanying witnesses who were dismissed and new ones who were called, Judge Hertz again rapped for order. At that point, the judge heard a request from Lee to approach the bench. When Aaron and Lee approached, Lee requested a postponement for the remainder of the day.

"May I ask why?"

"A person I would like to question is out of town."

"Was he notified properly?"

"An attempt was made, Your Honor."

"To what result?"

"He has been and is still removed for specialized dental work."

"And he will be here?"

"Yes sir, of that I have been assured."

"Under the circumstances, we have no choice." To the clerk, he said, "You have heard this request. Please reschedule court space and dismiss everyone."

The judge and court arose. Dismissal ensued.

* * *

After supper, Maggie asked, "Wonder what happened to Charles Davis?"

"I hope he has said nothing like what was said today."

"I like this man. He knows when to talk."

CHAPTER 37

"So, Mr. Davis, you deign to favor us with your presence."

"I'm sorry, sir, but I had a broken wisdom tooth."

"Did you lose it?"

"Sir?"

"Did you lose it—the wisdom tooth, that is?"

At that moment Charlie said nothing, being reminded of advice from Aaron, to be aware of haste." Lee Brazelton will try to confuse you with nonsense and haste, he'll try to slip you up," Aaron had said. "Think before you speak."

"Sir," Charlie finally responded to Brazelton, "I strongly suspect we are referring to vastly different things; me a tooth, you a mental concept. A bit different, don't you think?"

Charlie smiled. For a moment, Lee was aghast. Such insight was unexpected. He would need to tread more carefully.

"So, Mr. Davis, shall we start again? Your name please."

"Charles Davis."

"Your occupation?"

"Attorney at law."

"And, why are you here?"

"I was asked by my employer, Mr. Mellman, to intercede in a situation that had developed over the Sunbury Bank and Ms. Lilly Ann Coleburn, our client."

"I don't understand."

"Neither had Lilly Ann when she discovered her account was frozen. Had been for two months—a third one and the bank could have seized the property she lived on. She would have been evicted, as she had assumed her payments on the property were current."

An eerie silence befell the courtroom. There was no murmuring, only silence, all listening closely, knowing a similar situation could happen to them.

"And what happened next?"

"After Lilly Ann had told Mr. Mellman, he assigned me to look into the situation. My assignment was to go to Sunbury Bank, open an account for Mrs. Coleburn and myself that would make payments on the property."

"Did you accomplish that task?"

"I did."

"That being so, why did you return?"

"Once we had secured her property and made sure her payments were current, Mrs. Coleburn made us aware of a safe deposit box in which she had all of her papers, the ones to her property—papers to all of her possessions. Of course, she was fully aware of the strong-arm tactics being employed to prevent her gaining access to her papers placed there to be safe, but now threatening her and her family's well-being."

Charlie continued: "Mr. Mellman asked me to scout the situation, which I did, and was able to provide a solution."

"Which was?"

"One evening, I entered the bank seven minutes before closing time."

Charlie gave a recounting of what then took place.

"And the papers you removed from Ms. Coleburn's safe deposit box that evening?" Lee asked after Charlie had finished talking. "Where are they now?"

"Locked in a safe in my office. I'm protecting them for her."

"And what if whatever she has proves worthless?"

Charlie looked at his interrogator uncertainly. "Worthless? Why would it be worthless?"

Lee paused a moment then smiled broadly at Charlie. "Thank you for your time, Mr. Davis. No further questions."

CHAPTER 38

Lilly Ann's banker appeared before the court splendidly attired. Hair parted in the middle and combed back. Pince-nez gleaming. Eyes focused. Having been sworn in, he sat erect, almost eager to respond to Lee Brazelton's questions.

Lee smiled down at the banker and asked, "Sir, please state your name."

"A. Michael Fine."

"And you are…?"

"A banker, sir. The Sunbury Bank has been in my family for generations. We are proud to say we have provided financial services to much of Sunbury and the surrounding area."

"I understand that you volunteered to testify before the court."

"Yes, sir. My employees have been accused of conspiring against Mrs. Coleburn to lose her bank records."

"Records? Sir, I don't understand."

"Somehow, Mrs. Coleburn's records were ordered to be denied to her."

"And you were prepared to do so?"

"The bank, my family comes first, sir."

"And?"

"That's why I'm here. We did nothing wrong. We did nothing wrong," he repeated.

His composure was gone. Pince-nez in hand, his white collar was lined with sweat as he breathed hard.

Fearing that he would not achieve the desired outcome, Lee dismissed him. "Thank you, Mr. Samuelson. No further questions."

CHAPTER 39

She felt clean. The judge had decided to not start new hearings that day. A home-cooked supper had consisted of warmed-up leftovers from the evening before. Dishes were washed and put away. All of this was accomplished quickly, at Maggie's insistence. Followed by a bath, and dressed in their robes and nightgowns, they retired to the couch. Maggie then brought out letters that she had been concealing until then.

"I picked these up as I came in but thought you should be relaxed to enjoy them," she said.

As she handed the letters to Lilly Ann, her daughter smiled and clutched them to her chest. She would open them later: one from Junior, the other from her daughter. Snugly in bed, she opened the envelopes, carefully unfolding the sheets of tablet paper. Mrs. Gorsuch, then it had become blatantly clear that Lilly Ann would be occupied for an undisclosed amount of time, Mrs. Gorsuch had moved in to Lilly Ann's home to help out with the chores, keep the farm and milking going, and make sure the children's homework was done. Lilly Ann read the letters, hugged and cherished them, then reread them. Phyllis, in big letters, told of day-to-day events, expressed her love, and provided an update of her siblings' well-being. Junior, smoothly, and sophisticated in his writing, told of similar events and expressed similar thoughts—though one different idea emerged. Football players who were currently on the team plus new hopefuls who were trying out for the fall season were being encouraged to exercise and run sprints to improve their physical condition. Though Lilly Ann knew perfectly well what she had read, she reread it, and went to sleep fondly thinking of her children.

* * *

Under instructions provided by the clerk of the court the crowded courtroom rose, fell silent, repeated the oath, and as Judge Hertz took his seat, was seated.

"Before we get started with the day's proceedings there is a question or two I would like to ask and have answered. First, I understand there are two sets of papers pertaining to the ownership of this property."

Someone in the crowd spoke loudly, "Counterfeiting is a felony."

"Since when did you become an expert?"

"Maybe I don't know much, but I know that."

"Mrs. Lilly Ann, I understand you have papers?" the judge asked.

Mellman rose, holding a satchel in his hand. "Yes, sir, we have."

Addressing the clerk of the court the judge instructed, "Take the papers, label them 'Exhibit A' and 'Exhibit B' and bring them into my chambers where I and a witness from each side will observe as I examine them."

The clerk moved as instructed.

"See that they are secured in the safe until needed."

At that moment, Attorney Mellman asked his question. "Sir, do I correctly understand you? Since we are to, if necessary, present various aspects of these documents, are we permitted to closely examine, even quote portions of them as we appear before the court?"

A clerk in Lee Brazelton's group approached Brazelton and whispered into his ear. Brazelton then turned and, addressing the court, said, "Judge, as long as such examination is under your control, then taking them to another site to do so, we have no objection."

"But…." the clerk said.

Attorney Brazelton raised his hand.

"I see nothing wrong with it. Friday would provide weekend time, and a weekend should prove sufficient."

All the while that he was talking, he was thinking of the weekend he had promised his wife— a bonus from Rhodes—and the extra fees it would generate.

An introduction to the Wolfe family and their estate, The Wigwan, he thought. *Just think of it! Being entertained at The Wigwan!*

The country estate occupied several hundred acres. Owned by one of the richest families in Columbus, and maybe in the county—or maybe even the state—who swam in their own pool, shot skeet on their private range. Big name bands considered it an honor to play in their ballroom after the guests had dined on steak from beef grown on the grounds. While he didn't say it, he knew they had arrived. His wife would be looking the part in a strapless gown with a multi-diamond necklace leased for the event.

The Wolfes and the Wigwan. Just think of it!

CHAPTER 40

"How soon does the train leave?"

"Which one?"

"The first one into Washington, D.C."

"The Pennsylvania. It leaves in forty minutes."

"Get me a round-trip ticket on it." He pushed the money at the clerk.

The Pennsylvania pulled up as scheduled. Mellman, holding a large suitcase, boarded. As the train pulled out of the station, he was reminded of his conversation with the forensics laboratory technicians. As they had agreed, as soon as they received the materials, a full laboratory investigation would be conducted. As explained to their supervisor, a close friend of Mellman's, the entire laboratory was available and had been prepared for a full examination of the materials that had been sent.

It was daylight when Mellman arrived at the station. A taxi cab delivered him to the F.B.I. Immediately, the lab workers took his suitcase and carefully removed the contents then handed the components to various lab assistants, who immediately set to work.

"Please, as my men work, you need a rest," said his friend We have arranged hotel accommodations. Staff will work all night. We will have answers by morning. Our service will drop you off and will be there to pick you up at nine o'clock in the morning, if that is good for you."

The vehicle had hardly moved when it arrived at the Willard Hotel. Once used to accommodate Civil War soldiers, it had been remodeled to house high-level government employees, foreign officials, wealthy businessmen seeking lobbyists to secure various business favors. Mellman, tired and half-asleep, quickly found his room, refreshed himself, sought the dining room, ate, bathed, and slept. Morning, with full provisions furnished by the hotel, came quickly, as did his return to the forensics laboratory, where he was greeted with a request to telephone as soon as he arrived. It was his friend, the supervisor. "Mr. Mellman, I'm sorry I cannot be there to greet you. I am pleased, however, to inform you that we accomplished one task; when the time comes I will be more than willing to testify as to our findings. Now, I must rush back to a meeting. Good-bye."

The train ride home transpired in a timely fashion. Before Mellman did anything else, he returned the papers the clerk of the court's office. Almost immediately, all of the principals, including Judge Hertz, appeared in the courtroom. Fatigued, Mellman accompanied Lilly Ann, calm and beautiful. Immediately, the judge signaled court to begin.

He sat clutching the huge portfolio. In a white shirt, black tie, suit, and shoes. All, including the black frame of his spectacles, had been chosen with care, but none personified a man occupying a position of more importance than a clerk—a chief clerk, at best.

"Chief clerk, what is that?"

"I direct a staff of men who collect, file, and maintain a record of who owns which piece of land—including the property in question: who owns it now and who amended it through the years."

"And you perform this function?"

"Yes, sir, my staff and I."

"How long have you been doing this?"

"Twenty-three years, sir."

"But the program…?"

"Sir, our records go back to the early eighteen hundreds."

"And if I ask you for the records, say the nineteen twenties, or the nineteen thirties, would you have them?"

"Oh, yes, sir, anything that is current is right here." The clerk patted the large, thick, heavy file book he clutched in his lap.

"Then would you please trace the history of the land now occupied by Mrs. Coleburn, and the land around Mrs. Coleburn's property that has been so tenaciously claimed."

"Sir, if you don't mind, I will place the volume on a small table and turn the pages as I describe what is requested."

A small table was provided, and the huge volume was placed atop it. Opening the tome, the clerk addressed the awaiting audience: "The volume reveals a history, so to speak, of the area. I know you know, but I will remind you that the federal government designated certain areas as land grant regions. In order to develop these almost unknown areas, the government decided to award one square mile of land to those who would venture onto it and, a most demanding requirement, develop it."

Turning to a specific section of the volume, the clerk said, "Here, it is recorded that in the eighteen fifties, Ireland suffered a disaster. An unknown fungus attacked the potato crop, destroying it. Thousands of people migrated to the United States. Among them, my ancestors, the McGuires, migrated; most settled on the East Coast but some—my ancestors among them—migrated to the Midwest. Ancestors of John McGuire. Having acquired so much land, more than they could possibly manage, they sold the land, until they finally ended with the approximately sixty acres that are being contested."

He stopped and looked around, realizing he had run on—to what result, he did not know.

To his surprise and delight, Brazelton raised his hand, smiled, and said, "Thank you, sir, I could not have explained it better if I tried."

Brazelton turned and half bowed to Mellman. "Sir, while I secured this witness for my own purposes, you are welcome to ask him any questions."

Aroused from his travel-induced drowsiness, Mellman addressed Judge Hertz.

"Sir, if I may, I do have a few things I'd like to address. But sir, I did not come prepared to address them today. I was told records, papers, and verbal matters would be presented by the chief clerk, thus the records I would need are back in my office. Sir, I beg your indulgence to permit me to come prepared tomorrow."

"Permission granted," the judge said, looking at the pocket watch he held in his hand.

CHAPTER 41

"Yes, I invited you here," Rhodes said, "to have a meal at the Maramor in the event that you have never been here before—if you have, enjoy."

Lee Brazelton simply smiled and thanked him. At that moment, a uniformed waiter served them two glasses of cabernet sauvignon.

"I'm told you enjoyed this year."

With that, Brazelton raised his glass, signaling Rhodes to follow suit. Almost simultaneously a waiter appeared with oysters on the half shell.

Rhodes raised an oyster fork as Brazelton said, "Shall we pray...?"

Rhodes' fork was poised in midair, and his mouth was hanging open. Momentarily confused, the oyster dangling from the fork, he then angrily slammed the fork down. He was about to curse the speaker, but he halted mid-word. Remembering the speaker, he calmed himself down.

"Yes, of course," he said irritably.

As lunch progressed, the court case crept into the conversation: lucrative aspects...hay crops from various seeds...charges that should be imposed on leased land. Any impediments to Rhodes and Brazelton's enjoyment of each other's company during the course of the meal had disappeared, and lunch ended with the relationship smoothed out by assurances that victory was guaranteed.

* * *

Official ceremonies over, Judge Hertz leaned forward, resting his arms on his desk. "Since this is an open hearing, I realize, now, that Mr. Mellman has had no opportunity to prepare for making the presentation, even though such an opportunity was offered to him. So, I have invited him to open this session with any questions or facts that may be of interest to the case."

Mellman rose, made his way to the front of the courtroom, and handed several papers to the judge. "Sir, if I may," he addressed Judge

Hertz, "I would like to present this statement, notarized, of course, that I must present in lieu of Mr. McGuire's testifying, which I cannot do, due to severe illness. I will not attempt to explain in detail, except to say it fully details the McGuires', shall we say, journey, from the date of their arrival in this country until now. It will reveal information concerning the land being contested."

The judge instructed his clerk to receive the papers and designate them as Exhibit C.

"Now sir, if I may, I would ask several questions of the chief clerk."

"Of course."

The chief clerk returned to the witness stand.

"You testified to—and presented records of—areas formerly owned by Mrs. Coleburn, but now claimed by Mr. Rhodes."

The chief clerk nodded. "Yes."

"And you stand by the information presented?"

Having been in the department he had headed for so many years and never having been challenged, the chief clerk tugged at his collar. He half smiled, and then he half twitched. "Sir," he said, "the records you have been permitted to see have been kept for hundreds of years. Accurately, I might add, and guarded from tampering."

"Then the sworn and notarized records admitted by Judge Hertz are accurate?"

Not seeing where the questions were leading, the clerk hesitated. Reminded by the judge that he had to answer the question, the clerk shook his head and raised both arms, saying, "I assume—" then, reminding himself about assumptions, said, "I guess—" then shook his head in dismay and fell silent. Judge Hertz, sensing his frustration and dismay, called the clerk by name and said, "You're dismissed," then asked Mellman, "Do you have any further witnesses?"

"Sir, as all concerned here have previously agreed, may I present Mrs. Gorsuch?"

Mrs. Gorsuch approached the bench. She wore an older hat, white gloves (as her lady friends had instructed), an old (but clean) dress (which was too long on her), and button shoes. Judge Hertz listened to her simply out of courtesy as she described to the court her Greyhound ride from Sunbury and her walk to the court to support her friend. Asking her to wait in the courtroom, he summoned both attorneys into his chambers. Simply put, he described Mrs. Gorsuch's predicament: her having had to secure friends to mind the farm while she was gone, her arduous trip to arrive in court in order to testify in support of her friend. Now the Judge asked if either party objected to Mrs. Gorsuch being allowed to testify, which neither party did.

Mrs. Gorsuch remained in the witness box. In response to a few questions from him, Mrs. Gorsuch described how she first met Lilly Ann when she had trudged through the snow and cold, begging for milk to feed her children. She went on, the judge permitting her testimony, until finally he thanked and dismissed her. Then, addressing the court, he said, "Thank you for your indulgence…but be reminded this is a court of law; while we may be saddened by the testimony we just heard, this case will be decided by law, not emotion." He banged his gavel. "Court dismissed for the day."

CHAPTER 42

An indeterminate sky brought on by clouds scuttling along the horizon, where lightning flared like a flashlight switched on and off, greeted them as they arrived at the Lilly Ann's farm. Sandy Stevenson stepped from his Nash; he opened the door for Maggie and Lilly Ann. Hearing the automobile, Mrs. Gorsuch rushed to the door and hastily opened it before rushing back to the stove, where her pots and skillets gave off scrumptious odors of the meal she was preparing. Junior and the children were out completing the day's chores before coming in to have their supper and start their homework.

"I'm sorry, but the children are out, though they will be in soon," Mrs. Gorsuch told the new arrivals as they joined her in the kitchen. "Obviously, we weren't expecting you."

"It's just as well," Sandy said. "I want to talk with Lilly Ann for a moment."

With a hand on her arm, he led Lilly Ann back outside. The sun, which had been hidden by clouds, chose that moment to shine. Sandy, still with a hand on her arm, led Lilly Ann from the house, guiding her up toward the orchard and a full view of the neighboring farm. Higher still, beyond a break wind, the air felt penetrating. Lilly Ann drew her coat closer about her. Seeing her, Sandy said, "I'm sorry, I didn't mean to expose you in this way."

Lilly Ann smiled. "Please, I'm all right. I've been here many times."

Relieved, he smiled. "What I wanted to talk with you about is our house on Cleveland. When my wife and I bought it, we were a family. Now she's gone, I'm in those ten rooms with only a housekeeper. If your mother will have me, we will be married, and we have discussed moving into a smaller house on the eastside of Columbus. Though we intend to keep an automobile, we will be within walking distance of a grocery store and the drug store. It is a small drive to the hospital, God forbid, if we need one."

"And do the children and I fit into this plan?"

"For a negotiable price, you would have to leave the farm, move into the ten rooms, where the children would have their own bedrooms, bathrooms, hot and cold running water, a furnace with registers in each room. Down below, the coal for the furnace, enough for the whole winter, is shoveled into a bin. Schools for the children are within walking distance."

"And Junior?"

"Central High School is within walking distance as well."

"And football?"

"Central has a team, whether or not he will be on it I cannot promise."

"It would break his heart not to be."

Once more, he grasped her arm. "I take it I have interested you."

Moving several steps away from him, she looked over the fence at the land, her farm, her children's home. "Now, back to the real world. Tomorrow, or soon, at least, I must sit in the witness's stand and testify."

"You'll do fine."

"Neither you nor I know that."

He smiled again. "As your mother says to me often, 'ye of little faith.'"

CHAPTER 43

The day opened without incident. Properly dressed and accompanied by Mellman, the ladies arrived, only to be greeted by a clerk, saying, "Judge Hertz is ill. You will not have court today. The courtroom is being reclaimed for several days, four or more, I would guess. But now that you are here, you might as well sit in on this federal case; see how the other half lives." He laughed at his wittiness.

Mellman smiled and thanked him while saying to the ladies, "I think that is an excellent idea. Having never seen a federal hearing, this will provide an opportunity to familiarize yourselves well with close observation of all that goes on in an important case."

"And what do we have to do?" Lilly Ann said.

"Just sit along with the other spectators, quietly observe and listen to how a lawsuit is conducted in a federal court."

"Is it any different?"

"Not really, perhaps a few rules that will not concern you are different—that's all. Law courts are law courts."

Despite his suggestion, Maggie, stating she wasn't interested in sitting all morning simply to watch the proceedings, elected to return home, where she hoped to have supper ready when they returned. Mellman instructed her to have his driver take her home. Then, Lilly Ann and Mellman entered the courtroom. At the command "All rise," Lilly Ann, along with the rest of the court rose. The judge entered the courtroom. Somewhat gaunt, wearing a disheveled suit under his judicial robes, Judge Aaron Atkins appeared then took his seat on the bench and signaled all to be seated. "Ladies and gentlemen, welcome. For a moment, please permit me to familiarize you with why we're here. As you are aware, we are here to settle the contention over a patent, a product, and the royalties that are derived therefrom. In keeping with protocol, I will take great time describing what the two sides are contending over, except to say one side holds the patent, the other side is producing and selling the product without paying royalties, in violation of the patent. Thus, we are here to decide this matter."

* * *

"Gas tungsten arc welding—the trademarked name is Heliarc…in any case, I learned it five years ago and I've been doing it ever since."

The speaker, perhaps a bit shorter than his muscular structure suggested, commanded attention in spite of his blue, denim trousers, which were covered by a blue, cotton shirt buttoned at the collar; his long sleeves were buttoned, as well.

"You worked for the company for five years?"

"Yes, sir."

"Welding the whole time?"

"Tested for the welding job, passed, and have welded ever since."

"The trademarked process Heliarc?"

"Asked and answered," Judge Atkins stated. "Move on."

"I was just trying to determine his experience."

"Move on."

The attorney, George Feldt, turned back to the witness. "Do you have a family?"

"Sir?"

"Do you have a family?"

Judge Atkins addressed the attorney again.

"George, I assume there is a point to this line of questioning?"

"Yes, sir, I want to determine if the witness realizes what is at stake. This is not a trivial proceeding," the attorney responded. He turned back to the witness. "Jerry…is your name Jerry Sandevsky?

"Yes, sir."

"You don't mind if I call you Jerry?"

"No."

"Then, Jerry, perhaps you will describe your model, I understand you brought one."

Addressing the judge, the welder said, "Please, Your Honor, I need to go to a table to show it."

The judge signaled a clerk, who left the courtroom but returned immediately, carrying a small table. The witness stood and grasped a cardboard box of some two feet wide by twenty inches deep. Placing it on the table, he carefully removed a wooden device from the box. Seeing it, Lilly Ann thought, *how curious.* Jerry had made the device in his garage, he now told the court, using common tools: hammer, saw, hacksaw, wood chisel, and a screwdriver. Hours of careful labor—blood, sweat, and, nearly, tears. Four corner posts were screwed onto a wood base—what Lilly Ann guessed was a square foot in size; in the center of the base a circular device rode on rollers, permitting it to swivel three hundred and sixty degrees. On that stood a triangular device that could tip over one hundred and eighty degrees in both directions; it had a steel cap on which aluminum could be welded—by the trademarked process Heliarc, the witness explained—while the welder sat turning and swiveling it, to weld the piece in question.

Lilly Ann listened and tried to understand as the welder's explanation went on. Finally, the judge interrupted. "Mr. Sandevsky, I thank you. Attorney Felati?"

Attorney Felati addressed Mr. Sandevsky. "Sir, I'm told you hold a patent for this device. Is that correct?"

"Yes, sir."

"And when and how did you acquire that? As you know, that is an expensive and time-consuming process."

Jerry looked to the judge and said, "Your Honor, I beg your indulgence."

At that the judge snapped erect, impressed with what he considered eloquent language for a welder.

"Yes?" the judge said to Jerry. "What is it you desire?"

"Please let my friend, who is more able to answer these questions, do so for me."

Eying the witness, the opposing attorney made an assumption—and a decision. "Your Honor," he said, "I see no problem with allowing Mr. Sandevsky to go; nor do I object to asking a question or two of the second witness, whom I'm told you have here in the courtroom."

"So, you have no objection to questioning this second man?" Judge Atkins asked. "And you will be satisfied with his testimony?"

"I said so, didn't I?"

Judge Atkins looked to his officer tending the door and said, "Bring him in. Mr. Sandevsky, you are dismissed."

A slim man entered, carrying papers that were rolled under his arm. Glasses framed his eyes and lent shape to his muscular chin, under which a blue-striped necktie peaked beneath a white collar. Gold links at the cuffs shown beneath a Hickey Freeman sleeve of a grey-striped double-breasted suit coat. Standing at strict attention, Attorney Kenneth Duke repeated the oath of office. Seeing Attorney Duke, Jerry realized he had not anticipated that anyone of Attorney Duke's renown or ability would be appearing at the trial. Known for his architectural skills as well as his *pro bono* work, he appeared today to be testifying at the request of George Feldt.

"Mr. Duke, Am I correct in assuming you are ready to proceed?"

"Yes, sir."

Then, turning to the judge, he said, "Your Honor, I was told I could request a folding blackboard on which I may display architectural diagrams."

With a quick signal, Judge Atkins directed a standing blackboard be brought into the courtroom. Once the blackboard was in place, Attorney Duke went directly to the board, with drawings and tape. From a coat pocket he extracted a telescoping pointer.

"This," he said, "is a replica of the drawing submitted to the U.S. Patent Office, from which was received a patent, a copy of which we have here in our portfolio. The model submitted to the patent office was made in a machine shop and is composed of copper, steel, and aluminum. While I could go into a lengthy and technical explanation, simply stated, it sets on a welding table and permits the welder to turn it one hundred and eighty degrees, three hundred and sixty degrees, as desired, while sitting. As an engineer as well as an attorney, I marvel at an invention so simple, so complex, and so complete."

As Lilly Ann watched the proceedings and listened to the attorney's testimony, she turned to Mellman. He smiled and whispered, "Now watch."

Slowly, the attorney who had been selected to present the defense's case rose. Addressing the judge, he said, "Your Honor, if I may, I too have a model to present."

At a signal from the attorney, an assistant entered, carrying a black-painted model that appeared to replicate the diagram shown on the blackboard.

"Is it true that a worker on your production floor invented this?" the attorney asked.

"I'm sure it happened. Workers are always coming up with what they claim are sure and unique ideas for production, and Jerry Sandevsky was one of them. I'm sure his wooden contraption is one of those models."

The Attorney directed his next question to Duke, "And what are you displaying here?"

"It is a production device created by technicians on the research staff and on which we—the corporation, that is—has a patent pending," Attorney Duke said.

The judge cut in with a question: "I'm confused. You say you have a patent pending. How can that be when there is already a patent on this device, a copy of which was displayed here earlier today?"

Attorney Duke simply remained silent.

"Sir, I am waiting for an answer."

The silence remained palpable. Then the attorney spoke, his voice half muffled by emotion. "Sir, if I may, I am not prepared to respond satisfactorily."

Judge Atkins remained silent while he stroked his chin. Then he said, "All right, I will delay a verdict until I receive and had time to study them. Meanwhile, I am ruling a preliminary injunction until I have had time to consider your submission. For that I grant three days. My concern is whether or not you violated the patent held by Mr. Sandevsky describing the distinguishing features of the device he created. With that, this court is dismissed, to be reconvened three days hence."

Mellman turned to Lilly Ann. "Well, what do you think?"

"From what I understand, the court will not meet again for three days," Lilly Ann replied.

"I hadn't anticipated such an action, but, certainly, you are right. We will not meet again for three days. I will take you home to use the three days as you see fit."

At Maggie's home, Lilly Ann found a letter awaiting her from the children. It was one she particularly enjoyed, for each of them had written something about what had gone on while she was away, about school, about farm life, about the birth of new calves, and even about acting in the school play. As she read, she smiled. Happy to be back at her mother's and Sandy's, she settled by the heat and dozed. The next day, after Maggie had cared for her and talked with her, Sandy came. After socializing with the ladies, Sandy said, "Lilly Ann, while we have time, there is something I want to show you. While you've been to my house, you haven't seen it all."

Conversing pleasantly, Sandy escorted Lilly Ann to his nearly new Model A Ford Coupe, which was black with golden wheels and had spare tires mounted on each side, and then drove her to the Cleveland Avenue mansion. At the front door to the house, Sandy did not use his key but rang the doorbell. Almost immediately, a small lady dressed in a maid's uniform opened the door. Greeting them politely, she said, "Mrs. Lilly Ann, ma'am, how are you?" as if Lilly Ann had always been there.

Lilly Ann smiled and nodded.

"As I told you yesterday," Sandy said to the maid, "I have brought Lilly Ann to see the parts of the house she has not yet seen." Signaling to Lilly Ann to follow him, he led her to a stairwell and, instead of climbing the stairs, he went downstairs to a full basement. Still leading Lilly Ann, he pointed out the furnace, which had pipes that, he said, led to registers in the floor above. He pointed out, too, a window through which coal could be shoveled, whereupon it would fall into a large bin that stood beneath it; near the coal bin stood a washer–dryer, gleaming in white enamel. To the side were rooms with carpeted floors.

"The children could play here in bad weather."

Turning and pointing out other features, he soon finished explaining the basement then led Lilly Ann back upstairs. "You have seen this floor, let's go upstairs."

On the third floor were two rooms.

"I once had a couple of servants, a man and his wife. The man, as did my wife, died of cancer. In case you're interested we were married twenty-seven years. Our children, two boys and one girl, graduated from Ohio

State University. One boy lives in Boise, Idaho, has an executive position with the J.R. Simplot Company. The other is in Hollywood pursuing an acting and directing career. My daughter has two children and is married to an executive at a brokerage house there. Enough of that. Since we yet have hours of daylight there is something else I would like to show you, but you must not mention it to Maggie."

Again, they rode through Columbus on Broad Street. Passing through a variety of streets and neighborhoods they finally came to a halt. At a handsome, small house Sandy approached the front door then removed a key from his coat pocket and opened it. Behind him, as she approached the house, Lilly Ann could see what appeared to be white, overlapping, aluminum strips...windows...doors of more white aluminum strips as well as solid areas. Inside the house she saw walls of all white. Across from the front room, which appeared to be the living room, a small space had been set off to the side to serve as an office. Directly behind that room was a dining room and a kitchen. Leading the way through these rooms, Sandy pointed to a bathroom fronting two bedrooms.

"Well, what do you think?"

"Is it for Mother?"

"If she'll have me—and this house. I don't own it yet, I've only made a small deposit. If she likes it and will not only marry me but is willing to move here, I'll pay for the house in its entirety. But I have yet to settle the one we just left. What I'm saying is, I must sell it. My children would hate me forever if I just gave it away. I must receive three thousand dollars, one thousand for each."

Now, suddenly, everything became clear in Lilly Ann's mind. All the plans that Sandy had told her of, and all the possible fates of the houses she had seen, depended on Sunbury, the farm, and the outcome of her lawsuit. Understanding the situation fully now made her breathing turn harsh, her nerves standing on end. But before she could react, Sandy extracted his pocket watch then pressed the small button on top, springing the front open. Scrutinizing the watch face he said, "Lilly Ann, we still have time for me to show you the high school Junior would attend."

Riding across the Scioto Bridge, Lilly Ann viewed all the scenery passing by, but she said nothing. After a short ride on the other side of the river, Sandy turned his automobile into a designated parking area. Then he stopped and pointed.

"That's Central High School."

Lilly Ann got out of the car. The large, white building appeared to be made of granite; it covered the city block. Lilly Ann later learned that the lower level of the two-story school had a machine shop and an automobile shop for young boys to learn automobile mechanics. On the other side, slightly downhill from where she stood, came the sound of a muffled school bell, and of students being released for the day. Sandy touched her arm and gently led her to where she could see a football field, complete with a four-hundred-and-forty-yard track circling around it. Down each side of the field were rows of seats for the opposing team.

"You told me Junior loves competing in football and track. Perhaps you'll be coming here to see him," Sandy said. "Now let's go back into the school so you can see it."

Inside, walking through the second floor of the school, where janitors were already starting the day's cleaning, she saw numerous classrooms. As they neared the end of the hall she also saw many of the school's offices. Descending to the first floor, Sandy pointed out the labs, the stone floor, and the walls especially designed to protect against chemical spills. A chart of the elements overlooked the lab benches, and rows of Bunsen burners sat on a long countertop.

Impressed, Lilly Ann glanced at Sandy. He said, "For students who will study chemistry and physics…. Let's move on."

As they resumed their tour, Sandy seemed about to speak again. Before he could talk, Lilly Ann interrupted, "Please, if you are going to say what I think you are going to say, may I interrupt? I understand you are taking us to see Ohio State University. I have heard about it for a long time. I want to see it, too, but not a drive-through only. I want to walk it, see it, and see what Junior has talked about."

"Oh, Lilly Ann, please forgive me, I had no knowledge of your interest. Of course, we will park, we'll walk, I'll show you the buildings where I walked to classes, studied, and graduated. Now, shall we go home?"

The next day they left for High Street and the short ride north to the parking area that bordered the university's campus. They walked past the fortress-like building of the ROTC, where Sandy stopped and pointed.

"The campus lies directly in this direction, until it reaches the Olentangy River, where, on the other side, lies the farm of the agricultural college. But before we go there we must go to the Horseshoe, designed and built by some forward-thinking men for eighty-plus onlookers and planted with Buckeye trees. There, the guidance and team spirit propelled Buckeye football to the fame it currently enjoys."

Looking back behind her, Lilly Ann saw that a good bit of the overall campus was surrounded by a small stream.

"Now, are you ready to see the Farm?"

Riding across the campus they seemed to move into another world, where university students lived and managed horses, cows, sheep, goats, chickens of all types, geese, and ducks. Sandy explained that the students studied them and developed new breeds for Ohio farmers.

"Now you have seen the university Junior might attend and where, perhaps, he'll play football."

Lilly Ann nodded thoughtfully. She remained silent as Sandy led her back to the car.

The trip back to Maggie's proved uneventful. It was only after they all thought they were settled that a knock came on the door.

"Are you Sandy Stevenson?" a young man asked when Sandy opened the door.

"And who are you?"

"A messenger from University Hospital. I was instructed to contact you and tell you Silas Hertz is gravely ill. I was told that the judge may not make it. If he is removed from the case, the case may be postponed indefinitely, until a new judge has been appointed and has had time to review Judge Hertz's work and the court reporter's records. Please. This is only what has been bandied about the hospital and is not to be repeated. If you tell anyone, I will deny every word of it. Now I have done my job. Good night, sir."

Lilly Ann stood some distance from the door and heard every word the messenger said. She looked to Sandy, who only shook his head. Less than a week later, she was informed of Hertz's passing; Mellman had come to tell her the news, fearing her reaction—or overreaction.

With her before him, he said, "Remember our three-day case? It's still on. I will pick you up as before. Be on time."

CHAPTER 44

They arrived early.

Lilly Ann was beautifully attired by the Lazarus staff, who insisted she wear yet another new outfit., "You're the best advertising we have," they told her. "You wear our clothing so beautifully, every woman must look on with envy, while every man watches you with admiration."

Hair styled, wearing a veiled designer hat and long, white gloves, Lilly Ann displayed a continuous, demure smile as the Lazarus ladies looked on and pointed.

As before, they were in the courtroom. When the court formalities were over, Judge Atkins spoke: "Gentlemen, when we were last here, I granted your request of a three-day hiatus for you to prepare a response to a charge of patent infringement and improper payment of fees, past and future, for use licensing the patent."

From the defendant's table a figure rose and addressed the judge.

"Sir, I am Ryan Miller, attorney for the defense. My assignment has been to research the origin of the invention claimed by the plaintiff. It has been interesting and informative—I'm referring to the details of this case. At the insistence of the involved parties, I shall use no names; rather they will be identified as Plaintiff and Defendant. Those in attendance here today will know who they are. I designate them such unless there is an objection."

Pausing for any objection to be raised but seeing none he continued.

"The plaintiff in this case is a young welder. A fine young man, perhaps, lacking the finesse of a university graduate—yet a fine young man."

Listening to Attorney Miller, Lilly Ann nudged Mellman.

"I know I don't know much about these things, but what does that have to do with anything?"

Mellman smiled and asked, "Do you know the term 'subterfuge'?"

Lilly Ann shook her head.

"It means a number of things, among them is talking about things when you have nothing to say. It also means he hasn't done his research. He is unaware that this young man holds a university degree. It will be interesting to see where he goes from here."

Unaware such thinking and talk the attorney continued.

"This—" pointing to the original wood model "—is purported to be the plaintiff's work. Maybe. But if so, who knows who he previously heard talking about the design of the device; perhaps he knew the best way to make this thing and then contacted a draftsman, convinced him to make a drawing that could be submitted to the patent office, and—they not knowing any better—issued the document, no questions, no proof, no nothing. Meanwhile, my client created a device, made proper models, drawings, submissions, then issued an official, trademarked drawing from which model devices could be lawfully manufactured and sold. Yes, we produce and sell the device, of which we are very proud."

Now in a full voice—and full of himself—Attorney Miller turned to Judge Atkins, saying, "Your Honor, given these facts, I reiterate what our submission has requested."

Judge Atkins addressed the attorney.

"As promised, I have allowed you time to prepare your submission. Also, as promised, I have thoroughly read it. I found it beautifully prepared and interesting. I thank you for complying with my request."

At that, Attorney Miller swelled with pride and landed back in his chair, thrusting his thumbs into his vest pockets.

The judge stared at the attorney. "Sir, before you get too comfortable, perhaps you should hear my decision. I find that you are illegally in possession of the patent, patent rights, and all resources emanating therefrom."

With that the attorney's tilted-back chair slammed to the floor.

"In addition," the judge continued, "at this time, it is ordered that a proper percentage of the funds resulting from the sales of the device be provided to the plaintiff. If that is done there is no necessity to submit the case to the attorney general for consideration for criminal prosecution for theft of all items mentioned."

"Is it over?" Lilly Ann whispered.

"Oh, yes, a huge victory for the man who brought the case. Our firm had some involvement, though we didn't argue the case of the court floor."

Standing, he reached in a vest pocket for his gold pocket watch.

"Oh, how beautiful," Lilly Ann said.

Mellman smiled broadly.

"I think so too. A Patek Philippe a client brought from Sweden and gave me. If you have a few minutes, I would like a quiet moment to talk with you. I know you know what has happened in our case."

"They contacted me at Sandy's."

"I don't know what to say to you. I never had such a thing happen to me. So, I don't know what to tell you except to go home, enjoy your children. You will be contacted when we are scheduled to return to court."

Lilly Ann went home to Sunbury. She returned directly from lunch, not detouring to change into simpler clothes. As she approached her home, Mrs. Gorsuch greeted her with an open smile. With pleasant surprise she exclaimed, "Lilly Ann!"

Reaching her beloved neighbor, Lilly Ann hugged her.

"And you look so beautiful! Oh my! Turn. Let me see you!"

Obediently, Lilly Ann pirouetted, half striking poses as she turned. Moving into the house, she removed the gloves and the veiled hat, and sat in her rocker near the stove.

"I was just starting supper, if you will excuse me, I'll remove the pans from the stove. I'll be right back."

She was gone only a minute or two. When she returned she pulled up a chair and said, "We are blessed to have you home, but how can you be here *and* at court?"

Lilly Ann smiled and said, "I almost wonder the same thing. The judge passed away. The proceedings are delayed until they find another judge and the new judge is able to review the case's records. Meanwhile, I will be here."

"Then, I guess, I'll be heading back home."

"Please don't rush. You and I haven't seen each other or talked recently. How have you been? How have the children been?"

With that, Mrs. Gorsuch relaxed.

"I almost forgot you haven't been here for some time. First, your wonderful children are well, making good marks in school and working hard when they get home. We're milking twelve cows right now, we have five calves. The price of milk has gone up, your attorney has seen to the business end. This has been one of the happiest times of my life!"

"Mrs. Gorsuch, you're sure you're not just saying that to make me feel good?

"Honey, no! I so enjoy being with children again. I had seven—two boys, all the rest girls. Naturally all grown now, all gone. All married, with children of their own. The boys all work for Nestlé. My husband is home, half crippled up from a life of hard work on our place. Leaves me alone, most times. Your children remind me of when I was young and useful."

She stopped and lowered her head.

"I run on."

Lilly Ann rose, went to her, and put her arms around her shoulders.

"Please, you're the one who saved me and my children when we first moved here. We were near starving. I'll never forget it, and you've been such a helpful friend ever since. We look on you as being family. My time here at home will be as long or as short as the new judge makes it. I need you now, but when the time comes for me to go back…I will desperately need you then."

Mrs. Gorsuch looked up.

"I know you're right. I'll go home now but I'll return." Quickly she stood, turned, and went home.

Lilly Ann was back. Lilly Ann was not back. Would she ever be back again? She didn't know. Earlier, properly attired, she had attended to the morning's chores. Quickly she discovered the cows could not be milked in the gloves she had worn in Columbus; she found a pair of Junior's gloves and put them on to protect her hands, in particular her painted nails. Mucking out stalls, pitchforking hay, and other similar tasks were facilitated by the old gloves. Her hands, about which she had not concerned herself before, were suddenly of interest to her. However, after her joyous reunion with her children on their return home from school, she realized, despite Mrs. Gorsuch and the nearly normal conditions she had maintained, the children looked to her to return the household back into the normal, beloved home they had always known.

Wanting to settle in as part of the homestead they had known and enjoyed, with the help of Mrs. Gorsuch days passed when all seemed well. Cows were milked, the barn was leaned. Proper feed was prepared for animals and humans alike. Lilly Ann had soon mostly readjusted to life on her farm, only occasionally being reminded that at a moment's notice she could be called back to the courtroom in Columbus.

One morning when the children were in various stages of preparation for the school bus, it came as a shock to her to realize that Harold was absent.

"Where is your brother?" she asked of no one in particular.

"He didn't get up."

Lilly Ann climbed the stairs to the boys' bedroom.

"Son, you will be late for school."

At that, Harold burst into tears.

"I don't feel good. My legs feel funny."

She went to him, held him, and eased him out of bed. Partially standing, the child wobbled, reached out to her, and toppled onto her, crying.

Holding Harold, Lilly Ann cried out for Mrs. Gorsuch.

"Please, come help me!"

Mrs. Gorsuch rushed up the stairs and asked, "What's wrong?"

"I don't know. If you will stay until I get back I'll take him to the doctor."

"Of course I'll stay."

"Please, will you help him dress? I'll be right back."

Rushing downstairs, she dressed warmly while boiling water in a huge pot on the stove.

Junior, seeing her, asked, "What are you doing?"

"Boiling water."

"I can see that, but why?"

"Son, help me. Warm cans of oil and carry them and the water and start the automobile. I am going to drive your brother to town to see the doctor."

Shocked by his mother's words, Harold said, "Mother, you have never driven."

"If I can drive a Fordson, I can drive a Ford."

"On the road?"

"I just need to keep my eyes on the road and keep going."

"You're going to do this? Why not let me do it?"

"I don't want you to miss any school."

Filled with the hot water and oil Junior had brought out, the Ford started. Lilly Ann found reverse, backed the Ford out of the drive, and left it running, knowing that Junior had filled it with gasoline before storing it to prevent the gas tank from collecting water.

Warmly dressed, Junior, Lilly Ann and Mrs. Gorsuch half carried Harold into the automobile. The automobile lurched forward as the gears scraped and clashed. Lilly Ann found the high gear and drove at a good pace until they reached the building housing the doctor's office.

Asking a passing man for assistance, they managed to get Lilly Ann's son into the empty office. The doctor helped Harold onto the slanted table. Covering him with a blanket, he turned to Lilly Ann.

"Mrs. Coleburn. What seems to be the problem?"

Lilly Ann shook her head.

"I don't know. For some reason he is having trouble trying to walk."

The doctor turned to Harold.

"Son, I'm the doctor, and you're here for me to try and help you. For a little while you and I will work together, if you can help me. I'll ask some questions, and then you will answer. Okay?"

Harold nodded.

"Does it hurt?"

Harold nodded his head, yes.

"Where does it hurt? Can you point to it?"

He pointed to his legs. "Mostly I can't feel them."

"All over or just some places?"

"All over."

The doctor repositioned Harold carefully, until he was leaning against the tilted platform. Then, rubber mallet in hand, he instructed, "Tell me if you feel this."

He tapped. Harold winced slightly but obviously felt little. The doctor stopped.

To Harold, he said, "Now, my young friend, we'll get back on the table and I'll cover you back up. Keep you warm."

To Lilly Ann he said, "Please, will you step into the hall with me?"

In the hall, the doctor said to her, "I'm afraid we may have a serious problem. Only University Hospital can perform the diagnostics to make certain."

Frowning and near tears, Lilly Ann said, "You know me. You know I have hardly any money…. A hospital? I just can't!"

He smiled reassuringly.

"Please, let's return to my office."

Once back inside his office, the doctor seized the telephone and motioned for Lilly Ann to take a seat. Speaking into the phone, the doctor asked the operator for a Dr. Shapiro. When he was finally connected, he heard Dr. Shapiro's jovial and familiar greeting: "And what can I do you for?"

"Wish I could be so happy, Sorry, I can't. I have a situation here I'm pretty sure about but have never personally seen. I've only read about it. In short, I think we have a case of polio."

A long pause ensued before Dr. Karl Shapiro repeated in a whisper: "Polio."

"Karl, I would not say what I just said to just any doctor. I would like to deliver this young man—I'm not certain of his age, I would guess about eight or nine. Karl, I understand Ohio State's College of Medicine is one of several universities selected to undergo a trial for an experimental polio treatment."

Dr. Shapiro replied, "You needn't go on. We welcome this opportunity and yes, please bring him in. We'll discuss this further when you arrive."

Again, Mrs. Gorsuch was asked if she could assist Lilly Ann, and she agreed to help. The ride to Ohio State from the farm took longer than Lilly

Ann expected due to congestion on the road. Once there, they were ushered into a special section dedicated to polio research. Met by Dr. Shapiro, Harold was handed to the orderlies and was undressed, bathed, and placed into a hospital bed.

Dr. Shapiro explained: "As I mentioned before, Ohio State, the Mayo Clinic, Johns Hopkins, the Cleveland Clinic, plus several others are participating in the early experimental use of a polio vaccine that we hope will eradicate the disease."

"But what is going to happen?" Lilly Ann asked.

"First, rest assured your son will be well cared for. The procedure is simple. We will take a blood test. Once we have the results back and confirm that Harold has indeed contracted polio and we've received consent from you, Harold will be injected with a known, active strain of the polio virus, followed by an injection of the serum. In the meantime, while we wait for permission to be granted, photographs will be taken, then attempts at walking will be conducted. We will make every effort for him to lead a normal, healthy life. We feel the entire experiment will take about ten days to two weeks. Does that answer your question? Dr. Shapiro looked down at his watch. "It's just about time for his supper. The documents that will give us consent are at the front desk. Take them home and read them. We can't do anything without those papers."

Lilly Ann returned Maggie's' home to be close to the hospital and waited anxiously. Despite every attempt not to imagine it, she envisioned a household with a child who could not move himself about and could not go to school; a child and a family for whom life would be tenuous, at best, and nearly horrifying, at its extreme.

Hearing an automobile, she rushed to the window to see Sandy and his friend, Dr. Hutt and approach the house. She rushed to the door, flinging it open.

Sandy spoke, "You left him in good hands at the hospital. Lilly Ann, please sit down so we can talk."

She sat, as did they.

The doctor then said, "Lilly Ann, you and I have known each other for a number of years, so you know I will only speak the truth as simply as

I can. We believe Harold has polio, which often results in the loss of use in one's legs. In preliminary tests, a newly developed serum has demonstrated some success in defeating the polio virus. Harold has been selected to participate in a nationwide trial of this treatment. All we need is for you to review the consent forms and approve his treatment."

Lilly Ann replied, "I know I've asked this before, but what are the alternatives?"

"Simply speaking, this procedure will, if it works, allow your son to regain use of his legs. If it doesn't, he will be a burden forever. As an attorney, Sandy can help you understand the legal risks involved in signing the release papers demanded by the hospital."

At that point Sandy broke in: "I have in my briefcase the release papers. With your permission, Lilly Ann, I will collaborate with your attorney, Aaron Mellman. We will take the papers to his office, where we will review them and give you our advice."

* * *

Sandy looked around and admired Mellman's office. It was tasteful, with a separate area furnished with a small table, four chairs, and a leather sofa.

"Welcome," Mellman greeted. "I have read through the documents, as I'm certain you have. Sandy, does anything strike you?"

"If anything, how thorough the hospital has attempted to be," Sandy replied.

"In any event, shall we go over them together and determine what's covered? We want to be certain before she signs anything. As I see the first stipulation, it relieves Ohio State of any responsibility, regardless of outcome."

"Yes, no *mea culpa* here."

"The second stipulation relieves all doctors involved of any responsibility should anything unforeseen happen to the patient."

"I agree. Doctors generally assume risks with all they do. Unless this protection is granted, no doctor would participate."

"And the third stipulation is what you and I are most familiar with. A catchall to cover any and all contingencies in the event we missed anything. Have I covered it?"

"Completely and thoroughly," Sandy responded.

"In that case I will ask my secretary to bring Lilly Ann in. I took the liberty to have my driver bring her to the office. We'll have the opportunity to reveal our findings to her, advise her, and accept the decision she must make."

Mellman rose, moved to the front of his desk, and pressed a button before returning to his seat. Shortly thereafter, the secretary entered with Lilly Ann. Both men rose while Mellman signaled for Lilly Ann to take a seat on the couch. The men turned their chairs, to sit on each side in front of her.

"Lilly Ann, please make yourself comfortable. You are aware as to why we're here."

Then, to the surprise of them all, he removed his pocket watch, ascertained the time, and said, "The Maramor is close.... If you please, I suggest we go there for dinner and relax before we delve in."

Lilly Ann, not quite sure what to expect yet knowing the seriousness of the matter, could only swallow hard and stare. The Maramor! She had known of it forever, how exclusive, and expensive, it was. She had never dreamed that she would be able to dine there.

"Shall we?"

She could only nod "yes."

At the restaurant both men were known to the staff and were greeted warmly. Once seated, Lilly Ann gazed about, looking at the gold and silk linens, all gloriously matched and displayed. A warm chocolate drink was served, in response to Mellman's request.

"Sir," a headwaiter said, addressing Mellman. "We have lobster, fresh asparagus, Waldorf salad, and mushroom soup for our specials today. And of course, we have our regular menu of steaks and chops."

Of Lilly Ann, Mellman queried, albeit already knowing the answer, "Have you ever had lobster?"

She was slightly embarrassed by her gawking at the opulence and shook her head. Mellman signaled the waiter, indicating that they would have the specials. They conversed pleasantly as they drank their hot cocoa. When the waiter arrived with their meal, he demonstrated the proper way to extract the lobster meat, which proved to be delicious.

Back at the offices they settled at the table. Mellman removed the documents from their folder.

"Lilly Ann, if you don't mind, I'll explain the conditions of the release documents. Then we can discuss how we think you should proceed."

Sandy looked over to Lilly Ann.

"Mellman and I are agreed," he said. "We advise that you sign the documents. They give the hospital permission to perform the experimental treatment on your son. If the serum works he will recover the use of his legs. Without it, we know he could lose his legs and perhaps other extremities. Our advice is to take the chance."

Without hesitation, Lilly Ann said, "Please, show me where to sign."

* * *

A day later, when she arrived at the hospital, Lilly Ann was shown into a private room, where she found a needle had been attached to her son's arm. The needle was connected to a cord that led up to a transparent bag of fluid. As she watched she could see the fluid slowly dripping.

"My son, how are you?"

"They tell me that if I'm sick, they will give me something that will help me walk again."

She nodded.

"Tell me, Mother, do you think I will?"

She hoped, wished, and prayed...but she didn't know. Now she was asked to commit.

"Yes, son, of course you will walk again."

Harold was constantly monitored, *continuously* monitored, while they waited for the test results that would confirm or rule out a diagnosis of polio. Harold's bowel movements and urine were collected then immediately sent to the laboratory for analysis. Meals, though made fragrant to render them palatable, were prepared so that they contained starches, sugars, and fats in precise proportions while also providing a precise number of calories.

Lilly Ann visited Harold as often as was possible. Observing her son, she could tell little. Most often, Harold would smile or nod. Occasionally, he would half raise his hand then almost immediately fall into an uneasy sleep. Lilly Ann observed the white-robed doctors moving about, notebooks in hand, recording the various gauges and dials monitoring the boy's condition. Standing there helpless, she knew she was neglecting her other children.

Back at the farm, redirecting her energy, she, along with Mrs. Gorsuch, took turns at the Singer while the other cut materials from patterns, first for Phyllis, then for the boys, from materials and patterns purchased with the increasing money the family received from selling the milk from her dairy cows. Once again, economic conditions were improving. They were working thusly when a knock came at the door. Lilly Ann opened it to find Mellman standing there.

"Sir," she said, "What a pleasure and surprise to see you."

Mellman stepped in and removed his hat, but she could see his smile appeared forced and his eyes were filled with worry.

"Lilly Ann, I have some news that concerns your son, along with something else I need to discuss with you. May I come in?"

Once seated with a cup of tea, Mellman began.

"The polio lab has sent their results."

Lilly Ann gave him a long look before asking, "Do you think the treatment will work?"

"Harold does not have polio, thank God. The doctors have conducted more blood tests; your son has encephalitis, which means inflammation of the brain. It's often caused by a virus transmitted by mosquitos. The only treatment he'll need will be time, and a little medication to relieve his symptoms."

Lilly Ann placed her hand on her heart and heavily exhaled.

"How I prayed that he would receive the polio treatment and that it would cure him. I never dreamed that he might not have polio. Oh, thank you, Lord!"

Mellman smiled and patted her shoulder.

"Lilly Ann, I have something I need to ask you. A very serious matter has come up that I must tend to. Will you please accompany me to the courthouse?"

"You mean the trial is on again?"

"No, we are going to meet with the new judge."

"I'll be right out, sir."

"When we are finished, I will take you to the hospital and have a driver bring you and Harold back. The doctor tells me that his medication can be administered at home. I'll wait for you in the automobile."

"You're free to wait here."

"No, I'll be fine in the automobile."

Dressed, they rode silently to the courthouse. In the judge's chamber sat a judge she had not met. He rose.

"I am Judge Jonathan Capeheart. When the time comes I will be resuming your case. Right now, I am overloaded, but Mr. Mellman, whom I have known for some time, asked that I meet with you."

Looking toward Mellman, he asked, "What was it that you wanted to ask?"

"Sir, as you may know, I am a Jew from Poland. My father, who was also an attorney, saw to it that I became a man who feared the Nazi Germans. We moved to the United States when I was twelve, my mother had passed away the year before from cancer. I did not know until my father was on his deathbed that he had an affair shortly before we left and that he unknowingly left his lover pregnant with twin girls. I learned that my half-sisters are well-known hand painters of Polish pottery and dinnerware. Perhaps you have noticed the beautiful pieces when you have come to my house for dinner.

"Briefly I will tell you of their situation. Both women had great skill, which produced good income; they slipped across the border, into Czechoslovakia, both hoping to continue to exercise their skill in order to make a living. Now, they are fearing for their lives as the Nazis grow ever more fearful and ruthless. Please, sir, I ask that you grant me leave to go bring them out. I am even now arranging for the necessary papers."

"Do you think you can accomplish this?"

"Sir, I must try. From long ago I speak Polish, Yiddish, and German. While it may have gone noticed, I have performed work here speaking my clients' language."

Looking to Lilly Ann, Judge Capeheart asked, "Please, madam, how would you feel if your case were delayed?"

"If by delaying my case we are able to save these people's lives, I say save them."

"So be it," the judge said. He turned back to Mellman. "Since this matter has not been docketed, I hereby grant you the time needed to accomplish this task."

Mellman understood the task could not be accomplished from Ohio. How, he was not sure. The Nazis...where were they? Would he himself be captured and thrown into a notorious prison, like Auschwitz?

CHAPTER 45

Carefully, working with his wife, Mellman prepared a list of essentials: passport, visa, a bank list of monies that must be taken: Polish currency, sufficient American dollars to use on the trip, and a list of where it was accepted. Clothing—not suits and accessories, but warm, woolen shirts, jackets, gloves. Other items light enough to be carried in a shoulder bag.

"Here, along with love and prayers, I bought this leather shoulder bag for your precious, necessary papers," his wife said.

It was a brown bag, maybe fourteen inches long, maybe ten inches wide, holding several pockets for his papers. Mellman could only hold his wife in his arms and murmur his love and affection.

The Columbus Station was serviced by the rail lines on two main tracks, the Pennsylvania Railroad and the New York Central, with switches to reach the other tracks. Mellman walked along the Pennsylvania sleeper to his designated car. Upon entering he was shown to his seat.

"Dinner commences promptly at five o'clock, sir. May I be of any service?"

Mellman shook his head. After receiving a tip, the porter said, "Have a smooth trip, sir," and left. After relaxing momentarily from the hurried morning, Mellman laid out and studied maps of both Poland and Czechoslovakia, knowing he must go to the area in Poland near Snezka and Liberec. Later he was to find that skilled Jews settled around Krakow. Researching further, he discovered the area had previously been developed by King Casimir III and, subsequently, by others. Securing as much information and knowledge of the area would be critical for him to blend in without arousing suspicion.

Dinner proved to be agreeable. Pennsylvania Railroad personnel had worked to make the trip pleasant. While dining he sat silently alone at the table once again and inspected his papers; any slip could be fatal, resulting in torture so excruciating death would be welcome. A military officer, a colonel, approached, and sat down. Offering his hand, he said, "I'm Colonel Aubrey Martin, traveling to a new assignment in New York on a mission concerning Germany, Nazis, and strategy."

"That's not the way it should be, is it?"

"No, it isn't."

"No, the stories almost traumatize me."

"But what shall we do?"

"Why? Are you planning on going to Poland?"

"Since we're confiding I see no harm in telling you. I'm going to Poland to rescue my sisters, two artisans, highly skilled in painting Polish pottery. As artists, they thought they would be safe, but now we know better. God willing, I will bring them to the States."

To Mellman's shock, the colonel spoke to him in Yiddish.

"You're not...?"

The colonel smiled, saying, "When we reach New York I will arrange for you to meet with an expert staff. They will have knowledge of the area and the streets you are traveling to. In other words, you may learn exactly what you need to begin. If only we could help you from there. Now, where's that waiter? I'm famished."

*   *   *

The next morning, rather than rush away after arriving in New York, the colonel availed himself, saying, "I know you're on a schedule but if you have some time I may be able to help once you reach Poland. I will find storage for your gear if you accompany me to the government offices."

Mellman was uncertain about what he would learn but knew any knowledge would improve his chances of rescuing his half-sisters.

"Yes, thank you. I am in your hands and need all of the help I can get."

Arriving at the guarded entrance of an inconspicuous building near the train station, the colonel was saluted. To Mellman, he said, "Please, the Pledge of Allegiance."

Mellman put his hand over his heart, stood at what he thought was attention, and recited. The guard opened the door. Inside, Mellman hesitated. The room was filled with long, low tables, where men were intently examining notebooks, charts, and mock-ups of various sites.

"Please," the colonel said, "this way. Here you will find a mock-up of Poland in fine detail. Poland is a large land, with many sections and cultures. The section you see starts here—" the colonel pointed "—and ends here."

"You mean I must enter off the Baltic Sea."

"I'm afraid so. Studying closely, you can see Germany borders the whole western side of Poland, here—" pointing again. "Czechoslovakia takes up the whole southern border. Here is Byelorussia. Ukraine is on the other side, with Lithuania and Russia bordering the rest of the country. Therefore, Gdańsk will be your port of entry, hundreds of miles from Krakow, where your search must start. As you can see, it is a tremendous undertaking. You still have a chance to call your search off."

"Sir, I am grateful for all you have done for me, but someone once said, 'blood is thicker than water.' With me it is. I must find my half-sisters and help them. If I die trying, so be it."

*   *   *

The ship, a freighter that accommodated a few traveling passengers in order to gain extra income, was loaded down to the Plimsoll line mark. Its cargo was grain.

Mellman's quarters were located a few steps along the main deck and contained a bed and a crude shower, washbowl, and toilet. He had chosen to travel by ship to allay any fear of being spotted and recognized by a passerby. Carefully, he removed and stacked his belongings. Once settled he stepped outside his door, into the dusk of evening. Against the ship's motion a continuous stream of cool air flowed, blowing his cap, which he clutched tightly.

"Careful, sir, you'll lose it," a crew member advised.

"I'm just trying to get some fresh air."

"Dress warmly. Wear something waterproof to protect against the wind and blowing spray."

"I'll go back in."

The crewman nodded. "Take care, sir."

The next morning, clutching his stomach, Mellman bent over and retched. When one of the crew came to check on him, he could only gesture to his mouth and stomach, the door, and the railing. On the third day two men came, led him to the mess hall, and fed him. His recovery was slow, and thankfully, after two weeks, the freighter docked at the port of Gdańsk.

Under the cover of darkness, a small motor skiff took him ashore, where, to his surprise, a young, friendly man approached.

"Mr. Mellman, sir?"

"Yes?"

"My name is Joshua. I have been appointed to help you, but from now on, we're just friends on a trip. Understood?"

Mellman nodded.

"Then come with me."

Moving casually, pretending to be carrying out daily chores, they loaded the small truck that would transport them over the first leg of the trip. The vehicle, of which Mellman had no knowledge, looked rusted and nondescript, while underneath the hood it purred with a smoothness that revealed that it had been overhauled to perform flawlessly.

Joshua said, "I am committed to accompanying you to find and rescue your sisters. I keep my promises, but I wonder if you realize what a task we are undertaking. We must travel several thousand miles. Right now, we are at the extreme north of Poland. It is six hundred kilometers to Krakow. We may be in a fine vehicle now, but we will end up on a mule-drawn wagon; there is no petrol, and food will be scarce. You still have time to turn around."

"I am aware of all that, but I must go. Family is too important."

With that grim announcement they rode in silence. Finally, Mellman said, "When it's safe, a restroom is needed."

"Is it urgent? We will reach a hamlet in about five miles. Can you last?"

"With gritted teeth I will."

When they arrived at the hamlet, Joshua directed Mellman to an outhouse, where he was finally able to relieve himself. When they finally arrived at the shack where they would pass the evening, Joshua handed him a pan of warm water and soap to freshen up for a supper of lamb stew, hard bread, and warm cider. Talking with their host over dinner, they learned that the Germans had just passed through, only stopping there to eat and relieve themselves. Their conversation had indicated they were headed to Łódź.

"Since we are headed that way, we should wait and spend the night here. Do you remember the country?"

"No," Mellman responded. "I remember the language, at least enough to converse when I arrive at Krakow."

"We cannot waste any time. While we're here, let me help you remember Poland so that we not only complete our mission but are able to get you and your sisters back out to safety. So, please see the country as I see it. Before the Germans came, I was a P-h-D student. Among the classes I've taken is one on geopolitics. The geography, I will share with you, if you're interested."

"Yes, of course I am. It's been so long since I've been here I remember very little."

"Very well. Our country is an old one, dating to well before the year one thousand. From then until the sixteenth century, Poland loomed as a great European power. For various reasons, among them conflicts with Russia, Sweden, and the Ottoman Empire, Poland was conquered and divided among Prussia, Russia, and Austria.

"When we travel through the country, try to envision the fortresses, castles, and towers as we pass by their ruins. We will pass through coastal lowlands, forested woodlands, and lakes. I used to work in lumbering. I used to swim and fish in those lakes. We will have to proceed carefully, especially since we must move through the flat farmlands in the central region. I don't know what has changed, but we may be able to get decent food and sleep there. We may pass through Warsaw, so you may be able to see that outstanding city. We will also pass through Poland's two great river systems: the Vistula and the Oder. After that we will go into the uplands, where there is one of the world's greatest coalfields, in Silesia. Then, onto the Carpathian Mountains; that is where we are going. The city of Krakow is home to Poland's oldest university and its iron and steel industry. The oldest and most populace Jewish settlements are there."

Joshua paused, then said, "I hope I didn't bore you."

"Not in the slightest!" Mellman replied. "This has been very informative, and I know where we are going, now."

*   *   *

Morning brought packing and a warm breakfast. Thanking their host, they loaded the truck and continued their journey. Mellman was admiring the scenery when he was jolted out of his reverie by the sound of very loud horns. Joshua quickly pulled off the side of the road as six Nazi vehicles with armed troops rode by, their rifles between their legs, pointed skyward. When they had passed Joshua turned at the first crossroad.

"With those troops ahead of us, it's not safe for us to proceed this way. We will have to travel on the side roads."

CHAPTER 46

On the farm, Lilly Ann toiled away. She milked, shoveled, and pitched hay as routinely as if she had not been away. But she had. She didn't know where the feeling came from, it just came: the feeling of despair. As she watched her children quickly and silently carry out their chores, she felt that she was no longer needed. Mrs. Gorsuch happily provided the little instruction they needed. They had joyfully welcomed her home upon her return, but now they had moved on. She wasn't sure what she had expected, but whatever it was, she hadn't received it. Lilly Ann felt alone.

"Mother, are you all right?" Junior inquired.

The voice penetrated her solitude. Almost without realizing it she responded.

"Yes, son, I am," she said, knowing she could not reveal her inner feelings to him.

CHAPTER 47

The Maramor constantly received subtle touch-ups to maintain and enhance its glorious appearance. Moneyed members expected it. Rhodes demanded it. The maître d' resented Rhodes and his arrogance. Far more important and wealthy clientele treated him and his staff with much more respect. Now, with feigned happiness, he greeted him.

"Mr. Rhodes, sir. Your table is ready. May I escort you, sir?"

Rhodes nodded and handed him his walking cane as he removed his coat and hat. "I'm expecting a guest."

"Oh yes, sir. Please follow me."

They moved to what Rhodes considered his exclusive table.

"In this decanter, sir, you will find, as ordered, twelve-year-old Johnny Walker Scotch. May I pour for you, sir?"

"Yes, and pour a glass for my guest, who will be arriving shortly."

Moving skillfully, the maître d' poured the two glasses of Scotch. "Whenever you and your guest are ready."

"Oh no, just send a waiter. I know you have more important duties to perform."

With a half bow the maître d' was gone.

Rhodes' guest arrived, dressed nearly all in black. Half bowing, he was signaled to take a seat.

Pointing to the decanter, Rhodes said, "I understand you prefer Johnny Walker.... Have a swig and see if it's to your taste."

The man did as he was told. Hacking a little, he swallowed, smiled and nodded.

"Well," Rhodes began. "Our legal matter, how does it stand?"

The man took another sip of his drink and spoke.

"As instructed, I have kept as current as possible on the activities of Mellman's farmland case."

"Yes, yes, get on with it!"

"We have inquired locally and learned that the court case has been delayed as requested by Attorney Mellman."

"And...?"

"We followed him—had an agent on the train with him. Unfortunately, somehow, we lost him in New York. We have a watch on his house; when he returns, we'll know."

Unsure how Rhodes would respond, the investigator took a long swallow from his glass. For his part, Rhodes sat silent.

"So...." he said, almost to himself. "We wait."

Unexpectedly, in a tone seldom heard from Rhodes, the investigator heard his dining companion say, "Good report. New York is a huge and complicated city. No matter my anxiety, we must wait it out. Let's eat."

CHAPTER 48

The outskirts of Białystok loomed in the distance as Joshua pointed out some familiar sites. "This will take us several days longer. I don't know your religious leanings but as a Catholic I believe I have a godly duty to safely guide you on your mission."

Wordlessly they traveled on, until Joshua turned the truck and slowed.

"We will stop here for food and amenities. Thanks to the Nazis, we should have gasoline the entire way. It appears that they have kept the stations open nationwide for their consumption."

Stealthily, sometimes in the dark, they fulfilled their needs. One evening, Joshua stopped and signaled Mellman to remain in the car. Upon returning he said in Polish, "I have found us food and lodging for the night."

Inside the residence, Mellman inquired about bathing facilities. He was shown to a bathroom with a huge cast-iron bathtub. In the tub Mellman lounged, relieving himself of the tensions of travel and of trying to save his family.

*   *   *

"It should be less hazardous as we pass through the lakes country. Try to enjoy the scenery. Although I've swam and fished in just about all of them, I still marvel at their beauty. Our rivers flow out of these lakes for over six hundred miles before they meet the Baltic Sea. Maybe you don't know, but Poland is one of the largest countries in Europe, second only to Russia. We still have vast territory to cross before we reach the ghettos of Krakow."

Mellman nodded and smiled, admiring the endless farmland that surrounded them.

"If we had continued the way we were going we would have passed close to Poznań, one of the greatest Polish cities. Going this way, we will reach Warsaw, which is directly north of our goal."

"Do you have any idea when we will reach our goal?"

At that Joshua snapped his head around.

"Sir, I warned you before we started. I have no idea. If you are anxious, know that I am as well—anxious for every moment of our lives. We both want us to get there safely. The Nazis are everywhere."

Joshua turned his head to look back at the road, saying, "Proceed carefully, live. Proceed hastily and carelessly, die. Take your choice."

Mellman raised his hand, palm out.

"Please, I apologize. I will not do that again."

They continued in silence. An hour later, Joshua slowed the vehicle.

"Near here are people I need to meet with. I will leave you with trusted friends, who will see to it that you are fed and safe until we can move on."

Joshua drove through two open doors that swung shut behind them. As promised, Mellman was soon alone with the household's occupants. After a shave, bath and a fresh change of clothes, he appeared before his hosts, who invited him, in Polish, to eat with them. He was pleasantly surprised at how quickly speaking Polish returned to him. They dined on bratwurst, sauerkraut, potatoes, and a strong, flavorful alcoholic beverage. Thick, unique-tasting bread accompanied the meal. When they discovered he would respond to their questions, they wanted to know everything about him. He answered, reminding himself that a careless response could be his downfall. After eating and pleasant conversation, he excused himself, indicating fatigue, and returned to his room.

Very sharp would describe the blade of the pocketknife Mellman used to sharpen the thick stub of pencil as he prepared to write in the four-by-six-inch tablet he had brought should he not survive but his notes did. Satisfied, he folded the knife and returned it to his pocket. Addressing his wife and children, he wrote:

> *My darlings, know that you are loved. I am here, about half-way on my journey to rescue our beloved relatives. I am currently near Warsaw and am safe. In a day or two Joshua and I will leave for*

*Krakow to begin our search. It is a journey I take
very seriously. I pray I can save them.*

*If I fail to return, it is only fair that I describe
to you the conditions. The Nazis are everywhere.
Anyone can be seized and whisked away at any
time. There are reports of the horrors being committed at the concentration camps. Of course, there
are no official reports; brutality does not begin to
describe any of it. 'Jews beware' should be the message, but no such warning comes, only soldiers,
trucks, and roundups. Men, women, and children
loaded like garbage to be hauled away and fed into
the furnaces.*

*To Lilly Ann, know that, as I told you, your
case has been postponed until I return. In the event
that I am not available, go to our law offices, where
another attorney will be appointed for you.*

In the darkness that enclosed him he could no longer see. By touch,
he returned his pencil and tablet to their places and went to bed.

* * *

Three days passed, which he spent trying to relax while feeling eager
to get on with it. Joshua returned on the fourth day and appeared calm.

"I have acquired some information. It appears that we are safe in
continuing on."

Since it was so close to dinnertime, they shared one last meal with
their hosts, said their thank yous and farewells, and departed. Driving
as fast as they dared, they were ever watchful. They stopped near a small
house, with an outhouse some distance in back of it. While one of them
was inside the other leaned against the building. Suddenly, a woman with
a shotgun, both hammers pulled back on the double barrel, appeared.
Cautiously, Joshua greeted her in Polish.

"Who are you?" she demanded.

"We are just strangers passing through."

"Who else is with you?"

At that moment, Mellman, stepped out of the outhouse. In English, Joshua spoke to him calmly.

"Move slowly two steps then stop. I don't know who she is but the shotgun dictates the terms."

Mellman obeyed Joshua's instructions.

To the woman, Joshua asked, "Please, I need to use the restroom. May I?"

With the shotgun she gestured at the door. Joshua disappeared inside.

"Who are you? Why are you here?"

"Madam," Mellman said in his very best Polish, "we are going to Krakow to find my sisters and bring them out."

"What is your name?"

"Aaron Mellman."

"Are you Jewish?"

"Yes."

The shotgun lowered.

"So am I. I am the only one left of a group of us who lived here. When they raided us, I was in that same outhouse. They did not look there. When I could no longer hear anything, I crept out to the house, only to find no one there. My husband, my children, everyone was gone. Now you can see why I approached you with a shotgun. I'm sorry."

"No need to apologize, I understand. As you can see, I have little more than the clothes on my back. If I can help you, I will."

"Please, I do need help. I have been able to survive on food that we had stored, but it is running out. I cannot stay here. Łódź is not far from here. I'm not sure of the mileage but we can reach it in a day or two. I have family there who can help us. Please, sir, help me."

"I must consult with my guide."

"Can I bring my few possessions?"

"I must ask Joshua."

"I will go gather my things in case he approves."

Leaving the shotgun, she left. Shortly thereafter, Joshua appeared, and Mellman described what had taken place. Joshua listened, and anyone watching could almost see his mind working on two alternatives: save the woman, or simply move on. Łódź might require an extra day, but his mission was to save lives.

"Tell her we will help."

Loading whichever goods were the most vital for their trip, they worked quickly. Picking up the shotgun, Joshua carefully inspected it. The breech was inlaid with silver and gold, forming the figure of an antelope on one side, a pheasant on the other. The stock, made of finely grained mahogany, shone in the dimming sunlight. Joshua carefully laid the shotgun down on the floor of the truck. He started the engine. The woman sat close beside him in the middle, with Mellman on the passenger side.

They reached Łódź early the next day.

Having found a safe place for the woman, Joshua climbed into the rear of the vehicle. He was temporarily out of site when two men, under the guise of helping with the unloading, began whispering in German.

"We have a great chance to grab this vehicle and turn these Jews in."

"What shall we do?"

"Let's make it look as if we're leaving here. We'll go about a mile or so. When they are asleep we'll grab them, tie them up, and turn them into the Nazis. Maybe get a coin or two. Then, we'll take the truck. We'll be way ahead. Let's walk away now and pretend we are leaving."

From inside the truck, Joshua heard the conversation. Peeking out, he watched the two men walk away. Soundlessly, he climbed down, retrieved the shotgun, and, keeping a proper distance, followed the two men, who jovially moved along a stream that ran some ten or twelve feet below the road. As the day progressed and the sky darkened, the men moved more quickly, finally reaching what they thought to be an appropriate distance from the truck. Joshua waited, keeping out of site while the two men backtracked. When they were within fifteen yards of Joshua, he raised the gun and, with both hammers pulled back, shouted in German:

"*Heil Hitler!*"

Startled, both men stopped and tried to snap into a Nazi salute. One bullet in each barrel snapped them in two.

Joshua carefully placed the shotgun on the ground. Seizing a two-by-four board, he rolled the bodies into the water. Standing close to the bank, he watched as the bodies were swept downstream by the rushing waters. Retrieving the shotgun, he swiftly returned to where Mellman stood waiting, a curious look on his face.

"Please, don't ask. We must leave immediately. Use the outhouse now, for we will not be stopping for a while."

They kept a steady pace, Łódź long behind them. Suddenly, they were forced to slow down as they approached a long line of stopped vehicles that stretched around a curve in the road. Armed Nazi troops stood by. At the front end, Nazis were inspecting each vehicle before waving it on. Up and down the road, civilians were walking toward and past the checkpoint.

Joshua turned to Mellman.

"It will be best if you join the crowd and walk through."

Mellman nodded, opened the door, and stepped out. Joshua grasped his arm to stop him. He released his arm, removed the floor mat and raised a small trapdoor built into the floor.

"Leave all of your papers, your visa and passport, here."

To the words "Go with God," Mellman stepped out, joined the crowd, walking on with them.

At the checkpoint, Joshua greeted the soldiers, hat in hand, head and eyes turned downward.

A soldier stopped him and asked in German, "What is in the bags?"

Joshua could only look ignorant, hands raised, palms up. From among the Nazis a man stepped forward and repeated the question in Polish. Joshua smiled while pointing to himself.

"I'm a baker. We are going to the countryside around Krakow, where the coal mines are, to help the soldiers and miners by providing fresh bread. You will help by letting us pass."

He made a gesture with his hands.

In German the officer said, "Feel those bags, see if he is telling the truth."

Several of the soldiers inspected the bags and nodded. The officer looked to Joshua and waved him on. While all this was going on, Mellman had crossed the border and was waiting. Joshua pulled up beside him and waved him in. They moved quickly on.

*   *   *

For the next several days, the two men simply lived in accord with the instructions they had received from their own helpers. They stopped only to use the restroom, sleep, and eat.

"We're close to Krakow, our destination. Unfortunately, it is now everyone else's destination, by order of the Nazis, due to the energy situation and the vital coal mines. Please, I ask you to endure it—the coal mines. Almost everyone who lives here is pressed into the mines."

"You mean go down into the mines?"

Joshua smiled. "No, my friend; the coal lies for miles on the surface or at most one to two feet below the earth. As we will do today, with what you will think are crude tools, we will extract and load the coal into railcars and ship them to Germany for use in their factories."

"So…we're aiding the German war effort?"

"Only so we can live!"

Mellman fell silent, downfallen.

With a pat on his back, Joshua calmed him.

"As I pointed out before, we will not appear together. I will provide you with a guide who will drive in and conceal the vehicle. When we are there we will be provided with food and lodging while working in the mines. You must hide all of your valuables. You will be a part of a group, mining during the day. You will find group showers, restrooms, and dinner."

Joshua patted Mellman again.

"Information drifts out so listen carefully. In the evenings, we will meet and share what we have learned. Luck, my friend, keep your ears open. *Idź z bogiem*"

"Dziękuję panu."

CHAPTER 49

Coal. Anthracite. Bituminous. Hard, shiny, and black. Dusty, lung-clogging killer in deep holes. Lilly Ann had begged for it at home. It fueled the boiler furnaces that kept the A.I.U. building warm and comfortable in the winter. In Poland, this type of furious desperation spurred production in the coal mines, which supplied the black rock to vast regions of Europe and North America. Now the need, the greatest need, came on Germany's behalf, and Mellman took part in satisfying that need; he dressed daily in work shoes, coveralls, and caps furnished by the commune.

The German foreman instructed, "Since you're assigned here I will guide and teach you. Pay attention, your life may depend on it. Removing coal is a complex operation made of many simpler tasks. Ours is the simplest of all, just place a stick in a hole. Ever use a drill?" he asked, displaying a handheld motorized auger. "Lean your body in, turn it on, and stay on it until you have it around two feet in. Next, stick in one of these pre-cut, pre-fused sticks of dynamite with a long Permacord. This is repeated five times. From a far, removed, and safe place attach the cord to the plunger box— the detonator. Pull the plunger out and thrust down. Now, any questions?"

"Sir, you have explained it carefully. I will watch you for a little while, and then I'm gone."

Mellman diligently labored at drilling and then carefully inserting the dynamite, inspecting and attaching the cords, and even more carefully moving the detonator box. He watched his guide raise the red flag, waving, waving, and then he plunged the detonator handle down to the sound of the muffled rumbling as the force thrust the coal to the surface, leaving it loose enough to be collected and loaded onto trucks. Back at the shelter, Mellman met Joshua again, and the two friends shared their findings with one another.

"I saw and heard nothing."

Joshua nodded and smiled.

"I may have done a trifle better. I heard several of them mention a woman who had been secretly hurried away as the scavengers swept through. Over the next several days I will attempt to gather more information."

Weeks passed. The men quietly labored in moving the coal, performing their task with what was almost—but not quite—obedience. Then, without warning, Joshua signaled Mellman for a meeting. Standing in the two urinals, looking carefully around, Joshua whispered his news.

"Start gathering your things and load them into the vehicle. When I give the signal, be ready. I have a solid lead regarding your sisters, now popularly called Yvette and Yvonne. We'll never know their Polish names."

Their conversation came to a halt when the door to the urinal opened and a man entered.

"Sunday, sir," Joshua said as he walked out.

* * *

Soundlessly, the shed door opened as they guided the truck out of the range of anyone who might hear it. Rolling it downhill, Joshua held the clutch and then let it out as the vehicle gained speed. The engine caught smoothly, and they were underway.

"I don't really know where we are going, only a general location," Joshua explained. "I learned their last names are Plouffe, we can try any and all names to see if anyone knows where they are."

Mellman was comfortable in the front seat after all of the walking, drilling, stuffing, blowing. He was barely able to keep ahead of the diggers, shovelers, and loaders. Coal…always more coal!

As they rode on, Mellman retrieved his tablet and pencil and began recording.

> *We are coming out with a firm concept of where we're going. With proper calculations, we will reach Katowice near the Czech border. Somewhere near there we hope to find the ladies and get them out. We hope to find them well, able to travel, and willing to follow instructions. Even though we*

*are making progress, we still have a great distance to travel
to make it back to the coast....*

Without warning, the truck came to a screeching halt. Mellman looked out of the window. Armed men moved about, talking loudly. Joshua raised his hand, signaling for Mellman to remain silent. Joshua then stepped down and crept quietly to the front of the pack of cars. He paused for a moment, returned to the truck, and removed the documents from the lockbox then carried them back to the front of the line. Within minutes he returned.

"We are free to pass. Your sisters are being helped by a group of friends."

Turning to see if their passage was clear he said to Mellman, "We have help; mostly unseen, but we have help."

The vehicle started smoothly, and Joshua slowly eased it forward, as he had been advised. Noticing the anxiety on Mellman's face, Joshua reassured him.

"Please, sir, have no fear. We are on the right path. After speaking with those men, I determined they are being sheltered in a secure area several days from here. They are expecting us. We will skirt the border with Germany. They would never expect us to be so brazen. At the proper location we will turn north, directly to Poznań, then go on to where we started in Gdańsk, where a ship will carry us back to the United States."

Mellman waved his hand in silent surrender and sank back into silent observation.

They motored on.

CHAPTER 50

"My tooth hurts," he said. "It hurt all night."

Holding her son, Lilly Ann forced Junior's jaws by putting pressure on his cheeks. The gums felt swollen and appeared full of angry blood. Despite her firmest grasp, she could not budge it.

"We will have to get the doctor."

Lilly Ann rode the school bus with her children. After the bus delivered them all, Lilly Ann guided her son to the doctor rather than to school. They were greeted cordially at the doctor's office. The doctor examined the vexing tooth.

"His wisdom tooth is partially impacted. It will never fall out on its own, it must be removed."

Lilly Ann nodded in assent.

The doctor administered a small shot of Novocain. Once the area was numb, he extracted the tooth.

"He will be sore the rest of the day but will be able to go back to school tomorrow."

As she prepared to leave, the doctor asked, "How is our friend in Poland?"

Startled, she stood open-mouthed, not knowing how to respond.

"Oh yes, I am familiar with Attorney Mellman and Poland. I too have been there to visit family."

Lilly Ann paused before saying, "I have heard nothing. I only pray he is well."

The doctor nodded as she led her son out of the office.

Back at the restaurant she waited for the school bus to take her and her son home. Lilly Ann sipped coffee while her son slumped in his seat, still hurting and groggy from the extraction of the tooth. A man approached their table.

"May I draw up a chair?"

Lilly Ann was only half aware and nodded for the man to sit.

"I am Attorney Eagen. I was told that you would be here and felt obligated to speak with you. I, too, anxiously await the return of fellow Attorney Mellman. Charles Davis and I are attorneys with Mellman's law firm. We want you to know that Mr. Mellman is safe, as are his sisters, who are somewhere in the Czech Republic. Never fear, he and the ladies will soon be home and safe."

Lilly Ann remained silent, wondering what she was to do. Her very life, that of her children, everything was at stake and relied on the activities of Mellman, who had elected to represent her *pro bono*. Even his associates were only vaguely aware of where he was or how he was faring. Her silence led Mr. Eagen to rise.

"Thank you for allowing me to speak with you; rest assured, all will be well."

Lilly Ann heard him but was not reassured.

CHAPTER 51

Knowing what they needed, the Czech men built a small kiln in which to fire the small pieces they had encouraged the ladies to paint. They had dug up and hauled the revered white clay many days ago. Once the pieces were fired in the kiln, the ladies dipped their brushes into their supply of colorful paints. Knowing the price for which the white, glazed pieces were being hauled and sold, the Czech men knew the hand-painted pieces the ladies made would bring considerably more money when they were sneaked past the Nazis, who viewed anything other than plain white a waste of their time. Thus, the painting ladies were hidden securely in various locations for their safety. Not to mention that the sale of these pieces provided the income that was needed to buy food, lodging, and all of the other necessities the women required.

* * *

"I am assured that we are on the right track with each contact we make on our stops," Joshua said. "With luck, in several days we will reach them."

The vehicle slammed to a halt, throwing Mellman sharply against the truck's front panel. Roused, Mellman snapped, "What's going on?"

Flashlight in hand, a man in uniform appeared at the side of the truck. In a hushed voice he said, "Joshua, you are headed into a trap. Somehow word has leaked out that not only are you alive but that you are trying to rescue two Jewish women. The route you are on is heavily guarded by Nazi agents waiting for you."

"But how?"

"Czechs seeking favors."

"And how do I know that you are not the very people you're warning me against?"

The man half smiled and thrust a bundle of papers toward Joshua.

"Papers, sir!"

Joshua grasped the papers in his hands and quickly surveyed them.

"I'm sorry, what do you want us to do?"

"We have been advised that the Nazis have received information that the ladies you seek are in the area; an elite espionage unit of the Gestapo are also here, two or more of them. We know where they are. They do not know where the women are. We do not want them to somehow be led to them. We're here to help keep that from happening. We know of your mission and of its urgency. We will help, with your cooperation. To achieve that, you must permit us to be your guide."

Joshua quickly lifted the shotgun from where he had concealed it. As he did so the man he had been speaking to calmly said, "Son, I've been told of you, your bravery and intelligence, but please, not now. As I stated, they are searching. The sound of a gunshot would lead them to us. They would kill the men and handle the women as they see fit. If you think you are safe hiding in the shadows, be informed they are waiting to try an experimental device called a gyrocopter, which can rise up, fly over, and look down, even at night. Please, let us proceed as planned."

Joshua was mortified.

"I apologize, sir."

Mellman had silently watched the confrontation. He felt somewhat relieved, knowing that they were finally in safe hands, and that he would soon see his sisters.

CHAPTER 52

"What the hell do you mean, you don't know—why the hell not?" Rhodes shouted from his seat in the Maramor.

The agent, hat in hand, lowered his eyes. Jaw muscles flexed, he shifted his weight from one foot to the other and said nothing.

"Well?"

"Sir, I have asked everywhere. It's as if he disappeared from the face of the earth. No one has seen or heard from him."

"Damn it, he can't have vanished from the face of the earth."

Tilting back his martini glass, he swallowed the drink deep and intensely. He muttered, "He can't...he can't." Almost apologetically he muttered again, half out loud and half to himself. "What can we do? I'm tired of waiting."

Not realizing the question was rhetorical, the agent responded.

"Sir—." He started to say, "Unless he is dead..." but didn't.

He tried again.

"He is gone. He will not stay. He will return to normal circumstances."

The return of the waiter with a fresh martini interrupted the conversation, and the agent disappeared.

CHAPTER 53

As Joshua reviewed the map he had been given, he saw that, in some respects, it would be a somewhat shorter distance than he had expected, since Poland narrowed north of Czechoslovakia and along its border with Germany. Traveling to Katowice would move him in the right direction to make his dash to rescue the women. Sharing the map with Mellman, he outlined his plan. Mellman agreed with it.

Quietly, with little fanfare, they eased along the roads. Once they arrived in Katowice, the waving of hands, or three sharp horn taps, indicated not only that they were on the right path but that they were being watched. Everything seemed to be in order when, after several days, and without warning, a vehicle sped up, passed them, and then slowed when it was in front of them, allowing them to catch up and proceed on their journey. Disturbed, they were unsure what action, if any, they should take. They continued on for seventy-five miles, until the car in front of them turned on their left blinker and slowly turned. Joshua and Mellman followed them to what seemed to be a small factory. Then the vehicle they were following stopped and signaled Joshua and Mellman to do the same. Two men from the lead vehicle exited it, entered the building, and returned, with two ladies following them.

The two men approached Joshua and Mellman's truck, and, in Polish, one of the men said, "The sisters greet you."

Mellman and Joshua stepped out and removed their caps.

"My God, is it really you?" Mellman asked.

There they were, the two sisters, Helena and Sabina; they looked quite identical for fraternal twins. Both women were five feet, four inches in height, had the same rounded face, soft, green eyes, and gracefully tapered hands.

One of the men leading the sisters explained to Joshua and Mellman that the sisters were glad they could finally use their real names again, now that they were going to be leaving the country. He then said, "Ladies, this is your brother," pointing to Mellman.

After they were all introduced, they were led inside to wash up and enjoy a warm meal.

"I suggest everyone get some sleep so we can rise for an early start," one of the men suggested.

Turning to the sisters, he said, "Helena and Sabina, you have performed a wonderful service by painting the pottery, which we will sell to reimburse your expenses."

Then, to everyone, he said: "Please prepare and secure your private papers and documents for traveling, and get as much rest and sleep as possible for our journey.

*   *   *

Just short of daylight everyone was awake. Bathrooms were busy, the kitchen smelled of bacon and toast. Outside, the men scurried about, assuring the vehicles were packed with as much of their personal belongings as could fit. Sunrise brought a clear view of the road and surrounding area. When the vehicles were packed, they all exchanged handshakes and hugs, and the men who had helped rescue the sisters gave Joshua and Mellman final instructions.

Then, they were on their way.

"Do we know, I mean are we assured of where we're going?" Mellman asked Joshua.

"No, but I must trust these men. They have assured me of their aid and, while there will necessarily be deviations to our plans, we will reach the Baltic Sea and the ship."

The start of their trip proceeded more slowly than Mellman had hoped. The narrow, hilly, curvy roads forced them to travel at a slow pace. Facing the back, the sisters sat close to each other on a mattress that was piled with cushions. Close about them were personal items, all they had left on earth. When Mellman asked them the state of their well-being, they quietly indicated, in Polish, that they were okay.

Theirs was a circuitous route, touching Czechoslovakia's border with Germany, then proceeding north, toward Wroclaw.

"Something's wrong," Sabina said suddenly. "I feel sick from the riding."

"We must stop," Joshua said, waving his arm out the window to signal to the driver leading the caravan. Seeing Joshua's arm in the rearview mirror, the lead driver slowed and pulled to the side of the road.

"She's sick," Mellman said to Joshua. "What shall we do?"

With calm patience Joshua helped ease Sabina out of the truck. Helena followed close behind. Sabina indicated that she was going to throw up. Joshua helped her lean to one side while she wretched.

Almost reflexively, Joshua asked, "Are you pregnant?"

Sheepishly, Sabina hung her head.

"He traded better food, a warm bed, and better treatment of me for sex," she said. "At least someone cared about me."

Joshua placed a hand on her shoulder.

"Pregnant?" Mellman asked. "What should we do?"

Without waiting, he answered his own question. Moving quickly to Sabina, he held her close.

"Darling, please," he said. "Given all that you two have been through, we are blessed that you survived the gas chambers that have consumed so many. We have come in search of you. By whatever means, you have survived. We have survived this ordeal, too, and you will deliver my niece or nephew at Ohio State University Hospital."

Joshua joined Mellman in providing Sabina some comfort. Once her nausea had dissipated, the caravan continued on.

Sabina's pregnancy alarmed the men. As if all that had happened wasn't enough, they were now responsible for any harm that came to the baby, whether through accident or mishap. Despite his apprehensions, Mellman turned his head toward Joshua, whose gaze was focused on the road, his hands tightly gripping the steering wheel. Concentrating on the task at hand, he gave no indication of fear of what lay ahead.

Although rescuing Mellman's sisters had so far been largely successful, he remembered Lilly Ann's case back in Ohio. Although he had a leave of absence, finding his sisters and getting them out of the country was taking longer than anticipated. Lilly Ann had entrusted her future, and her children's future, to his hands. Would his being here and not before the court result in Lilly Ann's betrayal?

Łódź.

Mellman had heard of it, as had Joshua; but neither had expected to experience the city. Now, in their anxiety to move quickly and get the sisters out of Poland, Joshua suddenly felt the weight his role carried. Pushing ahead whenever possible, they nevertheless stopped as often as needed.

"Nazis…there were Nazis," the man said as he pumped gasoline.

"They were part of a sweep, I heard them say."

Joshua looked about then asked, "What else did they say?"

"They were searching for two women."

"Did they say why?"

"They were grousing about orders forcing them up here. They believed that any remaining Jews would be closer to Krakow or had already sneaked into Czechoslovakia."

Joshua said nothing but knew that if conditions remained the same their chances of reaching the coast were much improved. With that knowledge, he could almost see them reaching their goal without incident. Moving up the rutted road, the sounds of the blowing wind and various scurrying wildlife intermingled while they drove in silence, until Mellman and Joshua heard rapping on the rear window that separated them from the sisters. Looking back, they saw Helena in tears, gesturing wildly. They pulled to the side of the road. From the opened rear end of the truck they pulled the mattress out and placed it on the ground. Sabina was laid out on the mattress while Helena hovered close by. The red of Sabina's blood was bright on the mattress' white sheets.

"If we don't stop the bleeding, she will die," Joshua said.

"What shall we do?" Mellman asked. "Tell me what I can do."

"Don't forget," Joshua explained, "although I am a guerrilla now, I was in my second year of medical school when the Nazis struck. I was forced to flee, yet, determined, I sought a new program and converted to a

P-h-D to not lose all my credits. I plan on completing my studies in medicine. Trust me. I will staunch the bleeding until we can get to a hospital."

"Please save her," Mellman begged.

Joshua removed Sabina's garments and carefully probed inside her. When he was finished, he sat back.

"It's stopped. We must load everything back up and keep her warm."

With care they reloaded the vehicle and drove as fast as possible, heading to Warsaw in order to find a major hospital. There, Sabina was loaded onto a gurney and whisked into the delivery room.

"You saved her life," the doctor told Joshua after the delivery was complete. "The broken blood vessel would have caused her to bleed to death. We must keep her for at least two days, and then she should be able to travel again."

"What about the baby?"

"Barring future complications, Sabina and the baby will be fine."

Mellman extended his hand with a smile. "Thank you and thank God."

The doctor smiled. "Amen."

Meanwhile, being back in Warsaw gave Joshua the opportunity to meet with his contacts and let them know all was well; he was also able to secure new information on Nazi locations and the best routes for safe passage. One important bit of news he learned was that no one was expecting them to be in Warsaw or to be heading north. The Nazis were still watching the Czech border and the routes leading to it. Feeling reassured, Joshua went about the city, restocking supplies, obtaining fresh bedding, and getting the truck inspected. With a new muffler and some differential oil, the truck started without hesitation and hummed quietly. One of Joshua's contacts supplied him with a carefully drawn map, indicating which roads were safe to use to reach the highway into Gdańsk.

Another day of rest found Sabina and Helena fit for travel. They were all anxious to get underway. After arriving safely in Gdańsk, Joshua secured lodging for Mellman and his sisters and set off to the pier and the ship that Mellman had previously arranged. Returning, he pulled Mellman aside.

"Your sisters are safe here. It will take several weeks to unload the corn we're delivering to the whiskey manufacturers and to load the charcoal we will be carrying back for the steel industries in Pennsylvania and Ohio. We will be comfortable here but still must take precautions. We can only take your sisters outdoors after dark. You and I will set off with the crew."

Day after day at the pier, the huge buckets swung over the ship's holds onto the waiting vehicles that trucked them to distilleries. Watching the process, Mellman marveled at the procedure's efficiency. Unhindered by the Nazis' powerful spotlights, they continued their operations twenty-four hours a day, seven days a week.

Mellman walked along the shore to stretch his legs, observing the men's progress on a daily basis and judging how much they had left to unload by how much the ship had risen, exposing its Plimsoll line mark as the corn was removed, only to sink as the charcoal was loaded and the ship was readied for sailing.

After many heartfelt thanks, accompanied by a touch of sadness, Mellman bid farewell to Joshua. In spite of Joshua's strong protestations, Mellman awarded his friend the shotgun he acquired there, a small bag of gold coins, and a final hug. They turned away from each other to avoid a tearful good-bye.

*   *   *

While the ship was still close to Gdańsk, the waters of the Baltic Sea remained calm and the sailing remained smooth, but, farther offshore, the waves began to pitch the ship, forcing it to rise onto the oncoming waves and then bob back down again. After the ordeal they had all been through, Mellman had forgotten about his seasickness. He was ill for three days, vomiting until only water came up, his stomach voided of all food.

Bathed, combed, and dressed in new, colorful dresses, the sisters were freed of the harshness they had experienced—all of the sneaking, all of the hiding, all of the exchanging their bodies to ensure their own survival. Finally, they were able to walk about and talk freely, though their opportunity to do so was limited, since they spoke only Polish. Sailing into New York harbor the group was met by an attorney from Mellman's firm who had secured their paperwork for admittance into the United States. Heading home via the New York Central Railroad, they jabbered, pointing out the windows as they sped toward Columbus, where they would stay with Mellman and his wife, their son being away in Hollywood, where he had gone in search of a career in acting.

Arriving at his offices in the A.I.U. building, Mellman was greeted by a roomful of his staff, all of whom applauded and praised him for his bravery and his success. He humbly thanked them and promised he would meet with them all individually to catch up on all that he had missed. He met with his secretary first: she entered his office suite, pushing a small cart holding the documents needing his attention. After receiving a briefing from her and reviewing and signing off on all of the necessary paperwork that had been delayed, he arranged for a driver to pick up Helena and Sabina to meet him at Lazarus Department Store.

When the sisters stepped out of the automobile they stared in awe at the huge plate glass windows displaying vibrantly colored dresses. Seated comfortably, the sisters were escorted by the sales clerks to choose their wardrobes from hundreds of beautiful garments; those selected where taken to the counter and purchased. This was repeated at the Union Company Department Store. When the sisters had finished, the car was loaded with their packaged purchases, and another car was delivered to return them home.

CHAPTER 54

Driving his Packard up to Sunbury, he observed Mrs. Gorsuch, Junior, and the younger children heading to the barn for their evening chores. Pulling over, he stood with his hands on his hips, surveying the property. He could see that straw, mixed with cow manure, was spread over the fields. Knowing the legal troubles Lilly Ann and her children were facing, her neighbors, he assumed, had helped out and hauled manure from the barn to the fields and then spread the manure with pitchforks.

Lilly Ann had helped with the milking, but her fellow farmers would not allow her to labor as she had done previously. Rhodes observed all this and couldn't have been more pleased. Back in Columbus, he sat in the Maramor with a bourbon and soda. When his guest arrived, he signaled the waiter for another of the same—and signaled, as well, for his guest to have a seat.

With irritation, Rhodes said, "Tell me where we are."

"Mellman's back."

"And...?"

"Court has been rescheduled in Judge Jonathan Capeheart's courtroom."

"Hell. I know that, but why?"

"Rumor has it that the women who returned with him are relatives."

Before a response could be given, Rhode's attorney miraculously appeared.

"I hoped I would find you here. I wanted to make sure you were aware that your case has been rescheduled for next week."

Rhodes picked up his bourbon and stared a long minute into his glass before taking a sip.

"It's about time. I've been ready. I just want to get it over with."

In his mind's eye, as before, he could see himself aligned with Nestlé.

"Are you ready?"

Out of deference, the reply came softly:

"To your specifications, sir."

CHAPTER 55

Lilly Ann, splendidly dressed and styled by the ladies at Lazarus, took her place in the courtroom. After Judge Capeheart's entrance, all were seated.

"With your indulgence," the judge began, "I will defer all of us to a sensitive and personal matter. I'm certain that you have heard the news, that Germany's Chancellor, Adolf Hitler, has declared war on Europe. I refer specifically to Poland. With the time I granted him, Attorney Mellman, Mrs. Lilly Ann's lead attorney, went to Poland and rescued his two sisters, who were in danger of suffering the same fate that has befallen many of Poland's Jewish population—death in concentration camps. The sisters were saved, momentarily, at least, because of their skill in hand-painting Polish pottery that the Nazis then sell. Attorney Mellman, at great danger to himself, went to Poland, rescued them, and is back with us today. Attorney Mellman, we applaud you."

A round of applause ensued.

Judge Capeheart then held up his hand for silence.

"Please indulge me one word further. This war, despite efforts to the contrary, will involve the United States. Our young men will be called; there is no doubt in my mind.... Now, may we begin with the proceeding?"

Junior Attorney Anson O'Donnell fidgeted and squirmed while he awaited his first question. Inwardly, he was uncertain why he was there. His boss, a man whom he had seldom spoken with, had requested his appearance. Recognizing the young man's consternation, Mellman spoke to him slowly, asking only basic questions that provided an overview of the case. Satisfied, Mellman thanked the young man for his appearance and dismissed him.

Mellman paused while he searched his files for a particular document. When he called her name, a hush enveloped the room. Lilly Ann rose. She was impeccably dressed, wearing a perfectly fitted hat trimmed with a small veil. When she took her seat in the carved, mahogany chair, Judge Capeheart signaled for court to resume.

Mellman approached Lilly Ann.

"Mrs. Coleburn, why are you here?"

"I'm here to prove that my home is my home."

"Please explain."

"My place, the place where my children and I live, is being claimed by Mr. Rhodes."

A concerned buzz radiated through the courtroom. Judge Capeheart raised his gavel for silence and the noise subsided.

"Mr. Rhodes. I see. Why are you here, standing up for your home, and not your husband?"

"My husband is dead."

"Oh, I'm sorry."

"On winter black ice, he overturned our automobile and was killed instantly."

"And you and the children—?"

"We have labored, each of us as we are able. Until now, we have succeeded."

"Let us talk about our friend, Mr. Rhodes. Please, if I may deviate for a moment. In college, I studied Shakespeare. In Hamlet, he wrote, 'God has given yourself one face and you have given yourself another.' He was describing Mr. Rhodes."

Mellman smiled at Lilly Ann and paused to let his words permeate the court.

"He has been responsible for all that has happened to us. Mr. Rhodes forced us close to homelessness, but God Almighty saved us. Sunbury saved us. The farm saved us."

"May I ask how?"

"Roy, my late husband…what he had lived and learned as a young-ster he brought to our farm in Sunbury. My children and I learned from Roy. He saw us as helping hands, and I wanted to learn. He taught me to drive the Fordson. I sowed and harvested those crops and provided income and feed that helped us survive."

"But women don't do men's work."

"When you're hungry and it's freezing cold, there is no such thing as men's work, just work—and nearly as critical is what's called 'Reading, Writing, and Arithmetic.' My parents taught me the need to be educated. If doing farm work is the price I must pay to save my children, I will pay it."

Before she could continue, Judge Capeheart raised his hand to interrupt.

"Please, if I may interrupt. While I have read the transcripts from the previous sessions, your testimony is critical. Thus, I propose we halt and break for lunch. We will reconvene at two o'clock."

A rap of the gavel dismissed the court.

"How do you feel?" Mellman asked Lilly Ann.

"A little exhausted. I did not realize what I was telling. Much has happened in the past several years." Pausing, she said, "For many, this case may appear trivial. But for me, my life, and my children's life, we are hanging by a thread, depending on the outcome."

Mellman placed his hand on her shoulder.

"If you will permit me, I will treat you to lunch at the Maramor."

"Isn't it too expensive?"

"Yes, but occasionally we deserve the very best. Your performance this morning deserves the very best."

After their meal, Lilly Ann strolled, admiring the opulent paintings, the woodwork, and the cherry and oak pieces. The beautiful, stamped, tin ceiling was painted gold, blue, and black, with fascinating patterns. Seated in the lobby, fed and calm, Lilly Ann dozed off as Mellman watched. Finally, he tapped her shoulder, and she snapped forward.

"It's time to head back to the courthouse."

The quick trip back found others arriving simultaneously. Once they reconvened, Judge Capeheart tapped his gavel.

"Please take your places so we can begin."

Lilly Ann returned to the witness box.

"As I related this morning, my husband died in an accident. I, with the help of my neighbors, created a dairy farm supported by Nestlé, who purchased the milk." Addressing the judge, she continued: "As instructed by my attorney, I have all of the papers related to my ownership of the farm."

Lilly Ann produced a metal box. When she unlocked it, she revealed all of the legal papers she had pertaining to ownership of the Sunbury property.

Judge Capeheart looked to Mellman. "And you propose to enter these as evidence?"

"Yes, sir, we do."

"To what end?"

"Sir, if I may, these documents establish that Lilly Ann and her husband paid, on time, every obligation they had pertaining to their property."

At that point, the opposing attorney started to stand. The judge stopped him.

"Attorney Brazelton, you were permitted uninterrupted testimony, now I expect the same from you. Do not interrupt Mrs. Coleburn. The papers will be admitted into evidence. Please, Mrs. Coleburn, do continue."

Mellman stood up.

"Your honor, I request that we continue tomorrow so that I can present my next witness, who is presently in school."

Judge Capeheart turned to the opposing bench. "Any objections?"

Brazelton nearly spoke out before the judge signaled for silence.

"Very well," the judge said, turning back to Mellman, "but understand he will not be treated as a witness, only as a friend of the court. I will meet with him privately to better understand all aspects of the case. Court adjourned."

*   *   *

A neatly dressed Junior nervously approached the witness bench. Judge Capeheart calmly and softly asked Junior his name. Junior looked up to his smiling mother and replied. Somewhat more confident, he began to relax.

The judge asked, "Son, I only asked you here to talk with you a little. Just say to me anything that comes to mind, for instance, how long have you lived on the farm?"

"Almost four years," Junior replied.

"Have you enjoyed it?"

Junior hesitated, then said, "Sometimes yes, many times, no."

"Why not?"

"Being cold, hungry, wearing homemade clothes, it's hard work grinding the corn so that my mother can make cornbread to feed us."

"What have you enjoyed?"

"School—Mother insists on it. Football...."

"I have been told you are quite the football star—congratulations. Tell me, what does my court mean to you?"

Junior worriedly looked at Lilly Ann, who smiled and nodded "yes."

"I'm not supposed to know but I've heard others talk. They're trying to take our farm."

"Who is doing that?"

"A man the students call "the Devil Named Rhodes.""

"And will he take your farm?"

"I've heard that he's taken so many others; he might...."

At that Judge Capeheart raised his hand.

"Son, I promised your principal I would have you back with minimal loss of class time. Thank you for coming out and sharing with the court."

CHAPTER 56

Seated in Judge Capeheart's quarters, Mellman and the judge met privately.

"Aaron, I'm so relieved that your trip was successful and that you made it back in one piece. I understand your sisters are quite lovely."

Mellman smiled and said, "I would be happy to introduce you, Your Honor."

"But I don't speak Polish."

"I'll be happy to translate for you."

Judge Capeheart blushed.

"Seriously, I asked you to come to my office and have delayed the invitation for far too long. I'm being pressured."

"Pressured by whom?"

"The word is not direct but comes from the top."

"Anyone I know?"

"I can't say but someone we both know has brought pressure to bear in many similar cases before yours."

*   *   *

The New York Central passenger train, complete with dining and sleeper cars, sped toward Columbus from Washington, D.C., with Dietrich Shossmann onboard. Normally, his boss would have made the trip, since it was his friend Aaron Mellman who had requested the help from the F.B.I.'s Forensics Division. Wonderfully fed, and lounging in his pajamas and robe, Dietrich studied the exhibits that he would present in court the next day. Slowly, the gentle rocking of the train encouraged him to return the files to their folder and make his way to his bed, where a thought of unknown origin entered his mind: "God helps those who God has helped; God knew."

With those words, he prayed that in fact God would help those who helped themselves and soon fell asleep.

* * *

After a restful night at Columbus's premier hotel, the Deshler-Wallick, Dietrich arrived at the courthouse early. Many helpers carried the materials for his exhibits into the courtroom; during this time, noisy confusion reigned in Judge Capeheart's courtroom. The judge sat with his arms folded across his chest and permitted spectators to half rise and point to Dietrich.

"There, that's him…from D.C. He's supposed to know something about the case."

Another spectator drolly commented, "Came a long way just to be a character witness."

It took several raps of the judge's gavel before the courtroom was silent.

"We have given our guest a near-royal welcome," the judge observed. "Now, please settle yourselves; court must resume."

In response to routine questioning, Dietrich identified himself as second-in-command of the F.B.I.'s Forensics Division.

"And why was your assistance requested?" Mellman asked.

"We were asked to determine the authenticity of the property deed."

"Were you able to do so?"

"With your permission, I shall."

Evoking a studied glance, Mellman firmly grasped Dietrich's arm when he passed by. Handed a pointer, Dietrich walked over to where the clerks had erected stands on which he had placed his exhibits.

"This first exhibit is of the document in question."

He signaled for another, and another, and another, explaining his process while he exhibited the fronts, backs, and left right sides of the documents. He went on to explain how he noticed the aberration. The magnification of the document revealed a thicker line among many thin lines.

"As strange as it may sound, we examined the document under a microscope to determine if we were seeing it all—which we were not.

Sandwiched between the two sides of the document were at least two others. These two documents are the ones that Attorney Mellman asked to examine and received permission to access."

With that Dietrich signaled to a crew of three men to come forward. One man carried a bag of implements as he approached; another man carried a toolbox. The men removed two thin pieces of wood from the bag and attached them at opposite ends of the document that had been submitted by Rhodes's attorney as his proof of ownership. Dietrich had one of the men hold the document—attached to the two pieces of wood—upright. Then, from a toolbox, one of the men extracted a thin blade. With skill, he carefully inserted the blade between the two sides of the paper. Slowly the blade created a space that indicated at least two papers lay within. The assistant continued to separate the two pages. When the document was half separated, two additional sheets of parchment paper were revealed. The additional sheets proved to be those removed from a government file—which, as Dietrich and Mellman well knew—was illegal to do.

Seeing what was happening, Rhodes leaped to his feet and howled, "The state's records, they're destroying them! I'll...."

Rhodes took several steps toward Dietrich when a state patrol officer grabbed his shoulders and forced him back into his seat.

"Sir," the patrol officer said to Rhodes, "you must remain quiet and seated."

Rhodes continued to squirm.

"Keep it up and I will restrain you!" commanded the officer, removing a pair of handcuffs clipped to his belt and holding them before Rhodes.

Rhodes slumped over and rested his chin on his chest. At that moment, Judge Capeheart rapped his gavel.

"Order, I will have Order!"

The judge signaled for two of the four law officers to take charge of the evidence and have the exhibits transferred to secure storage for further examination. He ordered the other two officers to take Rhodes into custody for a minimum of forty-eight hours. Expressing his gratitude for Dietrich's testimony, he called it a day; court would resume at ten o'clock the following morning.

*   *   *

Seated in the courtroom, she heard it repeatedly: "She's beautiful! She's beautiful!"

Standing alongside Mellman, various colleagues, and staff, and knowing they had won, Lilly Ann was dressed and made up as only the ladies from the third floor of the Lazarus Department Store could make her. Smiling, she knew they spoke the truth. The courtroom went silent when Judge Capeheart appeared.

"I have arrived at a decision, but before I render it, I will make a few remarks based on the circumstances that have impacted this case. First, the passing of Judge Hertz brought me onto this case. Second, the time I had granted for this case took longer than anticipated due to Attorney Mellman's trip to Poland and his extended leave of absence. The time required for Attorney Brazelton to deliver and execute his stratagem to prevail in the Sunbury Land–Farm case also took longer than expected.

"God helps those who God has helped. There is a saying about the F.B.I.'s Forensics Division: 'They don't work for evidence; they work for facts.' That certainly was the case here. The F.B.I. has supplied us with all the facts needed in this matter. Having taken additional time to review the documents discovered by the F.B.I., I find them to be legal and proper. The defendant, Mrs. Lilly Ann Coleburn et al, owns the Sunbury property, as contended by Attorney Mellman. Also, I have been informed by the Nestlé Corporation that, pending the outcome of this case, an executive is being sent to the Sunbury facility: the company has offered five thousand dollars for the purchase of Mrs. Coleburn's farm. She has accepted the offer. She will also receive a payment of one thousand dollars in punitive damages. This case is closed."

PART 4

CHAPTER 57

"I won't go!" Junior exclaimed.

"I don't understand," his mother replied

"Yes, you do! What I meant is that I will not leave Sunbury. This is my senior year. I'm top back on the football team. I have three track meets…and several girls like me."

"Where do you suppose you will live? What do you plan to do?"

"I'll work for the principal, where I work in the summer. He needs a hand; the man he had left the state. I'll live in that little house on the property; I looked it over when I worked there over the summer."

"What if I say no?"

"I'll do it anyway. You all move to Cleveland Avenue. I already know, everybody has been talking about it."

"And the principal has agreed to take you on?"

"Not yet, but I know I will be…."

Lilly Ann half smiled and said, "My son, I love you."

Junior felt exuberant as he walked. He would not have to leave Sunbury High School. He had it all planned out. He would go to school during the day, play football where an Ohio State football scout would see him; then the Ohio State scout would select him for the freshman squad. In the evenings and during weekends he would work for the principal and live in the house for hired hands. He would cook, sleep, and bathe in his own place. He would be his own man.

Reaching his destination, he approached the small house.

"May I help you?"

The voice startled Junior. He looked up to see a large man standing at the top of a ladder slanting against the house.

Recovering, Junior said, "I came to see the place I'll live in."

"And you are?"

Junior told him.

"What makes you think you will live here?"

"Principal Scott practically promised me that, if my mother won her case and we moved."

"I was told to expect you. I'm Bill Grayson, the new hired hand," he said.

Only then did Junior closely inspect the man. Of more than average height and weight, he was muscular and wore a tool belt around his waist that held a hammer and small saw. Climbing down the ladder that was leaning against the house he noticed Junior's downfallen face.

"Your father told me he didn't want you to be a farmhand. That's all I'll ever be. You have the opportunity to go higher, Ohio State maybe, and as you grow bigger, the football team may take a look at you. I hear you've made quite the record at Sunbury."

Junior was crestfallen.

"Cheer up, son; it's not the end of the world. I have an idea. Come hand me those shingles while I work on repairing this roof."

Bill worked slowly and made the job last longer than necessary, hoping it would relieve Junior's disappointment. When the roof was repaired, Junior rushed home to Lilly Ann in tears.

"In case you haven't heard, Central High School in Columbus has a football team, too."

* * *

Any trepidation she might have felt disappeared as she entered the bank with Mellman. The banker approached them smiling. Days before, a Swiss envoy had met with Mellman regarding Nestlé. A new executive coming to the facility wanted to live on a small dairy farm and thought Lilly Ann's farm would be ideal. While he did not believe in extravagance, cost was no object. Mellman's firm oversaw the negotiation of the sale and prepared the documents. A date to vacate the premises was agreed upon, and Lilly Ann would have all the goods she had not agreed to leave, such as the stoves, removed.

Lilly Ann presented the agreement to Sandy, who could now move with Maggie into a smaller house on Columbus's East Side.

CHAPTER 58

Speaking to his waitstaff, the head waiter said, "As you all know, Mr. Mellman has asked us to provide a special supper for Mrs. Lilly Ann Coleburn. Mr. Mellman and Mrs. Coleburn have just won an important legal battle and we shall help them celebrate. Tonight's menu includes a standing rib roast au jus, asparagus in hollandaise, Waldorf salad, and Parker House rolls. Cabernet sauvignon will be served with dinner. For dessert, we will serve crêpes suzette. Now, it looks like our guests have arrived. Go and silently celebrate with her."

In the Maramor's dining room for special guests, they sat one more time. Knowing how special this occasion was, the ladies of Lazarus outdid themselves. Lilly Ann walked in wearing a sky-blue satin dress and a matching veiled hat that offset her thin strand of pearls.

"I never expected this," Lilly Ann said to Mellman.

"Good. Our intention exactly," Mellman responded, with a broad smile.

"But you have done too much already!"

"As you know, I'm required to provide a certain amount of *pro bono* legal services each year, but as the case progressed I came to realize that an evil man meant to deprive you of your livelihood. I wanted to prevent that from happening."

"I can't thank you enough. You saved our lives."

"All I ask is that you care and protect those children. Now, join me in this sumptuous meal they have specially prepared for us. I know you don't drink, but would you have a glass of this fine wine with me?"

After dessert and a last glass of wine they stood up to leave. Mellman escorted Lilly Ann to the driver waiting to take her home to Sunbury. As she eased into the automobile, Mellman softly grasped her arm.

"Lilly Ann, although this case started as an obligation, we have become close. Know that you and your family will always be welcomed and I will always be your friend."

When she arrived home, Lilly Ann quickly changed her clothing and was relaxing in her rocker when Mrs. Gorsuch and the children entered. Seeing them, Lilly Ann raised her arms; her children swarmed around her. When they removed themselves, they hurried to complete their chores.

Approaching Lilly Ann, Mrs. Gorsuch embraced her.

"My daughter, I love you and the children. I'm so happy with your court outcome, the radio has been full of it. And the farm?"

"Sold."

"And the Fordson, the tools, the animals?"

"Sold, all sold."

"Do you know where you'll live?"

"On Cleveland Avenue, in a ten-room house. The children will all have their own rooms instead of being scrunched together as they are now."

Mrs. Gorsuch came around and seated herself.

"How soon will this happen?"

"We have three months."

Suddenly, Mrs. Gorsuch snapped erect.

"I'm late. The children will be finishing their chores and I'm not there."

She turned to rush out when Lilly Ann halted her with a gesture.

"Mrs. Gorsuch, please. I can't express my thanks enough for all that you've done for me and my children."

For a moment, longer Mrs. Gorsuch hesitated, a wry smile on her face before she left to help Lilly Ann's children.

CHAPTER 59

"I don't feel well," Lilly Ann told the family as they ate breakfast while she shifted her food from one place to another. "If you will excuse me, I'll take one more day off and rest."

Her family worried about her, but she shooed them off, telling them to finish their morning chores and play outside. When they returned for dinner they attempted to be silent so that their mother could rest. Mrs. Gorsuch cooked supper for the children before leaving to prepare dinner for her and her husband.

*　*　*

Only when Lilly Ann did not arise the next day did Mrs. Gorsuch react with silent apprehension. Lilly Ann lay half-awake, wheezing slightly, her face pallid. A thermometer registered over one hundred degrees, but Mrs. Gorsuch's subsequent search of the medicine chest revealed nothing that would help, even had she known what was wrong.

"Shall I contact the doctor?"

Despite not knowing what ailed her, Lilly Ann was hesitant, fearing another bill. She wouldn't so much as dare to be sick, not with her children depending on her and looking to her for guidance and advice.

At that moment, her body flared with pain.

"I think someone must go into town."

Arriving at the house after having been summoned from his office, Dr. Hutt sounded jovial as he neared the bed.

"Lilly Ann, you are not permitted to be home in bed on such a fine day."

From her bed, Lilly Ann half waved her hand and smiled.

"Let's have a look," the doctor said.

Moving carefully around the bed, he took Lilly Ann's pulse, timing it with his pocket watch. After examining and gently prodding her prone body, he confirmed she had a fever.

"Can you get her to University Hospital?"

Nodding, Mrs. Gorsuch prepared Lilly Ann for travel while Dr. Hutt and his driver waited. After they had all arrived at the hospital, orderlies met the vehicle with a gurney and wheeled Lilly Ann into the emergency room. Observing her shiver, the orderly procured blankets, and the intern arrived. From where she lay, Lilly Ann could hear snippets of their conversation. Under the heated blanket her fever broke, and she began to feel a little better. For a period of time she lay there alone, until she was admitted. Soon an extensive examination ensued, with X-rays and blood tests. Various specialists looked in on her, checked her records, nodded, and then left. On Lilly Ann's third day, a doctor wearing glasses and a warm smile pulled up a chair and sat down beside her. Calling her by name, he introduced himself.

"I'm Dr. Warren Davis, the hospital's psychiatrist."

Saying nothing, Lilly Ann thought, "They think I'm crazy."

Seeing her expression. Davis said, "No, we don't think you're crazy."

Startled, she sat with her mouth opened, wondering how he knew what she had been thinking.

"Please, I'm simply here to talk."

"About what?"

"Anything you'd like to talk about."

At that moment, a middle-aged lady entered the room.

Seeing her, the doctor said, "Lilly Ann, this is our resident psychoanalyst, Dr. Irene Smithfield. She will listen in and be in consultation with the doctor. Now please, what's on your mind?"

Lilly Ann listened to this highly educated woman with admiration. In her hospital gown she seemed small, her hair braided and pinned carefully to her head.

Lilly Ann closed her eyes.

"I'm an only child, maybe that's why I have so many children. As a child, my mother closely guarded over me. Is that what you want to hear?"

"We are here to listen to everything you'd like to share about your life."

"I was lonely. Mother guarded me so closely. I read and studied and looked forward to high school. I was not allowed to attend school dances but I taught myself, listening to the neighbor's radio."

The memories brought a smile to her face.

With a sudden urgency, she continued: "I was happy when I was permitted to work at the tuberculosis hospital as a nurse's attendant. Jimmy, my stepfather, would drive me to and fro. I made friends there with the staff and some of the patients. When my mother became ill, I had to quit and help with the cooking and cleaning. Then I met Roy."

At that point, a nurse came in and asked Dr. Davis and Dr. Smithfield to step outside while she took the patient's vitals. Meanwhile, the medical group conferred, exchanging observations to determine how they would treat Lilly Ann.

Once back inside Dr. Smithfield asked, "Do you mind if we discuss Roy's accident?"

"Must we?"

"Yes, I believe we must."

"Really, there's nothing to it. Black ice caused the automobile to slide and roll over. He died. We had to go on without him."

"And?"

"Without Roy, I had to become the man of the house. I became both a father and a mother to my children. Denims and all, I raised my children, helped with their schoolwork, and taught them how to work the farm. When they first saw me in men's work clothes they hooted and hollered. But my neighbor, Mrs. Gorsuch, quieted them down. She saved our lives. When we first met, she lent us milk when we were running out of food." Lilly Ann paused. "I'm tired."

The team snapped erect.

"Of course. Only a little more, if we could continue tomorrow," Dr. Smithfield replied as they stepped out of Lilly Ann's room.

Finally alone, Lilly Ann tried to feel better. She wasn't certain but she recognized that she had not cried or become hysterical. Maybe the team would let her return home tomorrow. She thought she heard country music playing from a radio somewhere. To that, she drifted off to sleep.

At various times throughout the night, nurses, technicians, even the on-duty doctor checked on her. Lilly Ann, for her part, roused, complied, and returned to sleep. In the morning, she was given a sponge bath and escorted to the toilet. After eating breakfast in her hospital bed, she settled back and dozed until her doctors returned. After they exchanged pleasantries, Dr. Smithfield told her they had a surprise waiting. Helping her up, they walked her to the window. There, she saw an unexpected scene. Four stories down stood her children and Mrs. Gorsuch. They all waved. Not permitted inside, they stood by the curb and simply smiled and continued waving. Seeing them, Lilly Ann waved almost uncontrollably. Her medical team stood by silently, giving her support when needed.

When her children were gone, they returned her safely to her bed and asked if they could pick up from their talk the day before. As they asked questions, she responded as best she could. Then it came.

"Lilly Ann," Dr. Smithfield asked, "have you ever felt anxiety? If so, could you please describe how it felt?"

At first, she hesitated and considered not responding. After Roy, no one cared about her concerns, they were too busy with their own. She had lost so much, starting with the dream house that Roy had built. She remembered Roy sitting on their bed, shotgun aimed at his chin; the move, the loss of a child, and the loss of Roy. She remembered hungry mouths, and no food.

As if sensing her thoughts, Dr. Davis said softly, "Please, Lilly Ann. See us as friends here to help you. We can barely imagine what you have had to go through. If you let us in, we will share your pain with you."

Lilly Ann explored Dr. Davis's face. Hearing his calming voice and seeing Dr. Smithfield's compassionate expression, she decided to trust them. Her outflow of emotions continued for more than an hour and a half. For the most part, her doctors remained silent, only interrupting to get clarification on some of her experiences. Then, sensing her exhaustion, Dr. Davis looked at his pocket watch.

"Lilly Ann, I'm sorry, but we have made arrangements to meet with other patients this afternoon. We will meet with you again to share our assessment with you."

When they left, she napped peacefully. When she awoke, she found him there, Charles Davis from the A.I.U. law offices. Seeing her awake, he smiled and gave a halfwave.

"You're awake. How are you holding up?"

Lilly Ann smiled back and shrugged her shoulders.

"I just wanted to check in with you and hopefully relieve any anxiety you have regarding your finances. Not only am I an attorney, I'm also a certified public accountant. On Mr. Mellman's instructions, I have examined all of your financial affairs. Later, if you wish, we can review your matters line by line; but for now, please accept my word that you are financially sound, that you own the Cleveland Avenue property, and that you have enough funds to furnish and decorate your new home as you see fit. In fact, I have several acquaintances who can help you save money, if you desire."

Lilly Ann thanked Charles while indicating how pleased and appreciative she was at being represented by him. Both wore smiles as Charles parted from her. She wanted nothing more than to snooze the rest of the day away.

She turned on the radio. WLW blared with a narration about Weimar, Germany, after World War I. Turning it down, she continued to listen. Lilly Ann learned more details about what her instructors had long ago touched upon in her history classes but had not stressed. For instance, she learned that despite Adolf Hitler's strange appearance, clothes, and mustache, when he took power in January of 1933 he was already a brilliant speaker. He was able to convince members of his Nazi party and his fellow countrymen that the Jews had been the cause of their downfall and would continue to be if they were not stopped, and that his Germany, Nazi Germany, was not equal to the rest of the world but superior to it.

At that point in Lilly Ann's thinking, a nurse walked in and listened to the radio that Lilly Ann had turned low.

"It's coming."

Lilly Ann looked up.

"I don't understand. What's coming?"

"The next World War. My parents told me of World War One's coming. Starting as the Austro-Hungarian Empire, then involving France, Germany, and other countries until the Unites States became involved. Now, one by one, the world is becoming involved again."

Lilly Ann could only say, "I see."

The nurse said, "I'm talking too much. Please, let me turn the radio off so I can take my readings."

After she was gone, Lilly Ann did not turn the radio back on; rather, she thought about what she had heard. Then the door opened to admit her two doctors.

"Lilly Ann, how are you feeling today? We wanted to share some of our findings with you and tell you more about our research program. This is an experimental program where, in Germany, psychotherapy is being conducted. We would like to share with you some of our findings. Hopefully, we can resolve any anxiety you might have, allow you to think about it, and have a final discussion in the next day or two. Please listen, we have tested for any physical disease, you have none. You do have what has been labeled by European doctors as chronic distress syndrome, with symptoms of the emotional pressure she had endured over a prolonged period of time. Little is known about it, but we will discharge you, asking you to follow our instructions. We want you to resume your life and continue raising your family. Love your children, as we know you do. Be close with them, allow them to love you. Eat well, rest, sleep. Your strength will return. Maintain the special relationships you have developed. Be kind in your thoughts, decent, and loving. Now, we must move on—but remember, you are in a hospital. You only need ask and help for almost anything and everything is yours for the asking."

* * *

They were there when she returned with the nurse from a walk along the hospital's corridors: Maggie and Sandy.

Grasping her in a strong embrace, Maggie said, "If you can walk around, you must be much better."

Sitting down in a chair beside the bed, Lilly Ann simply responded, "I am."

Sandy said, "We want you to know we have, from time to time, looked in on Mrs. Gorsuch and the children. She has seen to it that the farm, the cows—all is well."

Lilly Ann moved forward and extended her arms, so Maggie and Sandy could each grasp one.

Smiling, she said, "I love you both. The doctors said I will be able to go home tomorrow."

To questions about her feelings she responded, "I know I'm still in the hospital, but I am much better."

Their conversation was interrupted by a knock on the door. Her doctors entered.

Sandy stood up.

"We should leave."

One of the doctors said, "Oh, no. You are her parents. I prefer that you stay. When she is back home she will need loving help. She is better, but only by being with her loving and caring family will she get well."

"But only when the huge hospital bill is paid will she be healed." Maggie sniffed.

"Then consider her healed, she owes nothing. In fact, she will be given a stipend for permitting us to investigate her condition as we have done. *Pro bono*," the doctor said, with a smile.

Lilly Ann had been sitting nearly erect. Now she slumped back, half choking as she said, "Thank you, thank you!"

Dr. Smithfield left. Lilly Ann's psychiatrist moved closer and spoke at length with them regarding her aftercare.

*   *   *

For several days Lilly Ann attired herself in gumboots, denims, and a slouch hat. She immersed herself in milking, shoveling. She found contentment in being involved again with the farm.

It was then that Mrs. Gorsuch asked, "I know everything else has been prepared for the move, but are you prepared?"

Breathless, Lilly Ann could only nod.

Later, half up the orchard's hill where fruit hung nearly ripe for picking, she thought about how the fruit were like her children. Both were in need of tending. Neglected, both would rot. Turning decisive, aware of her responsibilities, she understood, once again, that her children needed her. At the house she informed Mrs. Gorsuch to be gone in two weeks.

Mrs. Gorsuch shook her head and sighed softly "I shall miss you, all of you. I am so proud of you. Your children will receive a better education in the city. They will learn city ways. Be careful though, war is coming. Well, I must be going, but I'll see you each day until you leave."

Thoughtful, not vague platitudes: Mrs. Gorsuch had impressed Lilly Ann as she once more climbed into the purple quince, Grimes Golden, and sour cherries. The fruit of an overripe orchard needed picking, canning, and preserving. She had always looked forward to these chores…but never again. Standing, looking over the vast land, in every direction were signs of recovery. For a moment she felt a twinge of remorse, but only for a moment. The greater development of the city would bring better education to her children, along with more opportunities.

Back at the place—she had learned to speak of it as her "place" since the trial— Lilly Ann gathered her children before chore time.

"Please sit down, I need to speak with you."

Everett interrupted, "But we know about moving, we heard you and those men talking."

"Fine, son, but I want to tell you all about where we're moving. We are moving into the city, into a ten-room house where we'll almost each have a room of our own. It's on a street called Cleveland Avenue. I want you all to remember that you'll live on Cleveland Avenue. Later, you will learn the number, but for now remember 'Cleveland.' If you ever need help getting home, if you say, 'Cleveland Avenue,' someone will help you get home.

"But from where? We all go on one school bus to the same school."

"Not all of you will be going to the same school."

"Will we still have to carry water and go to the bathroom outside?"

"The bathroom?"

"You know, that little shed we got out back."

Lilly Ann laughed.

"Oh my, no. Water is provided in each house by the county through the city, and there are indoor toilets."

Junior had remained silent, but when he spoke, silence prevailed among the other children.

"Until now, each of us knew what was expected. Now where we're going, none of us knows anything."

"Son, no matter how lonely you think you will be, you'll be surrounded by family and friends. Sandy will be there, Maggie, too. They will be there to provide help of all kinds, when it is needed."

"But what about football?

"Son, you will play at Central High. The school is near our new home. If you make the team there, Ohio State will soon have someone looking at you—and if they think you're good enough, they might offer you a scholarship."

"Do you think so?"

"Son, what I think doesn't matter. You know I love you, and I want everything you want to happen."

*　*　*

Dusk hung in that ambivalent interval between light and dark. Having seen to the final chores, Lilly Ann now eased away from the kitchen. Having placed several Grimes Golden apples in the small bag she carried, she walked down the hill, seeing her Barney come to her. She extended an apple to him, and, biting into it, he dropped half. Lilly Ann patted the Percheron and looked around. Up the hill she could see the house and barn...the silo that she helped erect. The farm, where she and her children survived.

Now, God willing, they would prosper.

*　*　*

From the Cleveland Avenue curb where they were parked Lilly Ann could see the house as she had never seen it before. Stretching three stories into the sky, its bricks were layered into an ornate pattern, with an entrance in the rear to permit the servants in residence to gain access without disturbing the family. A spacious yard surrounded the property, and a large, multicolored garage provided space for three automobiles. Pairs of mahogany sliding doors were built into much of the first floor, enabling the family to divide the home into smaller, more private sections. In the dining room there was a dumbwaiter, permitting the staff to serve meals while remaining unseen. Lilly Ann marveled at the spaciousness, especially when she compared it to her small country home, where the children had slept head to toe.

A gentle touch on her arm shook her from her musings.

"May I speak to you?"

Lilly Ann turned to see an elderly white-haired lady wearing glasses.

"Yes, of course."

"I'm Mabel Thornton. I have lived here, on the third floor, with my husband, for twenty-seven years. We provided service to the Stevenson family. The children have grown up, and when Mrs. Stevenson passed... well, you know the rest. "

Lilly Ann nodded, and Mrs. Thornton continued.

"I'm a little old to work, anyway. My daughter asked me to come live with her, but I thought I would stop by to meet the new owners."

"It is a pleasure to meet you, Mrs. Thornton."

The lady pointed to show Lilly Ann the two copper lines that hung parallel to each other over the street.

"The city bus runs off those lines; at the corner you can catch the bus and travel all over the city, but there's rumors they will be stripped down to provide copper for the war that's coming."

Having heard such talk before, Lilly Ann nodded.

"I tell you this for two reasons. One, the rumor says young men will be drafted. Two, a man, a doctor, was approaching Mr. Stevenson with offers to buy this property. Right after you move in, you will be approached. Just south of the city lies Fort Hayes. The military will need housing, and the doctor could stand to make a fortune."

Hearing this, Lilly Ann thought immediately of Sunbury and Rhodes.

"Mind you, these are only rumors."

Lilly Ann had seen the articles in the *Dispatch*, describing the activities of Hitler and the Nazis in Europe. She thought of Junior and Everett. The thought of them going to war sent chills through her body.

Seeing the look of worry that clouded Lilly Ann's face, Mabel patted her arm.

"I just want you to be aware. They are rumors, just rumors, but please, watch them."

Lilly Ann walked about her new home. It was perfect. In the dining room, dinner was laid out. The table was loaded with roast pork, succotash, fresh baked bread, and salad. The smell of peach cobbler permeated the air. Someone had helped the children wash for their meal.

"We'll be going now," one of the helpers said to Lilly Ann.

"Before you go," she replied, "I want to thank you for everything you've done for us…. Please, would you join us in a prayer of thanks?"

* * *

As darkness descended a light drizzle fell on the earth. After dinner, Maggie went to Lilly Ann.

"My daughter, you have been placed in such a lovely home; I know you will care for it."

Lilly Ann hugged her mother as she whispered, "Thank you for everything…I will."

When Maggie left, Lilly Ann climbed the stairs to tuck her children in. On the third floor, she looked in on Junior and Everett, who were breathing steadily. On the second floor she peeked in Phyllis's room, then glanced into the room with her two youngest boys; everyone was fast asleep. Satisfied, she made it to her room and marveled at the beauty of it. She readied herself, then immersed herself in the elegant porcelain tub. After a long and relaxing soak, she dressed in her nightgown and climbed into bed.

* * *

Days passed while everyone settled into their routine. Once school had started Lilly Ann walked about her neighborhood, finding the grocery store, a dry cleaner, and the general store. Returning home, she found a man in overalls pushing a lawn mower. Seeing her, he introduced himself and explained he had been paid to mow her lawn. He said the season was nearly over, but that he would return in the spring. Again, as she walked into her home, she marveled at how organized Sandy and Mr. Mellman had been. A moment later, there was a knock on the front door. A man appeared to deliver coal to the basement.

"Coal?" Lilly Ann said.

"Oh yes, ma'am. We will deliver fifteen tons. It's all been paid for."

Lilly Ann followed him and watched as he resurrected the bin from under the basement window where the coal had been left. that had been left. Over the next several days the man returned, and the coal was delivered and piled into the bin.

"When the time comes we will return and start the fire, all you and your boys will have to do is bank it at night and fire it up in the morning. You'll have heat all winter."

Days slid by as Lilly Ann guided her children into adjusting to their new circumstances. She, too, was adjusting. One afternoon, while she was leaving for the general store, she was startled to find a man standing in front of her door. The man was tall, though slight of stature. He was dressed in a fine, three-piece suit and wore a Stetson on his head.

Nodding to Lilly Ann, he said, "Mrs. Coleburn, I am Dr. S. Thomas Redford. May I come in?"

"Yes, please, do come in."

Opening the front salon's sliding doors, she motioned for him to enter. After a brief exchange of pleasantries, Dr. Redford came to the point.

"Mrs. Coleburn, I have come to buy this house. I'm prepared to pay cash."

Lilly Ann smiled politely and replied, "I'm sorry, but I have no interest in selling this house. I have always dreamed of having enough room for my children. God has answered my prayers and my home is not for sale."

"Maybe so, but I want it and will acquire it, one way or another. The state is acquiring land for the new highway, a freeway, they call it. Sooner or later, they will inquire about the property, and I intend for them to have me to answer to."

Lilly Ann changed the subject.

"From time to time, my family and I will need a doctor. Would that be you?"

"Momentarily, but not for long. I plan on acquiring more properties to sell to the state. Maybe buy a fine house and a new car. Spend the winters someplace warm…maybe Florida or Jamaica. Who knows?"

Dr. Redford abruptly stood, grabbed his hat, and made for the door. He turned back to Lilly Ann.

"Remember, I'll be returning."

Lilly Ann watched as he left. Then, she chuckled to herself. Although her address had changed, life and its complexities would remain, and she would just have to accept that she would be involved in them forever.